1001 Dark Nights
Bundle 16

1001 Dark Nights
Bundle 16

Four Novellas
By
Jennifer Probst
Tessa Bailey
Elisabeth Naughton
and Laura Kaye

1001 Dark Nights

EVIL EYE
CONCEPTS

1001 Dark Nights: Bundle 16
ISBN 978-1-948050-68-5

Somehow, Some Way: A Billionaire Builders Novella
By Jennifer Probst
Copyright 2017 Triple J Publishing Inc

Too Close to Call: A Romancing the Clarksons Novella
By Tessa Bailey
Copyright 2017 Tessa Bailey

Hunted: An Eternal Guardians Novella
By Elisabeth Naughton
Copyright 2017 Elisabeth Naughton

Eyes On You: A Blasphemy Novella
By Laura Kaye
Copyright 2017 Laura Kaye

Foreword: Copyright 2014 M. J. Rose

Published by Evil Eye Concepts, Incorporated

Sign up for the 1001 Dark Nights Newsletter
and be entered to win a Tiffany Key necklace.

There's a contest every month!

Go to www.1001DarkNights.com to subscribe.

As a bonus, all subscribers will receive a free copy of
Discovery Bundle Three
Featuring stories by
Sidney Bristol, Darcy Burke, T. Gephart
Stacey Kennedy, Adriana Locke
JB Salsbury, and Erika Wilde

Table of Contents

One Thousand and One Dark Nights

Once upon a time, in the future…

*I was a student fascinated with stories and learning.
I studied philosophy, poetry, history, the occult, and
the art and science of love and magic. I had a vast
library at my father's home and collected thousands
of volumes of fantastic tales.*

*I learned all about ancient races and bygone
times. About myths and legends and dreams of all
people through the millennium. And the more I read
the stronger my imagination grew until I discovered
that I was able to travel into the stories… to actually
become part of them.*

*I wish I could say that I listened to my teacher
and respected my gift, as I ought to have. If I had, I
would not be telling you this tale now.
But I was foolhardy and confused, showing off
with bravery.*

*One afternoon, curious about the myth of the
Arabian Nights, I traveled back to ancient Persia to
see for myself if it was true that every day Shahryar
(Persian: شهريار, "king") married a new virgin, and then
sent yesterday's wife to be beheaded. It was written
and I had read, that by the time he met Scheherazade,
the vizier's daughter, he'd killed one thousand
women.*

*Something went wrong with my efforts. I arrived
in the midst of the story and somehow exchanged
places with Scheherazade – a phenomena that had
never occurred before and that still to this day, I
cannot explain.*

*Now I am trapped in that ancient past. I have
taken on Scheherazade's life and the only way I can
protect myself and stay alive is to do what she did to
protect herself and stay alive.*

*Every night the King calls for me and listens as I spin tales.
And when the evening ends and dawn breaks, I stop at a
point that leaves him breathless and yearning for more.
And so the King spares my life for one more day, so that
he might hear the rest of my dark tale.*

*As soon as I finish a story... I begin a new
one... like the one that you, dear reader, have before
you now.*

Somehow, Some Way

A Billionaire Builders Novella
By Jennifer Probst

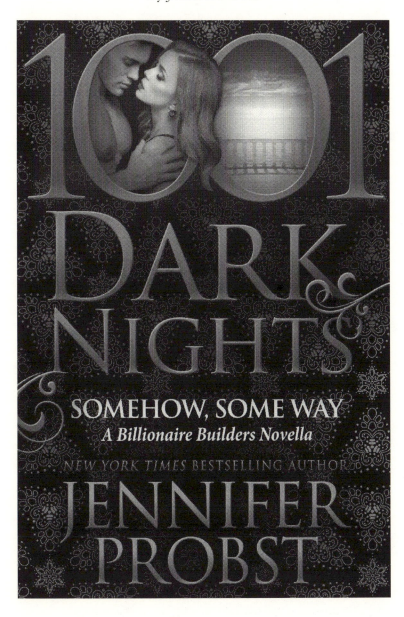

Acknowledgments from the Author

Huge thanks, kudos, and squishy hugs to the fabulous Liz Berry and MJ Rose. This 1001 Dark Nights family you've built is so much better than the mob. And much safer too. I'm so honored to be part of this.

Thanks to Kim Guidroz for the wonderful edits and feedback. Thanks to Jillian Stein for being one of the best bloggers in the entire planet and integral to this team.

I cannot tell you how many more fabulous authors I got hooked on by reading these books. You've all done a service to readers who love a great love story. That is your greatest success of all.

Dedication

Anyone who's read my books know I love to write about strong women.

I'd like to dedicate this book to Rosemary Conlon – my godmother and beloved Aunt, who taught me about all the fabulous things in life. Thanks for being an important part of my life and always believing in me. I love you.

Chapter One

"It's not the beauty of a building you should look at; it's the construction of the foundation that will stand the test of time."—David Allan Coe

Her gaze ate up the gorgeous build before her. Oh, this one was hot. Her hands ached to touch, stroke, enjoy. Immerse herself in the dirty, sweaty actions that would fulfill them both.

No.

She paused, pressing a hand to her mouth. What was wrong with her? Why was she always attracted to the ones needing so much damn work? It was like she craved to be the savior, restoring all the broken parts to achieve wholeness and beauty. How many times had she been bitterly disappointed by the result? By her investment in time and energy that never seemed to be enough?

Could she stand to take another risk?

Charlotte Grayson squeezed her eyes shut and struggled with the raw lust shooting through her body, competing with her sensible, overworked brain that screamed for her to walk away.

"Earth to Charlie."

Her lids flew open. And once again, she succumbed to bad-boy charm and the lure of the challenge. "I want him."

Her contact lifted a brow. Gage was a bit cutthroat in business but held a soft spot for her. No one ever took him as a serious competitor. His uniform was a backward red baseball cap, jeans with holes in the knees that weren't fashionable, nerdy white sneakers, and a T-shirt that declared BEER IS GOOD. With his nondescript features, unshaven jaw, and casual attitude, he looked like he'd rather be smoking weed in the garage than flipping dilapidated properties for a profit. Another reason Charlie liked him. People had been misjudging her forever, and it was nice to meet another of her kind. "How come you always call them he?" he asked curiously, scratching his head.

She shrugged. "Probably my warped way of controlling men?" she suggested. "I get to do what I want, when I want. Give them a makeover. Be their one and only for a while." She shot him a mischievous grin. "And I also get to be the one to break up with them. Kind of poetic, right?"

"Kind of weird, but you've always been a bit quirky." Gage grinned back and they both surveyed the house. "We'll need to close quick. I had a few other contacts interested but I showed this to you first."

"Always knew you had a crush on me, Gage." She batted her lashes, confident their relationship was on solid ground from any sexual minefields. His partner, Tom, would kick her ass if she tried to lure Gage to the land of women.

He snorted. "I just knew you'd be loony enough to grab it."

The sweet sizzle of foreplay flowed rich in her veins. The house was a horror show. From the sagging porch, broken shingles, cracked windows, and weed-clogged lot, it was tucked down the back end of a street in a crappy neighborhood. Most flippers would stay far away, but they didn't have her vision. Already, her hands itched to begin to restore and see how she could transform the brokenness into something truly beautiful.

Finally, she had her own project. She'd been saving money furiously in the past year for this very moment. Her first house to renovate on her own. It was a heady thrill that rivaled the feel of drinking too much champagne.

"Wait till you see him when I'm done."

He glanced around the deserted neighborhood. "Trapps isn't the best area. Don't make me regret selling you this by working out here alone."

She sniffed. "I'm not stupid, Gage."

"I know. They had a drug bust a few blocks over last week. Just want you to be careful."

"Land is getting scarce in Harrington, though. I like the idea of working within the outskirts of town before some billionaire beats me to it. There's tons of investors looking to scoop up property. I intend to be one of the first they buy."

His brown eyes lit with admiration. "You're too cool for a girl, Charlie."

She sighed. "I know. It's hard to find friends who want to spend their spare time ripping apart houses instead of doing their nails."

"Still at Pierce Brothers?" he asked.

"Yeah. I really like it." Her job at the customized builders had morphed to full time, and she was finally beginning to carve out a name for herself. This project would give her the extra push for her career. If she did this right, and Pierce approved, she'd get more opportunities, and maybe even a raise.

"Good. Maybe they'll help you out with this atrocity." He winked, taking the sting from his words, and pivoted on his sneakered heel. "Let's go sign some paperwork so I can get home in time for dinner. Tom's making Irish stew."

Her stomach grumbled on cue. Damn, she was always forgetting to eat. "How'd you get so lucky to hook up with a chef?"

"I date actual people. Not houses who are pretend boyfriends."

She laughed, not taking offense.

After all, he was right. Not that she had any issues with real men. She even liked sex, when she was able to tear her gaze away from a renovation long enough to satisfy her physical needs. The main problem was the quality, not quantity. She'd never had a problem securing dates, compliments, or interest from the opposite sex. It was keeping her attention that was the issue. Most men she dated seemed...flat. Once any physical chemistry faded, she was left with an itch to move on. Of course, men seemed to love the whole challenge aspect and immediately gave chase until she ended up having to either lie to spare their feelings, or hand out brutal honesty that sucked. She hated hurting people. Hell, she didn't even know what she wanted in a man anymore, so maybe that's why they got confused. She wouldn't mind a steady relationship, as long as it wasn't serious. Or boring. Or demanding. Or draining.

Ah, hell, it was so much easier to stick with houses.

She followed Gage back to the office, pushing away her thoughts, and concentrated on the new boy toy that would soon be all hers.

Chapter Two

"You need a plan to build a house. To build a life, it is even more important to have a plan or goal."—Zig Ziglar

Brady Heart crossed his arms in front of his chest and stared at the woman seated in his office. Already, prickles of heat sizzled on his skin like a heat rash. Good thing he knew it wasn't an allergy. He'd dealt with this before and knew the official term for his outbreak.

Irritation.

This seemed to be the normal reaction when he was in the vicinity of one single female.

Charlotte Grayson.

His penetrating look usually did the trick in quelling any type of opposition. He knew the art of silence and used it accordingly. Most women her age would be squirming in their seat and trying desperately to come up with clever quips to soothe his temper.

Not her. Even worse, she didn't even look like she was trying to challenge him back. She just looked...bored. Which pissed him off to no end.

Because when he was around her, he was everything *but* bored.

He clamped down the urge to scratch his skin, which was suddenly stretched too tight over his body. Especially in certain areas of his anatomy that seemed to gleefully rise to the occasion whenever Ms. Grayson was around.

"I told you before when I drafted the plans, I'm not going to change them again. Maybe you need to learn how to make up your mind so your renovations don't become a mismatched puzzle. I prefer organization and planning when I work closely with someone." His tone was mild, with a touch of disapproval—the perfect balance when dealing with stubborn coworkers who carried around a cloud of chaos like Pig Pen carried a cloud of dust.

Except she didn't look impressed. Dressed in another ridiculous outfit that made her look like a high schooler, she faced him with a mulish expression. For God's sake, hadn't anyone taught her to dress professionally? Her leggings were a wild mix of painted pinks, yellows, and blues, shades that startled an onlooker with all those bright colors hitting at once. Her T-shirt was basic, except for the way it pulled tight across her impressive chest and scrolled ANGEL in pink script. It was the type of outfit that emphasized the ripe curves held in a petite frame. Her sneakers were a metallic shade of silver that looked like a disco ball when she walked.

It wasn't just her clothes, either. Her hair was pin straight, with shaggy bangs. The strands weren't just blonde but a combination of cedar, honeycomb, and timber, all shaded together. Her hazel eyes were big—too big for her heart-shaped face—and framed by thick lashes. Her nose was pert, and her lips were perfectly formed. She rarely wore makeup, but liked to apply a glossy balm so her mouth resembled a juicy, shiny apple. Not Red Delicious. More like McIntosh, that held a nice pink color.

WTF?

Why the hell was he thinking of fruit and her mouth? She drove him nuts and was everything he wasn't attracted to in a woman. Including her sassy attitude. Like now.

"I think it's a shame you haven't been taught to be flexible," she retorted. Her purple nails flashed in the air. "Sometimes, creativity is more important than coloring within the lines. The house warrants our very best. I apologize if you need to redraft the plans again, but isn't that your job?"

Oh, she liked to push him. He got along with everyone else at Pierce Brothers, but as soon as they hired Charlie, he knew she'd be a challenge. What surprised him the most was her confidence. She seemed to have the ability to make him feel judged, even after years of experience in being an architect. The worst part?

He sensed she found him lacking.

"And I thought your job was to settle on a plan for renovation after carefully sifting through each option. Not to play with experimentation on my time." He kept his voice cool and impersonal, though temper heated his blood. How many times had he imagined shutting her up with his mouth over hers? He chalked it up to being sexually frustrated along with primitive emotions enclosed in a tiny workspace. Emotions that included anger and irritation logically extended to sexual attraction. He'd learned early on that being impulsive only led to disaster. He might be physically attracted to her for some strange reason, but they'd be a complete wreck after a few hours together. There was one thing he avoided at all costs in his personal relationships.

Mess.

"I did. But you kept pushing me to your timetable and now I need to redesign it." She raised one brow in pure challenge. "Would you rather our work be good? Or great?"

"My work is great," he fired back. "But you need to stop acting like Picasso with these renovations so we don't get backed up. Did you secure permission from Tristan to change the plans again?"

"Yes. He agreed." She paused. Her voice came out grudgingly. "But he said the final decision was yours."

A smug grin curved his lips. Oh, she hated having to ask him for things. He knew she considered him an uptight control freak. Maybe he was. But she needed to hone her creative outbursts and passion for ripping up houses on impulse without a solid architectural plan first.

"Hmm, funny, I didn't hear you ask me anything. Seemed more like a demand to me."

He gave her credit. She still didn't crack, but her eyes gleamed with a spark of temper that intrigued him. Why was it so much fun to rile her up? Because she seemed to dismiss him so easily in the office? Was it his ego or something more?

"I'm asking you to redo the plans because it's the right thing to do." Her tone was patient, as if trying to explain to a toddler. "It took me longer than I expected to get the right vision. I apologize if my request is causing a problem in your extremely busy schedule."

Only this woman could make an apology sound like a backhanded insult. He leaned back in the chair and studied her for a few moments in silence. As usual, she was comfortable enough in her skin to sit still and wait him out. He clicked on his keyboard and brought up his calendar to check the rest of his afternoon.

"Fine. I'll come out and see the property with you."

Her hazel eyes widened slightly. "Oh, no need. I have the photos in the office."

She seemed a bit too hasty to keep her distance. Another wave of irritation hit. She didn't act like this with the other men. Hell, he'd seen her laughing and joking with Dalton, Tristan, and Cal. It was only when he was around that she stiffened up and tried to avoid him. "I work more effectively when I can walk the site," he said. "We can head out now. I'll drive." Without another word, he stood up and straightened his tie. "Unless you don't have time in your busy schedule?"

She tightened her lips and rose. The word ANGEL sparkled with tiny pink sequins, emphasizing the lush curves of her breasts. The ultimate contradiction. Did she expect to retain the crew's respect when she worked at a site dressed in such an outfit? Not that he'd seen her in action. Only flitting in and out of the office, driving him mad with changing her design and treating him like an afterthought rather than the man who made it all happen for her. If she believed life was about impulse, fun, and following her muse, she should never have gotten into the design business. Without structure and a solid foundation—the actual plans that building and renovation revolved around—there was chaos.

Brady despised chaos.

Her tone was sugary sweet when she spoke. "I'm always up for a fun road trip. Lead the way."

He did.

* * * *

Charlie tried not to fidget in the expensive leather seat of his Mercedes-Benz. How much had this car cost him? It looked like a pilot's cockpit, with buttons, gadgets, and a big, shiny computer screen. He probably could've gotten a better deal with an American carmaker. On a holiday weekend. With a leftover model instead of the must-have newest one. Such a waste of money.

She bet he didn't care. The architect didn't seem to mind paying for luxuries if it made his life easier and more manageable. She'd pegged him the first moment they met, when his nose wrinkled and his gaze swept over her clothes, finding her lacking. The man wore a classic suit, like he was running for Congress rather than dealing with architectural plans. Always polished, groomed, with manicured fingers and a smoky, gravelly voice. It was funny because Tristan Pierce dressed like Bond himself, but never seemed to judge her wardrobe, occasional bawdy jokes, or tendency to work in disorganized chaos. He'd welcomed her to Pierce Brothers with an open mind, and when he saw her work on the first few jobs, he quickly doubled her workload. He also didn't hover or second-guess her instincts. He allowed her to lead on some jobs and told her he was impressed. He didn't care how she did her job as long as she was successful.

Not Brady.

He liked surface image. Polished women, with graceful manners. Word spread quickly around the office he only dated women who were soft spoken, well mannered, and let him lead in every way. The thought made Charlie shiver with loathing. She couldn't imagine giving her freedom over to a man just for his ego. Guess the man had no self-confidence. That would be the only reason he'd want to date a doormat or robotic Stepford Barbie.

Not that she cared.

She'd dealt with all types in the renovation business and usually could handle herself well. Too bad his lousy personality was hidden behind his looks. There was one thing she was forced to admit.

The man was hot.

Super hot. Sexy hot. Though his name was pure English, he looked all Latino, with gorgeous brown skin, sooty dark eyes, and inky, glossy, thick hair holding subtle shades of blue. One rebellious wave always fell loose over his forehead, giving just a touch of the disheveled look. His nose was a sharp blade that dominated his face. His lips were full and defined, with a slight curl to the bottom like he held a perpetual smirk. His body was hard and tight, and though he was average height, he used every one of those muscles to emanate a lean power that popped from his aura.

When he shook her hand for the first time, her skin had literally prickled with awareness. He was…intense. Thank God he wasn't her type, and she had little use for a chauvinistic male with an inflated ego.

No, thanks.

She remembered the exact moment she realized he wouldn't be the warm and fuzzy type. His judgy gaze traveled over her figure with dismissal; his mouth firmed into a thin line of disapproval, and he'd actually questioned Tristan if they really needed another employee to handle renovations.

It had taken all of her discipline not to give him the tongue lashing he deserved. He was a jerk and just plain rude. Sure, her clothes weren't conservative or polished. Yes, she looked super young and inexperienced. She might not talk like a Harvard graduate, but he didn't know her and yet he leapt to conclusions. Another trait she despised. She'd stood there, feeling a bit awkward, and Tristan had laughed and smoothly launched into a positive spiel about how much she'd help them out and how talented she was. Instead of apologizing or softening, Brady had just nodded, given her a clipped "Welcome to the team", and marched away like she wasn't worth another word.

After that, Charlie had declared a silent war on the architect. She went out of her way to make his life miserable. Oh, she wasn't proud of stooping to the level of petty vengeance, but she craved getting some kind of reaction from him. Since he'd rarely shown anger, interest, or respect, she figured she'd stick to the one she seemed to master.

Irritation.

The Mercedes purred low and sleek, like a graceful cougar. She tried to hold her tongue, but as usual, lost the battle. "How much did this car cost?"

He shot her a look, arching his brow. "A lot. Don't you think your question is a bit impolite?"

She gave a snort. Even his words were all proper. "Why is everyone so uptight about talking money?"

"It's a sensitive subject. Like politics. And sex."

Was that a deliberate pause or her imagination? The word fell from his lips like a crudely uttered curse. He seemed a bit shocked he'd uttered such a statement. Seems Brady didn't like to say the word aloud. Amusement flickered. She bet he'd be way too polite in the bedroom. Probably asked nicely for everything from start to finish, like a business dinner instead of a dirty roll in the hay. She liked a man who took what he wanted in private and seduced her into saying yes to everything. Politically incorrect, but she couldn't help what turned her on. She reached for her water bottle to take a sip and concentrated on the conversation. "If people were more honest, less miscommunication would occur."

"My car cost me $70,000."

The liquid slid down the wrong pipe and she fell into a coughing fit. He handed her a napkin, that faint disapproval flickering in his sooty eyes. He was probably terrified she'd drool on the leather. "Are you nuts?" she asked. Her voice sounded a tad shrill as she dabbed at the tears. "My truck cost ten thousand and it runs like a workhorse." It was a washed-out red with a kick-ass engine, and she loved it with a passion.

His nose wrinkled. "I've seen your truck. It's loud and obnoxious. Also ugly."

"But I got it for a steal," she retorted. "I could buy two houses with what you spent to drive around in luxury. Does sitting on a cushy car seat mean that much to you?"

"Actually, it does, especially when they're heated with an option for massage. And that is exactly why people don't talk about money."

She opened her mouth, then snapped it shut. "Sorry. Guess I'm a bit frugal."

"Some would say cheap." He flicked her a glance laced with suspicion. "Are you the one who spearheaded the movement to stop the pastries at morning meetings?"

She puffed up with pride. "Yes, I told Sydney by switching to bagels instead of those tiny overpriced sweets, you'd save money."

He groaned. "I loved those damn pastries. I looked forward to them."

She shrugged. "I just increased your bottom line."

"Fine. I'll pay for them out of my own pocket. Satisfied?"

She smothered a laugh. Questions whirled in her brain regarding how he fit in with the Pierce brothers. He was the only one who wasn't technically family. How did he get to be a partner? She'd watched him among the brothers, and he was treated like one of them—not an outsider. Pushing the impulse to blurt out a bunch of questions he'd refuse to answer anyway, she stuck to neutral topics. "Have you always wanted to be an architect?"

"Yes."

That was it? Someone needed to give him a class on how to carry on a conversation. "Cool beans." Forget it. She sure as hell wasn't going to search for safe topics to have a boring one-way conversation. She turned to the window and began to play her favorite game. Pick a house, imagine who lived there, and renovate to an imaginary world that perfectly fit her imaginary family. She'd spent hours driving around neighborhoods with her mother, peeking into windows at night, spinning tales of the families who lived behind the walls. If she had been a decent writer, maybe she could've been an author, but writing a business letter was enough for her. She liked anything that involved hands-on work that built something.

He made a grunt beside her. His next question was a bit reluctant, but she gave him credit for trying. "How did you get into home renovation?"

"I hate waste."

He lifted a brow. "Care to expound?"

"Like you?"

He stiffened, seeming a bit awkward, and she took pity on him. "I like the idea of using what's there already to make it better. People are obsessed with new. New clothes, cars, jewelry, houses. I look at the constant upgrades this world is obsessed with and it makes me sad. They're missing the potential of transforming ordinary into the extraordinary by making a few changes in what they have already. We've become a throw-away society and it pisses me off. So, yeah, to answer your question, when my friend told me she wanted the new Barbie dream house 'cause hers was old, I took it apart, renovated it, and she loved it all over again. Made me feel good. Here's the turnoff."

The car took the turn with competent ease. He shot her a strange look, as if she'd managed to surprise him, but he didn't respond and she shrugged the whole thing off. The rich scent of his cologne, a delicious mix of clove and musk, drifted to her nostrils. Probably cost a fortune. She'd always been an Old Spice type of girl.

He pulled up to the curb and cut the engine. The latest project for Pierce Brothers was a Tudor build that looked graceful from the front, but when they got inside, it was as if a puzzle had been mismatched and held together by old glue. The rooms had no flow and were individually contained in tight spaces rather than the open floor plan most customers coveted. She headed into the living room and pointed to the staircase that had been stuck in the back corner of a room solely meant for comfort and entertaining.

"Either the builder or the architect should have been jailed for this atrocity," Brady stated, his gaze registering the fireplace squooshed next to the stairs and a built-in cabinet in dull oak that had no function other than to visually assault. She laughed, already itching to transform the room into a cozy haven meant for a future family she'd never meet.

"Since we can't take them to court, let's fix it," she said.

"I already did. I gave you perfect plans already. Why do you want to change them?"

One thing she'd never fault him for was his work. His designs and outlook of a building were an art. She knew from working with other architects who were only able to see the technical aspects rather than the creative design that it limited options. Brady wasn't afraid to stretch out of his comfort zone. But he was still stubborn as hell about changing what was initially drafted. "There was nothing wrong with them. I've just come up with a better plan. If you can make it work."

"I can make anything work." His clean-shaven jaw clenched with the verbal challenge. "You have to convince me if it's worth it."

She rocked back on her silver sneakers and pointed to the ridiculous staircase. "Our first plan kept the staircase, removed the built-in, and destroyed the fireplace. Yes, it works functionally and visually, but I'd rather block off the staircase here, and extend it to the back of the room by the front door." She walked backward, her arm extended as she made sweeps in the open air. "We keep the built-in and have Dalton finish it in a rich mahogany. We keep the fireplace, restore the natural brick, and gain all this excess space that can be used as a full living room."

He tapped his finger against those carved lips, his dark brows drawn in concentration. He took a while to study the layout, examining the staircase with an intensity that intrigued her. Could he possibly have a sliver of passion buried beneath all those stringent rules and barriers?

"It's doable. But extra work with no solid purpose. It can work just as well if we keep the staircase as is."

"There's purpose. I'll have this open area where the stairs were to break through this wall and combine the dining room so we have one giant space. Come with me." She led him back to the front door and regarded the layout. "It makes no sense to have a back entrance to the upstairs and leave all this extra space open with no function. It also changes the appearance when you first walk through the door. There's no structure."

"Why now instead of when we met for the original design?" he challenged. "Sometimes if you make a mistake, you need to commit."

"Why?"

He stared at her. "What do you mean? To learn a lesson. To build discipline. To respect your coworkers. You can't go through life with a long line of unfinished products or half-assed work just because you can."

Oh, he was so uptight she wondered if he'd ever gone commando or skinny dipped or eaten ice cream in bed just for fun. "Actually, you can," she shot back. "Life isn't about putting your head down like a good little soldier and following the rules. It's about changing your mind, and making a mess, and surrendering to the moment when creativity strikes. I didn't see it before. Now, I do. The real question is do you walk away knowing it could have been better but you just didn't want to admit you were wrong the first time? Haven't you ever been wrong, Brady?"

A muscle worked in his jaw. "Of course. Everyone makes mistakes."

She tilted her head and studied him. "I know. But does everyone forgive themselves for making mistakes? I do. I want to fix it. Do you?"

His gaze met hers, and an odd heat simmered between them. "How old are you?" he demanded.

She stuck her chin in the air. "Twenty-five."

His lips twisted in a mockery of a smile. "I'm thirty-five. I've built my reputation on quality work and consistence. You want me to fix the house to suit your new vision? Fine. I can do that. But don't think making excuses to rationalize an error makes you some free-spirited, impulsive artist who knows more about life than I do."

Her mouth dropped open.

He spun on his polished heel and walked to the door. "By the way, I forgive you."

"Forgive me?" she managed to squeak out. Her vision blurred to a pale red. She'd always wondered if that cliché was true. "For what?"

"Making a mistake. I have to get back to the office. I'll have your new plans drawn up by end of day."

He disappeared through the door before she could launch herself after him and… Well, she wasn't sure what, but shaking that arrogant, cool exterior off his gorgeous face would be her first priority.

After a few moments of simmering, she stomped out, got in the car, and refused to talk to him for the rest of the drive back.

He was such an asshole.

* * * *

He was such an asshole.

Brady snuck a glance at her profile. Weak rays of sun streamed over her face, highlighting the smooth, soft skin of her cheek. An aura of steam hung over her head like a storm cloud brewing. Her gaze was trained out the window, arms clasped tight around her body, stretching the soft cotton over the lush curve of her breasts. Immediately his dick stirred to life. If he stopped the car, yanked her into his arms, and kissed her, would he finally figure out what made him so attracted to her?

He'd been hot for women before. He rarely leapt when a well-laid plan for seduction always worked better. He actually liked the foreplay and tension that flickered to a brilliant, white-hot flame. Enjoyed the play of banter and dialogue, of knowing what was to unfold between them, of the endless possibilities.

Unfortunately, he'd been wrong too many times before and he'd turned a tad cynical. Sure, he'd had some long-term relationships he'd hoped would become permanent, and many women had actually shared his same goals. Settle down to raise a family. Let him be the breadwinner and shoulder the financial responsibilities. He'd watched his father take care of his family, and now his two sisters had settled into domestic bliss. He refused to apologize for knowing who he was and what he wanted out of life. Yet each time he thought of making a permanent commitment, his soul balked. There was a restlessness inside him that never seemed to calm, and damned if he'd marry without being all in.

He knew all of his requirements, his fantasies, his needs, and his wants. When *the one* burst into his life, his heart and gut would sense his partner and everything would click into place.

Right now, he only knew one thing.

His soul mate was *not* Charlotte Grayson.

But he wanted her.

He cut her another glance, brooding over his assholery back in the house. Why did she always ignite his temper? The way she passionately pleaded a case, painting herself as a figure who raced through life grabbing every opportunity and following every impulse, while she mocked him for the very thing that brought him success.

Order. Knowledge. Control.

Probably the ten-year difference. She was a baby. She'd probably lived a pampered life, secure in her parents' house with her parents' money. She'd graduated from a proper college and decided to have some fun with rehab. Oh, she was good at her job, but this wasn't permanent for her. She had an itch to scratch, and he felt he needed to protect Pierce Brothers if she decided to go out on her own and steal any of their clients.

She couldn't do anything now, but he suspected once she found the next yellow brick road to follow, she'd be off to discover a brand new Oz. The last thing he needed in his life was a flighty woman.

But he wanted her.

He shifted in his seat, cursing under his breath. So stupid. He just needed to get over it because he sure as hell wasn't making a move. She'd probably spit in his face and sue him.

Charlotte Grayson would be shocked at some of the things he wanted to do to her. She called herself a free spirit, but he bet she'd be the type of lover to fight him on every move, questioning, pushing, until the entire episode became too complicated to be any fun.

No thanks.

He'd stick with the plan that had been working well between them. Keep his distance and limit his interaction with her. It gave him a better opportunity to be less of a dick. She didn't deserve to be insulted.

He pulled up to Pierce Brothers and cut the engine. "Charlotte, I apologize. I—"

"Don't call me that. I hate it."

"Fine. Let me explain—"

"No need to explain. I get it." She turned to him and those stunning hazel eyes regarded him with a spark of temper. "You haven't liked me from day one. Let's just agree to be polite at work and not pretend we'll ever be more than what we are—coworkers forced to share the same space."

A sting of shame hit him. "Listen, I—"

"I'll make sure from now on I get the plans right the first time so we have no further issues. Thanks for the cushy ride."

She jumped out of the car and didn't look back as she entered the office. Brady smothered a groan, rubbing his temples. Dammit, he hadn't meant to hurt her feelings. She churned him up inside and he couldn't figure out why.

Maybe it was better this way. He only worked with her on a limited basis, and it shouldn't be hard to keep his distance. He'd deliver her plans when she asked and schedule walk-throughs with Tristan so they didn't have to be alone again.

It was for the best.

Chapter Three

"Regard it as just as desirable to build a chicken house as to build a cathedral."—Frank Lloyd Wright

Charlie climbed up the broken steps, juggling the mass of supplies in her hands, and walked into the house. The scent of rotted wood and dust filled the air. Her ears strained with the sound of screaming silence. There was something so sad about an empty house. It cried of lost memories and loneliness.

She intended to fix it.

Dropping her toolbox, she grabbed her notebook and began taking inventory of the main things she wanted to accomplish. Finally, she had her own project to dive into. Her heart slammed against her ribs in excitement and anticipation. The dumpster was coming this week, but so far, she had been unable to book any extra help. Besides the expense, schedules for all her contacts were filled with Pierce Brothers work.

Ah, well. She could do the whole thing by herself. It would just take more time. She didn't have to deliver for a client. This was her baby, and she intended to make sure her first house was filled with her trademark creativity and restoration materials. Besides saving buckets of money, it would give the place a personal touch every homeowner appreciated.

She made notes in her pad, sketching out various ideas for the rooms. The roof would need replacement, but the structure itself was solid. The shingles were basic brown and easy to fill in. The basement was small and stuffed with various junk and insects galore, but it wouldn't need to be gutted. Everything was salvageable. That was the primary reason she'd wanted the property.

Humming under her breath, she lost herself in the magic of endless possibilities, ending in the tiny bedroom off the Jack and Jill bathroom. Checking light fixtures and computing square feet, her brain clicked madly until she noticed something out of place.

A blanket with a small oil lamp was set up neatly in the corner. A pile of books lay by its side, stacked in perfect precision. Charlie frowned, walking over to examine the odd setup. The blanket didn't look old, and the books had no dust on them. The lamp seemed to have a surplus of fluid and looked recently used.

Odd. A chill ran down her spine. The house was set on a block far enough away from the occasional violence and drugs that sprung up on the outskirts of town, but what if her house was being used for squatters? Or people doing drugs?

Dragging in a breath, she inspected every inch of the house but found no proof of needles, weed, or any other paraphernalia that pointed to crime. The front door was locked, and the main windows were cracked but not busted open. Where was the point of entry? After another half hour, she came up empty. She shook her head, making a note to check on it more tomorrow, and headed back out.

Shadows were beginning to chase the sun down, but a few leftover rays warmed her face. She got in the truck and turned the key.

Nothing.

Ah, crap.

She tried again but got the grindy sound that confirmed she was going nowhere. Muttering a curse, she popped the hood. She went through her normal checklist of diagnostics but found nothing strange. Probably the battery. A simple jump would work, and she had the cables. She looked around, and with a sinking heart, realized no one was there to help. No doors to knock on, and she wasn't comfortable enough in the neighborhood to begin walking around. Better to just call in some help.

She grabbed her phone and tried Sydney first.

"Hello?"

"Syd, it's Charlie. Are you still at the office?"

"Yes, I'm working late tonight and Becca is with the sitter.

What's up?"

"My car broke down and I think it needs a jump. I hate to bother you, but do you think you can come help me? I know Raven is at the bar, but I can check with Morgan if you can't get me."

"No, it's time I got out of here anyway. Give me the address." Charlie recited it to her. "I'll be there in fifteen."

"Thanks."

She clicked off, got back in the truck, and waited until she saw Sydney's car. She waved her friend over, directing her close to hook up the cables. "You rock. I didn't want to get stuck waiting for Triple A."

Sydney's green eyes filled with concern. "What are you doing out here?" she asked, her gaze taking in the empty street. "This place is deserted and on a dead end. You know there was a drug bust a few blocks over last week?"

Charlie laughed. "I'm fine. This is the new house I bought to flip." She waved her hand proudly in the air. "Gonna fix it up, make it nice, and sell it."

Her friend's mouth dropped open. "Girlfriend, please tell me you are not working on this all alone, late at night."

"Of course not. Eventually I'll hire some help, and it's not late at night. It's only seven pm."

Sydney crossed her arms in front of her chest and gave her *the look*. It reminded her a bit of her own mother. Since Sydney was a mother of a six-year-old, it wasn't a far reach. "This is dangerous," she said firmly. "I'm all about flipping houses and changing the neighborhood, but you didn't even tell anyone about it. Let us help."

"I'm fine, I swear. I like doing things on my own, and this is separate from Pierce Brothers work. Plus, I always carry pepper spray and a bat in case something happens. Can you gun your engine for me? I'm going to try to start it."

Grumbling under her breath, Sydney obeyed, and in a few minutes, the pickup roared back to life. Charlie shot her a thumbs-up signal and disconnected the cables. "Thanks so much. I'm good to go."

"I'm following you out of here. What made you buy this property?"

"It was the cheapest, and it has great potential. Look at the land." She pointed out the generous lot, infested with weeds, mud, and rocks. "Most of the houses in this area are squeezed tight together. Since this is on a dead end, it can be a great haven for someone who needs it."

Sydney shook her head. "You got it bad. A true rehab addict. Listen, I'm thrilled you're doing this on your own terms but you need to be safe. What if it's being used for other stuff like gangs or drugs?"

Her mind flashed to the quiet, neat corner with the books. "I didn't see any evidence of anything criminal. Just looks like a squatter needed a warm place to stay. I'm sure he or she will leave once I begin work."

Sydney's mouth dropped open. "Someone is living here!? What did you find?"

"Just a lamp and some books. I'm sure it's harmless."

Sydney frowned. "I'll help you with the project," she announced.

A pang of affection hit hard. She'd only been working with Sydney and the Pierce Brothers under a year, but already she felt as if she had a family. They took care of their own. "Syd, I adore you, but between work at Pierce and your daughter, you have no extra time. Besides, I want to do this on my own. Now stop being a worry wart and get your ass home."

Charlie blew her a kiss and got back into the truck. Finally, Sydney pulled out, carefully following her to the town limits before they went their separate ways. Charlie drove to her apartment with a smile on her face. It was nice to have friends who cared. She'd make sure she checked in with people when she was at the house and put an extra bottle of pepper spray inside. She'd learned in college how important it was to take care of herself. When an overly enthusiastic male backed her into a bedroom at a party, ignoring her repeated *no*'s, she'd lashed out and screamed *fire* at the top of her lungs until someone took notice.

He'd ended up with a social media smear as she warned everyone to stay far away from him.

Afterward, she'd taken defense classes so she felt more confident fighting back.

She pulled into her parking space and headed to her apartment. Immediately, the space settled and pulsed with warmth around her. Kicking off her boots, she collapsed on the couch. Her place was cozy, with everything she needed to live happily, and dirt cheap. The apartment building might look like crap from the outside, but inside she had appliances, warmth, and wifi. She'd decorated the rooms with her usual creativity, and now it was a feast for the senses. She'd painted her own canvases and hung them on the walls, interspersed between photo collages and shelves containing fun trinkets. She'd sewn her own throw pillows in happy colors like lemon, lime, and tangerine, brightening up her dull beige sofa sleeper, which was the most comfortable thing she'd ever sat her ass on. Much better than Brady's Mercedes. The coffee and side tables were restored wood she'd refinished. The television was a much smaller screen than most people demanded, but it was clear and color and half price. The chandelier had been created by beads bought at the craft store, and matched the various genie lamps she'd grabbed at a garage sale. A few bucks of polish and some elbow grease had restored them to glory.

Her place was eclectic and fun and made her happy.

She wondered what Brady's place looked like.

The thought flickered so quickly, she jerked and pushed it out of her head. For the past week, they'd left each other alone. Everything was finally coming together for her. She'd carved out a place at Pierce Brothers, and she had her own house to flip.

She closed her eyes with a smile on her face and dreamed of a perfect future.

Chapter Four

"The dialogue between client and architect is about as intimate as any conversation you can have, because when you're talking about building a house, you're talking about dreams."—Robert A. M. Stern

Dalton peeked his head in. "Dude, Cal called an emergency conference. You free?"

Brady nodded, grateful for the interruption. He'd spent too many hours bent over his desk, gaze trained on his computer. "Anything wrong?"

"Don't know. Just said it was important."

"Okay, let me grab some coffee and I'll meet you in there." He headed to the kitchen, which was stocked with every piece of machinery needed to work 24/7. From the stainless steel refrigerator, cappuccino maker, soda machine, vending machines, and mahogany cupboards stuffed with goodies, everyone made sure cravings could be satisfied. He headed to his stock of specially ground Kenyan coffee, anticipating that first whiff of pure bliss, lifted the airtight cover, and found...something else.

He frowned and took a sniff. This wasn't his coffee. The scent of fake beans drifted to his nostrils, weak and wimpy and painful to his coffee-loving soul. Clenching his hands into tight fists, he marched to the front desk. "Rachel, why was my coffee switched out?" he demanded.

The older woman was in her sixties, but looked a decade younger. With smooth skin and a polished appearance, Rachel would be the one to know what he was talking about. She was ruthlessly organized and on top of supplies. A smile wreathed her face. "Charlie found a supplier who sold in bulk and saved us tons of money. She said it's exactly like the brand you like but half the price. Is it good?"

Son of a bitch. He glowered, trying to yank back his temper. "No."

Her face fell. "Oh. Well, I guess I can switch it back if you'd like." She paused. "Seems like a waste of money, though. Charlie said the amount we save could go toward the local pet shelter to help the animals. Wasn't that a great idea?"

His temper hitched a notch higher. Now she was spreading her frugality around the office. He gave plenty to charity, and he refused to have his few indulgences yanked from him. He'd already lost his pastries. "I'd appreciate if you switch it back."

She nodded, her eyes flaring with disapproval. "Of course."

"Thank you, Rachel." He headed toward the conference room, skipping the coffee. The men were already seated around the polished table. Cal took the head, sprawled out in his usual battered jeans, T-shirt, and work boots. Dalton was popping Hershey kisses into his mouth, looking the most relaxed of the crew. With his surfer hair caught in a man bun and long, tapered fingers drumming the table, he didn't seem nervous about the emergency meeting. Tristan sat between them, clad in his high-powered, custom suit. He sat completely still, a slight frown on his brow from the interruption of his tight, controlled schedule.

Brady took his customary place to Caleb's right. He'd grown up with these men and looked at them as family—not friends. He'd met Cal in college freshman year and been invited to his house for the weekend. Instantly, he'd clicked with all the brothers and began splitting his time between them and his family, who lived a few towns away. He'd been fascinated with Pierce Brothers Construction from the first day, loving the idea of working for a family firm. He got his degree, passed the architectural board tests, and was hired immediately by Cal's father, Christian.

Of course, the tight-knit family he'd signed on to had finally splintered into pieces after they'd lost their beloved mother, Diane Pierce, driving all the brothers in separate directions. Tristan had headed to New York City to do real estate, and Dalton fled to Florida to open a wood restoration business. Brady had stayed with Cal and become a constant in the business, drawing up all the plans for houses and even doing some home renovation when needed.

When Christian died of a heart attack, the will had stated the brothers must work together in the family business for one year or it would be sold. They'd agreed to do it, and after a hard road, they eventually forgave each other and moved onward. When Brady looked at all of them now, a sense of brotherly connection and fierce loyalty shimmered in the air. Having them all back was a gift. He was now a full partner in the company and helped drive all the decisions. He had everything he'd ever dreamed of—financial security, a job he loved, a dream house, and friends who were family.

If only he could find his damn wife.

He pushed his distracting thoughts out of his mind and concentrated on the conversation. As usual, Cal got straight to the point. "We have a problem with Charlie."

Dalton cocked his head in surprise. "What's the problem? I thought her work was stellar."

Brady jumped right in. "I knew it. I didn't want to be the one who said I told you so, but I had doubts from the beginning."

Cal rolled his eyes. "There's nothing wrong with her work. And I still don't understand why you two can't be in the same room together without sharing dirty looks. Sydney came to me about something that concerns me."

"Is she in trouble?" Tristan asked. Concern lit his amber eyes. "If she is, we'll help her."

"She bought a house on her own to flip."

Dalton grinned. "Good for her. She's come a long way since I met her."

Cal snorted. "And a longer time since you tried to make Raven jealous by pretending you were interested in Charlie. I still love that story."

"Didn't she give you a shove and a tongue blistering in the parking lot of My Place?" Tristan jumped in.

Dalton groaned. "Leave me alone. I was screwed up and didn't realize Raven was the love of my life. I paid for my sins."

Brady remembered Cal telling him about that incident. Seemed Dalton and Charlie became friends, but when he broke up with Raven, he tried to use Charlie to make his ex-lover jealous. It backfired when Charlie confronted him, refusing to break female code and giving him a few hard truths.

Dalton's skin turned a shade red. "I should've never told you. I was drunk at the time."

"That's when we get all the good stuff," Tristan commented. "The Raging Bitch IPA does it every time."

Brady laughed. He was constantly entertained by the crew, but he brought back the purpose of the meeting. "So, Charlie bought a house to flip. Why is that a problem? Isn't she able to do her own sideline as long as it doesn't affect Pierce Brothers?"

"Yes, but I found out the property is on the outskirts of town in Trapps. I happened to do a drive-by today and several things concern me."

"That's not the best area," Tristan said. "It's pretty close to some of the hot spots. How many houses on the block?"

"Only a handful. It's on a dead-end street, so no immediate neighbors. Good lot. Crappy house, but structurally sound. Has potential," Cal said.

Tristan steepled his fingers. "She's got an eye for property."

Brady kept the surprise from showing on his face. He had no idea she had enough money to invest in her own house to flip, let alone know how to pick one. Sure, she was enthusiastic about her job, but he figured she wouldn't be around on a long-term basis. "Who's her crew?" Brady asked.

Cal leaned back in his chair. Worry glinted from gunmetal eyes. "No one. She's doing everything herself. Sydney says she intends to do her work in the early evenings after Pierce Brothers and on weekends."

Brady stared at Cal. "You mean she's working alone, in that neighborhood, at night?"

"That's right," Cal said.

Dalton groaned. "We can't let her do that. If something happens, we'll never forgive ourselves."

Cal nodded. "Agreed. Let's put a plan in place and bring her in for a discussion."

"Who do we have available to help her out?" Brady asked.

"Jason?" Tristan suggested.

"Nope, he's on a job for the next few weeks. Actually, all my main crew members are booked for the next two months."

"Maybe we can get her to delay the work," Brady said. "Wait until we can offer her some help."

Dalton shot him a look. "You don't know Charlie very well, do you, dude?"

He glowered. "I know she's a real pain in the ass."

Dalton grinned. "You like her."

His mouth fell open. He closed it with a snap, embarrassed at his obvious reaction. How juvenile. Dalton loved to jab at him and try to get him flustered. Some people thought it was part of his charm. "I have no opinion on her," he said way too stiffly. His dick stirred and screamed him a liar. Dammit, he had to focus on the problem at hand. "Dalton, why can't you give her a hand a few days per week?"

"Can't. I'm helping out Raven with the bar, building Cal and Morgan's new house, and have a ton of side jobs."

Cal rubbed his head. "It's the height of summer and we're at our peak. I'm slammed."

"Same here," Tristan said. "I'm traveling a lot and cramming in renovation on a few projects. There's just no damn time."

Silence settled. Very slowly, all the men swiveled their gaze to him. It took him a few moments to realize their intention.

"Hell, no," he bit out. "I work on renovation only when there's no other option."

"I think this fits the guidelines," Cal said. "You did mention you were caught up on most of our clients. Can you make the time?" Cal asked.

Frustration zipped through his blood. "I'm caught up, but there's always a ton of work. I can't afford to get behind by playing babysitter."

Dalton winced. "If she heard that, she'd come after all of us. She may be small, but Charlie is scary when she gets mad."

Brady smothered a groan at his friend's expression. When had they all become whipped by their women? Tristan seemed to be the only one left with some common sense, so he directed his words to him. "Look, I agree she needs someone at the site, but can't we hire an intern for her?"

Tristan regarded him thoughtfully. "Not a bad idea. I can ask around and see if there's an alternative. In the meantime, I think you'd be perfect to help her out. You can book your mornings out for clients, then spend late afternoon to evening working on the house. I'm sure I'll be able to find someone who wants extra money or to learn the trade."

"We'll help cover the overload on your work schedule," Cal added. "I just need to know you're on board before we bring Charlie in to tell her the plan."

The men around the table waited for his answer. A strange foreboding shivered down his spine, as if he knew things were about to change but he didn't know how. He quickly thought over his options and realized he had none. She couldn't be alone in that neighborhood, and he was the best one to help out until they found someone else. It would only be temporary. "I'll do it."

Cal let out a breath. "Thanks. I appreciate it. Now I just need to find the right way to tell her so it doesn't look like we're bullying or forcing her to accept help."

He shook his head. "Just explain to her it's not safe for a woman alone, plus she's getting free help. Win/win. She'll be grateful."

Cal and Dalton burst into laughter. He glared at them but noticed even Tristan was barely holding back a grin. "You really have no clue, do you?" Dalton asked. "I can't wait till you finally fall for some hot-tempered Latina woman who tells you how it really is."

He arched a brow. "I've always told you the perfect woman in my life not only respects my decisions, but listens. I have no problem claiming the leadership role."

Tristan lost the battle and grinned. "Can't wait to meet her. Guess you plan on being single a long damn time."

He shook his head at their good-natured jabbing. They'd been on his case for years about the type of woman he sought out, but Brady knew what was important to make a long lasting relationship. He'd seen it every day. If his father gave an order, everyone listened. Things ran smoothly and respect layered the relationship. Was that so bad? He wasn't some monster who wanted to order his lover around. He craved a give and take, with the knowledge he'd protect them both. It may be old-fashioned, but it wasn't wrong, and damned if he was going to keep apologizing for it.

"Okay, let's get this over with and call her in. I'll try to present it in the best way possible. Everyone ready?"

They nodded, and Cal opened the door to get her.

* * * *

Screw the Pierce Brothers.

Charlie seethed as her gloved hands began ripping out various junk from the house and dragging it to the dumpster. They had the nerve to summon her to the office and dictate who would help renovate her house? The house she'd invested in alone? And by renovate, they clearly meant babysit. A watcher. A keeper. Some big strong man to handle any trouble thrown her way, like she couldn't protect herself.

Hell, no.

Gritting her teeth, she threw her pissed-off energy into the cleanup, going over the entire episode in her head. Cal had taken the lead, but it was Brady's quiet judgment that made her crazed. He stared at her with a touch of disapproval, as if her rejection of their proposal was yet another stupid move she made because she wasn't smart enough to accept their help. He figured she'd be grateful. When she'd thrown it right back and told them no, thank you, they had the gall to practically threaten her. It had gone so bad she'd stormed out, almost tempted to quit and go on her own.

Almost.

But she needed this job. She wasn't far enough along on her own, and Pierce Brothers had the perfect setup. It would be easier to quit if she thought she was being placated by men who didn't respect her, but deep inside, she knew that wasn't the case. They were protective of all their employees, and had clearly explained they only wanted to be sure she was safe in the neighborhood. Yes, she appreciated their concern, but she wanted to do this job herself.

At least she'd made her opinion quite clear when she politely thanked them for their concern and promised to kick anyone's ass who showed up on her job site without prior approval.

Yeah. That had gone real well.

Blowing out a breath, she spent the next hour moving crap into the dumpster, only pausing for a water break. The junk removal was the easy part. She needed to attack the wall dividing the kitchen and family room, but she'd need a set of finalized plans. She refused to ask Brady for a favor, and if she paid him, he'd only treat her like a chore rather than a client. Her backup architect wasn't as good but would have to do. Then she'd concentrate on getting rid of the crap cabinets. She had her eye on some functional, low-cost ones at Anthony's in stark white. It would brighten the place up. She guzzled water, enjoying the silence. Dalton always worked with boy bands blaring, and Cal loved his metal eighties stuff, but she loved the quiet. Nothing needed but the flow of her thoughts and the movements of her hands as she restored and rebuilt. Her soul practically sang amidst the sawdust, mold, and rotted wood.

She was on her last trip when she spotted the small shadow on the front lawn, staring at her. A young boy—definitely a teen—stood on her property, a shocked look on his face. Seemed he hadn't expected her presence. He had large, dark eyes, beautiful brown skin, and long, lanky legs. He wore black cargo shorts, a gray T-shirt, and orange and white sneakers. Resentment practically beamed her like a laser. Obviously, she wasn't wanted. "Hi," she called out. "I'm Charlie."

He blinked but didn't move. Shifted his weight back and forth on those fancy sneakers. "What are you doing here?" His voice held the sharp edge of youth, with the high pitch of puberty. "This ain't your property."

She regarded him curiously, sensing no aggression but more of a possessive inflection of tone. "Actually, it is," she said lightly. Tugging off her gloves, she took a few steps closer. "I bought it. Plan on renovating it and selling. Are you from this neighborhood?"

He jerked back, averting his gaze, but not before she caught the flare of anger and grief in his dark eyes. Ah, she'd finally figured out who her visitor had been. The books, the lamp, and the blanket told her he'd been using her house as a crash pad. Normally, she'd let it go and urge him to be on his way, but something about the boy called to her.

Hands clenched into fists, body tight, he seemed to fight with himself before shaking his head and pivoting on his sneaker-clad heel. "Nah. Forget it." He'd taken a few steps before she called out again.

"It's your books in my house, isn't it? *The Outsiders?*"

He stiffened, slowly turning back around. He lifted his head with pure rebellion. "Yeah. It is. I wasn't trespassing. Didn't know anyone lived there."

"I know. I just recently bought it. Was trying to figure out how someone got in there."

He shrugged. "It was open."

Her lips twitched. "Oh, my bad. Do you like the book?"

He blinked. "Huh?"

"*The Outsiders.* It was on the top of your stack. Surprised you're reading it."

"'Cause you don't think kids like me can read? Think I'm more into comic books?"

She jerked back, frowning. His tone shimmered with resentment. "No. I didn't think the book was well known in your generation. Figured it was a bit out of date, you know? It's from the eighties. And I take offense to both statements. A kid is a kid, and comic books rock."

Her words had the intended reaction. A quick grin slid across his lips before quickly being squashed. She wondered why he was holing up in an abandoned house. Trouble at home? Friends? School? It could be anything, but he'd be prickly if she didn't mind her business.

"I saw it on TV," he admitted. "Looked cool. The book's good."

"I had such a crush on Matt Dillon when I first saw it," she sighed.

He rolled his eyes. "Can I have my stuff back or you gonna call the cops?"

"Nothing to call the cops for if the house wasn't locked. Come on in." She turned and went inside, not stopping to see if he followed. Slowly, he trudged through the sagging door, his gaze taking in the space now cleared of junk.

"Where's the other people?" he asked.

"It's just me. You gotta problem with that?"

Again, that grin came and went. Charlie liked the way it softened his features and took away the edges. "No, just seems like a lot of work to rebuild a house where it's only gonna get trashed again."

"Why? The neighborhood is solid enough. I figured a family will want in, and I like the property. I also intend to renovate it, which is quite different from a rebuild. Besides, you must like something about it to be hanging around."

He studied her with a gaze way too shrewd for his age. "I like a place where no one bothers me. You really think someone will buy it?"

"I really do." She crossed her arms in front of her chest. "I'll even make you a deal."

Right away, he stepped back, poised to run out of the house. "Don't make no deals."

She nodded. "Good. Means you're smart. Just saying if you're ever interested in seeing how to renovate, I'll show you some stuff."

"You don't even know me."

She shrugged. "Just an idea. If you have nothing to do, I'll be here working every day from 4 pm on. Got electricity now so no need for the oil lamp. But you can't sneak in anymore. And I don't allow friends or anyone else on my property when I'm not around. If I find that, I will call the cops. I have to be careful, too."

Interest flashed over his face. "What kind of stuff?"

"I'm tearing down that wall, then gutting the kitchen."

"With big machines?" he asked.

She laughed. "Nah, with my sledgehammer."

His eyes widened. Interesting. Too many kids weren't keen on manual labor. They liked sleek computers, video games, YouTube, instant gratification, and conversations that never occurred face to face. Renovating a house bored them to tears. Hell, she didn't judge. She had been the oddball her whole life. But if this kid wanted to learn, she'd love the company.

Much better than Brady Heart.

"I'll think about it," he stated.

"Cool. Let me get your stuff." She returned with the blanket, lamp, and books and stuck them in a plastic grocery bag. "What time does school let out?"

"Three. I have basketball on Tuesdays and Thursdays."

"If you want to work here, you need to let your mom and dad know."

"Mom doesn't come home till six."

"How old are you?"

The defenses shot back up. "Old enough."

Latchkey kid. Most were with both parents needing to work. She'd been the same, sometimes staying alone till late, making her own dinner and putting herself to bed. She was used to her own company and had no issues or excuses about being abandoned. Her mother had done her best and given her all. Charlie had been one of the lucky ones. She backed off, not wanting to spook him. "I know. I was ten when I started staying by myself."

He studied her face, finally nodding. His shoulders relaxed. "I'm thirteen."

"Ugh. Crappy age."

He laughed, seeming surprised. "Better go. Thanks."

"Hey, what's your name?"

"Jackson."

"Good to meet you, Jackson. Hope I'll see you here so I can get a little help."

He lifted a hand in the air and disappeared through the door. She thought about him for a while, wondering about his circumstances, wondering why he intrigued her. Maybe she'd see him again. Maybe not. Either way, at least she wasn't spooked about her mysterious visitor any longer.

If she told Brady, would he back off?

Probably not. He pictured himself the white knight ready to rescue a damsel, except it wasn't in a castle with a dragon, but a dilapidated house on a back end alley.

She checked again on her stash of pepper sprays readily available and her baseball bat leaning against the entrance to the kitchen. Hmm, if she wrapped it in barbed wire, would it be extra scary? Like Lucille from *The Walking Dead*?

Nah, that'd just be more like serial killer.

A giggle burst from her lips as she imagined Brady catching sight of her with a deadly bat. His appalled face would be almost worth it.

She glanced at her watch and figured she'd squeeze out another hour. Might as well hit the gross, scary, serial killer basement.

Glancing back and forth in the quiet, she grabbed her pepper spray just in case and headed down the rickety stairs.

Chapter Five

"Each new situation requires a new architecture."—*Jean Nouvel*

Brady stared at the house and wondered what the woman had gotten herself into.

Trapps wasn't the best area to begin with. Drug dealers were known to haunt the adjoining neighborhood, and it was all too possible for them to wander over to expand their distribution. His assessing gaze took in the structure, and he began a slow inspection around the property, noting the half-full dumpster. Hmm, she'd gotten a lot done. Of course, after she'd stormed out of the conference room, why wasn't he surprised she'd decided to work alone as a big "screw you" to everyone?

The house was small but solid. At least she got that right. The outside would need to be stripped and re-sided or painted. The lot was extra large for this area, but was now filled with overgrown weeds and creatures who probably had made a happy home. The cracked windows needed replacing, and so did the roof. He hoped she hadn't invested in a house with electrical or plumbing issues. That'd be the main costs. Surface was easy enough. Bad wires, pipes, or mold killed you each and every time.

Guess he'd find out now.

He shook his head. Honestly, she was acting like a child. He didn't want to be here either, but it was best to have some type of buddy system in a questionable neighborhood, especially when working alone at night. Did she want to court trouble for attention? Or was she so selfish she didn't care about anyone else who'd worry about her?

Tamping down a sigh, he knocked on the front door, already prepped for her attitude. She'd be pissed he showed up, but he'd made a promise to his friends, and he was sticking with it.

She didn't answer.

He knocked again, but after a few moments, he turned the doorknob and let himself in. The creak in the air should have alerted her, but when he called out her name, there was only silence. Where was she? And didn't she have the sense to lock the damn door? Sydney had told him about the mysterious visitor Charlie didn't seem to be worried about. What if the person consistently breaking in decided to pay her an impromptu visit? Smothering a curse, he walked further, examining the rooms.

Definite possibilities were here. It could be a cozy family home, even though the bedrooms were small and the kitchen needed updating. He took his time investigating, until he finally heard a clatter rise from the basement. Hmm, she probably hadn't heard him come in. Real smart. Thank God he'd shown up because she definitely couldn't be trusted to work here alone. His temper simmered at just the thought of the trouble she could be in if he'd been someone dangerous.

And then he saw the baseball bat.

His mouth fell open. Propped up in the corner, the large wooden bat was the perfect extra addition to help a criminal get further. He pressed his lips together, fighting the urge to throw open the basement door and stomp downstairs, giving her the scare of a lifetime.

Would serve her right.

He picked up the bat, running his hands down the smooth surface, and moved back into the kitchen. Who'd done her architectural plans? And why the hell wouldn't she have asked him? Irritation prickled his nerves. She might not like him, but he figured he'd earned her respect with his work. Did she dislike him so much she refused to ask him for sketches? They were coworkers, and he wouldn't have charged her.

Finally, he heard the door open to the basement. He opened his mouth to call out her name, then decided not to warn her. Maybe if he startled her, she'd realize anyone could have just walked right in the front door and availed himself of her only weapon.

He took a few steps into the family room, his shoes creaking slightly over the worn floors.

"Aghgh!"

Before he even managed to clear the corner, the warrior shriek hit his ears at the same time a foot smashed into his crotch. Exploding pain crippled his balls. The bat clattered to the ground. He bent over, grabbing his poor dick, which had retreated into his intestines.

Blinking through the agony, he tried to speak but a sudden shock of spray blasted his vision.

He didn't remember if he screamed or not. Later on, he'd deny it on the Bible, not even caring if his mother promised a trip to hell for lying to God. At that very moment, hell was right in front of him, with his streaming eyes and throbbing dick, and snot pouring from his nose. He stumbled back, his ears ringing, and began rubbing furiously at his eyes, completely blinded.

"Brady!"

The feminine voice barely registered. He was intent on trying to live past the agony. His brain splintered on which was worse—his burning eyes or his weeping testicles.

"Oh, my God. I'm so sorry! Oh, my God, I thought you were a criminal! Here, sit down. I'll call 911. Do you need an ambulance? A doctor? Oh, my God!"

The words bubbled in the air and he desperately tried to make sense of them. Strong hands grasped him and lowered him to the filthy floor. A bunch of towels were pressed into his grip, and he tried to dab at his stinging eyes. His tear ducts had exploded, and wetness dripped down his cheeks. Had that whimper come from him?

So embarrassing.

"What the fuck did you do to me?" he managed to grate out.

"Pepper spray." She shoved something at him, but he couldn't see it. "Here, hold your head back. I'm going to pour water in your eyes to see if I can flush it out."

"Son of a bitch!"

The water hit his eyeballs and more stinging commenced. He uttered a stream of Spanish—the only damn words he remembered were the curses—and wondered if Charlotte Grayson had not only taken away his vision but also his ability to ever pleasure a woman again. He craved to crawl into a ball and be left alone, but she kept pouring water on him, wiping at his snotty nose and edging way too close to his injured anatomy.

"The spray is only supposed to be temporary, but let me take you to the hospital. You look terrible."

He still couldn't see her face, just a rough shadowed outline of her figure. "You kicked me in the balls and sprayed me with that shit!" he bellowed. "Are you crazy? And I'm not going to the hospital." If anyone got wind of this story, he'd be done. He'd never live down the gossip.

"You broke in! I came up from the basement and heard a noise and saw a shadow holding my bat. I thought you were going to kill me!"

"You left the fucking front door open! I knocked, but when you didn't answer, I came right in. You would've been dead if I had been a killer."

Was that a snort or was he imagining things? "Doesn't seem like it. Looks more like you would've been going straight to jail since I took you out."

Rage mixed with pain. He reached his hands out toward the fuzzy figure in an effort to throttle her, but she jerked out of his reach. "You took me by surprise," he managed to choke out. "If I'd been a real killer, I wouldn't have waited. I would've trapped you in the basement."

"That's why I brought the pepper spray down with me. And I did lock the front door. Hmm, I wonder if that's how Jackson was getting in. Probably need to install a new dead bolt. I'll get that done by morning."

Was she trying to have a rational conversation with him or had his head truly exploded? He had no idea how long it took him to stumble to his feet, but he shook off her efforts to help and leaned weakly against the wall, fluid still streaming from his membranes. "Pepper spray won't stop a killer," he muttered, swiping at his eyes and nose. "You stormed out of the conference room like a toddler."

Through a haze of fuzz, her mouth dropped open. He couldn't mistake the fury laced in her tightly wound tone. "Maybe if you didn't treat me like a toddler, I wouldn't have to act like one. No one has any right to tell me what I can do with my own property. Or act like a bunch of overprotective big brothers bossing me around. Hell, no. I've got it handled. Now, are you going to the hospital or not?"

He glared through his tears. "Not. I'm fine. Just need to let the stuff work its way out. Funny, I seem to remember them taking you in for an internship and never treating you like an outsider. Cal and Dalton and Tristan trust you. You're not just a worker there anymore, Charlie. You're family. Don't you get it yet?"

A brief silence settled. Oh, good. He'd managed to counter some of that stubborn rebellion. A flash of admiration shot through him, taking him off guard. What was that about? Yes, he liked her spunk, even if it was a tad too intense. Yes, he respected her work ethic and pride and vision. It was a quality he didn't see very often, in either men or women. Maybe that's why it was hard for him to deal with. Not that he had to. If she was his woman, he wouldn't allow her to be fixing up some old house in a crappy neighborhood without supervision. End of argument.

But she wasn't his woman and that was good.

This time when she spoke, her words were a bit softer. "I appreciate it. I do, but you have to understand I'm used to running my own life. How would you feel if you had a project that was important to you and Cal decided you needed a supervisor?"

He'd be pissed. Her point hit home. Brady wiped his eyes, finally able to see her form more clearly. "I get it. Listen, I'm asking you to let me help. Not because I think you can't do this on your own, but if something were to happen, none of us would forgive ourselves. You're one of us now. That means we help each other out. Who's doing your plans?"

She rocked back and forth and took a while before answering. "Don't know yet."

"You don't trust me with your house?"

"No, you're a great architect. I just don't want you to feel obligated, especially if I change stuff."

A flash of regret hit him. He'd been a bit hard on her. "I won't. I'll do the plans at no charge, and I'll help you renovate in the evenings. I'm sure you could use an extra hand."

"I've never seen you involved in renovation. You never leave the office."

She sounded slightly accusatory, which made his lips twitch. "I've done rehab in the past when needed. I prefer the office, but sometimes it's good to switch things up. Get my hands dirty."

Was she nibbling at her lip? His vision was still blurred and the burning pain lingered. How long would it take for this crap to leave his system? "We can try things out," she finally said. "After a week, we'll reassess."

She didn't trust him at all. Not that he blamed her. Maybe it was the sexual attraction that threw him off. Being mean because he wanted to drag her into bed. God, how juvenile. Like pulling a girl's hair because he liked her. He'd thought he was better than that.

Evidently not.

"Agreed. Let's get the new deadbolt installed before anything else. I'll draw up plans once you tell me what your vision is. Who's Jackson?"

"Oh, I figured out who was breaking into the house. Young teen. He'd been using the house for some alone time. Brought his books and stuff. I offered to let him help me work on the house if he wanted."

He frowned. "Think that's a good idea when you don't even know him? He could be into drugs or staking out the house to bring his friends over. You can't trust everyone you meet."

She laughed, surprising him. "I don't. I go with a gut feeling, and this one told me he may like learning how to renovate. He may not even come back."

Another good reason he'd be here to help. "We'll see."

They fell quiet. He sensed her studying him for a while, but he was oddly comfortable under her stare. "I'll need something from you though, in order to move forward."

Suspicion leaked through him. "What?"

Her grin was pure cheekiness. "Admit I kicked your ass."

He couldn't help but laugh. Damn, she really had given it to him. "Only if you promise not to tell anyone. My man card may get yanked."

"We'll see how much you piss me off."

He shook his head, wiping his face with the towel one more time. Finally, his balls had stopped throbbing and tentatively lowered back down. She had a wicked kick. "Fine. You grabbed your opportunity and took me down temporarily."

She pursed her full, candy-pink lips and blew out a breath in disgust. "That was a sucky admission."

"Best you're gonna get after you almost castrated me."

"Whiner."

He laughed again. "Can we get out of here, please? Call it a night?"

"Sure. Let me just dump this last batch from the basement. Do you need me to drive you home or can you see?"

"I'm fine." He moved a bit slowly, but by the time she was done, he felt able to see enough of the road. "We can work up the plans tomorrow."

"Okay." She paused by her ugly red truck. "I'm really sorry. I never meant to hurt you like that."

He waved a hand in the air. "Raven would be proud of you. Let's just hope my date tonight doesn't notice I look hungover."

"Date?"

Her surprise made him frown. "Yeah. There're actually women out there who like my company and don't want to pepper spray me."

She laughed. "Got it. Have fun."

She got in her truck and drove off.

At least they'd come to some agreement. The Pierce brothers would be happy it was settled and they got to help her out. And Brady could handle a few evenings per week in her company. In fact, this strange attraction might fade after spending some time with her. This might be the best thing for him.

He drove home to get ready for his date, trying not to be concerned at his total lack of enthusiasm. This was his third date with Marissa, and she had all the qualities he was looking for. Besides being a stunning, quiet beauty, she was intelligent, soft spoken, and completely on board with a traditional type of relationship. He'd been thinking of seducing her tonight now that they'd gotten to know each other, but he always let his gut lead depending on what he sensed his woman wanted, or more important, needed.

He just hoped his poor dick was up for it after Charlie.

Chapter Six

"One of the great beauties of architecture is that each time it is like life starting all over again."—Renzo Piano

"Ready for the reveal?"

She took a deep breath and nodded. "Bring it on."

She tugged on her work gloves and tried to wipe off the sweat pouring from her forehead. August was a bitch in the northeast. Muggy, clingy heat kept the air heavy. She'd heard the West brag about their dry heat, but nothing was worse than a hot day in Connecticut when the air thickened and refused to move. Especially when working in a house with no A/C.

They'd done the complete walk-through, finalized plans, and finished up cleaning out the basement from hell. Now, it was time to rip out the carpets and see how bad the floors were. Sure, she always hoped for actual wood to refinish, but if they were bad, she'd just invest in new carpeting. Still, her heart beat with the thrill of the unknown and what could be.

They cut away the edges and pulled together, taking their time until the muddy, crusted fibers were carted away and the floors were naked to the vision.

She studied the faded wood, a dull oak color, walking around to examine the edges. Looking up, she broke into a joyous smile. "They're gorgeous! A little re-sanding and stain and we have new floors!"

Brady nodded, a small smile on his lips. "You got lucky."

"Hell, yes, I got lucky!" She broke into a happy dance, swinging her hips and waving her hands in the air to the music she heard in her head. "This is going to be awesome. Good floors automatically raise the investment value. Mo' money, mo' money! Come on—do the money dance with me."

He shook his head but she didn't care. She bet the man didn't even know how to dance. Poor thing. Charlie knew she could never get serious with a man who couldn't accomplish some badass moves on the dance floor. It spoke of a confidence and eroticism that was important in a relationship, at least to her. Plus, she refused to go through life dancing alone at weddings, parties, and all social functions.

His assessing gaze swept over her figure. Lush, dark lashes lowered to mask his expression. "I wouldn't get overexcited. The bathrooms aren't terrible and the pipes are decent, thank God. But the kitchen will cause you trouble. Did you see the cabinets? They're unsalvageable, and that wall boxing in the kitchen is load bearing. It can't come down, and it's a complete eyesore."

She stopped dancing and crossed her arms in front of her chest. "Boy, are you a Debbie Downer. I know, but I'm thinking of a plan."

"The roof needs replacement and so do the windows. Plus the shingles are crap."

"Waaa, waaa, waaa."

Was that amusement glinting in those sooty eyes or just her imagination? He turned and bent to pull the last rug remnants away, causing those jeans to stretch over his ass, emphasizing the muscled curves. Damn, he had a smokin' hot body. She liked seeing him in casual clothes for a change—even though his jeans weren't faded or old and his navy blue T-shirt seemed freshly pressed, even in the crippling heat. But he still cut an impressive figure, whether dressed in those sharp business suits or down-to-earth outdoor work clothes. It was an elemental male dominance in his aura he carried with him, as if he assumed everyone around would do his bidding. Probably another quality that made him so successful.

He walked back in and pointed to the entrance to the kitchen. "You want to knock this one down, right?"

"Definitely."

"You'll lose cabinet space."

"I can live with that. I have some ideas. Can you help me with the last of the basement junk? Then we can attack the wall tomorrow."

"Sure."

She grabbed her bat and pepper spray, ignoring his eye roll, and headed down the rickety stairs to the serial killer basement. At least it was unfinished space, which could house the washer and dryer, and eventually be converted into a family room. The last of the shelving held an array of mismatched paint cans, poles, boxes, and various junk. Grabbing a few boxes, they began sorting.

The question popped out before she had a chance to think about it. "I never asked you about your date last week. How was it?"

He arched a brow, not pausing in his pace. "Good."

"Steady girlfriend or new prospect?"

"Third date."

"Ah, the closer."

"Huh?"

She grinned, pushing the stray tendrils of hair from her eyes. "You know, the third date rule? You either sleep with them or decide to move on. What'd you decide?"

He stopped, gazing at her with faint astonishment. "Do you really ask anything that pops into your head or do you just like shocking people?"

"Don't think it's that shocking. Why are you so uptight?"

"I'm not uptight. I just happen to respect a person's privacy, which evidently, you do not. Some topics are inappropriate."

She snorted. Oh, he was fun to torture. "Nothing wrong with being honest and asking what you're genuinely curious about. I'm trying to get to know you better. I pretty much know nothing about you other than you're an architect. Oh, and you curse in Spanish when you're pissed, and look Latino but of course you're not."

He cut her an irritated glance. "I am Latino. And sometimes people don't want to share personal things with strangers. It's a matter of trust."

"How can you build trust if you don't take a risk and try to share things that are important to you?"

"It's called time. Obviously, you're young and impatient."

"Does that mean you're old and slow?" She smothered a delighted grin as he actually humphed. Maybe working with him wasn't so bad. It was certainly amusing. "Sorry, I couldn't resist. How can you be Latino with a name like Brady Heart?"

"Brady is a nickname. My grandfather was English and my grandmother Latina. They had three sons, one being my father. My father married a Latina, but I still inherited my grandfather's English name."

She cocked her head, fascinated. "What's your birth given name?"

He stiffened. "I don't share that with anyone."

"Oh, my God. Is it something really bad? Like Dudley? Or Dick?"

"No, and I'm not discussing it further."

"Gaylord? Elmo?"

"No."

She wrinkled her nose. "Well, now you got me all curious, and I won't rest until I figure it out."

Suddenly, all that seething dark intensity turned on her. His eyes gleamed with warning, and his figure radiated with shocking energy. Her breath caught in her lungs at the sudden change. His voice lowered to a rich, gravelly velvet that shot shivers down her spine. "I'd be very careful, Charlotte," he warned. "There are certain things that shouldn't be challenged."

Electricity crackled between them. His gaze held hers and dug deep, and yearning rose inside her for something she didn't understand. She shifted her feet. "I told you I don't like that name."

A smirk touched those carved lips. "I do. It's elegant. Musical. Traditional."

She snorted. "Everything I'm not and that's why I hate it." Odd, though. For some reason, her belly dropped when he spoke her name. It seemed almost...intimate. She shook off the strange energy between them and went back to her interrogation. "Do you speak Spanish?"

"Only a few phrases. My parents only spoke English in our household. Though my father calls my mother *querida*."

She smiled. "I like that. I always wanted to learn another language but I barely made it through English class. Do you have brothers or sisters?"

"Two sisters."

"Younger? Older? Are you close?"

He gave a long-suffering sigh, as if the whole getting-to-know-you game was beginning to wear on his nerves. "Older. They're both married with kids."

"I bet your mama wanted that third date to work out for you, then."

He laughed, and her heart leapt at the sound. She liked making him laugh. He was so serious all the time. She wondered who was able to lighten him up besides the Pierce brothers. Of course, she'd caught him teasing Sydney and Morgan on occasion, but he'd always been so closed off around her. It was interesting to think there were other layers hidden under that starched shirt.

"I love my mama, but I know exactly what I'm looking for."

They finished two boxes and started on the next round. Oh, this was too interesting not to investigate. "Well, now you need to tell me what you're looking for in a woman."

"Why?"

"I'm curious. Women are always curious about what men are interested in." She threw up her hands at his suspicious look. "I swear I won't judge."

"Why don't you tell me what you're looking for first?" he challenged.

She dropped a rusty lawn sign into the box. "Fair enough. Unlike you, I have nothing to hide and don't mind people asking questions. I think it's a fascinating study in human behavior and figuring out our deepest needs."

"You're stalling."

She screwed up her face and went over her mental list. "Well, I want a man who has a great sense of humor and doesn't take himself too seriously."

"Serious how? Like ego? Pride in his work? In his manhood?"

She blinked. "Umm, you know, someone who can make me laugh and doesn't think he's better than me."

"Ah, so you don't like a man with an inflated ego."

"Right."

"Go on."

Off balance, she went back to her list. "A man who's open to explore various paths in his life with his career."

"A Peter Pan, huh?"

She stopped, cutting him a glare. "What are you talking about? That's not a Peter Pan."

"Sure it is. You're just sugarcoating it. You're saying you don't want a man to commit to a serious career path and pursue it even though there are obstacles. Sounds like you enjoy those starving, brooding artist types." He gave a shudder of distaste. "Good luck."

She gasped. "You're twisting my words! I'm talking about being open minded to life's curve balls and able to adapt to change."

"That's different than what you originally said. Do you mean a man who can fall on bad times but is able to focus on the good for both him and his partner?"

Did she? Yeah, that sounded better, somehow, but she didn't like the way he was hijacking her list and bending it to his will. "Yes, that's what I said."

"I must've misunderstood. Continue."

"This one is very specific but important. I want a man who can dance."

His groan snapped her temper. "Wait, let me guess. You want some *Dirty Dancing* dude to sweep you off your feet, believing if he's good on the dance floor, he's good in bed."

Her cheeks turned red. Ugh. How did he make it sound so...lame? He was probably mad because he couldn't dance, so he was trying to make her feel guilty. The words practically sputtered out of her mouth. "No! I just believe a man who can dance is confident and assured and not afraid what everyone else thinks of him."

"What if he just happens not to have rhythm and doesn't want to embarrass YOU? If you meet this perfect man and he sucks on the dance floor, you'd cut him loose?"

She squirmed. "No. Yes. I mean, it depends. It may not be a make or break, but it's a quality I look for. Is that okay with you? Can I get back to my final requirement, please?"

"Of course. I apologize. I'm dying to know what comes next."

She yanked out a carton of old rusty tools and dropped them with a loud clatter. "Gee, thanks. A man who makes me happy." She tossed him a triumphant look. He couldn't pull that one apart.

Brady frowned. "That's not a serious requirement. In fact, it's quite juvenile."

She spun around and shot him a nasty glare. "Excuse me?"

He ignored her, continuing to throw things at the box without even glancing over. "Someone who makes you happy is a total cop-out. What if you're wrong or disagree with his thoughts or actions? He's not making you technically happy at the moment, but he's doing it for the greater good because he loves you. You can't be happy all the time. Relationships grow and change and arc. That's what makes them interesting. Being happy all the time is a lukewarm quality on your list. Frankly, I'm disappointed. I expected so much more from you. I think we're done here. I'll start bringing the stuff to the dumpster."

And with that, he pivoted on his heel, grabbed the box, and headed upstairs.

She stared at the empty basement, frustration and temper whirling in choppy waves through her body, and wished to God she could hit him with the pepper spray again.

Oh, she so didn't like him.

* * * *

Brady tried not to laugh at her obvious ploy to ignore him and take the higher road. She was so delightfully emotional, it was impossible for her to hide her disdain and temper at his dismissing words. He knew she was dying for him to share his own list of traits but he didn't offer and she was stuck with the silent treatment for a while, so she had to just suck it up.

Damn, she was sexy.

Her shirt was canary yellow with hot pink piping. The deep V at the neck hinted at a yellow bra that was driving him a tad insane. What woman wore a yellow bra? Did her panties match? He'd always been a man who preferred black for its sexy sophistication. What was happening to him? Her jeans had holes in the knees and flared at the ankle. When she bent over, he noticed the pockets had bright rhinestone bling in the shape of hearts. Her work boots were pink, which reminded him of Morgan. He wondered if she ordered them from the same place.

Her multi-hued blonde hair was pulled back in a high ponytail, and her face was free of makeup. Those huge hazel eyes dominated her face and were so expressive it was like looking into the windows of her soul, just like the cliché. It was rare he saw a woman without polish or cosmetics as a barrier. Was she so confident in her looks, or did she truly not care what others thought? If it was the latter, was it possible she had that much freedom in her soul?

Freedom in the soul translated to freedom in the bedroom. Freedom to all possibilities on the physical and emotional plane. Freedom to every erotic demand he wanted to give her.

His dick sprang to life, and he smothered a groan. Holy hell, he needed to get himself under control. Playing a good game of banter was one thing. Getting intrigued by her sweet body was another. They'd never cross that line for a variety of reasons, but the biggest one hit him as hard in the balls as her kick had.

She wasn't interested.

She looked upon him as a tightass. Too old. Too rigid. Too judgmental. She dreamed of a creative soul who'd torture her and present pain as passion, twisting her up inside and then saying his good-bye. He'd seen it before, many times. But it wasn't his damn business, and he wasn't getting involved in anything other than renovating this house.

Focus was the key. Having some fun along the way would make it interesting, but he knew he had to watch himself. She was too tempting, and she was too damn much trouble.

He wanted a wife, not a roll in the hay, no matter how mind blowing it might be.

He repeated the mantra to himself and got back to work.

Chapter Seven

"Renovating old homes is not about making them look new... it is about making new unnecessary."—Ty McBride

"I'm going to restore the cabinets."

His look was all too familiar, and one she was well versed in. "Those can't be saved," he clipped out. His hand ran over the chipped façade of cheap green paneling and the torn linoleum countertops. The knobs were busted, and the insides were torn up. "You told me you were getting rid of them. In fact, this whole kitchen is a problem. There's not enough space for a table. Little storage, especially if we remove that wall."

"I've been thinking about it all night." Her irritation with him had finally faded enough and taken on another outlet. Since he refused to leave her side as her protector, she'd work him to death and satisfy her curiosity. It had a double bang effect since it would annoy the crap out of him. She'd been way too much of an easy target and he'd played her well a few days ago. Now, she'd gotten her composure back and realized his game.

She was going to play better.

Charlie bounced on her heels, channeling her favorite Pooh character, Tigger, and expounded on her brilliant idea. "You know all that wood I made you save from the basement?"

"The scraps I advised you to get rid of that are now cluttering up the yard?"

"Yes, those. I'm going to do a two-pronged approach. First, I'm keeping the top tier of cabinets because they're the best of the worst.

I'll strip off the surface, put in new shelves and knobs, and paint them bright white."

"Why don't you get new ones?"

"Too expensive."

"It still won't be enough. You need to add bottom cabinets or the buyers will have nothing. It'll devalue the house."

"Ah, but I have a plan! I'm going to use the scrap wood from the basement and build them a corner cabinet here"— she pointed to the dead space on the end of the main counter—"and I'll make all the counters a beautiful stained plank wood."

He examined the space, his face doubtful. "You're going to give it a farmhouse look? Doesn't fit with the rest of the house."

"Not done. I'm going to build a high-top counter from that old headboard I snatched from that amazing store—the Barn—and put in stools. It gives eating space, modernizes the kitchen, and keeps it from being too farm looking."

He didn't answer, taking in her suggestions with a seriousness she was getting used to. She understood now Brady needed time to process all her ideas. Her brain worked different, exploding into a riot of color and graphics she made sense of. He needed time and space before the vision took hold. These past few days had given her a better glimpse into his work habits. "Maybe."

"Not done," she sang, clapping her hands together and dancing to the back of the kitchen. "See this here? I'm going to take the two windows I'm tearing out and make them a built-in cupboard for the rest of their storage."

He blinked. "You're taking those awful windows and turning them into a cupboard?"

"Yes! I've done it before and it's a great way to save money. We just have to make sure when we remove the windows we don't chip or break around the frame."

"I've never seen that done before. Won't it look cheap?"

"No. I've been studying renovation with old materials for a while now. I can make it look seamless."

"What about that dead wall?" He pointed to the massive empty space doing nothing but choking off the room. "There's no painting or built-in that will make that wall look good. Especially when people are eating at the counter with nothing to look at."

"I found the solution. I'm going to paint a graffiti design mural on it."

She hugged herself with excitement, waiting him out. The seconds dragged into minutes. Finally, he gazed at her with an expression of pure horror.

"You're kidding."

"No! I'm going to paint a big-assed, gorgeous graffiti-type wall in the kitchen. Isn't that genius? Brilliant?"

"You can paint? Graffiti?"

"Of course I can paint. You should see my apartment. I made these fabulous paintings out of old pizza boxes."

"No, I mean you're an artist-type painter? You studied art?"

She rolled her eyes. "No, I didn't actually study it, but I make things all the time and I know I can pull this off. What do you think?"

"I think you've officially lost your mind. If you're stuck on this idea, hire a real artist." He walked out of the kitchen, shaking his head. She followed him, refusing to be deterred.

"Too expensive. You need to think outside the box, Brady. I'm telling you, I can pull it off."

"I believe you think you can, but I've never seen a house with a graffiti wall in the kitchen. Or old windows converted into cupboards."

"It's gonna be awesome. For now, I don't want you worrying your pretty little head about it. We have a wall to take down and cabinets to work on."

He glared. "I'm not worried. This is your world. I'm just living in it."

"Cute. Let's remove the last of the counter from the kitchen so we can put it with the scrap wood."

They worked in silence for a while, the buzz of the saw and the slam of the hammer music to her ears. "I've decided it's time you hold up your end of the bargain," she said.

"I'm already working my ass off for you."

"No, your list. For what you want in a woman. Have you graduated to date four yet?"

Irritation skittered across his features. She tried to tamp down her delight. "Not yet." She waited him out, learning he liked to space out his responses. "I'm seeing her again this Friday," he added grudgingly.

"Ooh, exciting. Okay, so tell me what floats your boat, Casanova."

He shuddered. "God, please don't call me that. Or talk like that."

"Sorry, I forget you're a bit high class."

"No, I just speak proper English."

"Stop stalling."

He looked away but she caught the edge of a grin. He'd be loath to admit it, but she made him laugh. And from what she'd seen, this man desperately needed someone to balance all that seriousness. It must be exhausting.

"Fine. What do you want to know?"

She practically clapped her hands with glee. "The same question I answered. Tell me the traits in your perfect woman."

His arms flexed as he worked the hammer, and her gaze snagged on the lean, sinewy muscles under gorgeous brown skin. Wood chips and dust clung to his figure but it only added to his attractiveness, giving a sense of ruggedness to his normal poised elegance. Yes, women would definitely seek him out for his appearance alone, but she wondered how many stayed after they got a dose of his attitude. He must be on his best behavior to trick them.

"I don't know why you're interested in this," he muttered.

"Tit for tat."

"It's simple, really. I know exactly what I'm looking for. I'm ready to get married and have a family."

"Right away?"

"Yes. My future wife will have a few core qualities that I won't compromise on. Loyalty, honesty, and dual respect are at the top."

She cocked her head, studying him. He'd managed to surprise her. "Very thoughtful. Excellent choices."

"So glad you approve. I need a certain amount of intellectual stimulation, as I'm sure she will, so she cannot be just a pretty face."

Huh. Maybe she'd been wrong about him. So far, she wholeheartedly agreed with his choices. "Can't argue with those."

"I don't need laugh-out-loud funny, but a sense of humor helps get you through hard times."

"Agreed."

"And then she needs to obey, of course."

The hammer swung. The wood cracked and he began pulling off the remains of the cabinet. She tugged on her earlobe. "I'm sorry. I didn't hear you right. What was the last one?"

"Obey. She has to obey me. I'll be the leader in the relationship, and she'll need to respect my decisions."

She pulled her lobe harder, but her sinking heart confirmed she'd heard correctly. "Did you say the word 'obey'?"

"Yes." He continued, oblivious to her sudden rising body temperature, pounding heart, and slow fist clench. "I'll need to make the proper decisions on finances, but of course, she'll be the primary with the children since she'll be home with them all day."

Her mouth opened and shut like a guppy. "What if she wants to work?"

"Oh, that's not allowed. There will be too much to do running a tight household. Trust me. I've seen the way my mother and sisters handle their time, and you need to be quite organized. Dinner alone takes a chunk out of the day."

Steam began to rise from her head. The room began to sway. "She's going to have dinner ready for you when you come home?"

He grinned. Actually grinned with pleasure. "Of course. There's nothing wrong with understanding and embracing the roles in a marriage. In fact, it's quite a powerful, freeing thing. Society pushes both women and men to do too much crossover, which ends up breaking the relationship at the seams. I won't have that problem in my marriage."

Her voice sounded a few pitches too high when she managed to speak. "But what if you fall in love with a woman who doesn't want to stay home all day with the children and finds fulfillment in her own career?"

He didn't even pause. "Then she's not for me."

The hammer dropped out of her fingers with a crash. He swung his gaze around, frowning. "What's the matter?"

"You're a monster," she whispered. "A chauvinist. A card carrying ego-driven prejudiced male!"

With a long-suffering sigh, he rose to his feet, brushing the dust off his jeans. "Are you going to throw another tantrum because my ideals don't match yours? Who's calling whom chauvinist?"

"You want a Stepford woman. What if she disagrees with you and doesn't think your word is God? What will you do then? Beat her?"

His dark eyes flared with intensity. "If she wants me to," he growled. "Nothing wrong with a good spanking now and then to reset things."

Her stomach dropped at the same time her temper exploded. "My God, you've time traveled from another century and missed the sexual revolution. Women don't obey, Brady. They are equal partners in a relationship."

Irritation bristled from his form. "She will be my equal partner, but she'll respect boundaries and trust I'm making the right decision for all of us."

"That's a dictatorship, not a marriage."

He took a step forward, closing the distance between them. "Hey, just because you're too scared to fully trust and surrender to another person, don't judge me. There's power in submission."

She snorted. "For you, maybe. What about her? Sounds like she has no say in anything, and that, buddy boy, is a foundation for a very unhealthy marriage."

"Did you just call me Buddy Boy?"

She ignored his softly spoken warning, caught in sheer outrage for his future dates. "How early do you let your dates know what you're really looking for? Do you try and seduce them first, then get them to agree? Do you play some Jedi mind tricks on them like on *The Bachelor*, to make them think they need to marry you at all costs? Does this woman you're approaching a fourth date with know what she's getting into?"

He leaned in, toe to toe with her. Her nostrils filled with his scent, a delicious musk reminding her of smoke and sex. He wasn't particularly tall, but his solid, muscular build seethed with leashed power, making shivers trickle down her spine. His coal eyes held a savage gleam, and in that one moment, he seemed almost primeval. The air thickened with a low hum of electricity, as if preparing for a storm. She wanted to spurt more outraged accusations, but his gaze pinned her with a ruthless determination that suddenly made the breath whoosh from her lungs. Her breasts got achy and tight. A low throb pulsed between her legs.

What was going on?

He was pumping out sexual, dominant vibes she'd never caught before. He was cold. Controlled. A bit pompous. A businessman through and through, for goodness sakes. A tad boring. Where had all this hidden intensity come from? And why, oh why was she suddenly weirdly turned on?

"I only sleep with women who know exactly what I want and how I want it. I make sure there's plenty of communication and agreement on both sides before moving forward. There have never been complaints and I expect none in the future." A wolfish smile twisted his sensual lips. "Did you ever stop to wonder what it would feel like to let go of all that control, even for one night? Don't you get tired of trying to do it all when so much pleasure is waiting for you on the other side?"

Oh, hell no. He wasn't going to play her with those dark Latin eyes and hot body. She knew exactly what he was doing, and he'd be the last man on Earth she'd ever fall for. Ignoring her achy body, she rallied and fought back. Lifting her chin, she met his gaze head on. "Oh, don't worry about me. I get plenty of pleasure without having to give up my independence and soul for an orgasm," she said sweetly.

"Maybe you haven't had the proper orgasm." His gravelly voice caressed her ears, and those inky eyes burned like charcoal. "More specifically, orgasms. If a man is giving you just one, he's plain lazy."

Her heart thundered and her palms dampened. She didn't even like the man but her body was strangely turned on with this hot sexual bantering. "Maybe you haven't been introduced to the cutting edge technology they have available that removes a man from the equation," she challenged. "My standards are already high. And multiples are already assumed."

Irritation flickered over his features, along with another emotion she didn't want to name. He moved a step closer. "You're a bona fide brat who needs a bit of taming."

"I'm not starring in *The Taming of the Shrew*. I still think that is the most sexist play ever created. Just tell me this. Does your date know exactly what's expected of her yet, or do you keep that as one of your special surprises?"

"Don't judge me, Charlotte, nor the women I spend my time with. At least I own my stuff and don't try to pretend I'm someone I'm not." His gaze raked over her figure. "I bet you still have no idea what type of man will truly satisfy you."

"Who cares? I only know one important thing. It'll never be you!"

They both stared at each other, caught in a powerful surge of energy that rooted her feet to the floor. She should be stomping away from him, but she couldn't seem to look away. He was so close their breath intermingled, their lips inches apart. Perspiration broke out on her skin. Her breath strangled in her lungs. She waited for him to do something, say something, anything to break her out of this trance. He murmured a curse word, jaw clenched, and his hands snagged her upper arms, ready to shake her, and—

"Stop! Stop right there or I'll bash your brains out, asshole!"

Brady jerked back and stuck his hands in the air. Charlie whirled around and found Jackson holding the baseball bat that was supposed to protect her. She smothered a groan. She had to get rid of that thing. Who would've thought it would end up being the ultimate weapon?

"Jackson, it's okay. This is Brady and he works for me."

The boy's eyes were full of suspicion. He didn't lower the bat, his gaze darting back and forth between them. "He was yelling at you. Grabbed you."

"We're coworkers and we fight a lot. I swear, there's nothing to worry about."

Brady kept his silence, hands up, and waited him out. A grudging respect came over her. She bet many men would have wanted to jump in to control the situation, especially with a teen. Brady let him lead. Slowly, Jackson put down the bat, a flush rising to his cheeks. "Sorry, man. I didn't know what was going on."

Brady lowered his hands and nodded. "Actually, that was pretty damn awesome. Just be careful of busting in on a scene that can get violent. Better to call 911 on your cell first before doing anything."

"Uh, oh, did you call 911?" Charlie asked nervously.

"Nah. I should've thought about it. I went on instinct. Heard voices and the door was unlocked. Didn't think about it until I saw the bat by the door."

Brady muttered something under his breath. "I told you to get the deadbolt fixed," he said to her.

She lifted a brow. "I did. You forgot to lock it behind you today."

Jackson gave a half laugh. Brady chose to ignore her quip and walked toward the boy with his hand extended. "Don't think we officially met. Brady."

They shook hands. "Jackson."

"You were the one crashing at this place?"

Jackson stiffened, but Brady was perfectly at ease, which seemed to relax the boy. "Yeah, wanted some time alone. Didn't know anyone was around." He shifted his weight, his hands clenching around the baseball bat. "Charlie said I could come by and check things out. Said she'd be tearing down a wall."

Brady laughed. "Yep. That's probably one of the most satisfying jobs in renovation. You wanna join us? We're ripping it out tomorrow. Today, we're focused on cabinets."

"Cabinets sound boring."

Charlie stepped forward. "Are you kidding me? It's all about creativity. Seeing what's not there yet and how you can make it different. It's the only time you harness power through your own vision. Come see."

Her tone brooked no argument. Jackson followed her in the kitchen, and she pointed out the half-ripped-out lower cabinets and the guts of plumbing, rotted wood, and empty space. "A good renovator takes this ugliness and sees something bigger. What do you see?"

He stared at her for a while before taking in the scene. "I see a mess."

"Wanna know what I see?"

"What?"

She smiled and floated around the cramped, clutter-filled space. "Right here are beautiful distressed wood cabinets that give off a touch of an older farmhouse look. Think deep sinks, faded-type wood, rustic. Instead of fancy, modern granite, we'll put in lighter wood counters for contrast, all from scrap wood. I'll show you how to make it shine like a deeper grain by using coconut oil."

"No shit?"

"No shit! Umm, does your mom let you curse? Probably not cool at your age. Girls don't like when boys curse a lot either."

"She doesn't like it too much either."

"Okay, so we won't curse. Now, for the top cabinets, I'm going to strip off that crappy green—is crappy a curse word?"

"Don't think so."

"Crappy green and see what I can salvage. I think it would be cool to have the upper and lower cabinets not match. I'm thinking rustic wood on the bottom and white on top."

Brady interrupted. "That sounds like a horror show."

"My mom likes when things match," Jackson said with a touch of worry. "I think most people do."

She wrinkled her nose. "Yeah, but I swear I can pull this off. If I make it homey but with a bit of an edge, I think a family will fall in love with the house because it is different. Who wants a cookie-cutter house? Sometimes it's like food. In your mind, certain ingredients don't go together, but then when the flavors explode on your tongue, it makes sense."

"True." He nodded, squinting a bit as he took in the kitchen. "I still can't really see it."

"Takes a lot of practice. I'll show you the steps if you can make it here after school. But no pressure, just come when you want."

"Cool. Thanks." He turned to Brady, still regarding him with a touch of suspicion. "Will you be here, too?"

"Yeah, I'm not crazy about Charlie working in this neighborhood alone, plus I like to renovate sometimes. I'm usually just an architect."

"You draw buildings and stuff?"

"Yep. And houses and additions and rooms. Anything that's wanted."

Jackson nodded. "Can I hang out and watch a little bit? Or will I be in the way?"

Brady grinned. "Grab a pair of work gloves and help me haul out some of this wood to the scrap pile. I'll show you some more stuff."

"Awesome!"

He dove into the project, and for the next hour, they worked together in a happy comradery. Brady watched him with attentiveness, but after a while, he seemed to realize Jackson was a good kid and had an honest desire to learn. By the time the cabinets were pulled out and she'd selected the pieces she wanted to restore, they were tired and bonded by good, old-fashioned sweat and hard work.

"I better get home," Jackson said with a touch of reluctance. "Mom should be back from work soon. Thanks for letting me help."

"Come back tomorrow and I'll let you smash a bit of the wall," she said brightly.

"Thanks. Bye, Charlie. Bye, Brady!"

He took off with the enthusiasm of youth and disappeared out the door. Brady closed it and clicked the deadbolt firmly into place. She fought a shiver, not wanting to think of their intimate scene before. They had gotten a bit riled up and emotions had turned physical. Simple to explain away, but she wanted no awkwardness between them. Thank God nothing had happened they couldn't come back from. But it seemed Brady had a different opinion. He walked over to her, standing a few inches away, arms crossed in front of his powerful chest, his sooty gaze locked with hers. "Seems like a good kid." He paused. "You're good with kids."

She swallowed, trying to sound light and cheerful. "Thanks. Kids are real. I can deal with real."

"Gotta admit you surprised me a bit today."

"Because I don't hate kids?"

A grin tugged at his full lips. "No. Because you're not flighty, as I originally thought."

She rolled her eyes. "Gee, thanks. But I still think you're a tightass."

"Maybe I have some time to change your mind," he said softly. His voice stroked some hidden parts deep inside—girly parts—that had never been ruffled before. She shifted her weight, nervously nibbling on her thumbnail.

"Umm, Brady—"

"Can I ask you a question?"

Damn. Things were getting out of hand, and she'd have to delicately tell him there was no way in hell anything would ever happen between them. He'd earned her respect by helping her and being cool with Jackson, but after his little speech today about what he wanted from a woman, it was evident they were universes apart. Even with the odd pull of sexual chemistry. "Well, see, I don't think—"

"Are you really going to do white cabinets with rustic wood together? Because I think that's going to be a deal breaker with people. You need to take some time to think about it."

As his words registered, there was only one thing left to do.

She laughed. He grinned back at her, and the last bit of awkwardness and tension drained away. "You just wait, Heart. I'm going to blow your mind when this house is done."

"Never said you weren't going to. Just worried in what capacity it'll be. Come on. Let's get out of here and call it a night."

They packed up their tools and headed out. He was becoming a better renovation partner than she'd originally thought.

Chapter Eight

"Whatever good things we build end up building us."—*Jim Rohn*

"What are you doing here?"

Charlie grinned as Dalton stepped over the debris, his sharp gaze traveling over the house. As a master woodworker, Dalton had been the one who suggested she start working at Pierce Brothers. One soul recognized the other. They were both madly in love with renovation and woodworking and had formed a tight bond over the past months.

"Checking up on you since I was in the area. Where's Brady?"

She tilted her head and gave him a look. "Dude, really? You checking to see if I have my babysitter? He should be here soon."

"Partner," he corrected. "Assistant. Not caretaker. And I'm checking to see if you need anything from me and how it's progressed. Taking down the wall today?"

"Yep. Getting there slow and steady. Hey, do you happen to have an extra circular saw I can use?"

"Of course. I'll bring it tomorrow. This is an exciting canvas. Whatcha doing with woodwork?"

She rubbed her hands together with glee and motioned him toward the kitchen. "Taking the windows and building an extra cabinet for storage space. Gonna build my own countertops and do a mismatch of cabinets."

He nodded slowly, interest piquing in his blue eyes. "Gutsy, but I like it. Let me know if you need an extra set of hands sometime. Be happy to help."

Her heart softened. She might have been pissed over the Pierces' overprotectiveness, but there was also a sense of family and shelter she loved. "Thanks. I'll let you know."

"How are you getting along with Brady?"

She regarded Dalton with curiosity. "We're managing."

Dalton gave a short laugh. "I know you two haven't been close in the past, but I was hoping this project would help bring you together."

She narrowed her gaze. "What do you mean?"

"What I said. It's easier if we all get along at the office, right?"

She relaxed. He had no ulterior motives. She was just being completely paranoid. They'd shared a small, tiny moment together, which meant nothing. It had all been based on annoyance and temper. "Right. So, you and Brady have known each other a long time, huh?"

Dalton walked through the rooms, studying the layout. "Yep. He met Cal in college and became almost like an adopted brother. He remained solid even during our period of hating one another. Never took a side—he was just there for all of us."

She wasn't surprised. Brady was loyal; that much was evident. "What about his family? I asked him about his background because his name was English and not Latino."

Dalton laughed. "Oh, don't mention the name thing. That's a hot spot with him. I only use his birth name when I want to seriously piss him off."

"What is it?"

"Can't tell you. He'll castrate me, and don't think I'm joking."

Damn, now she really had to know. She was very good at getting her answers, so she launched into the famous diversion attack. Her mother had always told her she'd be deadly in a courtroom if she ever wanted to be a lawyer. "Fine. Is he close with his family? What are they like?"

"He eats dinner with them every other Sunday. The other times he's at our house. They're awesome. His mom makes fabulous dinners, and his sisters really look up to Brady. They're a tight-knit crew, but very traditional."

Ah, ha. "Traditional how?" she asked casually.

He examined the moldings, running his fingers over the inside windows, and seemingly calculating distance and ideas in his head. "Are these the windows you're using as cabinets?"

"Yes."

"Interesting. Can't wait to see the finished product."

"How is his family traditional?"

"Oh, his sisters both defer to their husbands, just like his mom. Guess the men in the family are raised to be the leaders. The women all stay at home to take care of the kids and run the household."

"You don't think that's a bit archaic?"

He shrugged. "I guess. It works for them, and they're pretty damn happy. Who are we to judge what's right or wrong for anyone based on societal expectations?"

She jerked back. The words hit her like a sucker punch, and a sense of shame trickled through her. She'd never really thought of it like that. She'd been so outraged at the idea, she didn't stop to think whether it was forced on women or freely chosen. In a way, she was being a reverse chauvinist. "I guess you're right. I'm sure there's plenty of ways his sisters can get what they want. Like his real name. If they know how much he hates it, I bet they've tortured him over that a few times."

Dalton laughed. "Yeah, I'll never forget that one time his sister Cecilia snuck out to date this boy, and he was yelling at her, acting all manly, and she just shouted his name in front of her date: 'You're not my papa, Bolivar!' and his date was like, 'What's your brother's name?' and Brady got all embarrassed and—"

Dalton trailed off. Slowly, horror leaked over his features, and he slapped his hand over his mouth.

Charlie's eyes widened. "His name is Bolivar?"

"Shit. Ah, shit! I swear, Charlie, I will kill you if you repeat that to him. No one is supposed to know."

Actually, she loved the name. It was formal and regal and full of pride. But knowing she had the secret weapon, like Rumpelstiltskin, gave her a rush of adrenaline. Oh, the ways she could use this to her advantage. She kept her tone sugary sweet. "Don't worry. I promise I won't tell."

He opened his mouth to say something but the door interrupted him. Brady stepped through, grinning in welcome. "Hey, dude. What's up? Am I needed at the office?"

Shooting her a warning glare, Dalton cleared his throat a walked toward him. "Nah, just checking in. Wanted to see the hou. and the progress. Looks great."

"Charlie's doing a good job." His words came out true and clear, and a thrill of pleasure caught her unaware. Seemed his opinion meant more than she had originally thought. "Hey, can we borrow your extra circular saw? We need to do some cabinet work."

Dalton raised a brow. "Yeah, I told Charlie I'd drop it off tomorrow." He shot them both a weird look, then shook his head. "Gotta head out. I have a dining room table that's overdue for a client. See you guys later."

They said their good-byes. Silence enveloped the room. She averted her gaze, afraid her face would give away the sheer glee of knowing his secret name. "Haven't seen Jackson yet, so maybe we should get started. But don't feel you need to stay with me the whole time. There hasn't been any trouble or people bothering me, and I think we both know it's completely safe here."

"What are you hiding?"

Her mouth fell open. She quickly shut it. "What are you talking about? I'm not hiding anything."

His narrowed gaze raked over her figure, probing way too deep. Holy hell, why couldn't she be a better liar? "No. You're holding something back. And frankly, it terrifies me."

Surprise flickered through her. "You? Terrified? Not of a woman who's only here to listen to your instructions and do as she's told?"

The moment the words came out, she regretted them. Especially after seeing the flash of hurt on his face before it was replaced by cold dismissal. "Think what you want. Let's concentrate on work." He grabbed the hammer, donned gloves, and began setting up.

She watched him in misery for a while. "Brady?"

"Yeah?"

"I'm sorry."

His shoulders stiffened. He didn't turn back around. "Forget it."

"No, I really am sorry. Listen, I may not agree with your outlook, but there are plenty of relationships that work well. Who am I to judge you or what makes you happy? I'm kind of ashamed I gave you such a hard time. So, I'm offering my apology."

_d_
_e_   ...ned around, met her stare head on, then slowly nodded.

...accepted."

...f flowed through her. She was glad Dalton had stopped in.

...se, she still knew Brady would eventually piss her off again,

...ing his name as her artillery was exactly what she needed to

...e the scales. "Thank you."

The knock on the door interrupted anything further. Brady
...alked over to open it, motioning Jackson in. "Good to see you.
...Thought you wouldn't be able to make it today."

"Me either." The boy trudged inside with a gloomy look on his
face. She exchanged a glance with Brady, noting the difference
immediately. Underneath the normal tough exterior Jackson liked to
emanate, he was enthusiastic and excited to learn new things. She
genuinely enjoyed his company and sense of humor, liking the way he
was able to soften Brady's usual crusty surface and get him to share
some real belly laughs. But now? Obviously, something had
happened. Shadows clung to his dark eyes.

"You okay?" Brady asked him.

"Sure. What do you want me to do?"

Charlie hesitated. She didn't know Jackson that well and had no
idea if it was right to push him to share. She tried to act casual. "Bad
day at school?"

He didn't answer. Just shrugged.

Sympathy tugged at her heart. God, school was sometimes so
brutal. Finding your way, finding yourself, staying sane. She wished
she could save children the heartache of growing up and dealing with
peers, but it was part of the journey and built the fortitude needed to
live life fully.

Still, it just plain sucked.

"Jackson, do you know how each job has something in it that is
the best part?" Brady asked.

The boy shook his head. "Like what?"

"Like if you're a writer, the best part is working in your pajamas
all day. If you own a bakery, the best part is sampling all the yummy
treats."

A ghost of a smile skirted Jackson's lips. "I get it. The best part
about being a teacher is summer vacations."

"Exactly!" Brady handed him a protective glass mask, smock,

and a hammer. "This is the best part of renovating a house. You get to smash something into smithereens without worrying about the mess or someone getting mad."

Charlie jumped right in. "Brady's right. When I get to take down walls, I imagine everything that frustrates me, makes me mad, makes me sad, and then I let it rip. Let's show you first how it's done, and then we'll let you take your whacks."

The brightness ignited in his dark eyes. They donned their protective gear and tools and stood in front of the wall. "Step back, Jackson."

He obeyed, stopping a safe distance away. Charlie looked at Brady and nodded. In sync, they arced the sledgehammers over their heads and hit the wall together in coordinated efficiency.

With a satisfying crack, plaster exploded. The hole was large, but there was more to be done. Charlie funneled all her energy into attacking the wall until there was a decent space in the middle. She motioned Jackson over. "Okay, stand with your feet braced apart. This hammer is heavy so be careful and watch your range. You want a smooth, full arc as you hit it. Don't forget to summon all that junk inside and let it out with the hammer. Ready?"

His voice shook slightly with excitement. "Ready."

He swung the hammer with little expertise and a lot of enthusiasm. The wall splintered and widened the space. He shot her a delighted grin and waited.

She grinned back. "Again."

Jackson hammered the wall under her supervision while Brady helped and pointed out tips along the way. By the time the debris littered the wood floors, and the kitchen now shone brightly through, no longer masked, she felt a bit lighter. From the dazed look on Jackson's face, she immediately recognized a fellow soul.

He loved it.

"That. Was. Awesome," he said. "What next?"

"Cleaning it up. See what a difference it makes in the layout of the house? More open and accessible."

He studied the new space, slowly nodding. "Yeah, I get it now. But I'm still not sure about those weird cabinets."

Brady laughed. "Agreed. We may need to pull her back from the abyss of bad taste, Jackson."

She shot them both a mock glare. "With you as partners, who needs enemies?"

Brady and Jackson shared a high-five.

They spent the rest of their time carting pieces of the wall to the dumpster and exposing the last of the beams. By the time Jackson was ready to go home, his step was lighter and his face had smoothed out to the carefree youthful expression she hoped he wore more often. His teeth flashed white in a wide grin as he rushed out.

Brady shook his head. "That was the best medicine for him today. Middle school is a nightmare."

She shuddered. "You're telling me. I was always being made fun of because of my clothes and my uncoolness."

Surprise flickered in his dark eyes. "You? Funny, I pegged you for the bubbly cheerleader type with a whole bunch of friends."

"Oh, Lord, no. My mom and I moved a lot, always trying to get cheaper rent, and I was so damn poor my clothes were bargain basement. You know how kids like the designer brand? Let's just say mine was the no-name brand."

"You were poor?"

She swept the floor with a broom, catching the last of the remnants. "Yep. We lived in a motel at certain times. Thank goodness for the backpack program and the food pantry to help us when things were really bad. But eventually, Mom got a decent job and we had an apartment and a car. But kids can be mean. I never really fit in, even though I finally made some friends."

He didn't speak for a while, but the silence felt comfortable. She continued sweeping. His voice deepened, rising to her ears like seductive smoke. "Is that why you're always looking to save money?"

She threw back her head and laughed. "Hell, yes. That's why I'm cheap. Frugal. Call it whatever you want. It's embedded in my DNA. I get off on saving money for some reason. There's such a waste in society today, it hurts my heart. People throw things away without seeing their real value. That's exactly what I love about a renovation project rather than a new build."

"What about your dad?"

His tone was soft and respectful. She paused in her sweeping and smiled. "Never knew him. Never missed him either. My mom is pretty great. She can fix anything, from a broken car engine to a faulty pipe. You know what I think?"

"What?"

"I think if we weren't poor and got to buy stuff, I would've never discovered I had a gift for renovation. Maybe I would've taken it for granted. I'm glad I found my passion in life while so many others drift by, looking for something more to fulfill them. Does that make sense?"

His gaze dove deep, saw everything, and stayed anyway. "Yeah. It makes perfect sense."

The silence shifted, grew, simmered. Suddenly uneasy, she swallowed and took a casual step back. There it was again. That change of consciousness, as if the universe was forcing them to see something neither of them wanted. Her skin prickled in response, and the scent of musk and virile sweaty male filled the air, pumping in waves around her.

She ripped her gaze away and propped the broom back in the closet. Her heart pounded so hard she swore he heard it. What was happening between them lately? Why was she suddenly so aware of him? She cleared her throat. "Sounds corny, right?" she forced out. "Like tricking your mind to believe the bad stuff is really good. Guess you'd call it juvenile."

"Don't." His voice was a whiplash, stilling her back into silence. He crossed the room and stood before her. Slowly, he reached out and tipped her chin up. A slight frown creased his brow, the expression he usually wore when confronted by a stubborn project or when she was driving him nuts with her banter. Only this time, his dark eyes seethed with raw emotion. "It's not corny. It's not juvenile. It's brave and good and damn humbling. I was wrong about you."

Her eyes widened. His finger on her skin burned, causing a rush of heat to pool and pound mercilessly between her thighs. "How?"

A muscle ticked in his jaw. "I judged you. Thought you came from a cushy background. Thought you were dabbling in renovation because you were bored. Thought you were reckless and silly."

The words hurt, but she met his gaze head on, sensing a shift between them. "What do you think now?" she asked softly.

"I think every day you amaze me a little bit more, Charlotte Grayson."

A tiny gasp escaped her lips. A surging sexual chemistry took them in a tight hold, and they stared at one another for seconds, minutes, centuries. He was so close his scent surrounded her with rich cloves, and her hands ached to drag him forward and feel those lips over hers just once.

Just once…

Instead, panic tore through her and she stumbled back, breaking the connection. Instantly, a shutter slammed over his face, and the sexual tension fizzled like a bottle of seltzer going immediately flat. Confusion swamped her. The jagged seesaw of emotion between them was too overwhelming. This was a man she worked with. A man who had completely different philosophies on relationships. A man who frustrated her on a constant basis.

This was one time in her life she could not afford to be impulsive.

"I'd better get going," she said. Her voice was a bit too high, but he followed her lead and turned away.

"Sure. I'll walk you out."

She didn't even get mad anymore at his insistence to accompany her everywhere. She'd gotten used to the protectiveness he afforded her. Lately, he seemed less domineering and more…sweet. He refused to leave the site without her safely in her truck, driving away. Once, she caught him behind her following her to her house. She'd parked, jumped out to yell at him, but he just sped past without a second glance. The man was pure stubbornness.

Like her.

Boy, they'd be a disaster together. They grabbed their stuff and locked up, walking to the car. Freaked out by the awkward silence, she burst out with the first question she could think of. "Have a date tonight?"

He stiffened. For one moment, she wondered if she'd glimpsed hurt in his eyes, but it disappeared so quickly she knew she imagined it. "No."

Instead of getting in her damn car, she kept making it worse, not able to silence her mouth. "Is she still on the hook or did you scare her away?"

The more familiar expression of irritation was back on his face. Thank goodness. Much more comfortable this way. She squashed the tiny flicker of regret, refusing to think about it. "We're seeing each other this weekend."

"Good. Really good. Does she seem like the type of woman you want?"

His gaze raked over her, probing in the darkness for something she couldn't name. Didn't want to name. He paused. "She seems...perfect."

She ignored the sharp pang that struck her. She was glad he'd found someone who was more of a match for him. Hell, the pang was probably envy he'd found the ONE. Who wouldn't be? Sure, she wasn't ready to settle down like he was or have kids, but didn't everyone dream about finding a soul mate? "That's great! Really, really, great." Ugh, why was her voice so high and fake? She was tired. She had to get out of here. "See you tomorrow."

He regarded her for a few moments while she held her breath. Then he nodded and turned away. "'Night."

She got in her car and drove away, wondering why her heart ached.

Chapter Nine

"Excuses are the nails used to build a house of failure."—Don Wilder

He was in a piss-poor mood.

Brady brooded as he watched her animatedly tutor Jackson in the art of flipping a window frame into a cabinet. The new windows were propped up, ready for installation, with a nice thick layer to insulate the house. The woman had gone on a hunt for the best deal, calling in favors and negotiating like it was a used car. She finally scored a bargain basement deal because Bakers Glass Warehouse had gotten tired of dealing with her.

She was the definition of persistence.

Sitting cross-legged on a blanket, she chipped away at the layers of cheap paint, an arsenal of products lined up to help her transform something old to something new.

Personally, he didn't think she'd be able to do it, but that's not what bothered him. No, it was much deeper than that. The woman was beginning to affect his personal life on a grand scale, and if he didn't get a handle on it, things were going to explode.

Marissa wanted to sleep with him. It was obvious from their last dinner together. She needed no further courting. They'd gone way past the third and fourth date in the last few weeks, and he sensed the beginning of her frustration. The good-night kiss and tame foreplay had reached an end. She was ready to take the next step, and so was he. The problem was more serious than he'd originally thought.

His dick just refused to respond.

No matter how hard he tried, he couldn't get excited about bringing her to his bed.

Because all he could think about was Charlie.

Brady smothered a groan and concentrated on his task. The thick humidity had finally drifted away with the end of summer, and a gorgeous late September breeze blew in like a gentle lover's kiss. Fall hovered, tempting the northeast with eye-popping colors as the leaves turned and the earth was drenched in golden light. It was his favorite time of year, and the height of the building season.

They'd been working together nonstop for the last two months and had found their rhythm. Though they still bantered and insulted, it had a softened edge. Respect had grown out of cramped quarters. And something more. Something dangerous.

It had been two weeks since their last encounter when he'd almost kissed her. That almost kiss haunted him on a daily basis. That almost kiss had caused a shift between them, igniting a sensual awareness that was with them every moment of every day. They both ignored the simmering attraction and stuck to business, but it was getting harder and harder to pretend he didn't want her.

"Hey, Brady, Jackson said next Friday his mom has a work thing so I thought we'd throw a pizza party here. If you don't have a date with Marissa, how about joining us?" she called out.

Jackson hooted. "Is she hot?"

He straightened his shoulders. "Of course. She's with me, isn't she?"

Charlie grinned and shook her head. Ash- and timber-colored strands of hair brushed her shoulders and clung to her cheek. "Egomaniac. She's only with you for the free dinners, dude."

Jackson thought that was hysterical, bringing a reluctant grin to Brady's lips. Somehow, they'd created a bit of a ragtag crew of three, all with one focus: restore the house so it could live again. Before, Charlie's chaotic work process had struck him as sloppy and disrespectful. Now, he saw how her vision of a house was so pure, she'd do anything to keep it. The work was part of her makeup and soul, striking him a bit like Dalton when he worked on a piece of wood. Brady had always respected that quality, even as he bemoaned the sometimes ragged timeline that screwed things up for him.

It was a different way of looking at things, and he was getting better at seeing the bigger picture. He'd gained a deep respect for her as a professional and a woman who'd overcome a challenging past to make herself better.

Too bad he still wanted to strip her clothes, part her thighs, and make her scream with pleasure.

"Earth to Brady. Next Friday good?"

"Sure."

She frowned, as if noticing his response was lackluster. "Come over here."

"Busy now. Later." Hell, he was sporting wood on a whole new level just by the image of Charlie naked. Marissa was beautiful and sweet. Her dark hair and eyes bespoke a Latina heritage he loved. She was soft spoken and never argued with him. She wanted a family immediately. She knew his parents through the church. She also gave plenty of indication she'd be open minded in the bedroom, which was a must.

Then why hadn't he taken her yet? Why wasn't it her naked form he was currently visualizing in his head?

Because he couldn't get Charlotte out of his damn head.

He slammed the window in, causing a loud shriek of protest from the shrinking wood. "Hey, be careful with my windows!" she shouted out. "Do you need help?"

He gritted his teeth. "I got it."

"Doesn't look like you got it."

"I got it, okay!" He shoved. With a weak protest, the frame slid in. "See?"

"I'll do the other one. I have a gentler approach."

"Stop being a control freak and paint your damn window cupboard DIY project!"

Jackson winced. "Umm, Brady, do you need to smash a wall or something? Bad day?"

Charlie slapped her hand over her mouth but not before a giggle burst through. With his dick hard, his hands smarting, and his heart confused, he glared at both of them, then stormed out. "I need a break. Gonna get some air."

He sat on the broken stoop and guzzled water, calming himself. Enough. He was going to fuck Marissa's brains out and he was going to love it. They were already falling in love. They'd get married in church, have beautiful babies, and she'd be the perfect wife. Done.

"Do you want to take off?"

Her soft voice stroked his ears and he half closed his eyes, wishing she'd go away. "No. Just want to drink my water in peace."

She ignored him, plopping herself beside him. Her wide, thickly lashed eyes were filled with concern. The tangy scent of citrus drifted to his nostrils. He'd discovered she had a weakness for grapefruits in the morning. He'd never imagined the scent could set off pure lust, but he was beginning to realize a whole lot of things lately. "You've been here every day, and it was wrong of me to begin taking you for granted. I don't know how it happened, but I feel like we've built this crew and you both belong to me. Stupid, right? Especially when I was against you even being here and we couldn't stand being in the same room together."

You both belong to me...

His inner caveman roared to life, wondering what it would be like to belong to Charlotte Grayson. He'd feast on her for hours, learning what every moan and whimper meant. He'd tear off those ridiculous clothes and taste and touch every inch of her beautiful body. He'd take her to places she'd dreamed about, and then take her there again and again. He'd fuck her, please her, claim her. A shudder wracked his body as a sudden primal need overtook him. He clenched his fists and breathed slow and deep, harnessing the arousal she didn't even seem to notice.

"But you have a life you've been putting on hold. Why don't you work with me every other day? Jackson has been great. There's no trouble here. Even some neighbors have come over to introduce themselves and say how happy they are to get a nice house to add to the neighborhood."

Damn her. First, she never wanted to even acknowledge the almost kiss. Then she insisted on treating him like some distant work buddy. And now she wanted to completely dismiss him? "We made a deal. I'm sticking to it, and you better do the same."

Her brows snapped together. Much better. He could deal with her when she was annoyed with him and he with her. Things were clearer that way. "I'm trying to be nice," she explained. "I just don't think I need you anymore."

Hurt lashed at him. Caught off guard, he fired back. "Glad to know I'm so dispensable. But even if you insist on making cupboards out of windows, and pizza art boxes, and ridiculous wall murals in the kitchen like a craft show gone bad, I made a promise to stay until the last damn nail is in. Got it?"

"Just because you're so narrow minded and scared to get outside the box, don't put your crap on me. I never needed you in the first place. You're the liability here! I'm practically carrying you along, so do us both a favor and we'll both tell Cal we're good to part ways."

Adrenaline pumped through his veins. He practically snarled the words in irritation. "Here's a hint. Going outside the box is sometimes not a good thing."

"What do you know? Have you ever been pushed to create something from nothing? I bet your own house is technically beautiful, with all the latest gadgets and a sleek, modern feel. But guess what? I bet it's all empty inside. No surprises. No creativity. And no soul." She spit out her last words in a staccato rhythm that made a smear of red blur his vision.

"Here we go again with the tortured, poor artist you like to bring out when challenged. Coloring inside the lines is not all bad, Charlotte." He sneered her full name with sarcastic intent. Her widened eyes told him it struck home. She'd gotten used to hearing her formal name from him and usually didn't snap back. Maybe she sensed the intention not to mock, but an underlying intimacy they both sensed and accepted.

But this time, his intention was to completely piss her off.

Choppy pants broke from her gumball lips. Hazel eyes blazed with scorching heat. Her body trembled and his responded instantly, unfurling with a crazed need to yank her against him and kiss her the way she should be kissed, by a man and not the boys he bet she dated. He reached out slowly, his logic long gone under the sting of her words and her attitude and her damn delectable mouth, and then—

"It may not be bad, Bolivar," she drawled, "but it's boring as hell."

He froze, staring at her with a growing horror, hoping he heard wrong. The smug arrogance glowing from her features told him he'd gotten it right the first time.

She knew his birth name.

Someone was going to die.

"What did you call me?" he asked softly, a clear warning vibrating from his chest.

She didn't even blink. "Bolivar. Your real name. Kind of cute, actually. All formal and regal. Full of male posturing pride. Not sure why you're so embarrassed by it."

This was not happening. His ears actually got hot, and he prayed they didn't look red. "You will never call me by that again. Do you understand? Who told you?"

She broke into a delighted grin. Why was she never afraid of him? Or even cautious? "No one. I just did my research. Now, you can decide to lose your attitude and come back inside to help or knock off for the rest of the day. I don't really care, *Bolivar.*"

He gnashed his teeth together and his hands fisted. He was going to choke her. He was actually going to murder a poor defenseless female, except she was anything but. "I swear to you, Charlotte, if you push me on this you will regret it."

"Okay." She jumped up from the step, dusted off her jeans, which actually boasted pink flowers on the sides, and grinned wider. "Bolivar, Bolivar, Bolivar," she sang in an off-key song.

He got up and reached for her, ready to spank her sweet ass, but she broke into giggles and danced away, his name still falling from her lips.

The door slammed behind her.

Brady closed his eyes and groaned. This was a nightmare. He fucking hated that name. He'd been tortured in school until he declared to the family he'd no longer answer to Bolivar and changed it to Brady. It had taken his parents a while, but he was so crazed and insistent, they finally listened. Even his sisters were afraid to use it.

But not *her.*

Like the damn fairytale, he had a feeling the secret of his real name would be his downfall. She'd torture him endlessly because she acted like a child. A woman child. Who could possibly handle her on a full-time basis?

No one. Including him.

Tempted to walk away, he forced himself to drag in a breath and stand. Best to get back in there and not mention anything.

Concentrate on finishing the window work, and he'd cut out early. He'd squeeze in an impromptu date with Marissa and get his life back on track where it belonged.

He refused to allow Charlotte Grayson to kidnap his heart.

He guzzled the rest of his water and walked back inside.

Chapter Ten

"Creativity requires the courage to let go of certainties."—Erich Fromm

"It's too big. No way will it fit."

His voice was full of impatience. "Of course it'll fit. Just use some more lube and relax. Why do you have to make things so difficult?"

"Me? You're the one who wanted the screw! I told you this whole thing wouldn't work."

He grunted. "Open up, dammit. You're not helping me at all here!"

"I swear, if you hurt me, I'll pepper spray you again!"

His hands clenched. Sweat dotted his brow. "I won't hurt you. Just relax. I'm going in, okay?"

"Fine, just do it!"

He pushed through the resistance and finally the cabinet slid in with a pop. Shaking out her fingers, she examined the frame for damage, noticing the wood hadn't cracked and everything fit perfectly. She'd argued against using the extra screws but Brady insisted it would be more stable. Guess he'd been right, even though she'd hate to admit it.

He puffed up his chest in macho pride. "See? Told you we just needed more lube."

An amused, masculine voice cut through the tension-filled air.

"Damn, that was hot. Am I interrupting something?"

Charlie jumped and swung around. Gage stood in the doorway, a huge grin plastered on his face. As usual, he wore nerdy white sneakers, old jeans, and a ripped Metallica concert T-shirt. His hair was mussed under his red baseball hat, and his jaw unshaven. He looked like he'd gone on a bender for a few nights, but Charlie knew it was part of his usual messy demeanor.

"Gage!" With a delighted laugh, she threw herself across the room for a quick hug. "What are you doing here?"

"Wanted to see how you were managing your difficult new lover."

Brady cleared his throat. "Umm, we're not lovers. Just work partners." His voice held a clip of annoyance, as if he hated the idea of them being linked. Charlie ignored the flash of hurt that caught her on the chin like a sucker punch. Damn, he still didn't think much of her, even after all this time. Had it been childish to hope these past months had bonded them? Maybe it was all in her head. Maybe he still looked at her as a chore and thought her ideas were juvenile. Her heart squeezed, but she fought past it, pissed that she still cared.

"He's talking about the house," she retorted.

"She looks at houses as men," Gage explained. "Kind of a weird love-affair thing to me, but damn, girl, you done good. He's looking great."

She beamed up at him. "Thanks! I told you I'd make you proud."

"You always do." He tugged on her hair with affection, then walked across the room, holding out his hand. "Gage Masterson. I sold Charlie the house."

Brady nodded, reaching out to shake his hand. "Brady Heart. I'm with Pierce Brothers. Helping her with the renovation."

"Nice. Finally took my advice and asked for some help, huh?"

She snorted at the same time Brady did. "Hardly," she muttered. "Let's say they insisted on providing me with a helper, whether or not I wanted one."

Gage frowned. "Why are you so damn stubborn? There's nothing wrong with needing help. Especially with a bastard like this."

"What did you say?" Brady asked.

Gage grinned and pointed to the ceiling. "Sorry. I meant the house. Charlie has me thinking about them in male terms and it's damn annoying. Wanna show me the rest of your place?"

"Yes, come with me and I'll give you the full tour." Without another glance, she ignored Brady and grabbed Gage's hand, tugging him out of the kitchen. "Let's start in the basement."

Son of a bitch.

Who the hell was this guy?

Brady fumed at her careless dismissal and began cleaning up. She'd told him before she wasn't dating anyone. He'd figured all her time was spent on the house or at Pierce Brothers, so it'd be hard to find someone new for a while. But if he'd sold her this house, maybe they'd been dating all along? The guy seemed nice enough, but a bit scruffy around the edges. Is that what she preferred?

The fact throbbed under his skin like a splinter. He'd never seen him around before, though, and she didn't mention him. Maybe it was a strictly casual relationship? Or a once in a while hookup? And why the hell did he care?

He shook his head, reaching for patience. Probably because he'd been unable to close the deal with Marissa. She'd gone away to visit her family for two weeks, so their next date had been postponed. He needed to stop worrying about who Charlie dated and concentrate on finishing up this damn house and moving on.

Trying to keep his focus, he cleaned up, his gaze taking in what Gage had seen for the first time. Like a child who had grown up before his eyes, he realized he hadn't noticed how well it was shaping up.

The new windows and floors gave off more space and light, and with the wall gone, the house had a flow it had been missing before. The disastrous kitchen was slowly taking shape. Charlie had stuck to her plan, rebuilding the cabinets in different forms for the upper and lower. They weren't painted, and the counters weren't installed, and the window frame they'd just shoved in to build a half pantry was unfinished, but he was able to spot the full vision. He couldn't believe it, but it was possible she'd pull it off. Of course, he couldn't imagine what type of mural anyone would want in their kitchen, but maybe he could talk her out of that. They still had the roof to replace, and the porch, but the main renovation was behind them. She'd even managed to find matching shingles and only had to replace a quarter of the outside.

Gage's voice floated up the stairs, blending with Charlie's musical laugh. Wind chimes. Why did her voice remind him of the happy quality of bells tinkling in the breeze?

"You're on," she said, entering the kitchen. "It's been way too long and it's already late."

"Done. We'll grab a bite there." Gage turned and shot him a look. "Hey, Brady. Wanna join us?"

"Where?"

"Heading to the restaurant and dance club Tangos. They have salsa dancing Thursday nights."

Charlie waved her hand in the air. "Brady doesn't dance."

"I'd love to come."

It was worth it to see her mouth open. Was she angry he was interrupting her alone time with Gage? Or did she even care? He probed her gaze but was only able to spot pure surprise. Satisfaction ran through him. Good. About time he threw her off balance.

"Great," Gage said. "Do you know where the place is? I'll meet you there in an hour or so? Just gonna head home and change."

"Sounds good," he said. "I'll be there."

With a frown, Charlie walked him to the door, then came back. Her teeth nibbled on her lower lip. "Umm, Brady? You don't have to go if you don't want to. Tangos may be a bit out of your league. The restaurant is small and it only serves tapas. The music is really loud and most people who go are there to dance. I don't think you'll feel comfortable."

Anticipation thickened his blood. He grinned real slow. "Don't worry about me, Charlotte. I can handle it. But I appreciate the heads-up. Now, let's get packed up and call it a day so I can go change."

Still nibbling on her lip, she nodded, but her greenish-brown eyes were filled with doubt.

Oh, he was really looking forward to this.

Chapter Eleven

"If opportunity doesn't knock, build a door."—*Milton Berle*

Charlie squeezed herself between Gage and Brady at the packed bar and ordered a Blue Moon. The upbeat music of trumpets and clave filled the air, revving up the crowd. Gage pushed a twenty dollar bill onto the bar, handing Brady his IPA, and motioned them toward a corner where they could take in the atmosphere and lean comfortably. Gage hooked his fingers through hers, making sure she wasn't bumped or jostled, and she fought a smile. Too bad Tom couldn't come tonight. He was stuck working late again at the restaurant, which was another reason Gage had been insistent on a night out. She loved taking turns dancing with both of them at the club, even though most assumed they were part of a ménage. At least, that's what she told herself as the reason men never hit on her here.

Brady shot her a cool look at their clasped hands, then glanced away. Her skin prickled with awareness. Ever since they'd left the house, she hadn't been able to rationalize the tension in the air. It was almost as if he was bothered by the idea of her and Gage being a couple. She hadn't told him about Tom—it was none of his business and Gage's call. But if he did believe they were together, why would he possibly care?

The image of that almost kiss slammed into her vision. She'd spent the last weeks burying the memory far underground, desperate to ignore the awareness between them. Instead, every day drove her a bit more mad.

His fingers sliding over hers when they adjusted a cabinet. The stretch of his jeans over that tight ass as he bent over. The dark, velvety pull of those sooty eyes as he gazed at her in moody silence, as if thinking things he didn't want her to know.

Bad things.

She shivered and pressed closer to Gage. Gage drummed his fingers on her hip to the music, content to watch the crowd and drink his own beer. She snuck a sideways glance at Brady, still surprised he'd actually shown up. Even more surprising was his comfort level. She'd expected him to be overdressed, uptight, and a bit awkward.

Instead, he seemed to fit right in.

His jeans were dark-washed and snug. His charcoal button-down shirt had a fancy navy scroll at the cuffs and neck, but looked amazing with his dark hair and eyes. His shoes were red Italian leather that was probably ridiculously expensive and impossible to dance in, but again, they looked good on him. He cocked out his hip, beer casually hooked from his fingers as he took in the dancers. His scent drifted from his skin in an intoxicating flavor of spice and sea salt, reminding her of the special caramels she ordered by the box and only devoured on Valentine's Day for her own special present to herself.

Not that she wanted to devour him.

Absolutely not.

She shifted her weight closer to Gage and surveyed the room. Tangos reminded her of those old jazz bars where people jammed together at too tiny tables to hear great music. It was hidden underground, with only one half-lit neon sign to advertise its presence. This was a club that wasn't on Facebook or heavily marketed, because the true fans of Latin music poured in on a regular basis. All forms of dance were highlighted, but salsa was the most favored. Here, the club demanded participation and took their dancing seriously. The darkness lent an air of mystery, and the pounding, energized music lent an air of sexuality. Bodies twisted together on the dance floor, highlighted by flashing red lights, squeezed tight yet claiming their own space by the demands of each couple. The air hung heavy with the ripe scents of sweat and skin, with alcohol and musk, with pungent arousal. The bar was separated from the dance floor by a low wall, and the dining area consisted of small round tables and wooden chairs jammed into every available space. Exposed brick walls collided with red accents, leading to an open floor area packed with dancers.

She'd taken salsa lessons a few years ago and fell in love with the fast, fluid moves that demanded skill, enthusiasm, and high energy.

Gage ducked his head to whisper in her ear. "Ready to dance?"

"Sure." She turned to Brady, speaking directly in his ear. "Gage and I are hitting the floor. Will you be okay alone?"

She expected him to make an excuse to leave, but he only nodded, those dark eyes filled with a mixture of emotions she couldn't name. "Go ahead, have fun."

She forced a smile. "Thanks." Then she allowed Gage to lead her onto the floor.

When she looked back, Brady had been swallowed up by the crowd. She worried if a woman asked him to dance, he'd panic, but then she was on the floor and the only thing that demanded her attention was the music. Half closing her eyes, she began to soften and relax, to embrace the music and release all the tension she carried with her, shedding her body of expectations and responsibilities and the cares of life.

Her feet spun, tapped, glided. Gage was a solid partner, holding her hands in a firm grip, yet allowing her to lead slightly since he knew she always enjoyed a say in the steps. Her hips swayed, her back arched, and she let herself go free.

God, she loved dancing.

Poor Brady. He had no idea what he was missing.

Brady watched her out on the floor, his gaze pinned to every movement of her body. God, she was gorgeous. He'd never seen someone so enthralled with the music, so able to surrender to the inner demands of the physical and emotional entwined together. Dancing the salsa required a delicate balance, a merging of release and precision, of control and surrender, and if done correctly, the outcome was pure ecstasy—almost orgasmic.

She had no clue he'd been raised on salsa dancing. The tango. The merengue. He'd been taught to embrace all Latin dances since his parents had been regularly dancing since he was a child. He'd actually been to Tangos a few times but had never seen Charlie or Gage here before.

She danced the salsa like she'd been born to it. Limbs loose and elegant, arms holding a firm frame to Gage, her hips rolled and her feet flashed as she spun to the jungle beat of the trumpets and horns and clave, the music encouraging the dancers to go deeper, get wild, lose themselves in the energy of the moment.

He'd almost thrown out his plan and dragged her right to the floor once he spotted her. The pink bling jeans were gone. The glittery T-shirts were tucked away, along with the sparkly sneakers. Tonight, she wore a lipstick-red dress that dared a man not to notice. With plunging cleavage and a skirt that twirled with every spin on the floor, those gorgeous, naked legs teased him with every turn. Her shoes were low heeled with a peekaboo toe and made strictly for dancing. He knew this because his own shoes had been custom made over a year ago. Her blonde hair whipped in the air, teasing her bare shoulders, practically begging him to fist all those silky strands in his hand and pull. Hard.

His dick wept, pressing against the ridge of his jeans. His breath was shallow, his muscles locked in anticipation of what was about to happen. For the first time, he was throwing rational logic away. He had one goal tonight and he wouldn't leave until it was achieved, no matter what the consequences.

Tonight, he was going to salsa dance with Charlotte Grayson.

Slowly, he dragged in a lungful of air. Steadied himself. Unbuttoned his cuffs and slowly rolled up his shirt sleeves. Undid the first two buttons of his shirt. Put his beer down on the ledge.

And went over to claim her.

* * * *

She was laughing as Gage masterfully led her into a tight spin. Pivoting on her heel, the room whirled around in blurred images until her gaze snagged on a figure walking toward her.

Charlie squinted, sure she was imagining things, until he stood before her. Leashed power radiated in waves, wrapping her within a snug circle of male demand. He nailed her with his stare, those sooty eyes seething with a raw emotion that drove the breath from her lungs. One blue-black curl fell across his forehead in disarray. He'd unbuttoned his shirt and rolled up his cuffs, exposing sinewy arms sprinkled with dark hair. "May I cut in?" His voice was formal, but his gravelly tone dripped with command. He never broke his gaze, lifting his hand and offering it to her.

In seconds, her skin prickled with goose bumps, and her nipples pushed against the thin jersey of her dress. She squeezed her thighs together, suddenly wet and aroused, her core throbbing with need. She blinked, staring at his outstretched hand in half fear, half fascination. What was happening? What was he doing? And why was he looking at her like a sleek panther who'd finally spotted his prey?

A chuckle drifted to her ears. Gage pressed her hand in Brady's. "Have fun, you two." He walked off without another glance, leaving them amidst grinding, sweaty bodies pressing against them from all sides.

"Brady, I don't think—"

With one swift movement, he pulled her against him, his hand pressed into the small of her back, forcing her hips to cradle his. Off balance, she automatically reached up to grab his shoulders. Her nails curled into those rock hard muscles, a groan rising to her lips. The pulsing sexuality of his body against hers short circuited her brain. Her swollen breasts rubbed against his chest, and his mouth stopped inches from hers. Carved lips curled at the corner in a touch of a smirk, but his eyes blazed with an intense sexuality she couldn't deny or escape. Her eyes widened at the evidence of his arousal, notched securely between her thighs.

"Are you dating Gage?" he demanded.

She blinked, completely disoriented at his direct question. "No. He has a partner named Tom."

Satisfaction carved out his features. "Good."

"I don't understand. You don't dance."

"I most certainly do dance."

"Why didn't you tell me?"

"You never asked." His gaze practically devoured her. His thumb slid a few inches lower, stopping at the curve of her ass. She shivered. "Dance with me, Charlotte."

This time, the sound of her full name caused a helpless shudder.

Confusion swamped her. "Why?"

"Because I want to. And I think you do, too."

She stared back at him, tilting her chin upward with a hint of a challenge. "How do I know you can keep up?"

His lip quirked. Damn, he was smoking hot. That combination of arrogance and dark sensuality was wickedly tempting. It was as if a filter had been ripped off her vision, and she saw him in all of his masculine glory. This was crazy. She'd never been attracted to Brady Heart like this before. Had she?

He lowered his head and spoke against her ear, his breath a warm rush of air. "Take the chance. I'll give you what you want. What you need." He pulled back slightly, meeting her eyes. "You just have to say yes."

Standing still on the dance floor as couples whizzed by them, Charlie came to her decision. A slow smile curved her lips. She wouldn't make it easy for him, though. She intended to pull out all the stops and see if he had what it took. That was the only way she'd allow him to suddenly transcend from irritated coworker to dance partner. And maybe more.

"Yes."

The blare of the trumpet foreshadowed the challenge ahead. Never breaking his stare, he positioned his arms in the closed position, his strong fingers wrapped around hers. His hand burned a scorching imprint in the small of her back. Then he began to move.

The salsa was a dance very different from the tango—the dance of love. The tango relied on full body contact and was a dance of seduction unfurled in the center of the floor. The salsa was a tease, a flirtation, a promise of what could be. If she had one thing to bet on in life, it was that Brady Heart wouldn't know how to dance the salsa no matter how much he wanted to try.

She was so very wrong.

He was a master on the dance floor. She'd been used to dancing with Gage and Tom, and was comfortable with her own moves and their easy leads. They played at the salsa.

Brady owned it.

He moved with a speed and grace that took her breath away, leading with a command she'd never experienced. He gave her no choice but to follow, to bend to his will and the will of the salsa, until her body rose with its own demand and gave him what he wanted.

She spun away, launching into a short solo, whipping her hair and shaking her hips to the percussion beat, daring him to match her.

And he did, pulling her in, forcing her into a series of turns while he guided her with strong hands that took control. His red shoes flashed, his onyx eyes blazed, and each time she challenged him, he gave it all back, demanding more.

They danced until sweat dampened their skin and their muscles ached, and still the music pounded in a jungle beat, refusing to stop. The crowd around them disappeared to a distant blur and roar. She was caught up in another world of vast space and physical freedom.

He pushed her, punished her, broke her. With each step her will lessened, until she was a beautiful extension of his limbs, his lean muscles, his inward grace and leashed sensuality. He pushed her away, pulled her in, bent her so far back her hair brushed the floor, then pressed her so tight against his body, there was no separation between them as they became one.

Each time he brought her close, his hands ran over her body, stroked the bare skin of her arms, the curve of her spine, the hard tips of her breasts. Her body was lit from within with a fire that ravaged and burned her alive. It was a dance of seduction and intention, of lust and primitive need. And still, he never stopped, forcing her to meet each one of his steps and give her what he wanted.

Everything.

A whimper broke from her lips. He stopped, dragging her against his chest, his hand fisting in her tangled hair to tug hard, forcing her head back. He studied her face, a curse blistering in the air, and lowered his head. "Charlotte."

She waited. Then she rose up on her tiptoes, the decision already made.

His mouth took hers.

Like the dance itself, it was a fiery kiss that defied logic, a raw mating of tongues and teeth and want, stripped down to its basic form. Her head spun as she opened wider for his thrusting tongue, thrilling to the fingers digging into her scalp and his dominant kiss. His teeth nipped and his tongue dove deeper, swallowing her moan. His taste swamped her with hunger, and she was mad for more, desperate to feel his lips on her naked skin and between her thighs, crazed to tear off his clothes and reveal every sleek, hard muscle.

He ripped his mouth away, dark eyes gleaming with fierce possession.

Time stopped. They stared at each other for endless moments, the world falling away and leaving them alone in a tunnel of raw emotion, burning hunger, and stunning silence.

His fingers lifted, grazing her swollen lips with the lightest of touches. "I've been wanting to do that for a long time," he murmured.

Her heart skidded, tripped, stopped. "About damn time."

That gorgeous mouth tipped in a smile. Before she could reach for him or say anything else, he dropped his hand and stepped back.

"Good night, Charlotte."

She watched in stunned silence as he left the dance floor and disappeared out the door, leaving her alone.

By the time she made her way back to Gage, she knew everything had changed.

She just didn't know what she was going to do about it.

Chapter Twelve

"Design must seduce, shape, and perhaps more importantly, evoke an emotional response."—April Greiman

When he walked through the door on Monday afternoon, she was waiting for him.

She hadn't slept in two nights. His image taunted her behind closed lids, tempting her with dirty, sex-filled scenes that made her body ache and yearn. He hadn't called or texted. Was he going to pretend nothing had happened between them? Did he believe they could just calmly go back to work without acknowledging what had happened on that dance floor?

Fine. If he could do it, she could too. She'd die before mentioning the kiss or the blistering connection or the way her skin burned when they touched. She'd pretend they'd never danced and melted into one another as if they were one. They could torture her and she'd refuse to admit there was anything else between them but work, friendship, and respect.

Her whole body prickled in recognition as he stopped behind her. She refused to glance back, concentrating on putting the finishes on her built-in cabinet.

"Hey, you're early," he said. "The cabinet looks amazing. Did you use the warm pine stain?"

Jerk.

She made sure her voice sounded light and airy. "Yes, the cedar was too red, and the kitchen needs a more open, casual feel."

His steps came closer. She practically felt his body heat pressing around her. "You distressed it, too."

"Yep. Again, this calls for a more worn look. What do you think?"

"Looks great. Didn't think you could pull it off, but once again, you managed to surprise me."

"Glad you can admit some things," she muttered, roughly sanding one ragged edge with a tad of violence.

"What'd you say?"

"Nothing. How was your weekend?" she asked.

She tried not to hold her breath. Had he seen Marissa Saturday night? Did he sleep with his potential wife after kissing her with wild abandon just a few nights before? She ground her teeth together and waited for his response.

"Kind of crappy. Went to my family's house for dinner. Had to do some work for Cal so that took up most of my time."

He could have texted her. A simple *How are you doing?* would have sufficed. She was on Twitter and knew he sometimes used the company account. Even a Facebook message would've been acceptable since she knew for sure they were friends.

"Cool."

She didn't say anything further. She concentrated on sanding, and practically felt him twitch with nerves behind her. Good. "How about you? Have a nice weekend?" he asked.

"It was great. Went out for drinks and dinner Saturday night." The lie sprung easily. Sure, there were drinks, but it was just a few glasses of wine alone in her apartment. Dinner had consisted of Gage and Tom taking pity on her and feeding her a three-course meal while they listened sympathetically to her complaints about Brady.

"Oh. Sounds nice."

Did his voice sound strained? Did he think she went on a date? She sanded the wood harder. "It was."

"Good." More silence. "Umm, I guess I'll finish the work in the bathroom."

"Great." She listened to his footsteps retreat, hating their ridiculously juvenile one-word conversation. Why did she suddenly feel like a teenager around him? And why did she care so much if he didn't want to talk about the kiss? Maybe it was just an experiment. Now that he'd satisfied his curiosity, he wanted things to go back to normal.

She groaned when she saw the uneven edge on the cabinets she'd sanded down like a madwoman and swore to get her act together.

She hadn't mentioned the kiss.

Brady ripped at the last of the tile with a bit of violence. He was acting like a fucking idiot. He'd planned to call her over the weekend, but every time he picked up his damn phone, he choked. What was he going to say? *How's it going? Great kiss Thursday night? I've been thinking about you nonstop?*

Everything seemed juvenile, so he decided to just wait to see her in person. He intended to talk about the kiss right away, but she'd refused to turn around, like she was embarrassed to face him. Did she regret the kiss? Had it been an experiment and one she now wanted to forget? Or had she thought about it endlessly on loop like he had, unable to sleep?

He uttered a vicious curse word in Spanish. She could've gone on a date Saturday night and put the encounter out of her mind. If he mentioned it now, it might look like he was a damn puppy dog panting for some attention. Probably better to remain cool, focus on work, and see where the day took them.

As the hours passed, the tension between them grew, twisting so tight Brady felt like any moment they'd both snap. Jackson's absence made it worse. By the time dusk fell, they'd managed to avoid each other, exchange tight one-word sentences, and pretend everything was normal.

"Think you're ready to wrap up?" he asked. They faced each other across the living room. He tried not to linger too long on the ripe swell of her breasts contained in a T-shirt that declared, *Dream Big, Love Bigger* in baby blue sparkle. Her jeans were too tight, her lips were too tempting, and her eyes were too full of questions he wanted answers to.

"You can go without me. I'll see you tomorrow."

Her chilly tone caused the rubber band of tension to vibrate in warning. "I'll wait."

"I'm sure you have better things to do. People to see. Dates to go on. Sex to be had."

He jerked back. Studied her with a narrowed gaze. "What did you just say?" he asked softly.

She practically spit and growled like a pissed-off cat ready to pounce. "You heard me the first time. In fact, I've been thinking you don't need to be here anymore. Why don't you go off and do what you do best—find a neat little project to work on and a nice little woman to obey? 'Cause I'm done!"

And just like that, he snapped.

All of his doubts vanished, and he knew in that instant, she was just as crazed as he was. She hadn't forgotten their kiss. The memory was in her glittering hazel eyes, her shaking body, her tightly drawn tension. It was in the simmering heat pumping between them. It was in the tight tips of her nipples pressing desperately against her T-shirt, and her squeezed thighs and the madly beating pulse at the base of her neck.

Relief coursed through him. Now, at least he knew what to do.

Brady smiled real slow. Then crossed the room toward her.

＊ ＊ ＊ ＊

Charlie watched him close the distance between them. The entire day had been torture. She thought she could play the game, but she just couldn't. She hated thinking he didn't care about their kiss and refused to be one of those superchic, casual women who blew off any intimate encounter with jaded flourish.

Screw that.

"Why are you so mad, Charlotte?" he asked softly, getting closer and closer.

She stretched to full height, refusing to cower, and marched halfway to meet him. "Really? You have the nerve to ask me why I'm pissed off? We share this amazing, earth-shattering kiss in the middle of the dance floor, and then you walk out without another word? And when I think maybe you'll reach out over the weekend to acknowledge such a kiss, I get nothing. Well, let me tell you something, Brady Heart. I won't be used as some kind of Frankenstein experiment while you go off on real dates with Stepford women who are good enough to marry!"

"You think the kiss was that good, huh?"

Temper struck her. "You're an asshole!"

She launched for him in attack, but he caught her close, bending her backward, holding her tight in his embrace. She panted for breath, ready to pummel him, but stilled when she saw the raw truth glimmering in his dark eyes. "I can't stop thinking about that kiss either," he growled against her lips. "Can't stop thinking about you, like this, in my arms. Can't stop thinking about you being mine."

And then he kissed her, long and deep and hard. His tongue claimed her, holding her still beneath his demands. She curled closer to him, opened her mouth wider, and gave it all back to him full power. Finally, he broke away, his expression fierce with hunger.

She tried to speak, couldn't, then tried again. "That was unexpected."

His smile softened her heart. "Yes."

"How long have you had the hots for me?"

"Too long."

"I had no idea. Well, even after our almost kiss, I thought you didn't like me."

His brows drew together. His hands stroked her cheeks. "Not true. We may argue and I may disagree with your ideas, but there's a lot of things I like about you."

"Name them."

He lowered his head, his breath a warm rush in her ear. "I respect your drive and your focus. You have great creativity. You have a kind heart, and you make people around you feel good. You're funny. You're passionate. You know how to salsa. And your body is super hot."

A laugh hovered on her lips. "Did you just butcher the English language and say super?"

His teeth nibbled on her lobe, biting gently, then licking with his tongue. She shivered. "Sorry. I got caught up in the moment."

Her hands stroked the lean muscles of his back, the broad strength of his shoulders. "Were you jealous of Gage?"

"Yes. I've been fighting my attraction to you for a while. Besides the work conflict, you're ten years younger, plus I didn't think you were interested."

Her knees grew weak as he nibbled on her jaw, bit her lower lip, and kissed her again. "I never let myself go there. But I was always sneaking glances at your ass."

He chuckled. "Brat." He kissed her again. And again.

She leaned into him, hungry and desperate for more. He whispered her name.

"Yes?"

"Come home with me."

The words rang with primal need and a hunger that rocked her foundation. Charlie had learned life was a gift of chances and opportunities that were ripped away with too much hesitation. She'd never regret any decision of risk; her only regrets were the what ifs. Right now, logic had no place in her world. Right now, she needed him and refused to think about tomorrow.

"Yes."

He kissed her again, locked up, grabbed her hand, and led her out the door. She buckled herself into the cushy seat of his Mercedes. He pulled away from the curb, reached over, and entwined his fingers with hers.

They didn't speak. The sexual tension pulsed in the tight quarters of the car. The drive felt like forever, but in reality, it had only been fifteen minutes. He pulled down a quiet end street and into a circular driveway. He cut the engine, getting out of the car, and quickly led her up the pathway. Charlie got the impression of sweeping lines of brick and glass, of multi-level decks and huge windows caught in shadows. They reached the porch. He opened the door, punched in a code to his alarm, and shut it behind him.

Then in one swift movement, he picked her up high in his arms, spun her around, and slammed her against the door. His body pinned hers until each of her curves cushioned his hard muscles. His knee slowly pushed open her thighs while his hands cupped her ass, holding her still.

Her breath came in rapid pants. Her panties were so wet, they were useless as any type of barrier. The primitive gleam in his dark eyes declared his intention, but it was his words that made her practically reach orgasm right there, right then.

"I need to know how you like it," he whispered against her trembling lips. His thumbs caressed her jaw. "If you don't like rough, I need to know now. Because I'm on the edge and I don't want to scare you."

Thrilled at his dark words, she parted her lips, running her tongue deliberately over the line of his mouth, then nipped with her teeth. "You couldn't scare me if you tried," she whispered back.

"Oh, the bad things I intend to do to you, Charlotte." He worked his knee higher, pressing against her throbbing pussy.

She half shut her eyes and fought the moan. "Then make them good, *Bolivar.*"

That did it. His grip tightened, and his breath dragged into his lungs with force. "What did you just call me?" he asked softly, in clear warning.

She nibbled at that delicious, firm mouth of his again. God, she was frantic to get him to kiss her, rip off her damn clothes, and fuck her properly. But she wasn't about to lose the first battle of the bedroom. "You heard me, Bolivar."

His low laugh promised retribution. "Have you ever begged, Charlotte? Really begged?"

Her tummy dropped. Her nipples were so hard they ached. "No."

"Oh, good. This is going to be fun."

He slammed his mouth over hers at the same time his knee pushed firmly in between her legs.

She cried out but he swallowed the sound whole. His tongue dove deep, dominating her mouth in delicious, wicked detail. She battled him back, tongues twisting, teeth gnashing, frantic for more of him to ease the yawning need devouring her. The barrier of her jeans was pure torture. His knee slowly rocked against her swollen folds, giving temporary relief, then ripping it away. Her clit pounded for more pressure, and she twisted in his arms, but he held her still, refusing to let her satisfy herself. He began rubbing his knee slowly back and forth, driving her out of her mind, until her fingers grabbed at the open collar of his shirt and ripped.

The buttons popped off and spilled to the floor. She tore at the fabric until his chest was bared, and her hands traced the gloriously hard muscles of his shoulders, his pecs, his rippled abs, scraping her nails along his hot skin.

He cursed. Yanked down the zipper of her jeans and tore them off. Fisted her T-shirt in one hand and guided it over her head, then threw the fabric to the ground. He growled in appreciation at the baby blue lace of her bra, but he divested her of it quickly, baring her breasts. He wasted no time, dipping his head to capture a hard nipple in his mouth. She arched against him at the same time his knee made torturous circles around her pounding clit, hazing her vision.

He sucked hard, plumping up her breast, flicking the tip back and forth before biting gently.

"Oh, God!"

"No, my name. What is it?"

"Bolivar." Damned if she was going to surrender this early on. She could hang on. Right?

He blew on her wet nipple. "Wrong answer."

His fingers slid under her baby blue panties and dove into her wet heat.

"Agh!" Her head banged against the door at the delicious pressure of his fingers deep in her core. His thumb played with her clit and he hit just the right spot to make her body explode with shivers, right on the verge of a shattering, mind-blowing orgasm. His teeth sunk into the tender curve of her neck while he added another finger, curling slightly and driving deeper. Lights shimmered in her vision, and her hips rolled with demand, seeking more, seeking...

"You want it? Ask me."

He was winning but she didn't care, not when she was so close to the best orgasm of her life. She rode his fingers in total abandon, digging her nails into his hips, head arched back.

"I want it. Now."

"Now, what?"

"Bastard. Now, please."

"God, you drive me fucking crazy. Yes. Come for me, Charlotte."

He bit her nipple, slammed his fingers into her dripping core, and flicked her clit.

She came. She screamed. She convulsed around his fingers, wet and throbbing, feeling so much pleasure it almost edged into pain. Instead of taking her down slow like most men did, he never stopped, pushing her further, rubbing her clit until she fell into a second orgasm whether she wanted to or not. Her legs clenched tight around his hips and she screamed again, awash in the sharp sensations attacking her from everywhere, flowing through her body like a river of hot lava.

She began to sag in his arms, and he scooped her up, carrying her up the stairs and entering a dark bedroom. He lay her down, the comforter soft and warm on her back, then quickly stripped off the rest of her clothes. Shadows slid and played over his figure. He unbuckled his belt and slid off his pants, then his underwear. Her gaze feasted on his gorgeous body. He stood with a sexy arrogance, hands on hips, feet apart, his large cock jutting out and making her mouth water.

Without thought, she crawled over the bed on all fours. "Let me touch you." She reached out and he slowly walked over, allowing her fingers to grip him, stroking from root to tip, catching the drops of moisture on the head. He groaned, stiffening more under her touch, and with a thrill of power, she dipped her head and took him in her mouth.

His taste was as delicious as his scent, musky, earthy, sexy. She licked and sucked, hollowing her cheeks and taking him to the back of her throat, humming slightly until he jerked in her mouth, and his fingers tangled in her hair, guiding her movements. Wild with need, she worked him until he ripped her away, cursing, and threw her back on the bed.

"I haven't even started and you already have me at the edge," he growled. "You're such a witch."

She pouted. "You made me lose control. Fair play, right?"

"Not in my bedroom."

"You chauvinistic, domineering, arrog-oh, God!"

She fell back on the pillow, gasping as his mouth hit her core. His broad shoulders kept her thighs wide apart, and he took his time tasting and exploring, his talented tongue using just the right amount of pressure on her clit, teasing her labia, bringing her straight to the edge again and keeping her there with a ruthless precision that made her want to weep and scream at the same time.

Her hips rolled in demand but he chained her to the bed, keeping his hands flat on her stomach and pinning her to the mattress. Her head thrashed. Her hands reached, her toes curled, and she did it again, dammit.

She begged.

He sucked hard on her clit and slammed three fingers inside her and she was coming again.

This time, he didn't wait. She heard a rip, he rolled on the condom, and with one quick plunge, he took her completely.

The burning, tight heat inside was almost too much. She whimpered, but he shushed her, pressing kisses to her swollen lips, stroking her breasts, gentling her for the invasion. Her body opened up, released, and he slid more fully inside. Rocking his hips, he kept up a teasing rhythm until the burning need was back in full force.

"Charlotte? Is this too much?"

She looked into his beautiful face. He gritted his teeth, and his jaw clenched with tension as he held himself back, waiting until she was ready. The graceful symmetry of his demand and patience, his dominance and gentleness, poured through her. She stroked his cheeks and wrapped her arms around his shoulders.

"Want more."

He pressed his forehead to hers and moved. Over and over, faster and faster, he fucked her more completely and fully than any man had before. His gaze locked on hers, never breaking the connection, drinking in every expression on her face. The wet slap of their bodies and panting breaths filled the silence, filled the darkness, and then the orgasm shredded through her, tossing her around the bed and wringing helpless cries from her lips.

He groaned and tightened his grip as he came right after, jerking his hips as he reached release. Bodies slick with sweat, the smell of sex ripe in the air, he held her close until she slumped into the mattress. "Be right back," he whispered. After a few moments, he climbed back into bed and cradled her against his chest. She didn't speak for a while, enjoying the tender strokes of his hand over her hair, gentle kisses pressed against her forehead. Completely boneless, deliriously giddy, a smile curved her lips as she lay in the darkness, enjoying the moment and the connection.

"You were right," she finally roused herself to say.

He stroked her hair. "About what?"

"You're a master at multiple orgasms."

He laughed, cuddling her closer, and her whole body sighed with pleasure. They fell into a comfortable, stretching silence for a while. She stroked his chest, letting her thoughts guide her words. "What about Marissa?" she asked. "I know we weren't thinking this through. What are we doing, Brady?"

Her heart galloped as his muscles tightened. She hadn't planned to jump into bed with him, but now that it had happened, she realized she wanted more. More time with him. More time to see the man beneath the surface and everything he'd been hiding. Would he give them a chance or was this just a one-night stand?

"We never slept together," he said quietly. "And I won't be seeing her again, Charlotte."

She held her breath. "Why?"

"Because I don't just sleep with women and walk away the next day."

She rolled over, propping herself on her elbows. Her gaze narrowed. "Listen up, buddy. If you just want to see me again to soothe your good guy responsibility, forget it. I'm a big girl and I can handle it. We both wanted to have sex, and it was pretty damn awesome. I know we're very different, and we didn't plan on this for the long term. So, don't get all high and mighty and play the martyr because of guilt. Got it?"

"You are such a pain in the ass."

In one swift movement, he flipped her over to her back, pinning her wrists to the mattress. She blinked in astonishment at him. His sooty gaze held resolve, lust, and resignation. "You should know me better than that. I'm no damn martyr, and I'm honest. I happen to crave you, Charlotte, and it's not going away anytime soon. I don't intend to promise anything right now, except that I want to see you again. I enjoy your company, and I'd like to date. Is that acceptable?"

"That's acceptable." She paused. "Bolivar."

His grin was pure male and sent a delicious tide of shivers down her spine. "Did you just term the sex we had pretty awesome?"

Her lips twitched. "Yes."

"Have you ever had a spanking, Charlotte?"

Her eyes widened. "No!"

"Good. I'm going to enjoy this. A lot."

He flipped her over so she was on all fours. He pressed one hand to her back, forcing her down and leaving her ass high in the air. The other arm wrapped underneath her stomach, pinning her in place for every depraved, filthy, dirty act he wanted to do to her.

Oh. My. God. She was so frickin' turned on.

He seemed to know, chuckling low, teasing her with swipes of his finger through her wetness. He dropped kisses on the small of her back, moving downward, his tongue dancing over her sensitized skin. She trembled, aching for more, and when his teeth took a bite of her flesh, she moaned.

"You are so sexy," he murmured. "Baby, are you on birth control?"

"Yes."

"I can use another condom, but I'm clean and get tested regularly."

She pushed her hips back unconsciously toward his deliciously wicked mouth. "I am, too."

"No condom needed?"

"No." She wriggled her ass in abandon. "For months I've been begging you to talk more. Does the bedroom suddenly make you chatty?"

A burning sting hit her ass. She jerked, her breath hissing out of her lungs. Holy shit. "That hurt!"

He did it again on the other cheek. Then again. Oh, she didn't like this at all. She must not be into spanking and all that crap about it turning into pleasure was just that. Crap. She opened her mouth to tell him to stop right now, but then his fingers plunged into her pussy. Her swollen, wet folds clenched on him with fierceness, and suddenly, she was rollicking toward orgasm.

"Oh!"

His tone held a bite of laughter. "Like that, do you? God, you're soaked. You're so fucking sexy. I want to eat you alive."

He gave her a few more slaps. She tried to jerk away, but he kept her in place with his firm grip, forcing her to take it. Just like before, the stinging burn turned into a hot pleasure, until she was desperate with need.

"Brady."

Her voice broke on his name. He seemed to sense her raw urgency. Dragging her hips back, he kicked open her legs and thrust into her in one perfect, full stroke.

She buried her face in the pillow, swallowing her cries and grunts. He fucked her hard, with merciless strokes that dominated and controlled, and she loved every moment. The climax dragged her under hard and fast, tossing her around, lighting her body with explosive pleasure.

She slumped on the mattress, boneless and exhausted. Barely able to move, she heard him get up and pad back with a damp washcloth. He cleaned her gently, pressing tender kisses over her skin, then tucked her under the covers. Never before had she felt so treasured and taken care of after sex. The light flicked back off. Then he climbed into bed, pulling her into his embrace. With his scent in her nostrils, and his warm, hard body cradling hers, Charlotte fell asleep with a smile on her lips.

Chapter Thirteen

"Creativity involves breaking out of established patterns in order to look at things in a different way."—Edward de Bono

"I have an idea."

Charlie set up the cans of paint in the kitchen and stared at the massive wall. Excitement nipped her nerves. She'd always dreamed of attacking a big-ass white canvas, and now she'd finally get to do it. She'd made some mock-ups of the image she wanted to create, but doing graffiti on such a large scale would be a challenge.

She glanced at Brady, who actually looked nervous. Those dark brows lowered in a frown, and he was studying the blank wall like it was a bomb and he was trying to disarm it. "What's your idea?" she asked, trying not to smile at his obvious doubt at her abilities.

"Wallpaper. We get some amazing wallpaper that makes the kitchen pop, and you don't have to ruin, er, paint the wall."

She shook her head. "This will be better than wallpaper. I deliberately went with wood and white cabinets, and underscaled the floors and countertops to balance out the artistic pop of a mural. It's going to blow your mind."

"I'm sure it will," he muttered.

She laughed out loud and rose, crossing the room to put her arms around him. Immediately he lost the worried edge, wrapping her in his embrace. Their bodies melded in perfect symmetry, and the scent of musk and spice rose to her nostrils. In seconds, she was hot, wet, and ready for him.

Two weeks.

Two weeks of nonstop, raw, carnal, hungry sex. It was something Charlie had never before experienced. They couldn't be in close quarters without needing to touch. The air seemed to crackle and come alive, as if it had been simmering the whole time, waiting to explode. So far, they'd spent almost every night together. She expected Brady to want to set up clear rules and boundaries—his entire persona was based around expectations and responsibilities for a relationship. Instead, when they ended work, they grabbed dinner together and headed back to either his house or her apartment, spending the entire evening naked and in bed.

Sheer heaven.

Deep down, she knew it couldn't last. Not like this. Eventually, they'd have to answer questions about what they were doing. But for a little longer, she embraced the moments with him, learning more and more each night. After endless orgasms, before sleep would claim them, they'd talk and share stories in the darkness, voices hushed, fingers entwined, slowly unveiling parts of themselves. The banter between them had also changed, softening to a lover's intimacy. Oh, they still argued with each other and differed with their opinions, but now the heat had a whole new meaning and was usually solved by ripping off their clothes the moment they were alone.

Unhealthy? Maybe.

Satisfying? Hell, yes.

"You're going to have to trust my vision on this one," she said, her hands slipping around to squeeze his ass. "Can you start work on the porch?"

"Yes. You're not going to paint girly type flowers, are you? 'Cause men use the kitchen too."

"Oh, really? I figured you'd peg the kitchen as the woman's domain. Doesn't Mr. Chauvinist expect his dinner on the table when he returns home from work?" she teased.

"Brat." His hand moved to her plump breast, tweaking her nipple through the fabric. Shocks of heat shot straight to her clit. He caught her expression and gave a very satisfied, male smile. "I have no problem with men cooking."

"Oh, really? Then what is it you truly demand from your woman?"

"What every man wants. A lady in the parlor. And in the

bedroom a—"

"Don't you dare!" Shaking with outrage, she pressed her palm against his firm lips. "I swear, you were plucked straight from the fifties and sent here to live!"

His dark eyes twinkled with mischief. "I was going to say a bad girl."

She pursed her lips, still mad. "Ugh, that's awful and cliché."

"Oh, yeah? What do you want from your man? And don't give me all that fake stuff about a sense of humor, nice eyes, and to make you *happy*. Be honest."

The memory of their previous conversation rose up and mocked her. He wanted the truth? Fine. She'd give it to him and have a bit of fun along the way. She bit her lip, looked down, and plastered a guilty expression on her face. "Okay, you want the real truth? The ugly stuff I've never admitted because I felt like it was really wrong?"

Now he looked intrigued. "Definitely. Just let it rip. I can take it."

"I want him to have a big, well, you know."

He blinked. "Big?"

She licked her lips and tilted her head back, widened her eyes in pure innocence. "I need it BIG, Brady. Really, really big. It's kind of a fantasy for me."

Did he look worried? "How big are you talking?" His voice hitched just a tad.

"So big it not only shocks me, but breaks me," she whispered naughtily. Her hands coasted down his chest, tracing the line of the buckle of his jeans. "Bigger then you can ever imagine."

Oh, yeah, he looked a bit pale. "I see. Umm, do you have an actual measurement you were looking for, or is this just general?"

She shrugged. "Just the bigger the better. Boy, am I glad I finally admitted it. You're not upset, are you? I certainly don't want you to feel like you're not big enough for me."

The paleness was replaced with red dots on his cheeks. Giggles threatened to escape. She'd never seen him this thrown off before.

"No! Of course, not. I'm just, just glad you shared that with me."

"You can work on it. You know, if you want it to get bigger."

His mouth dropped open. "Excuse me?"

"Sometimes practice makes it grow."

"What?"

"Like random acts of kindness. Or charity work. Or just sacrificing for someone else in general," she rambled on, as if clueless to his growing horror. It took a few moments before her words really hit him, and then she knew she was in trouble.

"Charlotte. What part of the anatomy are you talking about?"

She smiled sweetly. "The heart, silly. I want a man with a big, big heart. What did you think I meant?"

His gaze narrowed and he made a move to reach for her. With a burst of laughter, she jumped out of his reach, backing up. "Oh, my, Bolivar. Was your mind in the gutter?"

"What time is Jackson coming today?"

The question took her by surprise. "Regular time. 3:30 pm."

"Good. Then we have plenty of time."

He stalked her with a slow, predatory grace. Her heart pounded as she looked down, making sure she wouldn't trip, and she managed to get into the living room. Uh, oh. He looked way too serious. "Umm, Brady, we have a lot of work to do. I was just kidding. A joke. Funny, right?"

"No."

She stumbled, regained her balance, and realized this was a very small house to elude a predator. "Don't make me pepper spray you again," she said desperately.

"Ah, thank you for the reminder. That's two punishments."

Was it wrong that her body practically wept with anticipation? She squeezed her thighs together, ignoring the wet achiness throbbing for relief. She was becoming a nympho and a spanking addict. Who would've thought her rigid, rational architect was so deliciously dirty in bed?

The thought hit her mind at the same time that her back hit the door.

Damn.

He wasted no time. In seconds, he laid his palms flat on the wood, caging her head. His hips pressed against hers, boldly dragging his erection over the notch in her thighs. Even through her jeans, the friction brought a moan to her lips. She gazed at his beautiful face, with his carved features, firm lips, strong, clean-shaven jaw. Those dark eyes seethed with lust but tangled with enough want and need to make her knees weak. That stray curl had once again escaped his neat style and lay over his forehead. Not able to help herself, she reached up and tucked it back, her hand stroking his rough cheek. Her breath whispered over his lips.

"You're beautiful," she whispered.

His eyes softened. Their gazes locked for endless seconds and something shifted between them. The lust became an aching tenderness that suddenly brought tears to her eyes. She battled her initial instinct to blink them back. Instead, she allowed him in, allowed him to see how he affected her. He sucked in a breath and his thumb dragged against her lips, his eyes delving deeper.

Her voice shook. "What's happening between us?"

She half expected him to step back, away from the sudden messy emotions surging between them. Instead, he smiled, dipping his head so his mouth was inches from her. "I don't know. You've ripped away my ideas and my plans and my control. You make me laugh, make me want to throttle you, fuck you, kiss you, take care of you. I thirst for you, Charlotte. Every damn day, I thirst for you."

The raw honesty of his words shook through her. She reached up on tiptoes, pressing her lips to his, the kiss so achingly tender the tears escaped and ran down her cheeks. He pulled her against him, wrapping her in tight, his tongue sliding between her lips to stroke and please. The kiss deepened, lengthened, stealing her breath and her heart and everything in between.

And that's the exact moment she tumbled head first into love with Bolivar Heart.

* * * *

Brady walked into the kitchen and took a deep breath. "I wanted to ask you a question."

"Hmm?"

She was up on the ladder, ass wriggling as she stretched to reach the top corner of the mural. He shook his head, fighting a laugh. She'd been obsessed with the painting, starting over three separate times and refusing to give up. Each day, he saw a bit more of the fuller picture, and though he was still doubtful, his intrigue was growing. The colors were muted earthy tones, reminding him of a Tuscan hillside. Mossy greens, muted golds, shaded burgundy. The blocks of graffiti were in 3D imagery that grabbed an onlooker, forcing them to give the wall their full attention. He might not be a fan of graffiti art, but he had to admit there was something compelling about the wall. Damned if he wasn't beginning to think she'd pull this off.

The real problem was her attention. The woman lived, ate, and breathed work, and as they neared the finish line, more of her focus revolved around perfecting every inch. The only way he was able to tempt her away from work was his body and the promise of endless orgasms.

He smothered a grin. He wasn't complaining. He'd never dated a woman so involved in her work. Most of his previous partners adjusted around his schedule and his career. He'd gotten used to making all the decisions, being the leader, and taking charge in all areas. Oh, he made sure he pleased every single one of them, both in and out of the bedroom. His satisfaction depended on the happiness of his partner, and he'd learned early being selfish brought disaster, especially to relationships.

But Charlie stomped on every single ideal he'd had for the woman he'd fall for.

She was vocal and had no issues stating exactly what she wanted and how she wanted it. Brady had never realized how much easier a relationship was when a woman played no games, or depended on him for happiness. From what they were eating for dinner, to how they renovated the house, to what DVD they wanted to watch, she negotiated the perfect balance of compromise. She was a giver, but also enjoyed taking, expressing her gratitude in such an honest way, it both refreshed and delighted him.

Both in and out of the bedroom.

She'd completely blown him away with her open hunger and sweet submission to every dirty, bossy, pleasurable act he wanted to commit. She owned it all on her terms, surrendering to her sensuality and bringing a whole new level to their lovemaking. He'd never been with a woman who could be so naturally submissive in bed, yet completely own it. There were no games between them, no pretending to be what they weren't, and in such acceptance, Brady felt more connected to her than any other woman before.

The more he learned about her, the more infatuated he became. He was changing, and he wasn't sure how to feel about it. Every time he took her in his arms, she chiseled off another part of him for keeps.

If things kept up, would he have anything of himself left? Was this a temporary affair that would eventually blow up and damage them both? He needed more answers, and there was one way to find out.

He tried to swallow back his nervousness. "Charlie? Are you listening? I need to ask you a question," he repeated.

"Sorry. Do you think brown is too dark?"

"No, I like it."

"Good. What's up?"

"I wanted to see if you'd like to come to dinner at my parents' on Sunday."

Her paintbrush froze midair. She swiveled around, pinning him with those expressive hazel eyes. "Wait. You want me to meet your parents?"

He shifted his weight, feeling ridiculously juvenile. "If you want to. I mean, I'd like you to but not if you're uncomfortable."

She broke into a joyous smile that made his heart stutter. "I'd love to have dinner with your family. I'm so excited to meet them. Will both your sisters be there?"

"Yes."

"Yay! I bet I'll get some serious dirt on you, dude."

He shook his head, grinning. "My sisters are well behaved, very unlike you. They won't share anything that may embarrass me."

She clucked her tongue and pointed the paintbrush at him. "You have no clue about women, do you?"

Her nose had a smudge of gold on the side. Her hair was covered by a ratty bandana. She wore old, baggy clothes, but her shirt was still carnation pink and her jeans had ridiculous pink bows at the ankles. She looked twelve years old and she was so damn adorable, he fought the urge to sweep her off the ladder and kiss her senseless. His throat tightened with emotion. What was she doing to him?

"I know more than you think I do. Shall I show you tonight?"

She threw back her head and laughed. "Yes, please. Oh, does

your mom like flowers? Wine? What shall I bring? What should I wear? I can't wait!"

Sheer pleasure flowed through him. He rarely brought home a woman. It was nice to see her genuine enthusiasm to meet his family. She always made him feel good.

The door opened, and Jackson strode in. He was at the site about three times a week, and his mom was also a regular visitor. She'd stopped by to personally check up on where Jackson had been spending his time, and they'd connected immediately. She now joined them for their occasional Friday night pizza parties. Seeing the boy's enthusiasm with renovation filled Brady with pride.

"It's Friday!" he shouted, pumping his fist in the air. "Plus we have Monday off for some conference!"

"Nice," Brady said, grinning. They high-fived each other.

"Hi, Jackson!" Charlie called from the kitchen.

Jackson called a greeting back, but motioned Brady over with a worried look.

"What's up?" he asked the boy. "You okay?"

"Did you convince her to do the wallpaper yet?" he whispered. "'Cause the last time I saw that mural it was pretty bad."

He fought back a smile. "Nope. You know how stubborn she is. But she redid it again and it's getting better."

"Again? Man, why is she so stuck on graffiti? Just because it's in a black neighborhood doesn't mean we like graffiti in the kitchen!"

Brady couldn't help it. He burst into laughter.

"What are you guys laughing about?" Charlie yelled.

"None of your business," he yelled back. "Keep your attention on the mural, please."

He heard a series of mutters. He turned back to Jackson. "Let's give her support and see what happens. It is her house. Her decision."

Jackson sighed. "Yeah, I guess. Can I work with you on the porch so I don't have to watch? It makes me nervous."

"Yes. Let's go. Do some man work."

Jackson nodded and gave him a thumbs-up. They trudged out to begin sanding before staining the treated wood. At least they'd been able to save most of it and didn't have to rip the whole thing out. Sure, it was a lot of manual labor, but he liked hanging out with

Jackson, hearing about school and his friends, sometimes just sanding and being quiet with their own thoughts like men did. Somehow, some way, Jackson and Charlie had become part of the fabric of his daily life and changed him. They brought out the best in him.

They made him happy.

Brady refused to think about what would happen once the house was done.

Chapter Fourteen

"Discoveries are often made by not following instructions, by going off the main road, by trying the untried."—Frank Tyger

They sat cross-legged in a tangle of sheets, passing a bowl of cold pasta back and forth. "Now my illusions are completely shattered," she mumbled between bites. "Brady Heart eats in his bed. Who would've thought?"

"I don't allow anything with crumbs," he pointed out, popping a forkful of noodles in his mouth. "Nothing crunchy or melty."

"So, no chocolate. No chips. What about pancakes?"

"What about them?"

"Well, they don't have crumbs but they can get sticky with syrup."

"I like my pancakes without syrup so they're allowed. Thinking of making me breakfast in bed?"

She dropped her fork in the bowl. Her mouth fell open. "Not if you eat pancakes dry. You have got to be kidding. That has to be illegal."

He grinned. "You have no right to judge. I caught you slathering chunky peanut butter on your nonfat granola bar. That's a complete contradiction."

She stuck out her bottom lip. "I needed more protein."

"I checked the label. It already had 7 grams."

"Are you spying on me?"

He grinned wider and had the nerve to grab the last portion of the noodles. Even worse, he didn't look sorry. "Nope. Just an innocent bystander."

"I can't believe I'm dating someone who has no respect for maple syrup."

"I'm a good lay."

"Oh, that's right. You're forgiven."

They stared at each other, smiling, and her heart did a little skip. Oh, Lord, he made her giddy. She loved the way he surprised her just when he thought she had him pegged. He was a delicious contradiction of rebel and rules.

Her gaze swept the gorgeous bedroom. Decorated in rich woods and dark navy, it held both warmth and masculinity. The bed was king size, with an intricately scrolled headboard that Dalton had built him. Mahogany floors and furniture set off tasteful accents in navy blue and silver. The master bath could fit an entire family and was outfitted with a steam shower, jacuzzi tub, television, and a fireplace. If she were Brady, she'd never have the motivation to ever leave the bedroom.

His entire house held the same type of appeal—large, warm, and masculine. There were no feminine touches, but she once believed his home would've been more like a museum, impressive to look at but at the heart, cold and remote.

Instead, the intricate architecture, from its floating decks, multi-level staircase, and open loft, emanated an artful creativity she admired. He'd used different shades of wood to mix and match, from African walnut to teak, to rich red cedar. He seemed to have a thing for unique chairs—each room showed off various fabrics and shapes, startling an onlooker. His home clearly showed there were many layers underneath the surface to the man she'd fallen in love with. She only wished she had the guts to tell him how she felt and brave the fallout.

But she couldn't. Not yet. Not when things were still so fresh and new and perfect.

She comforted herself with the knowledge that he wanted her to meet his parents. If she wasn't important, he would have kept her away. Charlie refused to analyze his intentions and kept surrendering to the moment. It had worked beautifully so far.

"You never answered my question," she said. "What made you want to be an architect?"

"When did you ask me that?"

She gave a long sigh. "That first time we drove to the Baker renovation property together. You were barely speaking to me at the time. Remember now?"

"Ah, yes. I do remember. But I think your question was phrased as 'Did you always want to be an architect?', and my response was a simple 'Yes.'"

"Damn, you're annoying."

"I try. Still want my answer?"

"Yes."

"I was always attracted to logistics. Balance. Numbers. My brain seemed to work well when I could grasp solid concepts and put them to use. But I also had a passion for architecture and drawing. My father suggested studying graphic design in college. I consider myself lucky that I knew exactly what I wanted to do early on."

"Dalton said you met Cal in college?"

"Were you asking Dalton questions about me?" he teased.

"Guilty as charged."

"Yes, I actually met Cal when we were in college together. His father was very generous to me and asked me to intern at the company. I loved working with everyone and it was a natural fit. After my degree, I became certified and immediately began working for Pierce Brothers. Eventually, I proved myself over the years and they offered me a partnership."

"I love that you embraced your father's suggestion. Teens are so rebellious. They'd fight their parents on anything."

He laughed. "My parents and I were always close. My father was strict, but we never had any issues, and I always felt like I was fairly treated. I had a good home life."

She squeezed his hand. "And you appreciated it. That's what makes you special."

He blinked in surprise, then gave her a lopsided smile. "Never really thought of it. But it's the same with you, Charlotte. The way you talk about your mom and growing up poor. You make no excuses. In fact, you make it sound like you were happy."

She shrugged. "I was. I had a great mom, and yeah, we had tough times but I always had her. And once she found a steady job, we managed to settle down and have a boring, normal life like I always dreamed about."

"Do you see your mom a lot?"

"Not as much as I want to. We lived in a small town in Pennsylvania. Our area wasn't the best to launch a design and renovation career. I came to visit my aunt and uncle and fell in love with Harrington. I just had a sense right away this was where I was meant to be. And I was right."

He leaned over and kissed her. She kissed him back, loving the leisurely stroke of his tongue, the gentle caress of his fingers trailing over her skin. The hunger was always there between them, burning bright, but as days passed, it grew into more tenderness, adding an extra layer that intensified the bond between them.

"Can I ask you another question?" she murmured against his lips.

"Anything."

"What is it about being an architect you love the most?"

He never hesitated. "Precision and numbers and control are all wonderful. But I'm really a planner of dreams. I help build a story, whether it be for an office or a house or an addition. That's the real value of my work, and that's why it never gets old."

Her heart stopped. God, she loved this man. The words hovered on her lips, caught up in a tide of emotion, but she kissed him again, and he pressed her slowly back into the mattress and then there was no more time for words.

* * * *

"I'm nervous," she blurted out. Her fingers clenched around the bottle of wine. He glanced over but he could barely see her from behind the huge bouquet of wildflowers she'd also brought.

"It's just dinner," he said patiently. "You're going to love my parents. And if you don't like them, let's set up a signal. If you kiss me, I'll know it's my cue to get us out of there."

"I'm not kissing you in front of your parents!"

"Okay. How about if you flash me your breasts, I'll make excuses and we'll leave."

"You are totally making fun of me."

"I am. We're here."

His family home always wrapped him up in the warmth and security of his childhood. It was a moderate-sized house, with dark shingled wood, a quirky tilted roof, and a cheery front lawn lined with bricks. His mother's vegetable garden took up the side lawn, and graceful weeping willows lined the property. There was no front porch—only a stoop—but the back deck was where everyone gathered for barbeques and parties. He'd offered many times to renovate his parents' home to their specifications, but his father refused, stating his mother hated to live in chaos with construction and strangers in her house.

He didn't knock, just led her through the door and headed straight to the kitchen. "Mama?"

"Brady!" She embraced him with open joy and enthusiasm, hugging him like it'd been months rather than two weeks since he'd seen her. "Who is this beautiful girl you've brought today?" she demanded, smiling at Charlie.

Why was his heart beating so madly? He felt like he was introducing his first girlfriend. "This is Charlotte. She likes to be called Charlie."

Charlie handed her the flowers, looking pleased at his mother's *oohs* and *ahs*, and hugged her back fully. His family was always touchy feely, preferring a hug over a handshake. Pride ruffled through him as he watched the embrace. He loved how Charlotte was so open and never exhibited distance.

"Thank you so much for inviting me to dinner," Charlotte said.

"If I had known you were coming, I would've made my special paella. This is the most wonderful surprise! I am so happy Brady finally brought a woman home."

Brady winced. Uh, oh. At first, he'd been surprised Charlie even agreed to join him for a Sunday dinner. He'd decided to avoid warning his family, afraid of the endless questions that would set off a barrage of phone calls. His sisters were nosy and his mother was panicked at the idea she wouldn't get grandchildren from him. He'd hoped to save them both the stress by just showing up with Charlie for a visit.

Probably not a great idea.

"Wait. You didn't tell your mother I was coming for dinner?"

He half closed his eyes. Yeah. The plan had definitely backfired.

Now he had two women glaring at him with matching outraged expressions. "Sorry. I forgot."

"You forgot?" Charlie's voice went to a high pitch. "So, your sisters don't know I'm here, or your dad, and your poor mother didn't have time to make more food? Really, dude? Really?"

His mother watched her in fascination as he was scolded. He cleared his throat, struggling to get back on firm ground. "Mama loves company. Also loves surprises. Come on, let's meet the rest of the family."

He marched her firmly through the kitchen, ignoring her hushed accusations, and thrust her in front of the family. "Hi, guys. Umm, this is Charlie. She's staying for dinner."

Silence descended. Everyone stared, not speaking, not moving, and the air thickened with anticipation.

Ah, crap. He should've warned them.

After all, it was the first time he'd brought a woman to meet his family in a long time.

A long, long time.

He'd screwed up and Charlie was going to kill him.

She was going to kill him.

She stared at the group of strangers in front of her. Even the children were gazing at her in astonishment, like she was an alien who'd flown in to visit from her spaceship. The three men were gathered around a big platter of various appetizers placed on a glass table in front of them. Two women, both dark haired and quite beautiful, stood in a corner with babies in their arms. One little boy with curly brown hair and his front teeth missing lay on the floor surrounded by toys. A little girl with pigtails and a pink dress clutched her doll close to her chest, frowning slightly in confusion.

Oh, my God. He hadn't told anyone she was coming to dinner, so no one was prepared. Was he crazy?

As the silence lengthened, Charlie swiped her damp palms over her dressy black slacks—which she'd picked out specifically for this occasion—and stepped forward. "It's such a pleasure to be here," she said in a bright tone. "Of course, I'm quite embarrassed Brady didn't tell you I was coming, but I hope you'll let me stay for dinner because everything smells delicious."

And just like that, the spell broke.

She was immediately enveloped in a swarm of family warmth. Brady's sisters—Cecilia and Sophia—chattered nonstop, holding out their babies—Armando and Angel—and introduced their husbands—Carlos and Michael. Brady's father, Bruno, hurried to pour her sangria, scolding his son for not telling them such a beautiful woman was coming to visit, and quickly escorted her into a comfy, overstuffed green chair.

The little girl—Alexa—jumped over, showing off her doll and peppering her with questions about how she met Uncle Brady and how did she get her hair to look so beautiful. They plied her with mini tacos, chips with guacamole, cheese and crackers, and crusty bread filled with spinach dip. Alexa sat on her lap, Cecilia and Sophia perched on the side of her armchair, and before the hour was up, Charlie had answered over a hundred questions and felt like she had a brand new family.

They were utterly, completely charming.

By the time dinner was called, she was already stuffed and had gulped down two sangrias, but then it started all over. She ate food she'd never been introduced to and became more amazed by his mother's cooking skills. Bowls filled with *menudo*—a thick, hearty soup with flavors of lime, red pepper chilis, and cilantro, danced with flavor in her mouth. Platters of steaming, tender pork shoulder, called *pernil*, paired with *arroz con gandules*, a simple, tasty rice with peas. The tortillas were stuffed with chunks of meat and seafood. The *mofongo*—a dish of fried mashed plantain with pork rinds— became her new obsession. The children sat in high chairs close to their mothers, babbling and eating happily as they were continuously fed tiny portions. Cecilia kept her baby perched on her lap, same as Sophia.

Charlie ate with enthusiasm, forcing herself way past her comfort zone, and finally fell back in her chair, dragging in deep breaths.

Cecilia laughed. "Ah, you're not used to the big Sunday dinners, huh? What do you usually cook for Brady?"

"Oh, I'm not a great cook," she admitted. "We've been switching on and off, or try to manage a meal together. Two cooks are better than one, right?"

Sophia stared at her in surprise. "Brady cooks for you?"

Brady groaned. "I can cook, Sophia. I'm not helpless."

"I know, but you prefer not to. Then again, you're in the honeymoon phase. I'm sure things will settle down once you two get into a routine."

Charlie blinked. Had she heard correctly? A warning flashed in her brain but she ignored it. "Settle down?"

Cecilia waved her hand in the air. "Sure. Even Michael spoiled me rotten for the first few weeks. Then we settled down, and of course I took care of all the cooking. God knows, that would be a disaster if I gave up my kitchen to a man."

Michael tugged at his wife's hair playfully. "Hey, I made you breakfast in bed for Mother's Day."

"Burnt toast and pitted orange juice. But it was the thought that counts." They shared an intimate glance, obviously warm and loving. "How long have you two been seeing each other?"

Brady winked at her. Charlie relaxed a bit. "Well, we've been working on the house for a few months, but we officially started dating a few weeks ago."

Sophia sighed. "That's so romantic. Building a house together and falling in love. When do you think you want to get married?"

Married? She swallowed, noticing Brady stiffen in his chair, tight with tension. He tore his gaze from hers, focused on his plate, and shoved mouthfuls of food into his mouth. "Umm, we haven't really talked about that. We're just dating."

"But you want to get married, right, Charlie?" Cecilia asked with a pointed stare.

Heat rose to her cheeks. Thank God, Brady threw her a temporary lifeline. "We haven't discussed anything like that, Cecilia. Don't go scaring her."

Brady's mother cackled, offering more food to her sons-in-law. "Ah, nothing to be scared of. Marriage is a blessing of God and brings great joy with the right person. And once the babies come, you become queen. Mamas are well taken care of, and I know my Brady looks at his responsibilities to family very seriously."

Babies? She fumbled for her sangria and took a healthy swallow. She would not freak out. She would not freak out. She would not...

Cecilia smiled at her like the subject was completely normal at her first family dinner. "I'm sure you want to enjoy a honeymoon period first, but I know how badly Brady wants kids. How many do you think you want?"

Brady groaned. "Cecilia, you're scaring her again."

Sophia frowned. "But you want babies, right, Charlie?"

Oh. My. God.

"Eventually," she squeaked.

"When do you think the house will be done?" Carlos asked.

"Umm, in a month or so. I'm very excited to flip the finished product. It's been taking up a lot of our time so we'll get a bit of a break."

"That's amazing," Sophia said. "I always wondered what it would be like to have a career, but there wasn't anything I felt passionate about. Except my children, of course." Her smile was brilliant. "They're a full-time job. Especially with the third on its way." She patted her stomach, which barely showed a bulge.

"Oh, congratulations," Charlie said. "That's such wonderful news!"

"Thank you, we're hoping for a girl this time around, but if not, we can always try again. Unless the third one finally does me in."

Carlos leaned over and pressed a kiss to his wife's cheek. "Ah, but you'd be bored without us," he teased.

She practically glowed with satisfaction. "I love it. Every part of it. And you will too, Charlie. Once you marry Brady and have his babies, you won't miss building houses."

Her fork dropped. "Wait a minute. Brady and I would never—"

Brady fell into a loud coughing fit, interrupting her and distracting everyone at the table. She stared at him, fuming, waiting for him to tell his family they didn't have that type of relationship and Charlie would never quit her career.

Instead, he chugged down water and quickly changed the subject. Before long, they were involved in a lively discussion about Carlos's job as a history professor. Charlie sipped her third sangria, watching the clear dynamics play out at the dinner table. The women murmured and chatted about the children, and the men talked about their careers and the challenges. When dinner ended, the men got up from the table and filed into the living room, leaving a table full of dishes, leftover food, and needy children.

"Where'd they go?" Charlie asked. "They aren't going to help clean up?"

The women stared at her like she'd sprouted horns, then burst into laughter. "Oh, now that would be a sight to see!" Cecilia said, getting up from her chair and grabbing a plate. "They play cards now."

"For how long?"

Sophia shrugged. "About an hour. We'll be done by then. But Charlie, you're our guest. Why don't you take a seat and chat with us while we clean up?"

She rose with the women, shaking her head. "Absolutely not. I need to work off some calories. I don't think I've ever eaten that much in my life. It was absolutely delicious."

His mother beamed. "Thank you. I can teach you how to make the paella and menudo. They are Brady's favorites."

She nodded, forcing a smile, but uneasiness flickered deep within. Was this what being with his family would be like? They were warm and gracious and wonderful, but would they actually expect her to give up her career? Dedicate her time to cooking and cleaning and raising kids while he owned the role of breadwinner? Did a relationship with Brady consist of becoming someone else? Or at least pretending to be?

She swallowed back her doubts and concentrated on helping the women. At one point, the two toddlers were wailing, but she engaged in a rousing game of peekaboo while they sat in their high chairs and soon had them giggling nonstop.

Brady's mother patted her shoulder. Charlie glanced up and noticed the dancing glint in her beautiful dark eyes. "I am so glad you came," she said quietly. "You are good for him. You make him happy."

"He makes me happy," she said simply. "But I don't want to mislead you. We're not, umm, we're not really serious. We're just dating."

The older woman cackled with merriment. "Brady doesn't bring someone home unless he's serious." She pointed to the two babies. "You will be a good daughter-in-law."

"Umm, I'm not—"

"Welcome to the family."

"But—"

She was pulled into a warm, loving embrace, quickly joined by Cecilia and Sophia, as if she'd just announced their engagement. And though her words sputtered in her throat, the denial hovering on her lips, a tide of yearning so intense crashed over her in waves, tempting her with an image she'd never believed could be a possibility.

The possibility of Brady loving her as she loved him. The possibility of his family becoming hers. The possibility of…more.

So Charlie said nothing and hugged them back.

Chapter Fifteen

"The most important part of design is finding all the issues to be resolved. The rest are details."—Soumeet Lanka

Brady wondered how certain silences could scream.

He glanced over and studied her face. After expressing how wonderful she thought his family was, she'd stopped talking. With each mile the Mercedes gobbled up, the tension grew between them. But not the usual hungry, sexual type he was used to.

No, this was the worst kind. The awkward kind. The kind he got after a bad date where he couldn't wait to flee the other person for a few hours to be alone.

He should've never invited her to dinner.

"Umm, would you mind if you dropped me off at my apartment tonight? I have some stuff to do."

He stiffened. It was the first time she was asking to spend a night apart from him. The searing pain caught him under the chin and knocked him back, but he gritted his teeth and kept his gaze on the road. "That's fine."

Back to silence.

Sweat broke out on his brow. Why had he done it? He'd always known his family thrived on tradition. It was the main reason he sought a woman who could offer him the type of lifestyle he'd grown up with. Charlie was a complete contradiction to everything he said he wanted. Marissa would've emerged from the visit steeped in happiness, ready to accept a ring on her finger and get pregnant on the honeymoon.

Charlie looked like she wanted to change her phone number, leave town, and pretend they'd never met.

He was such an idiot.

Anger ruffled his nerves. He grabbed onto it, liking the emotion so much better than the hurt threatening to overwhelm him. He'd never lied to her about what he wanted. He refused to apologize for his family dynamics because it worked and everyone was happy. When he came into the kitchen and found her wrapped in an embrace with his mother and sister, his throat had tightened and he'd barely been able to speak. The idea of Charlie being part of his life in such an intimate way made his heart soar. But when he caught her expression as he stepped forward, he'd crashed immediately.

She'd looked completely panicked.

Brady pulled up to her apartment building and waited.

"Thanks so much. I had a lovely evening. I'll see you tomorrow. Good night." She leaned over, pressing a kiss to his cheek, and started to get out of the car.

His fucking cheek.

No fucking way.

He flicked his wrist and cut the ignition. "I'll walk you up."

"Oh, you don't have to."

"I didn't ask."

He got out of the car and walked around. She seemed tempted to respond to his statement but decided to let it go. She slid the key in the lock, opening the door, but he gave her no opportunity to dismiss him again. He walked right inside and shut the door behind them.

His gaze swept over the room. They usually stayed at his house, but he was comfortable at her place. It was a standard issue, one-bedroom basic apartment, but she'd made it unique with her flair for design. Done in tones of pale pink, cream, and chocolate brown, the furniture was comfortable, with tons of throw pillows, shag rugs, and a rustic chandelier she'd created herself. The famous pizza box art she boasted about lined the walls of her sunny yellow kitchen, done in bright turquoise and pinks, adding a shock of color. Glass vases stuffed with various wildflowers sprouted from accents of mismatched wood shelving, homemade cabinetry, and a giant coffee table converted from a headboard. It was one of the most visually arresting, homey places he'd ever been.

"Umm, I really need to go to bed early, Brady." Her tone was the high, false one she used when she was nervous. "Can we talk tomorrow?"

"No." He put his hands on his hips and faced her. "I want to know one thing. How bad were you spooked?"

She jerked back. He waited, drinking in her expressions as she seemed to struggle with telling him the truth or giving him an excuse. Finally, she tilted her chin and met his gaze head on. "Very spooked."

"Better. I'll take honesty over bullshit any time. What spooked you?"

Temper flickered in her hazel eyes. "Don't try to bully me," she warned. "How dare you not even warn them I was coming! And what was that crap of you pretending to choke on your water to avoid telling them I'm not your baby-making machine?"

He took a step closer. "I wanted to buy some time, okay? My parents have always had a traditional marriage, and so do my sisters. They expect the same type of life for me. And don't you dare use that expression. My sisters are happy being homemakers and I refuse to allow you to judge them."

"I'm not judging them, you idiot! I adored them. You dare to think I have a problem about women choosing to do what makes them happy? 'Cause if you think that, you can march your ass right out of my apartment and don't come back."

"You certainly seemed freaked out."

"Because they didn't even stop to think I didn't want that type of life. I'm not them, Brady. I never pretended to be."

He stood in front of her, seething with a bunch of tangled emotions that made him roar like a pissed-off lion. "I never pretended to hide what my family is like or what type of woman fits with my lifestyle."

She breathed hard, cheeks flushed, fists clenched. Damn her. Why did she have to be so sexy and hot when she argued with him? Why was he so attracted to a difficult, bullheaded woman who'd choose career over love? "Is that what you want then? Because if you do, what the hell are you doing with me?"

"I don't know! I never planned on you. Never planned you'd wreck me and make me want you so bad, I'd do anything to have you."

She gasped, pressing her fingers to her lips. The room hummed with electricity. Those hazel eyes burned with a raw emotion he'd never seen before she quickly banked the flames. "Even give up your ideals? Your detailed plans for the future? Because I will never be that woman. I will never want to cook and run a household and watch the children while you go out every day to live your dreams." Her voice broke. "It would destroy me."

The truth choked him with fear and need and pure confusion. What did he want? Could he give up his own dreams of a future with a wife who suited his needs? Or had he believed in something for so long, he never questioned the possibility of falling for someone else? Someone with different plans in life. Someone who made him hunger from his very soul and filled him with a peace he'd never experienced.

"I know it would," he ground out in the shattering silence. "I'd never ask that of you."

She wrapped her arms around her chest as if seeking comfort. He fought back the impulse to cross the room and pull her against him. "How can we keep going on like this?" she asked. "We fell into a sexual affair and it worked because we asked nothing else of the other. We lived day to day. But eventually, we were going to have to face the truth and decide what we both really want from each other."

"I'm not ready to give you up."

His stark admission fell between them and lay there, waiting for her answer. He couldn't bear the idea of losing her. Panic hit him from all directions, and he felt like a wild animal locked in a cage, desperate to move.

"During dinner, when your family assumed my career meant little to me, you never defended me. Never said what you wanted or that my choices were just as important as yours. Are you ready to tell your family our relationship will never be like theirs? That I'll never be a traditional wife?"

"Do you want children, Charlotte?"

He asked the question with nausea burning in his gut. His dream of a family was important. Could he possibly give that up for her?

"Yes."

His chest loosened and he let out a breath.

"But not now. Not for a few more years. I don't have a blueprint of my life like you do. I'm passionate about my career, and I want to build and renovate houses. I want to get married and have kids and have a beautiful house and a life full of chaos and joy. That's important to me. But not now. And I don't know when. Can you accept that?"

He studied the stubborn tilt to her jaw. The trembling of her lips. The too-wide hazel-colored eyes filled with fear and need and truth. That she'd never be enough for him. That eventually, he'd regret putting his own future on hold for a shot at something that might never work out. Was the risk just too great for both of them to take? He'd always longed for the type of family he was raised in, with solid roles for both sexes and a secure household. He'd never felt confused growing up or dismissed due to other obligations. He'd lived the happy, secure childhood he dreamed of for his own kids. Could he change his ideas for her? Be a different type of man? Or would their entire relationship be built on a lie?

He answered in the only way he could.

"I don't know."

Tears filled her eyes but she nodded, refusing to let them fall. "I understand. You have to go."

He knew then if he left, it would be all over. The light of day would rip them apart with rational conclusions and neat answers that made sense. He couldn't lose her like this. He wouldn't allow it.

"Brady—"

"You tell me that you don't want me." He closed the distance, reached out, and yanked her against him. "You tell me you don't want me to rip off your clothes and kiss you. Fuck you hard and deep until you come for me so many times, you forget why we shouldn't be together."

"Bastard! Why are you doing this now? I'm giving you what you want! I'm letting you leave nice and neat and tidy, just the way you like things!"

She pummeled his chest, but he knew it wasn't to get away. Her body was already burning, melting against him, her hips arching, her tight nipples evident from the sheer fabric of her shirt. He let her pound at him a few more times before snatching her wrists and pinning them behind her back. His other hand thrust into her hair and pulled hard, exposing her throat. His gaze raked over her face, taking in her parted bubble-gum lips, the hazy sheen of need in her eyes, and the pounding pulse at the base of her neck.

"I don't want you nice and neat, Charlotte," he growled, scraping his teeth down the vulnerable curve of her neck, sinking his teeth in the sensitive hollow of her shoulder. She shuddered. His dick strained against his jeans. "I want you dirty and needy. I want you begging. I want you so hot for me you'll do anything I demand."

"We can't make this about sex." Her voice was desperate, and he took advantage by running his tongue up her jaw, nibbling on her mouth, teasing her with tiny bites and licks that he knew would drive her crazy. Her low whimper was music to his ears.

"It's not about sex. It's about want. Need." His gaze crashed into hers. "It's about everything."

Refusing to wait another second, he slammed his mouth over hers, kissing her deep, his tongue thrusting over and over until she was a wild, writhing animal in his arms. Groaning, he lifted her up and carried her into the bedroom, laying her out on the comforter. He gave her no time to protest, quickly stripping her clothes off, then his, and joining her on the bed naked.

He was starved for her, and his slightly shaking hands showed her his desperation. Brady stroked every inch of her naked body, sliding over her lush breasts, teasing her tight pink nipples, tracing the gentle curves of her hips, the bare, swollen lips between her legs, all the way down her muscled thighs to her poppy-pink-colored toenails.

She cried his name, twisting under his touch, then arching to meet his tongue as he began to taste everything he'd touched. By the time he'd worked his way back up to her mouth, she was clinging, hooking her feet around his hips and arching for more.

"Damn you, Bolivar," she whispered against his mouth, eyes glassy with need. "Finish what you started."

A fierce rush of possessiveness seized him. This woman was his. She belonged to him, and they could fight, run, deny—nothing mattered in the end because she would always be his. He spread her thighs wider and reared up, poised at her dripping entrance.

"Yes, Charlotte."

Then plunged deep.

Buried to the hilt inside her, he practically roared with pride, feeling her swollen tissues clench around him, squeezing and holding him tight. She arched, shuddering, taking him all in, and then her head began to thrash side to side, her nails digging and tearing his skin with command.

He cursed and grasped her hips. He pulled all the way out, then slammed back inside her. Again. Again. Harder. Always harder.

She took it all, begged for more, and surrendered completely. Brady became a madman, completely enthralled with her smell and touch and feel, and it was never enough, so he bent forward to kiss her, his tongue mimicking his rolling, thrusting hips, demanding every part of her be open to him.

She screamed and thrashed and then his fingers found her hard clit and he rubbed gently, then harder and harder, and she came around his dick, drenching him with her climax, and he bit her neck as he shuddered and followed her over the edge.

He wondered if an orgasm could last hours because that's how it felt as the endless waves of intense pleasure rang through his body. She whispered his name in the dark, and he kissed her, feeling as if the earth had shattered and everything he'd once believed in was gone.

"What is it, baby?" he asked gently.

"I love you."

He pressed his forehead to hers, the joy exploding through him. "I love you, too."

"But I don't know if this will work."

It would. It had to.

Because he wasn't giving her up.

"Sleep now, Charlotte. We'll talk in the morning."

This time, she chose to obey. Soon, he heard the deep steady beat of her heart and her even breathing and he knew it had to be okay.

Chapter Sixteen

"Design is an opportunity to continue telling the story, not just to sum everything up."—Tate Linden

Charlotte tried to ignore the nerves jumping in her belly and concentrated on putting the last touches on her wall mural. It was all coming together. She had to finish sanding and staining the floors, paint the entire house, and deal with the property. She wasn't the best at landscaping, so she'd have to get someone to do some magic. And of course, the roof. Unfortunately, she was low on funds, even by saving on some other projects. She'd had to replace the refrigerator and stove, which came out higher than she thought after deciding to get a higher-level brand. The kitchen was the core of the house, and damned if she'd offer crappy appliances to a family. She'd have to wait a bit longer to save up for a roof, but she'd get there.

There was no reason Brady needed to be here to paint or work on floors. The main portion of the renovation was behind them, which meant his time was coming to an end.

And their time together.

She'd left before he woke, slipping out of bed around dawn.

She dragged in a breath, trying to ignore her aching heart when she thought of not being with Brady. Last night, she'd told him the truth. She was in love with him. What she hadn't expected was the words given back with a truth that devastated her. But she had already made her decision, and nothing would change her course.

Brady had always been truthful about his needs. He had a right to marry someone who would fit into his family. Someone who wanted kids quickly and embraced the role of housewife and mother. Someone happy without a career or the constant need to challenge her husband's leadership.

Someone who wasn't her.

They were opposites, a complete mismatch of wants, and furthering their relationship would only hurt them more when it ended.

She couldn't do it. Every day she fell deeper in love with the man. He spoke to her soul in a way she'd never experienced and transported her body to places she'd never gone. He was the man of her dreams, but because she loved him so much, she needed to let him go.

To find the woman who was meant for him.

"You did it."

She spun around at his familiar voice. He was looking at the mural, his expression full of respect and a touch of awe. Her voice was a bit creaky when she forced herself to speak. "You like it?"

He walked farther into the room, taking in the picture. She'd stuck with a Tuscan theme, but instead of gently rolling hills and distant colors, she'd created a pop-out graffiti effect of a house with a red tiled roof perched on the top of a tall hill. Earthy colors and splashes of burgundy contrasted with dots of stark white. It was a piece of art that seemed to pull a gaze and hold it; a mural that would never get boring and always be a conversation starter. The colors and image blended with the wood and white cabinets and gave the room a completely new look.

"Yes. But I'm not surprised. I should've learned to trust you from the beginning." He paused, then met her gaze. Her chest ached with need for him when she looked into his beautiful, dark eyes. Those lush lashes. Brown skin. Cleft chin. Wavy black hair. He was so gorgeous everything hurt just to look at him, because yesterday she had the right to touch him, kiss him, laugh with him.

"You could say the same with me," she said quietly. "I guess we changed each other's minds."

"I guess we did." He studied her for a while. "You left."

"Yes. I had to."

"Why?"

Her voice was steady but her heart was already in pieces.

"Because I don't want to be with you anymore."

He jerked back, pain flickering over his face. She tamped down the need to go to him and soothe the hurt. Take her words back and say she'd do anything to make it work. But this was the only way and she had to follow her gut.

"Why?"

"I can't do this anymore. Please understand. You said it well. I'm ten years younger than you. I don't know yet what I want or when I even want to settle down. If we stay together, you could lose too much time looking for the woman you're meant to marry. A woman like your family wants."

"We can take it slow. Take more time. See what happens."

He winced, as if knowing his tone sounded desperate. Knowing he'd give up his pride to fight for her made her want to cry out, but she had to see it through. "Nothing will change. It's better this way. If we keep going, it'll get harder for me."

He took a few steps forward, then stopped. The scant distance between them yawned like a canyon and tore at her insides. His voice broke. "You said you love me."

This time, she couldn't hold back the tears that stung her eyes. "I do. But you were right. Sometimes, it's better to plan and follow your head so things don't get chaotic and end up destroying the very person you love. We want different things. It's time to be realistic and do what's right for both of us."

He spun around. Curses blistered the air. Her entire body trembled, waiting for him to come to the only conclusion left.

"We need to finish the house."

His flat tone ripped through her with sheer agony. She practically choked on her words. "I only have the floors and the paint job and minor landscaping."

"The roof needs to be replaced."

"I know, but it's not in my budget right now so I have to wait. Jackson can help me paint and do the floors. Gage said he has a guy who does good outside work for cheap. I'm almost there."

"You don't need me any longer."

She bit her lip, hard, to keep from crying out. God, how she needed him. Even now, she was practically shaking with the need to touch him, stroke back that unruly curl, smooth her palm over his forehead, and press her lips to his. He'd become a part of her in a few short months, and she had to relearn how to live without him.

She opened her mouth to respond, then fell silent. There was nothing else to say, and she was a few seconds from breaking down and begging him not to leave her.

"Very well. I'll see you back at the office."

And then she watched him walk out the door and out of her life.

* * * *

"Why aren't you at the house with Charlie?"

Brady glared at Cal and snarled his response. "Because the job is practically finished. Because she doesn't need me anymore. Because I'm trying to get this fucking plan together for Tristan, who didn't give me enough notice. Does that answer your question?"

Cal narrowed his gaze. "Yeah, it does. Get your ass in the conference room."

"I'm busy."

"Tough shit. Now."

He turned and Brady cursed at his back. All he wanted to do was concentrate on his damn job and he kept getting distracted. He was not in the mood to get into it with Cal, but he got out of the chair and marched into the conference room. Instead of sitting, he began to pace, needing to move. Lately, his skin felt stretched too tight over his body. He hadn't slept for over a week. He'd locked himself in the office until late, then went straight home and stayed there. He was either hopped up on caffeine or having too many beers at night.

He was fucking miserable.

Cal shut the door and took a seat at the head of the table. "What's going on?"

"I told you. Nothing. I'm busy. Charlie's at the end of her renovation. There's no danger—she's made friends with some of the neighbors and can take care of herself."

Cal rubbed his hand through his hair. "I'm missing something and you're gonna tell me. You've been a bastard this week. Sydney said you yelled at her regarding the new plans for Summit Avenue."

"They weren't ready to be filed."

"Syd showed me your handwritten note clearly telling her to file it."

"Fine, I made the mistake then. You wanna crucify me? Kick me off the board? Do whatever the hell you want—just leave me alone."

Cal's mouth dropped open as he stared in astonishment. "Holy shit, you slept with Charlie!"

Brady simmered with anger, treating his friend and partner to a nasty glare. "That's none of your business."

"Of course it is. You're like my brother."

The simple words were so truthful, the fight drained out of him, leaving him empty.

"Tell me what happened. You can talk to me."

In that moment, he realized he needed to dump the whole story to someone he trusted. So he did. He talked at length for a long time, confessing the ups and downs of the relationship and the final scene between them. When he was done, he felt a bit lighter. He forgot how Cal was able to listen and understand him as only a long-term best friend could. He'd been so careful to keep Charlie a secret, he'd stripped himself of an important support system in his life.

Cal tapped a finger on the mahogany table. "You know, Dalton bet me you had a secret crush on her but I told him he was crazy. Now all that animosity makes sense."

Brady sighed, dropping into the seat next to Cal. "Yeah. I wanted to deny the whole attraction because I knew it would change my life. And it did. Reminds me of Sydney and Tristan. They're so cold to each other, it's obvious something big is going on."

"They'll be forced to deal with their past sooner rather than later." Cal paused, cocking his head to study him. "You know, I see why you and Charlie ran into a problem. Would be so much easier to just stay in bed with our women, wouldn't it?"

Brady laughed. "Hell, yeah."

"I felt the same way when I first met Morgan. The problem doesn't seem to be how you feel about each other—that's the simple part. It's more about expectations of the future. Listen, Brady. I've known you a long time and you've always had a specific idea of the perfect woman in mind. You got thrown a curve ball. I guess you have to ask yourself, will this curve ball make your life better? Make you happier? Can you step away from what you *thought* your future would be and embrace what it could *actually* be? There's no guarantees with Charlie."

"I know and it's haunted me. I always wanted what I grew up around. Clear roles. Clear leadership. It seemed easy."

"Did you ever talk to your parents about their relationship?" Cal asked curiously. "As a child, you may have seen things a different way than what they did. Maybe you need to talk to them about Charlie."

Brady shook his head. "They adored her, but once they learn she's not going to be the traditional wife, they'll tell me to break it off. I know them."

"Sometimes people can surprise you. Remember when Morgan and I first got together? It took us a while to work things out, but I almost walked away when I found out she couldn't have children. My vision for my future included a bunch of kids and I didn't know if I would be okay accepting a different path."

"You're going to marry her this year. Do you have any regrets?"

His friend broke into a smile reflecting pure joy. "Not one. Not ever. Because I realized she's my person. My soul mate. She was my curve ball and it was the best thing that ever happened. She's my family, with you and my brothers and my dogs. And maybe we'll adopt or foster kids in the future. Your life can be anything you want it to be, Brady. As long as you're happy."

Brady stared at his friend for a long time, feeling something shifting inside.

Cal leaned over, clapping him on the shoulder. "Think about talking to your parents. In the meantime, I'm here for you. I don't want to step into your business, but I also want Charlie to know I'm here for her, too. Whatever you both decide, she's a part of the team, and we need to find a way to make things work."

"We will." Brady stood up. "There's one thing I need to do for her, though. The house is almost done but she can't afford a roof."

Cal frowned. "Are you kidding me? For everything she does in the company, I can send her some workers and get the roof done quickly. We'll give her a loan with no interest so she can pay it back whenever she wants."

Brady shook his head. "No, Cal. I'm already taking care of it. I need to. What she's done with this house is amazing. Her talent is something I rarely see—she sees things no one else can. I want to give her the damn roof, I just need the go-ahead to use some of your crew to schedule the work this week."

"Of course." He tilted his head, regarding him. "Did you ever think you'd be bored to tears with a traditional type woman? It's pretty rare we're able to find partners with the same passion for our work. I love working with Morgan. I know Dalton loves working with Raven. You share a special bond that many don't realize. Just a thought."

Cal walked away, leaving Brady with a lot to ponder.

Chapter Seventeen

"Great love and great achievements take great risk."—*Dalai Lama*

"Did you guys have a fight?"

Charlie turned toward the quiet voice. Jackson knelt on the floor, paintbrush in hand, concentrating on the back and forth strokes of his brush. But she knew immediately he was troubled. Dammit, she was making such a mess of things. Brady hadn't been here in the past week and it was affecting Jackson. She'd tried to explain Brady had other jobs to accomplish, but it was obvious Jackson didn't believe her. She realized lying to him was wrong. He deserved the truth.

Charlie put down her own brush and faced him. "No, we didn't have a fight. In fact, I think I'll always love him. He's kind and funny and fair. He's brilliant. And he was my friend."

Jackson stiffened, not moving. Then slowly, he turned and met her gaze. His wide dark eyes filled with wariness. "You loved him?" he asked quietly.

"Yes."

"Then why did he leave?"

She didn't want to have this conversation but it was important. Jackson faced his own problems on a daily basis. She knew he was being raised by a single mother. She had no idea about the relationship between him and his father, or if it even existed. He should know not every breakup was done to harm the other. Sometimes, it was just the opposite.

She sat cross-legged and blew out a breath. "I don't know if you're going to understand this completely, but I'm going to try.

Brady and I started out not liking each other, as you probably saw from our fights."

A small grin curved his lips. "Yeah, you guys did like to fight a lot. But it was funny."

She smiled back. "Yeah, it kind of was. Then we became friends. Good friends. And then we began to fall in love the more time we spent together. But we realized as much as we cared about each other, we wanted different things to make us happy. We didn't want to end up hurting one another, Jackson. So, even though it completely sucks, and we're both sad, I want Brady to find the type of woman that will make him really, really happy."

Jackson scrunched up his nose. "Does he like redheads or something? 'Cause you could dye your hair."

She laughed. "Oh, I wish it was that easy. No. It's a lot more than that."

"My dad left because he didn't want a baby. Didn't want me." He uttered the words in defiance, his gaze hard. "I don't care though, 'cause we don't need him. One day, I'm going to do something great in life and he'll be sorry."

Her heart shattered, but she also knew she couldn't show her pain or sympathy. Jackson was an extraordinary boy, and he deserved his pride. "You're right," she said. "He's missing out on the best thing possible, and I feel sorry for him. Your mom gets all the good stuff. She got you."

Jackson nodded, his face softening. "Yeah. I'm gonna buy her a big house one day."

"Maybe you'll build her a house instead. You have talent. In fact, Pierce Brothers always takes on interns. I started as one. Maybe we can keep working together after this house is done."

His eyes widened. "You're going to get another house?"

"Hell, yeah. A ton more houses. And I kind of got used to you as an assistant, so maybe we'll talk to your mom and figure out a good schedule. If you're interested, of course."

"I'm interested."

They smiled at each other. "Then let's get back to work," she said, turning around so he wouldn't see the sting of tears in her eyes. "We'll order pizza tonight."

"Cool."

The knock at the door made her look up in surprise. "Wow, a real visitor. Let me check it out."

She peeked through the window and recognized Gary and Peter from the Pierce Brothers crew. Their truck was outside and a trailer was behind them with materials. She unbolted the deadbolt and greeted them. "What are you doing here, guys?"

Peter jerked a thumb toward his truck. "Ready to do the new roof."

Confusion swamped her. "What new roof?"

"This one. Was told to install the roof today for you and finish up the work tomorrow. Do you need us to come back another time?"

Oh, no. Caught between a rush of gratitude and pure stubborn pride that this was her project, she shook her head. "I think there's been a mistake," she said firmly. "I can't afford a new roof right now so this won't work. Sorry you had to come out here. I'll talk to Cal about it."

Gary grinned and thrust out a piece of paper. "Yeah, we were told you'd say that. Read this."

She opened up the note.

Charlotte,

I know you're going to try to send the guys back and say you don't want the roof because you need to do it yourself. I'm asking you to accept this as a present from me. For allowing me into your life, for changing me, for humbling me with your amazing talent and vision. I want to give you this roof so I will always carry a piece of you and Jackson in my heart, and in the house you allowed me to help renovate. Please.

Brady

Her throat tightened. She read the note again, almost sinking to her knees at the rippling waves of pain that crashed through her from his words. And she knew there was only one thing to do, for both of them.

She gave a nod. "Yes. Thank you so much. Today would be great."

"Cool, we'll get started."

She turned to Jackson, her eyes glittering. "We're getting our roof."

The boy let out a whoop, putting down his paintbrush. "Can I help? Or watch? Or carry supplies? Or do anything but paint?"

She laughed. "Go ahead. Tell Peter and Gary I vouched for your skills."

Jackson ran out of the house in excitement and Charlie hugged the note to her broken heart.

* * * *

"Son, are you okay? You're scaring us."

Brady looked at his parents, staring at him with slightly panicked expressions. He reached out and grabbed his mother's hands. "No, Mama. I'm sorry to scare you. I'm fine. I just wanted to talk to you both about a personal thing."

"Thank God." Her muscles relaxed, and she refocused on getting him to eat. "Have a snack. What else can I get you?"

His father smiled, staring lovingly at her. "*Querida*, let our son talk. He doesn't need anything right now."

His lips twitched. His mother lived to serve and loved every moment. It was part of the culture he'd grown up with, and his sisters had happily incorporated the qualities into their own marriages. "I want to talk to you about Charlotte."

His parents both lit up. His mother's voice filled with affection. "We loved her. So sweet and funny and smart. It was like she fit in perfectly here. And we've never seen you happier. You practically glowed in her presence!"

His father nodded. "Agreed. She's special. I've always hoped you'd find what your sisters had. Do you love her?"

"Yes, I love her. But we decided to break up."

His mother gasped. "What? How is this so? What happened?"

He laid his hands flat on the table and told them the truth. "I'm confused. Mama, Charlotte isn't like any of the other girls I've dated. She's different."

His father frowned. "Different how?"

"She's ten years younger."

"So what?" his mother burst out. "Cecilia is five years younger than Michael!"

"It's bigger than that. She's not the traditional wife I've always wanted."

His father's frown deepened. "Traditional how?"

Brady let out an irritated breath. "Like you and Mama. Like Cecelia and Sophia. She loves her job and never wants to quit her career. She has a passion for restoring houses and it's part of her soul—she could never leave it behind her to raise children and stay home. She won't be the type of wife to cook and clean and listen to me. Hell, I'd be lucky if she listens to me at all! She's stubborn and chaotic. She's the type to want her own checking account and challenge my every decision and probably drive me crazy. She won't be…easy. Nothing like your marriage or my sisters. You all have everything perfect."

He waited for his mother to jump from the table and tell him he was better off without this woman who was the model image of everything she was against for her son.

Instead, she threw back her head and burst into laughter.

He stared in astonishment as his father grinned, shaking his head.

"What's going on? What's so funny?"

His mother wiped her eyes and shared a look with his father. "Should I tell him or should you?"

"You, *querida*."

"My poor, sweet, confused boy. Your father and I certainly did not fall magically into these roles, and things are never perfect in a marriage. It is a living, breathing, fluid thing that changes as people change. We married very, very young because we were passionate about each other but I never thought my life would be about changing diapers and cooking dinners and meekly listening to your father's every command."

"You didn't?"

His father snorted. "Hell, no. We had two years where we traveled and partied. We fought a lot, we made up a lot, we figured out who we were. Then you were born and things changed."

"I was depressed at first," his mother admitted. "I used to work at a small retail store selling fashion and I loved it."

"You worked?"

"Of course. I gave it up when you came along but it wasn't easy for me. Your father and I fell into certain roles because they fit for us. He liked paying the bills, and I eventually loved staying home with you children. I began cooking with traditional Spanish dishes, and I found it satisfied a creativity inside of me."

"I got a promotion and the money was good, so there was no reason for your mother to go back to work. But do you honestly think I would've told her she wasn't able to work outside the home if that is what satisfied her soul?"

The room tilted. It was as if everything he'd ever believed suddenly changed, and he didn't know how to keep up. "Well, yeah. I thought you told Mom what to do!"

"I do," his father said in amusement. "Sometimes she listens. Sometimes she doesn't."

"Cecilia told me she'd like to go back to school once Angel gets older. Part time, of course. Sophia is happy being home with the kids and adores being involved with the mommy groups. She thrives. But I don't think Michael ever demanded she be a particular way. It's what works best for them."

"But—but everyone said they expected her to quit her job once the babies come."

His mother shrugged. "That was our expectations based on no solid information. But it's not yours. Not Charlie's. You run your own life and your own relationship. Is this why you broke up with Charlie? Because she wants to work?"

"Or does she not want children?" his father asked.

"No, she does, but not now."

His mother gave a relieved sigh. "Thank goodness. So, it's just a matter of timing for you two."

Brady rubbed his temples, trying to find his footing. All this time. All this worry about what his family expected from him. It had all been in his own head.

"Son, you have to ask yourself some important questions. If you actually want a wife who won't work and wants to raise children, that's a different story. Sometimes you can't change who you are inside," his father explained. "But if you're confused because you think we want you to have these things, you're wrong. We want you to be happy. To be passionately in love with a partner who satisfies you and makes you a better man. That's what marriage is about. Not who cooks or cleans or pays the bills."

And, suddenly, magically, his path was completely clear.

He didn't care about a traditional marriage, or who made money, or who cleaned or cooked. It had all been a distant mirage of perfection that didn't even matter. He craved a partner, a lover, a friend. He craved a woman who made him better.

He only wanted one thing to make him happy. One thing he'd been missing and searching for, over and over, believing it would fit his ideals and slide neatly into the perfectly square pegs of his life.

Charlotte Grayson.

The round peg. The one who shouldn't fit, but did. The one who rocked his body and his soul and his heart. The one he refused to live without for another minute.

"I have to go."

He stumbled from the chair, looking at his parents. "Thank you. I don't know if I say it often enough, but I love you. You've given me a life to treasure and showed me everything I need to know to be happy."

His mother covered her mouth with her hands, eyes shining with tears. "Good luck, my son. We love you, too."

His father nodded, and damned if Brady didn't spot the moisture in his father's eyes also.

Brady jumped into his Mercedes and sped off to claim the woman he loved.

Chapter Eighteen

"To design the future effectively, you must first let go of your past."—Charles J. Givens

"No! Fix it—don't list it, you idiot! Ah, what a waste of good money," she groaned through a mouthful of popcorn.

HGTV was so damn stressful.

She grabbed her wine, taking a few sips, and continued yelling at the stupid couple who was about to get into more debt for no reason other than they liked new.

The doorbell rang.

She stilled. Who could that be? She wasn't up for company tonight. After spending the day at the house finishing up details, she couldn't get over the present Brady had sent her. A new roof. So much better than anything she could've imagined. The man *got* her.

He just couldn't be with her.

She'd gotten so damn depressed she decided to order take-out, get in her old terrycloth pink Victoria's Secret robe with matching fuzzy slippers, and have a TV night. She'd eaten four slices of pizza, half a bag of potato chips, three chocolate chip cookies, and was about to demolish an entire bucket of popcorn. Her hair was stuck up in a Pebbles ponytail, her face was swollen from crying, and her mouth felt slick with grease.

Oh, no way in hell was she opening that door.

The bell rang again. Then again. Shoving the bucket off her lap, she marched over and peered through the slot.

Brady peered right back.

She jumped, slamming her palms over her mouth to muffle her cry. What was he doing here? The roof was his good-bye present, his final love letter; she knew it as well as he. Why would he go on torturing her with his presence? She was already dreading dealing with working with him day after day, but she'd grit her teeth and do it. But here, at her apartment, where they'd spent hours ripping off each other's clothes and playing sexy, naked, dirty games?

No.

He began to pound. "Charlotte, I know you're in there. I saw your eye. Open the door. I need to say something to you."

She looked down and groaned. "I can't. Now isn't a good time. Come back tomorrow."

His low laugh echoed through the door. "No, it has to be now. Right now."

"I was going to thank you for the roof."

"It's not about the roof. Open the door, now, or I swear, you're going to regret it."

"You can't talk to me like that! Demanding I open the door to my house after we broke up and you gifted me a roof? Who do you think you are? Go away."

"Open the door or I'll break it down."

"You wouldn't."

"Hell, yes, I would, and then your punishment will be worse when I spank your ass."

Her head spun with arousal and a blood-pumping anger. "You bastard! How dare you bring up sacred things we shared when we're not together anymore!" She turned the lock and flung open the door, glaring. "I don't know what games you're playing but I don't like them and I'm not the type of woman to let you walk all over her with a thank you so you better—oh!"

He jerked her forward and crushed his mouth to hers.

Her toes curled and her body sighed with bliss as his tongue dove deep to gather her taste, while he hitched her high up against his body to keep her still. She didn't fight, just wrapped her arms around him and kissed him back with all her own demands.

A long time later, he raised his head. "Pizza and popcorn?"

"I'm depressed."

He kicked the door shut and pressed a thumb over her lips. His dark eyes seethed with a naked hunger and something else. Something so wonderful she was terrified to hope. "You're so fucking beautiful," he murmured.

"What are you doing here?"

"Can't stay away from you any longer. I fucked up. I'm sorry."

Her lips trembled. "Oh, God, don't. 'Cause I can't send you away again. Please, go. Go and find someone who will make you happy, Brady. You deserve it."

"I do. And the only woman who will make me happy is you."

Misery shuddered through her. "I'm not good for you. Nothing's changed."

"Everything's changed. I realized I was being an asshole. I found the woman who owns my soul and I sent her away. But I figured it out, and I'm not leaving again. I love you."

"What about marriage and kids and your family?"

"I spoke with my parents. I was wrong, Charlotte. I cast them in a certain light and believed sticking to some roles would make my marriage perfect. The only thing that makes a marriage perfect is who you're with, and all I want is you. I want the woman who eats and breathes renovating houses and who's so cheap she makes cabinets out of windows. I want the woman who makes me laugh, makes me mad, and whose body I crave on a constant basis. That's you. And I don't give a crap about when or if we'll get married, or when and if we'll have kids. It can be two years, five years, or ten—I just want you for every single one of them."

The words were too much. The words were everything. But it wasn't just the words that made her realize what had changed. It was the open love and happiness carved in his features, the truth glinting in the depth of his sooty eyes. Somehow, some way, this man had fallen in love with her and wasn't going to let her go.

She jumped up, wrapping her limbs around him and kissing him. Her fingers twisted in his hair and she moaned with need as he walked her to the couch and they collapsed onto the cushions, still kissing.

"I love you and missed you and oh, God, you feel so good."

"You too," he growled, nipping at her neck.

"I look terrible," she moaned in between breaths.

"You look stunning. Even better once I get these clothes off."

She laughed as he tugged them off, and then they were naked and falling into each other like a beautiful poem where every word and stanza fit into the whole to achieve perfection. As he filled her completely, she cried his name. As she fell apart, he caught her. And as they lay sated in each other's arms, Charlie smiled. The future looked bright.

On their terms.

Epilogue

"I'm rich!" Charlie jumped up and down, clapping and dancing, while Brady shook his head and watched her. "I'm going to pocket $100,000! And not only that—Gage offered me the lot across the street for dirt cheap! The bank foreclosed and nobody wanted it and now it's all mine!"

She shook her hips, did a sexy wriggle, and tried to get him to dance with her. It was time to get her back to Tangos. "Congrats. I saw the new neighbors. Jackson seemed really excited to have a boy the same age move in."

"He's over the moon. And I'm so happy Cal liked the idea of doing a young internship program. I can't wait to have Jackson help me work on this house. This entire neighborhood will be transformed, slowly but surely—"

"House by house," he finished. She settled, and he gathered her close as they looked at the SOLD sign perched on the front lawn of their house. To him, it would always be their house, a reminder of their own personal love story played out plank by plank.

The couple who bought the house had two boys and they'd fallen in love with Charlie's renovation, offering full price. They were thrilled over the mural and the quirky touches that made the house special. It was as if it was made for them.

"Hey, I forgot to tell you Gage invited us over to dinner Friday night," she said. She tucked her arm around his hips and leaned in. "Figured we could go to Tangos afterward."

"Sounds good. Don't forget dinner at my parents' on Sunday."

"Already on my schedule. My place or yours tonight?"

She tilted her head up and gazed at him. His heart squeezed, and he fell deep into those hazel eyes that promised him the world and gave it to him on a daily basis. "Yours. I want you to show me how to make pizza box art tonight."

She giggled. "I can't wait to see this one. Just remember you can color outside the box."

"Don't be a brat, Charlotte."

"Don't be a hardass, Bolivar. Great art takes letting go."

"Great art takes discipline."

"Let's see whose is better. We'll let Cal, Dalton, and Tristan judge."

"Done. What does the winner get?" he demanded.

She whispered in his ear all the filthy, dirty ideas she had in mind, and in seconds, his jeans were way too tight.

"I can't wait."

She smiled up at him amidst the streaming rays of the sun.

"Me neither. For…everything."

Then she kissed him.

The End

* * * *

Also from 1001 Dark Nights and Jennifer Probst, discover Searching For Mine and The Marriage Arrangement.

About Jennifer Probst

Jennifer Probst is the *New York Times*, *USA Today*, and *Wall Street Journal* bestselling author of both sexy and erotic contemporary romance. She was thrilled her novel, *The Marriage Bargain*, was the #6 Bestselling Book on Amazon for 2012, and spent 26 weeks on the *New York Times*. Her work has been translated in over a dozen countries, sold over a million copies, and was dubbed a "romance phenomenon" by Kirkus Reviews. She makes her home in New York with her sons, husband, two rescue dogs, and a house that never seems to be clean. She loves hearing from all readers! Stop by her website at http://www.jenniferprobst.com for all her upcoming releases, news and street team information. Sign up for her newsletter at www.jenniferprobst.com/newsletter for a chance to win a gift card each month and receive exclusive material and giveaways.

Also from Jennifer Probst

The Billionaire Builders
Everywhere and Every Way
Any Time, Any Place
All Or Nothing At All

Searching for Series:
Searching for Someday
Searching for Perfect
Searching for Beautiful
Searching for Always
Searching for You

The Marriage to a Billionaire series:
The Marriage Bargain
The Marriage Trap
The Marriage Mistake
The Marriage Merger
The Books of Spells

Executive Seduction
All the Way

The Sex on the Beach Series:
Beyond Me
Chasing Me

The Hot in the Hamptons Series:
Summer Sins

The Steele Brother Series:
Catch Me
Play Me
Dare Me
Beg Me

Dante's Fire

Discover More Jennifer Probst

The Marriage Arrangement
A Marriage to a Billionaire Novella
By Jennifer Probst

She had run from her demons…
Caterina Victoria Windsor fled her family winery after a humiliating broken engagement, and spent the past year in Italy rebuilding her world. But when Ripley Savage shows up with a plan to bring her back home, and an outrageous demand for her to marry him, she has no choice but to return to face her past. But when simple attraction begins to run deeper, Cat has to decide if she's strong enough to trust again…and strong enough to stay…
He vowed to bring her back home to be his wife…
Rip Savage saved Windsor Winery, but the only way to make it truly his is to marry into the family. He's not about to walk away from the only thing he's ever wanted, even if he has to tame the spoiled brat who left her legacy and her father behind without a care. When he convinces her to agree to a marriage arrangement and return home, he never counted on the fierce sexual attraction between them to grow into something more. But when deeper emotions emerge, Rip has to fight for something he wants even more than Winsor Winery: his future wife.

* * * *

Searching for Mine
A Searching For Novella
By Jennifer Probst

The Ultimate Anti-Hero Meets His Match…

Connor Dunkle knows what he wants in a woman, and it's the three B's. Beauty. Body. Boobs. Other women need not apply. With his good looks and easygoing charm, he's used to getting what he wants—and who. Until he comes face to face with the one woman who's slowly making his life hell...and enjoying every moment...

Ella Blake is a single mom and a professor at the local Verily College who's climbed up the ranks the hard way. Her ten-year-old son is a constant challenge, and her students are driving her crazy— namely Connor Dunkle, who's failing her class and trying to charm his way into a better grade. Fuming at his chauvinistic tendencies, Ella teaches him the ultimate lesson by giving him a *special* project to help his grade. When sparks fly, neither of them are ready to face their true feelings, but will love teach them the ultimate lesson of all?

All or Nothing At All
The Billionaire Builders, Book 3
By Jennifer Probst

HGTV's *Property Brothers* meets *The Marriage Bargain* in this third novel in the Billionaire Builders series, an all-new sexy contemporary romance from *New York Times* bestselling author Jennifer Probst.

* * * *

Chapter One

Sydney Greene rushed into the office of Pierce Brothers Construction, frantically calculating how she'd make up the twenty minutes she lost in morning madness. Her daughter, Becca, had insisted on wearing her hair in a French braid, then raced back to her closet to change twice before school. If she acted like this at six years old, what would happen when she reached high school? Sydney shuddered at the thought. Juggling her purse, laptop, and briefcase, she dug for the key. She was a bit of a control freak when it came to running the office where she'd worked since she was sixteen years old and liked to arrive before everyone else started. Order was the key to dealing with chaos. Her life had been such a series of sharp turns and fear-inducing hills, her soul was soothed in the one place she could not only control but thrive in. Her job. And finally, she was ready to take it to the next level. The office was quiet, immediately calming her. She dropped her stuff on her desk, then headed to the kitchen in a hunt for sanity.

Or, at least, some clarity. The kitchen was high-tech, from the stainless steel refrigerator to the cappuccino maker, soda machine, and various vending booths. With skilled motions, she quickly brewed the coffee, then grabbed her fav Muppets mug and filled it to the brim. Trying not to gulp the wicked-hot liquid, she sipped and breathed, bringing her focus to the upcoming presentation. After years of running Pierce Brothers as executive assistant and general office guru, she was about to make the pitch of a lifetime. It was time to take the next step and prove her worth. It was time to be promoted to CFO. And they had no idea it was coming. Nerves fluttered in her stomach, but she ignored them. She walked back into her office with her coffee, her Jimmy Choo high heels sinking into the plush carpet. She'd dressed to impress in her designer Donna Karan apple-green suit and even managed to pin up her crazed curls in a semblance of professionalism. Her black-framed glasses added a flair of style and seriousness. After grabbing her flash drive with her PowerPoint presentation loaded, she quickly set up the conference room with her handouts and laptop, then brought in a tray of pastries from Andrea's Bakery with a pitcher of water. Nothing wrong with a little bribing, especially when it involved sweets. She double-checked the room. Perfect. She was ready. She picked up her mug for another sip. She'd calculated this quarter's profits and could clearly show the margin of growth once she brought in this new— "Morning." She jerked at the deep, cultured voice breaking into her thoughts. Coffee splashed over the edge of her mug onto her jacket. Cursing, she swiveled her head, her gaze crashing into whiskey-colored eyes that were as familiar as her own beating heart. Familiar yet deadly, to both her past and her present. Why did he have to be the one who was here first? The man owned an inner alarm clock that detested lateness. She still hated the little leap of her heart when she was in his company, but it'd just become part of her routine. Kind of like eating and breathing. Anyone else would've brought a smile and a bit of chatter. But Tristan Pierce didn't talk to her. Not really. Oh, he lectured and demanded and judged, but he refused to actually have a conversation with her. Not that she cared. It was better for both of them to keep their distance. "You scared me," she accused. "Why don't you ever make any noise when you walk into a room?" Those carved lips twitched in the need to smile. Unfortunately, her presence rarely allowed the man to connect with any of his softer emotions, so he kept his expression grim. They'd been dancing around each other for over a year now, and still struggled with discomfort in each other's presence. Well, he experienced discomfort in the form of awkwardness. She experienced discomfort in the form of sexual torture. "I'll work on it." He gestured to the new brown stain on her clothes. "Need help?" "I got it." Her body wept at the thought of him touching her, even for a moment. Down, girl. She grabbed a napkin, dipped it in water, and dabbed at her suit jacket. "I didn't realize we were having a meeting today. I have some appointments."

"I rearranged your schedule. This is the only time that everyone was able to meet." "Another board meeting?" "Sort of." He didn't ask any other questions. He rarely did. She tried to ignore the masculine waves of energy that emanated from his figure. He'd always been the quiet one of his brothers, but he never needed words or noise to make his presence known. When he walked into a room, everyone noticed—men and women. He held a demeanor of competence and power in a whole different way from his brothers, Caleb and Dalton. As the middle child, he was a peacemaker and able to make decisions with a confident quickness most admired but never duplicated. His thoroughness was legendary. Tristan was able to see a problem at all angles and attack it with a single-minded intensity and level of control. He'd once brought that same talent to the bedroom, concentrating on wringing pleasure from her body with a thoroughness that ruined her for other lovers. She studied him from under heavy-lidded eyes. His suits were legendary—custom made with the best fabrics and cut that emphasized his powerful, lean body. Today he wore a charcoal-gray suit, a snowy-white shirt, and a vivid purple tie. Engraved gold cuff links. His shoes were polished to a high sheen and made of soft leather. He always reminded her of one of those jungle cats who prowled with litheness, amber eyes lit with intention, taking their time before deciding what to do with prey. His analytical mind was as drool worthy as his body. Hard, supple muscles balanced with a beautiful grace most men could never pull off. His hair was thick, perfectly groomed, and a deep reddish brown. His face was an artistry of elegance, from the sharp blade of his nose to his square jaw, full lips, and high cheekbones. Lush lashes set off eyes that practically glowed, darkening to an intensity that made a woman's heart beat madly. He was beauty incarnate, a feast for the senses a woman could never bore of while spending the rest of eternity studying every angle and curve and drowning in his cognac gaze. She'd once been that woman. Of course, that was centuries ago, before the ugliness between them sprouted from dark corners and swallowed them up whole. Didn't matter. She only dealt with Tristan for work now, though the past year had been more difficult, as she was forced to spend so much time in his presence.

Those five years after he'd moved to New York and been away from Harrington were hard, but she'd finally grown up. Become a mother and made her own niche in life, rather than waiting for him to dictate her wants and needs. If only she weren't still attracted to the man. Already, the room surged with the innate connection between them. Some things never disappeared. They'd always had chemistry. Now it was just a matter of accepting it as fact and ignoring it. Most of the time she managed. "Let me settle in. We'll start in fifteen?" he asked. "Yes, that's fine." She turned away, discarding the napkin, and he left. She practically sagged in relief. Having him too close threw her off, and this morning she needed to be a poised, cool, confident professional.

Twenty minutes later, the team was assembled around the conference table. She tried to keep a smug smile from her face as they immediately attacked the tray of pastries, arguing good-naturedly over who got what and who saw what first. She'd decided on a sneak attack for her presentation. She knew these men well, and taking them by surprise would lower their defenses and allow them to really listen to her presentation without preliminary assumptions. The biggest problem working with Pierce Brothers for the past decade was also her greatest asset. She was like family. Unfortunately, this meant being treated like a little sister, which was also frustrating. She needed to convince them she was the best person for the job as CFO based on her business history. Not because of familial relations. "Who called this meeting?" Cal asked between bites of his favorite cinnamon bun. "It wasn't on my schedule originally." As the oldest brother of the crew, he was the most no nonsense, with a simple, rugged manner. He wore his usual uniform of old, ripped jeans, a white T-shirt, and work boots. His face was as rough as his appearance, from his hooked nose to his bushy brows and gunmetal-gray eyes, but he was always protective and held the wisest counsel she knew. He'd led the company along with his brothers when it was almost lost due to his father's will, but now they stood together, bonded once again by affection. "Not me." Dalton had his legs stretched out and propped up on the opposite-facing leather chair. She held back a sigh at the lack of professionalism. "I have no issues to discuss." As the youngest, he'd always been the wildest, and his woodworking talent was legendary. Stinging-blue eyes, long blond surfer-type hair, and an easy charm made women fall happily in line to warm his bed. Of course, now he was settled and in love with Raven. He'd grown and matured over the past year, and she had never seen him so happy. They both looked at Tristan, who shrugged. Elegantly, of course. "I was told my calendar was rearranged just for this meeting." The final member in the crew, not related by blood, was Brady. He lifted his hands in the air. "Nope. Have no idea what this is about." As the architect and longtime family friend, he'd carved his own niche for himself in the company. With his dark, Latin looks and commanding manner, he'd been essential to their success and easily held his own. Time to gain control of this meeting and do what she came for. "I did." All gazes turned and focused on her. She gave them a cool smile and flipped on her laptop so the first slide of her PowerPoint presentation flashed on the screen. After quickly distributing the stack of handouts, she stood at the head of the conference table. Already, she took in Tristan's fierce frown as he began flipping through the pages of her proposal. "What's this about, Syd?" Cal asked, finishing up his pastry. "As you know, I've been working at Pierce Brothers a long time. I started as file clerk, worked my way up to secretary, then executive assistant. I've been in charge of accounting, marketing, and managing the office staff." Cal cocked his head. "You want a raise. You don't need to hold a meeting for this. You deserve a pay bump."

"I don't want just a raise, Cal. I want to be promoted to CFO of Pierce Brothers. I want to be part of the board of directors." Dalton whistled. A grin curved his lips. "Man, this is gonna be good," he drawled, taking a bite of a simple jelly doughnut. Brady sat back in the seat, a thoughtful look on his face. Cal nodded, urging her to go on. She refused to glance over at Tristan. She didn't need any negative energy affecting her presentation. "I've been in charge of the accounts at Pierce Brothers for years, which goes beyond the standard accounts receivables and payables. Besides budgeting, I'm involved in negotiating with our local vendors for discounts and securing new jobs, and I have built solid relationships that keep productivity at increased levels. I've included a breakdown of the past quarter's profit margin." She clicked steadily on the slides, which were also included in the work sheets. "As Pierce Brothers has evolved, the workload has doubled, and all of you are consistently in the field. I've been able to fill in the gap by being more involved in the design aspect. Three months ago, I secured a new contract with Grey's Custom Flooring with a significant discount to our clients. I was able to do this because of my relationship with Anthony Moretti. Building up my main base of contacts keeps Pierce Brothers viable and able to keep offering unique materials to our clients." Cal tapped his pen against the desk. "I was impressed with Grey's. The quality is top-notch, and they've been easy to work with. You did a great job." She gave a slight nod. "Thank you. I'd like to show you how those savings affected our bottom line." She clicked steadily through the slides, breaking down each of her skills and leading up to the main event. It was time to bring it home. "I believe it's time to move forward. We're financially stable and ready to take on a bigger job with our redesigning and renovation projects." Tristan glanced up, frowning. This was the delicate part of negotiations. She was directly stepping into Tristan's territory, but it was time he realized what she could bring to the organization on her own. "I've been in talks with Adam Cushman. He's been very interested in securing some homes in the Harrington area and on the lookout for an opportunity. I believe he's finally found one." "Cushman?" Tristan narrowed his gaze. "He's the big developer in New York City. I worked with him briefly. How is it you know him well enough to be involved in such a conversation without my knowledge?" His voice was chilled, like one of those frosty mugs Raven used in her bar. She fought a shiver, determined not to let him intimidate her. Not anymore. "If you remember, you were in a bidding war with him for the property on Allerton. He came into the office one day, but no one was here, so I took the meeting. You ended up winning the property, but he kept in contact with me regarding future opportunities in Harrington. We both hold a similar vision on developing more family-friendly homes with touches of unique designs to court a solid middle-class-income bracket." "What properties is he interested in?" Tristan flicked out the demanding question with a touch of impatience. She gave a tight smile. "It's there in the proposal you're holding." She clicked to the next slide of her PowerPoint, sketching out a block of houses. "He'll be purchasing a total of eight houses on Bakery Street." Dalton stared at the screen, shaking his head. "Bakery? Those houses are in bad shape. Most of the tenants abandoned them, and no one's been interested in renovation for an entire block." "Exactly." She pushed the button for the next screen. "Adam has been able to purchase the entire lot and plans to renovate them all together, then flip them. This is the breakdown of approximate costs. We still need architectural proposals drawn up and design specifics discussed, but he's on board and wants Pierce Brothers to take the job." Tristan studied the papers in front of him like he was a lawyer about to take the bar exam. Brady scribbled notes in the margins, nodding. Dalton shot her a proud grin. It took everything not to smile back from his obvious admiration, but she kept her gaze focused on Cal. "Ambitious," he said slowly. "And brilliant. How'd you sell him Pierce?" "I want to use local suppliers for the entire project. I convinced Adam to go local instead of using the main manufacturing plants. We're concentrating on unique kitchen and bath features to appeal to middle income. Fenced-in yards, smaller-type decks, and appealing front porches for the lot." "Have you confirmed all our local suppliers will be on board with this?" Tristan demanded. "Many of them refuse to work with the bigwigs. They prefer local developers. Not city slickers, as they term them." "I've made initial contact and received definite interest.

I'd meet with them and get everything in writing before moving forward." "Well done," Cal murmured, still tapping his pen. "This is a huge job, Sydney. Do you have specifics?" She clicked to the next screen, which showed an organized calendar of tasks, assignments, and proposed time slots. "This is the working plan, but of course it will be tweaked as we discuss further." "I would've appreciated a heads-up before this meeting," Tristan clipped out. "I have another project in the works, and this will take up my calendar for the next several months. Why didn't Adam reach out to me before this?" She practically purred with satisfaction as she delivered the crushing words. "Because Adam wants me to lead this project. Not you." The men stared at her in slightly shocked silence. She smoothly continued her pitch. "Adam trusts me. He knows I'll retain his vision and be the main contact throughout the project. The only way he'll allow Pierce Brothers the job is if I'm in charge. And the only way I'll agree to be in charge is if you promote me to CFO." Sydney snapped the laptop closed. The screen went dark. "I need something more. I deserve this opportunity. I know we'll need to hire another person to take over more office responsibilities, but I think Charlie may be interested. I know her primary love is doing renovation and rehab, but learning the business from the ground up intrigues her." Brady nodded. Charlie had come to Pierce Brothers as an intern, then slowly made her way to becoming indispensable for her skill in pulling apart houses and putting them back together. She and Brady experienced their own fireworks, beginning with intense dislike and moving to grudging respect and then something much more. Though they seemed like opposites, they fit together perfectly, and it was obvious how in love each was with the other. "Charlie actually mentioned she'd like to take on more work," he said. "It's definitely a possibility." "I have no problem hiring another person," Cal said. "Securing this project can be a big asset, especially for the future." Dalton grabbed another jelly doughnut. "I think it's amazing, Syd. Great presentation." "Thank you." Suddenly burning amber eyes pierced into hers. Tristan's lips pressed together in a thin line of disapproval. "You giving us an ultimatum?" She met his gaze head on, refusing to flinch. Refusing to back down. "I'm giving you a proposal. A smart one. And I'll be waiting for your decision. Adam wants to move quickly on this, so I'd like to be able to get back to him." "Fair enough." Cal rose to his feet. "Give us some time to discuss. We'll have an answer for you soon." She smiled. "I appreciate it." Scooping up her laptop and empty coffee mug, she walked out of the conference room with her head held high. She'd done it. Whatever happened next, she'd made her pitch and fought for what she deserved, for both her and Becca. After all these years in the background, it was finally her chance. She intended to take it.

Too Close to Call

A Romancing the Clarksons Novella
By Tessa Bailey

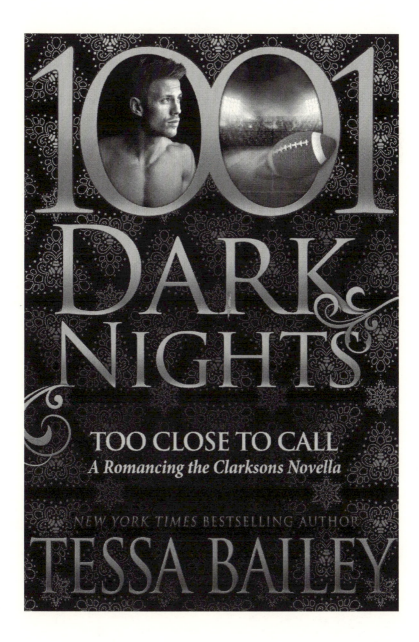

Acknowledgments from the Author

Thank you so much to the 1001 Dark Nights team, including Liz Berry, MJ Rose, Jillian Greenfield Stein, and all the wonderful editors and designers. Thank you as well to Madeleine Colavita at Forever Romance, my family (especially my husband who watches the NFL Draft, which inspired this story) and as always, the readers. Love you all.

Chapter One

Draft Day was *nothing* like Kyler had pictured.

"With the ninth pick in the 2017 NFL Draft, the Los Angeles Rage select…" Kyler Tate's parents sucked in breaths on either side of him. "Kyler Tate, receiver, University of Cincinnati."

The tense atmosphere inside the event hall exploded with wild cheers, exclamations, and boos. His shoulders were slapped by thousands of hands, kisses landing on his cheeks. Like falling out of a kayak into a rushing current, bashing into rocks on the way toward a waterfall, Kyler stood, put his head down, and proceeded toward the stage. Cell phones rang at every table he passed, terse conversations taking place as the deadline timer for the next announcement started. Players he'd faced on the gridiron sweated in their suits, mothers fussed, water glasses were refilled.

This was it. Years of training, icing down injuries, two-a-day practices, glory, pain, and mental fatigue. All for this moment.

And it was…utterly fucking incomplete.

Before he could reach the stage, panic set in. Set in real good, like claws digging into fertile ground. A moment earlier, everyone in the room had looked familiar, but they were strangers now, spinning in a kaleidoscope. Sweat popped up on his forehead. His shoulder blades tightened, a harsh sound puffed from between his lips. From behind the podium, the announcer gave him a strange look, the Rage jersey lowering in his grip. *Are you okay?*

The man's mouthed words barely penetrated over the sudden rushing stream of images. Of her. Bree Justice.

Since middle school, he'd been imagining this day. Late at night, his head nestled into the pillow of his childhood bedroom, staring up at a poster of T.Y. Hilton on his ceiling, he'd heard the announcer saying his name. But in every single one of his dreams, he'd leaned over to kiss Bree before making his way to the stage.

Bree wasn't there, though. She was a thousand miles away in Indiana, same place she'd been since he left for college. Same place she'd been since breaking up with him the night before he climbed aboard the Cincinnati-bound train and sped off, doubtful he would make it one day without her.

In a way, he hadn't.

A vivid memory swept into the chaos of Kyler's mind. Another time he'd climbed a stage what felt like a million years ago...and he was powerless to do anything but let it play out.

"Bloomfield High! It's the moment we've all been waiting for. Your votes have been counted!" The smiling cheerleader bounced up and down on the stage, a microphone in one hand, two gold sashes dangling in the other. "Your pick for prom queen is..." She squeaked and did a little dance. "My friend and yours, the incredible Hailey Faye! Congratulations, Hailey!" Kyler smiled and pulled Bree tighter against his side. Lord Jesus, he couldn't tear his eyes off her tonight. Any night, really. But in the ice blue dress that brushed her knees, all that curly black hair twisted up into some fancy style, she was even more beautiful than usual. His heart hadn't stopped beating triple time since Bree floated down the stairs, her father watching with hawk eyes as he pinned on the corsage.

In the back of the gymnasium, they were surrounded by a mixture of Kyler's teammates—most of them sneaking sips of vodka from flasks stowed in their jackets—and Bree's Animal Care Club friends. It was an odd mix, to be sure, but ever since Kyler and Bree had gotten together in middle school after being randomly paired for a science class presentation, they'd proceeded as if the eclectic blend was normal. So everyone had followed suit.

Years later, they all traveled in a pack, meeting at Nelson's Diner on Friday nights, sneaking out to the creek that ran through the town woods on summer Saturdays. On a monthly basis, couples were formed or dissolved within the group, but Kyler and Bree stuck together like glue through it all.

Kyler loved Bree. Bree loved Kyler. Nothing would ever change that.

The applause was beginning to die down from the prom queen announcement and Kyler's teammates began nudging him between the shoulder blades, making wise cracks about how pretty he looked, how adorable it was that his tie matched

Bree's dress. He merely shot them the bird. "Your choice for king should come as no surprise," called the cheerleader from the stage, rolling her eyes good-naturedly.

Everyone turned to look at Kyler and he forced himself to smile, nodding politely. Earlier that year, he'd captained the team and led them to the state championships. In a football town like Bloomfield, title winning touchdowns, like the one he'd scored, tended to remain fresh in their minds. News of his full-ride scholarship to the University of Cincinnati had blown through the town like wildfire this week, making it impossible to walk two feet without receiving the kind of effusive praise he'd learned early to be thankful for.

At one time, he might've wished for a football helmet to tug down over his head to escape the scrutiny, but he kept his chin up in the face of the attention now. The people of Bloomfield drove to his games every week, made signs, chanted his name—a fact he still couldn't believe—and he wouldn't hide from that type of kindness.

Bree slipped her hand into Kyler's and went up on her toes, whispering in his ear. "I'll meet you out back after your dance."

"You don't want to stick around and see my oversized head in a crown?"

"I'll see you in it later." Her slow wink sent warmth sliding into his belly. "But everyone is going to stare at me while you're out there, wondering how I feel about you dancing with another girl." She shivered. "You know I don't like the attention."

"I do know that." His mouth started to curve with the secret he was keeping, so he planted a kiss on her forehead to hide it. "Or maybe I forgot. Again."

Suspicion snuck into her expression. "Kyler Joseph Tate—"

"You know what? I'm not even going to announce his name," said the cheerleader on stage, sending laughter rippling through the crowd of dressed up high school students. "I'll just say this. It's a well-known fact that Kyler Tate doesn't dance with anyone but Bree Justice. No matter how hard all us ladies have wished he would." Laughter, sighs, gagging noises, and camera flashes went off around them, but Kyler kept his gaze trained on Bree, his pulse hammering as she tried to hide beneath his arm. "So we're bucking tradition tonight. Your queen is going to dance with her man. And Kyler is going to dance with his Bree. Everyone clear a path to the dance floor. DJ? Drop that slow jam."

It took Kyler several gentle tugs to get Bree out on the floor, but when they finally got there, he knew it would be a moment he remembered for the rest of his life.

Because it was the first time he'd seen her heartbroken.

"Son, would you mind getting your ass up on the damn stage?" the announcer said in a gruff whisper, his big hand covering the microphone. "The next team is on the clock and we need to get a picture before their pick is up."

You don't understand. This is all wrong. Dressed in an ironed suit beneath the television camera lights, Kyler had never been more aware that he was being swept along in the current, nowhere to grab hold. Doing his job inside the classroom and out on the field had made it easier to forget the pain. But now? His future had just been sealed. Being only than a few hours' drive from Indiana, his absence from home—from Bree—had always seemed temporary somehow.

Once he left for Los Angeles, it would be permanent.

He would be permanently without Bree.

"I, uh…yeah." Kyler rubbed the heel of his hand against his stuttering heartbeat. "Sorry, sir. It's all happening so fast, is all."

"It's the cameras, right? Get used to them," the announcer said out of the side of his mouth, gripping Kyler's hand in a tight handshake, his lips spreading into a white-toothed smile for the cameras. "Welcome to the pros. Cameras and assholes are going to be in your face everywhere you go, asking you a bunch of questions you don't know how to answer. Good news is, today all you have to do is smile, celebrate, and get laid." He boomed a tight laugh. "Make sure there are no cameras around during that last part."

Kyler forced a pleased expression onto his face, holding up the jersey he'd been handed. "That advice coming from personal experience?"

"Son, I've got three ex-wives in the crowd. What do you think?"

"Right." Kyler spotted his mother crying in the audience, his father looking bemused by the whole proceeding. No Bree, dammit. If she were there, she'd be cracking a joke to make Kyler's father relax while handing his mother tissue, all graceful and easy. Not having her there was wrong. *Everything* was wrong.

White winked in front of his eyes as more cameras went off in a barrage of blinding light. The announcer thought he'd been taken off guard by the chaotic media presence, but he wasn't. No, he'd been expecting the cameras. *Waiting* for them with something akin to helpless loathing. After all, the flashes and scrutiny were a major part of what had cost him Bree.

Perhaps what happened next could be credited to Kyler's competitive spirit, those lenses being his opponent. Or maybe it was the love for his ex-girlfriend that had never dimmed, not one single iota. As Kyler stood there, having his image captured and replicated millions of times across computer, television, and cell phone screens, a sense of determination crept in. Slowly at first. Then it swelled and crowded his insides like rising dough.

He'd won championships. Been named an All-American. Drafted by a professional organization. Dreams and goals being ticked off a list, one by one. But that night in the woods after prom, when Bree had tearfully ripped out his heart, he'd lost the most important battle of his life. He'd been in too much agony and shock to fight hard as he should have. Too resentful. And as a result, none of the glory that had come after losing Bree seemed real. None of it.

Nor would anything that came after.

No way in hell I'm going to Los Angeles without her.

Chapter Two

No rest for the weary.

Bree climbed out of her truck and bent forward to touch her toes, groaning at the pull of muscles in her lower back. Who needed Pilates when she could spend the night tending a dairy cow with an infected hoof? Everything ached, she looked like a dumpster fire, and she only had fifteen minutes to guzzle a gallon of coffee before her next appointment.

Pinning her messy curls on top of her head, she kicked her wellies against the truck tires, hoping to lose some of the caked-on mud. No dice. The nasty brown stuff climbed her weathered jeans and even dotted her T-shirt.

The family business was thriving—which was a *great* thing. But her father's advancing years meant more responsibility for Bree. More all-nighters at local barns without anyone to relieve her. More exhaustion.

Not complaining. Bree straightened her back and marched toward the diner, knowing nobody inside would be surprised or offended by her appearance. No, the diner and a host of familiar voices would wrap around her like a warm hug, same as always. This town ran in Bree's veins and she counted it a blessing that every morning she had the privilege of waking up inside its borders. If she ever found herself daydreaming of what lay beyond, well, she shut it down quick enough.

The people of Bloomfield were farmers, small business owners, construction workers, teachers, all of them working honest jobs. Content with what they had, even if they struggled from time to time.

Bree was no exception.

Night classes had been manageable when her father was able to run the business alone, but since he'd slowed down, the workload had fallen on her shoulders. In the four years since high school, she'd completed her pre-veterinary studies degree while training constantly to follow in her father's footsteps. She'd become a trusted animal care specialist in her own right, but even with tuition saved up, actual veterinary school seemed like a pipe dream.

Someday.

Right now, her most important job was paying the mortgage, making sure the business continued to thrive, and adding to her sister Kira's college fund.

Well worth the sore back and mud-soaked jeans.

As soon as Bree walked into the diner, she knew something was up. For one thing, no one was sitting down. Every patron was on their feet, crowded together on one side of the restaurant, food left untouched on tables.

She wiped her boots on the welcome mat and treaded toward the counter, hopping up on one of the stools. The clock above the grill said she only had ten minutes now to wrangle some coffee, but no one was behind the counter to take her order. A swell of murmurs and laughter went up in the crowd where they stood congregated about twenty feet away.

And that's when she heard his voice.

Kyler Tate.

Bree's heart shot up into her throat, her fingers fluttering there, as if she could reach in and dislodge the obstruction. Oh no. Bad. *Very* bad. Since he'd left for college, she'd managed to avoid him almost every time he'd come home to visit. Apart from a couple quick sightings in the grocery store, she hadn't even *seen* him. No matter that her eyes and chest ached with the need to catch a glimpse of him now, it wasn't happening. Too many memories, feelings. Regrets?

No. She refused to have those.

How had this happened? There was always a buzz in town whenever the star football player descended. How had he snuck in without warning at the tail end of July? Very inconsiderate of him to deprive Bree of her usual method of avoidance. Whenever Bloomfield welcomed him home, she holed up in her house until he had the decency to skedaddle. If she was forced to leave the house while Kyler was in town limits, she sure as hell didn't do it dressed like a drowned rat.

Bree slipped off the stool and crept toward the door, praying none of Kyler's many admirers would turn around. His deep, rich voice drifted across the separation—humble as always—causing a hesitation in her step, but she managed to keep going. Having him so close was doing terrible damage to her insides, tangling them up like gnarled tree roots. A vision caught Bree in the throat, forcing her to gasp for breath.

Kyler, dressed in a tuxedo on that long ago prom night, bow tie loose and hanging down, his face the picture of devastation. *That* man. The one she'd hurt beyond repair.

He was *right there.*

It didn't escape Bree's notice that she was bolting like a coward, same way her mother had done all those years ago, but what choice did she have? Stick around and come face to face with her past? Or live to fight another day? It was a no brainer.

Nearly every day of her life, she walked in and out of Nelson's Diner. Yet somehow she forgot about the gumball machine. Her wellies connected with the red plastic base—hard. It sent a boom through the diner and a reverberation of denial coursing down her spine. "Shit almighty," Bree muttered, squeezing her eyes closed. When she turned toward the gathering of people, every single eye in the joint was on her. "Oh. Hey, y'all."

Sly looks were traded, elbows were shoved not so discreetly into ribs. This was why she didn't leave her house when Kyler came to Bloomfield. Because as much as Bree loved her small town, they were a pain in the rear end when it came to relationships, past and present. Nosy as all get out, every last one of them.

"Funny you should stop in when you did," called one of the waitresses, Sharon, propping hands on hips. "It's like you knew something about something."

"I don't know something about anything," Bree sputtered, backing toward the door. "I was just stopping in to see what pie was on special. And now I know. Peach."

Sharon raised a gray eyebrow, all lazy-like, rolling her neck in the process. "You don't want your usual coffee to go?"

"Just remembered I have some in the truck, thank you."

"How is that?" one of the old timers called. "You've been out on Gamble's farm all night. Was it them that gave you the coffee?"

"They're decaf drinkers," Sharon supplied. "Did you make the switch?"

"I don't understand the need for specifics." Panic and the urgency to flee gripped Bree when the crowd began parting. Any second now, she would see Kyler. They would make eye contact. Another flash of him on the creek bed, his face stark in the moonlight, made Bree bump back into the door. "You all have a good day now—"

"Bree." Her blood snapped with electricity at the sound of her name, said in that low drawl. Kyler stepped to the forefront of the crowd. The green eyes that still graced her dreams zeroed in, raking over her like they couldn't help it.

Heaven above, four years looked incredible on him. Extra inches had been added *everywhere*. His height. The athletic breadth of his shoulders. The corded biceps that tested the stitching of his T-shirt sleeves. Even his thighs, which were wrapped up in faded denim, were exploding with muscle; thighs she'd spent a good portion of her youth perched on since Kyler never allowed her to sit anywhere but his lap, no matter where they were or whether it was appropriate. "Hello."

"Hello," she whispered. "You're in town."

His slow nod was so familiar a ripple moved through her. "Here for the week. Can I get you that coffee?"

"No." She flushed over her own abruptness. "I meant to say, I can't stay. I'm going to be late for an appointment."

"Fine. I'll walk you out."

His expression *dared* her to say no. Challenged her. And for the first time since Kyler left, sexual awareness danced in her middle, sending a swift tremble down the length of her legs. Because her body hadn't forgotten what often lay on the other side of those challenges. "Fine," she breathed. "Suit yourself."

For all his sexual energy, Kyler was a gentleman, straight down to the soles of his feet. So Bree wasn't one bit surprised when his long gait ate up the distance between them. He reached over her head to push open the glass door, sending his scent crashing into her senses, the combination so familiar, Bree's nipples tightened until she winced. Grassy fields and Nautica Blue aftershave.

Their gazes clashed, but Bree couldn't decide if he'd worn the scent on purpose. His steady eyes gave nothing away. Before *hers* could betray her curiosity, Bree turned and passed through the door Kyler held open. And hell if it wasn't the longest walk in history, his presence behind her looming larger than a mountain. Every eyeball in the diner was sure to be on them and the attention made Bree twitchy, her fingers yanking on the strings of her hoodie.

She needed to get this reunion over with as soon as possible. Being around Kyler would only make her wonder what might have been. That kind of thinking was pointless. Destructive. Wanting more than a comfortable life is why her mother had walked out a decade earlier, leaving Bree to run the household. To care for her younger sister and heartbroken father. Bree took pride in those responsibilities now. They were what life had handed her and she would be *content.*

Back in high school, the writing had been on the wall when it came to Kyler. Everyone knew he'd been destined for greatness. That he would shake off Bloomfield and put his name in the history books. She'd been selfish to stay with him for so long, absorbing his love and attention, all the while knowing she'd wave good-bye to him someday. The decision was a painful one, but it had been made and now she would stick to it.

Bree gripped the truck's door handle and sent a casual smile over her shoulder. "Thanks for seeing me to my vehicle. You've earned your Boy Scout badge."

Kyler kept walking until Bree couldn't open the truck door without hitting him. Which meant he was close. Close enough to make her nerve endings sing in falsetto. "I think you'd need to be a little old lady for me to earn that badge," he drawled.

"Feeling pretty old today," Bree murmured without thinking, glancing down at her muddy clothes.

When she lifted her face again, his easy smile had slipped. "You look tired."

She nudged his shoulder, determined not to acknowledge it was made of stone. "Back in town five minutes and already pouring on the compliments."

"When I don't like something, I say it out loud. You remember that about me, don't you." Not a question. "Bree looking tired is high on the list of things I don't like."

"Good thing it's my business, then." Bree forced a polite smile, mostly for the benefit of their audience. She'd never fooled Kyler with phony smiles a day in her life and wouldn't start today. "Not yours, Ky."

He opened his mouth to argue, but closed it, his throat muscles shifting. "You've got new rain boots. What happened to the ones with the yellow ducks?"

Was he intentionally bombarding her with shared memories? That didn't seem like Kyler's style, but he might as well be shooting blow darts into her chest. "I, um…" She nudged one rubber toe against the other. "I rocked them long as I could. Last time I wore them, my pinkie toe was peeking out."

"See now, I'm sorry I missed that." Inching closer, he shook his head. "Always did think you had the cutest feet."

"When do you leave?" Bree blurted, making him flinch. "I mean, how long are you in town?"

He stared at a spot in the distance. "Week or so. Need to report for training camp out in California in August."

"Yes. Training camp." More polite smiling. She even gave a little pageant wave at the gawking row of town people staring at them through the windows. "Well. A week is a nice visit. Not too short. Not too long."

"I aim to take you out for dinner while I'm here."

"Pardon?" Bree snapped straight, her pulse flashing like erratic lightning. "What for?"

"What for." His eyelids dropped, then lifted to reveal…nothing. A wall. "Just two friends catching up is all, Bree. We don't need to play this game."

"Game?"

"Yeah. The one where I come home and you burrow into the ground like a gopher."

"Oh, fine. Now I'm tired looking *and* a gopher."

"Don't deflect."

"Oh, fine. Now I'm a tired, deflecting goph—"

"Bree Caroline Justice," Kyler warned, using her full name, same way he always used to when his temper got riled. "We're going out for a meal, you and I. This nonsense has gone on way too long. You broke my heart. I went away and healed it up. Now we're going to be friends."

The air left her, her organs trembling. "You just put it right out there."

"Somebody had to." His voice had softened, but that wall he'd built behind his eyes was still standing. "You have plans tonight?"

"Besides washing my hair?" They traded a quick smirk. "I'm chaperoning the church youth group dance. For Kira. She's going to be a senior in the fall."

"Shit, that went fast." His lips lifted in a fond smile, calling to mind how much Kyler used to spoil her little sister, bringing her flowers to ease the sting of being left at home while he took out Bree. "Is she the hell raiser we suspected she'd be?"

"Yes." Bree wrinkled her nose. "She's got boys on the brain and goes through them like a chain smoker does cigarettes. Hence me volunteering to keep an eye on the dance tonight. Told Kira if I didn't see daylight between her and her dance partner, I'd break out *my* moves."

"That sounds less like a threat and more like a promise." For just a split second, his wall lowered itself. "You never could sit still for long when music was playing."

"Only because you didn't let me."

"True enough." He propped a hand beside her on the truck, his scrutiny thickening. "Now that you sit still instead of dancing, are you happier?"

Dammit, she hesitated. "Yes."

"That so."

Feeling exposed, as if she'd suddenly been robbed of four years' worth of maturing and moving on, Bree took advantage of Kyler being distracted. She curled her fingers around the door handle, opened it, and hefted herself into the truck. "Maybe I grew up," she mumbled. "I'll see you, Ky."

When she pulled out of the parking lot moments later, Kyler was watching her in the rearview, fingers hooked in his belt loops, eyes narrowed.

For now, she'd escaped without making that dinner date. But she didn't have a doubt in her mind Kyler wouldn't give up after only one attempt.

Chapter Three

Kyler pulled his truck into the church parking lot and turned up the air conditioner, reckoning he should sneak in once the dance was already in full swing. Wouldn't want to give a certain someone another chance to pull a Houdini, now would he?

By a certain someone, he meant the beautiful, skittish animal lover who'd evaded him this afternoon. Not before they'd traded words, though. Memories. He thought he'd missed Bree for ten thousand reasons, but after seeing her again today, that number seemed like an underestimation. No one spoke, moved, smiled, smelled like her. Each of her little qualities had remained buried beneath his skin. And today his need for all those unique parts of Bree had swelled to the surface, just having her close.

Lord. His muscles were still in knots. Not getting right up into Bree's space and stating his intentions to win her back had been the hardest challenge of his life. He'd had no choice, though, had he?

Here was the thing. Bree Justice hated surprises.

Sophomore year of high school, Kyler had organized their classmates into singing happy birthday to Bree on her sixteenth birthday when she walked into the cafeteria. They'd taken it to the next level by serenading her on tabletops and throwing makeshift confetti fashioned out of notebook paper.

She'd promptly dropped her tray and gone to hide in the ladies' bathroom.

One would think Kyler had learned from that first incident, but no. Later that year, he'd asked her to homecoming during halftime of a game, climbing into the stands and getting down on one knee, still decked out in his football gear.

See, while Bree hated public interest, Kyler *loved* it when Bree was the main attraction. Even when she tried and failed to give him the silent treatment afterward, Kyler felt it was worth the advantage of making sure everyone knew she was special. And *his*.

In high school, riling Bree up and coaxing her away from her anger had been fun. Like flirting. Later on…foreplay. Yeah, they'd been real big on foreplay.

Kyler dropped his head back against the driver's seat and groaned, memories of Bree flooding in from all sides. Grappling hands, straining thighs, and gritted teeth. Challenging each other was their national pastime and they'd never missed an opportunity, whether it was over chess, getting the highest grade on a test…or seeing who could go the longest without a kiss.

Her competitive nature, coupled with the way she always seemed to slide from his grip *right* when he got comfortable, had always been an aphrodisiac to the athlete inside of him. A call to battle. Well, not a damn thing had changed in that regard. Just like when they were teenagers, Kyler was restless and heart-heavy and yes, horny beyond belief, thanks to having Bree mere inches away that afternoon.

The younger man he'd once been wouldn't have wasted a single second pretending to want only friendship from Bree. He'd have cut right to the chase, explaining he wouldn't go to Los Angeles without her. Would. *Not*.

But they weren't in high school now. Futures were on the line. The happiness he'd been attempting since leaving for college was all a sham without her beside him. So he would finally take what he knew about the love of his life…and apply it. Going against his very nature, Kyler would play the long game. One foot in front of the other, nice and easy. Right now, Bree was spooked simply having him in Bloomfield. If he came on too strong, she'd go hide in the ladies' bathroom—and he'd have a much more complicated obstacle course to complete.

Some surprises were in order, however, or Kyler would never get his chance to win back Bree. Which meant he'd be chaperoning a church dance tonight.

Kyler shut off the ignition and climbed out of his truck, snatching up the bouquet of sunflowers he'd bought at the last minute. Striding up the cobblestone walkway, he marveled over how the church seemed to shrink a little more every time he came home for a visit from Cincinnati. Music drifted on the summer wind as he skirted around back to the rear entrance. A minute later, he walked into the gym. It looked half the size of the one in his memory, but he still had to pause in the doorway, held there by the rush of the past.

Refreshment table to the right. Bleachers to the left. Dancing in the middle. DJ booth in the corner. Nothing had changed except the faces.

Through the darkness, there was one feminine figure sitting in the bleachers he would recognize ten lifetimes from now, her right leg jiggling to the beat. Seeing Bree with her hair loose, an amused smile on her face, Kyler's arm lost power, the bouquet slapping down against his thigh. As if she'd heard the smack of paper on denim, Bree's head turned, back straightening.

Good thing he stood between her and the exit.

Holding up his free hand in a conciliatory gesture, Kyler approached Bree where she sat quivering in the bleachers. In his wake, exclamations went off like little explosions; eyes bugged out. Kids stopped dancing. It was unfortunate he couldn't walk into a room in Bloomfield without making a scene, but he'd learned that if he acted casual, most people would follow suit. And keeping his focus locked on Bree wasn't difficult. Not in the least. Not when she was wearing a white summer dress. Not when he could remember her sitting in those same bleachers years earlier, tucked into his side.

"Evening, Bree."

"Ky," she returned with a suspicious look. "This sure is a coincidence."

"Isn't it?" Keeping his features schooled, he tipped his head in the direction of the dance floor. "My cousin's wife's nephew is out there. When I heard he'd be in attendance, I just had to volunteer my services, same as you. Keeping the next generation honest is a team effort."

"Uh-huh." Humor sparked in her eyes. "How many cousins did you call before finding a connection?"

"Just one." Her skeptical eyebrow lift made his lips twitch. "It's more of a phone tree situation."

"Is it now?" She sized him up with a glance. "First night in town and you're skipping out on your mama's dinner. She can't be happy about it."

He conceded her point with a nod. "You reckon I should save these flowers for her?"

"If you brought them for me?" Her chin lifted, hands folding over one knee. "Yes, give them to Mama instead."

"They're for your sister."

As he'd known it would, the fight fled her in a giant wave. Tension deserted every line of her sexy body, leaving her pliant against the bleacher step behind her. A visual reminder of how Kyler used to rob her of tension in a very different way. *God,* she looked hot. Even while pouting. "Aw, why'd you have to go and do that?"

Kyler sat down on the creaky wooden step beside her. "You're glad I did."

"I know. You don't have to point it out." Chewing her lip, she cut a glance at the dance floor. "I was sitting here trying to decide something."

"Lay it on me, supergirl."

Her lips parted at the nickname he'd bestowed on her years ago. After her mother left, Bree had assumed so much responsibility, playing mom to Kira, helping her father run the family business and never once letting her grades suffer. The first time he'd called her supergirl, she'd sobbed for an hour in his arms, showing Kyler how much the added responsibility had taken a toll. How hard it had been to face every day, no matter how difficult. Afterward, she'd tearfully asked him if he still thought the nickname fit. *Fits even better now,* he'd said.

It took Bree a few seconds to continue, but she didn't ask Kyler not to call her supergirl anymore. So he considered it a victory. "Kira's *date* didn't bring her flowers tonight. Didn't even come to the door. Have boys changed so much in four years or..." Something seemed to dawn on her. "You know what? Never mind."

A laugh worked its way up from Kyler's chest. "You were asking yourself if boys have changed or if they were always useless. And maybe I just happened to be the exception."

"That's *not* what I was going to say." The metal was back in her spine, lips pursed together in a way that drove him crazy. "Actually, I was wondering if being a big college star would give you an ego. You just answered my question."

"Liar." He winked to soften the accusation. "And *you* were the exception. Not the other way around. That's why I brought flowers and shook your daddy's hand at the door. I knew there'd never be another Bree Justice."

Damn. Now maybe he shouldn't have said that, seeing as how his strategy was to play the long game. He'd never been much good at keeping the truth to himself, though. Bree stared over at him from beneath her eyelashes, that pulse he used to kiss every chance he got fluttering at the base on her neck. "W-well, maybe there were no other *Brees*." She nudged him with her elbow, but the effort was half-hearted at best. "But I bet there's been gaggles of Mindys and Beckys and Crystals over the last four years, am I right?"

His throat ached with the sudden need to shout. If she only knew how *wrong* she was. When he'd first arrived in Cincinnati, he'd been so damn angry and hurt that he'd wanted to accept every single proposition that came his way. Women flocked to college football players like bees to honey—and once he'd been named an All-American, the whispered invitations had been inescapable. Constant and blatant. A few times, he'd even gotten as far as saying yes. Right before growing sick to his stomach and canceling at the last minute.

Truth was, he hadn't been with a woman since prom night with Bree.

The night she'd shattered him.

If he told her the truth now, there would be no chance of getting those broken pieces back together, though. Best to evade and clear up any misunderstandings later.

"Sure, you know how it is," Kyler managed around the golf ball in his throat. "No one special, though."

Her expression didn't change. If possible, it turned to stone. But when she went back to observing the dance floor, Kyler saw that her fingers were clutched together in her lap. "Yeah, I know how it is."

Wrong. It didn't matter *how it is* or how the athlete-groupie lifestyle operated. It didn't operate *him*. And if there was a hope in hell of him convincing Bree to build a future with a professional football player, she needed to have no doubt about that. About him.

And he would convince her. He *would*. But now was not the time to freak her out.

Stay the course, Tate.

"What about you?" He already knew the answer—he grilled his mother about Bree during their weekly phone calls—so he forced himself to relax. "Anyone...special?"

"Not yet. I've been so busy." Her voice sounded unnatural and his heart lurched in response. "I-I mean, there is one guy—"

"Come again?"

It occurred to Kyler in a blinding flash that his mother might have been trying to guard his feelings by assuring him every week that Bree remained single. And good God almighty, the very possibility gave him the urge to throw up. Then maybe go for a casual rampage through Bloomfield, overturning cars and uprooting trees.

Totally normal, right?

"I don't get calls out in Hashtown very often, but their local vet fell ill a few months back, so I traveled out that way. A sick mare. Beautiful creature." She rubbed her palms against her knees, her voice back to normal, totally oblivious to Kyler's mounting agony. "The farm's horse trainer hung out while I worked. He's the one who asked me out, but I said no. I flat out didn't have time. But he must have convinced his boss I was the better doctor because I get called out there for all manner of animal injuries and sicknesses now."

"And this fella keeps asking you out."

"Right."

"But you've been saying no."

"That's the gist of it."

Feeling like he'd been doused in gasoline and lit on fire, Kyler shot to his feet. "I don't like it, Bree Caroline."

Bree rose slowly and crossed her arms. "Don't you dare use my middle name, Kyler Joseph Tate."

"Kyler Tate! Is that you?"

They both turned thunderous stares on the interrupter.

Clearly undeterred, Kira Justice launched herself into Kyler's arms anyway.

Chapter Four

Bree wasn't prepared for seeing her little sister hugging Kyler.

In those early days, when Kyler had just left for Cincinnati, Bree lived with tunnel vision. Getting from one day to the next without a crying jag, throwing herself into learning her father's trade so she couldn't revel in missing him. On more than one occasion, being without him had gotten so unbearable, she'd considered boarding a train to the university to go get him back. Only the staunch belief she was doing the right thing for her family kept Bree putting one foot in front of the other.

For all the time and effort she put into supporting her family, however, she hadn't taken the time to consider how her sister had been impacted by the sudden lack of Kyler's presence in their lives. Clearly, Bree hadn't been the only one missing the star receiver after he left for college. No, it appeared Kira was still feeling the giant hole he'd left behind. Bree wasn't, though. Not after four years.

Certainly not.

Bree swallowed the bitterness on her tongue and focused on her sister and Kyler. It was a well-known fact that teenagers could be irreverent jerks on occasion, and Kira was smack dab in the midst of the classic know-it-all phase. When her face wasn't buried in her iPhone, it was complaining, being critical, and rolling her eyes. In between, though, the amazing woman Kira would be someday soon shone through the cracks. Just like Bree, Kira was a wizard in the classroom. Ambitious. Unlike her big sister, however, Kira loved the spotlight.

She certainly had it now. The dance had ground to a halt, and phones were up and filming the reunion. But for once, Bree's little sister seemed completely unaware of the envious attention she'd drawn. No, every ounce of her focus was fastened on Kyler. Tears made her eyes shine, one rolling free when Kyler whirled her in a circle.

"I thought it was just a rumor you were in town," Kira said, swiping away her running mascara. "And I told everyone it wasn't true. If you were in Bloomfield, my sister would be finding reasons to stay home."

Heat blasted Bree's face, but because avoidance was her best friend, she feigned deafness, picking at an imaginary thread on her dress. More cameras were being lifted, the pinhole sized lights sending Bree stepping back, out of the frames.

Kyler caught the move and frowned, but thankfully didn't join her sister in humiliating her. "How've you been, sweetheart? You been staying out of trouble?"

"Most of the time." Kira gave an exaggerated flutter of her eyelashes. "Me and Daddy saw you on the television. Drafted to the NFL. I can't *believe* it." Her eyebrows drew together. "What happened when you were climbing the stage, though? You looked like you'd seen a ghost."

Bree watched curiously as Kyler seemed to search for an answer. She'd thrown herself into work the day of the draft, afraid of what she'd feel seeing Kyler moving on to the next phase of his life. "I'd just realized I'd forgotten to do something important," Kyler said finally, catching her with a look.

"Like calling before showing up?" Bree asked, still picking at that thread. "Pretty bad habit you've picked up."

Kyler let out a big, booming laugh. "Something like that." He put an arm around Kira's shoulder and turned her toward their grinning, fascinated audience. "Which one of these lucky Bloomfield men is your date, huh? Point him out."

Before Kira could finger the accused, Chuck Brady raised his hand from behind a camera phone, flushing to the roots of his faux-hawk. "That'd be me, sir."

Kyler tucked his tongue inside his cheek, stepping back with Kira in tow to size the kid up. "And have you danced with her yet?"

"Not much of a dancer, sir." Another boy standing beside

Chuck shouted *it's true*, earning himself a shove. "I'm better on the football field."

Heads were whipping back and forth between Chuck and Kyler. Clearly, that comment had been made in an attempt to impress the town legend. It didn't work. "Is there a rule that says you can't do both?"

Chuck's friend finally got around to pushing him back. "No, sir."

"In fact, I'm not seeing much dancing between dates going on at all," Kyler said. "Boys on one side, girls on the other is what it looks like to me." He sent Bree a slow grin, eliciting dreamy sighs from every female in the gymnasium. "Correct me if I'm wrong, supergirl, but I do believe this calls for a dance off."

Equal parts terror and...exhilaration tumbled in Bree's stomach. Terror because, hello, everyone knew high school students were the scariest individuals alive. Dancing in front of them was the stuff of nightmares. And exhilaration, because, damn, she hadn't felt her blood pumping, hadn't experienced that wicked belly twist since the last time she and Kyler were in that very gymnasium together.

Which sent her spiraling right back into terror because she couldn't deny anymore that a huge, long ignored place inside of her had missed him. No one had ever succeeded in dragging her out of her comfort zone and making her enjoy it. No one but Kyler freaking Tate.

Scariest of all, Kyler always made her wish for...more. The way her mother had done before walking out on them, going in search of that elusive something *else.*

Bree had balked at his final offer to do just that, though, hadn't she? Cincinnati. Beyond. So far away from her comfort zone and those she loved—those who needed her—she never would have had the option of climbing back into it. Their plan had been to apply to the same colleges and attend as a unit.

Only, she'd kept her *real* plan tucked inside until she couldn't anymore.

"You better not be looking over here at me," Bree called, sitting back down and crossing her legs. "I'm happy right here on the bleachers."

"Gentleman, grab your partners. *Politely,*" Kyler instructed, ignoring her. "Oh, we're going to find out who has the best moves.

Yes, we are, Bree."

"No, we're not," Bree said. "Not me. No, thank you." She repeated those words right up until a minute later, when Kyler twirled her into his arms on the dance floor, laughing while she groaned. "How do you always manage to make me cave?"

The old disco ball spun above his head, sending little silver spots gliding over his smiling face. "Because deep down you want to."

Their bodies were still a few inches apart, as if they were worried about brushing together and giving off sparks. And they idled there, separated by a few breaths, Kyler's smile dimming from its position above her. Bree swallowed several times but couldn't seem to flush her heart out of her throat. His thumbs rested in the crooks of her elbows, brushing back and forth, making every bit of her skin sit up and give him its undivided attention. Eyes that had been so good-natured and sweet minutes ago were now dark, like rainclouds that absorbed memories instead of moisture. Just waiting to storm.

When a slow song—"Remind Me"—started to pump low and heavy through the crackling speakers, Kyler slipped an arm around the small of her back and tugged Bree close. Fast. As if propelled by a burst of anger. They were suddenly pressed so tightly together she could feel his warm breath at her forehead. The rises and falls of his every hard muscle, of which there were many.

"Whoa there," Bree whispered shakily. "This is a church dance."

Her words seemed to bring him back from whatever land he'd been teleported to. "Right," he rasped. "We're supposed to be setting an example."

"Yes."

"So I should definitely stop thinking about sucking on your lower lip."

Bree's thighs pressed together, her gasping inhale shivering all the way down into her tummy. Lower. "Stop that right now."

His gaze remained zeroed in on her mouth. "Stop thinking about it or saying it out loud?"

"*Both*." Trying desperately to remain indignant in the face of *that* face—and that drawl, those muscles, his familiar scent—Bree warned him with a look. "You said we were going to be friends. There's nothing the least bit friendly about lip sucking."

"I don't know." He hummed in his throat and tightened his hold around her waist. "Seems like letting me do it would be mighty friendly of you."

Bree tamped down a laugh. "Friendly or stupid?"

"Stupid?" Kyler frowned. "Why?"

"Because we both know where it leads."

Shit almighty. How had it come to this? She was plastered against her ex-boyfriend—whom she'd yet to shake completely. He looked delicious enough to eat, and now they were having a conversation about sex. And—*and*—she was wearing her feel-good dress. The one she wore when her hair was down and everything was shaved and waxed. Had she primped because Kyler was back in town? It was too infuriating to speculate on.

"You're getting pretty worked up down there, supergirl."

Bree sniffed. "I am not."

"Since you're already worked up…" he murmured into her ear, raising goosebumps down the length of her spine. "Tell me exactly where it would lead if I sucked on your lip."

Four years hadn't changed a single thing, had they? If one of them wasn't throwing down a gauntlet, the other picked up the slack, without fail. Case in point, when they'd been paired up for that fateful science presentation in middle school, they'd both been adamant about *their* idea for a subject being the best. So they'd worked on the project separately, hell bent on outdoing one another. Only to walk into class on presentation day and realize they'd written the same speech, almost word for word.

That day, midway through the oral presentation, Kyler had asked Bree out in front of the whole class. She'd stammered a yes. Then they'd promptly begun boasting about who could pick the best location for their date.

"All right, Ky," she purred, trailing a finger down the back of his neck and watching his shit-eating grin vanish. "*If* I let you that close to my mouth…it would end in your truck."

A rumble moved in his chest. "Yeah?"

"Yeah. We'd drive out to the creek, out where no one could hear us, and climb into the back bed. It's so hot out tonight, isn't it?" She tilted her head and allowed the air conditioning to cool her neck while Kyler's eyes devoured the curve of flesh hungrily. "We'd both be a little dewy from wearing clothes in the humidity…but it wouldn't stop us getting sweatier, would it, Ky?"

"No," he groaned. "Nothing ever did."

Bree almost felt guilty when she felt his erection rise to full mast. *Almost.* Because her own arousal overshadowed everything else. Throat dry, limbs restless, a warning siren went off inside her head. They were moving into dangerous territory. How had they gotten there? "Um…" She sucked in a breath and focused on swaying to the music, but her body clamored against his, furious with the lack of friction. The absence of satisfaction. "We'd get sweaty because…"

His hand fisted in the back of her dress. "Tell me, Bree. Tell me how I'd make you sweat."

"Because I'd be starving and you'd have bought me tacos," she blurted. "Spicy ones."

"Damn, you're cruel." He released a pained laugh into her hair, followed by a groan. "You'll pay for that."

"How?"

"For now?" Kyler's eyes were almost black when he pulled back, but his smile was determined. "In the dance off."

"This wasn't it?"

"Nope."

Suspicion fogged on. "Wait a minute. This is how I'm paying *for now*? What happens later?"

Kyler moved in and brushed his lips along her jawline. "Depends on how good of friends we want to be." One hand lifted to squeeze her hip, slow and possessive, that low voice directly against her ear. "Me, Bree? All due respect, I want to be the kind of friend who takes your panties home in his pocket. The kind of friend who sucks your lower lip until your fingers start fumbling with his zipper. You need a friend like that?" His labored breath matched hers. "Because trust me when I say I'll be your best fucking friend."

* * * *

Funny how plans made themselves.

Especially when you were all goal and very little game plan. The shocked expression on Bree's face was well warranted because he'd definitely just implied he'd like to fuck her mercilessly while in Bloomfield.

And yeah, he did. Christ on a pogo stick, if she'd finished that story the correct way—without the surprise taco twist—she'd be in a fireman hold over his shoulder and halfway to his truck. Hell, he'd *lost* himself in that story, seeing, tasting, feeling himself rocking into Bree while his truck creaked beneath them. That white dress would be pulled down to her waist so he could suck her nipples, rucked up around her hips so he could thrust without obstruction.

Easy, man. He was standing in the midst of dozens of high school students daydreaming about finally, *finally*, getting Bree back underneath him… And those thoughts were causing a seriously unfortunate situation in his jeans. As in, he had enough wood to build a log cabin. Not good when everyone in the place was taking pictures of him and whispering. Although he no longer knew if they were whispering because they considered him some kind of celebrity. Or on account of his up close and personal dance with Bree. It was a coin toss.

"Are you two finished *re-u-niting* so we can start this dance off?" Kira asked, stepping between him and Bree. The younger girl's intrusion poured cold water on the fire below, thank God, but when she waved a hand in front of his face, Kyler realized he was still staring hard at his gorgeous ex-girlfriend. At least Bree was staring back just as hard. That had to mean something, right? "Are we doing boys versus girls?"

"Yeah," Kyler answered, clearing the rust from his voice. "Boys under the scoreboard. Girls by the bleachers. Pick your best five." He shot a wink over Kira's head. "As long as one of them is your sister."

Bree, still visibly dumbfounded by his blunt speech, seemed to rouse herself. "You know what?" Her beautiful eyes flashed, speeding his need for her back to the forefront. "It's *on*, Kyler Tate."

Jesus, he loved her. Couldn't she see it? That he would never love another woman as long as they both lived? "Oh, it's on, is it?" He gave a sharp whistle that sent every dude in the gym hustling toward the scoreboard. "We battle last, supergirl. That ought to give you time to prepare."

"Prepare for what? To make you look foolish?" She jerked her thumb in the direction of the bleachers and the girls ran past her, giggling. "But you're doing such a good job of it yourself."

Both sides of the gymnasium weighed in with a simultaneous

"*Ohhhh.*"

"You know what? I'm going to let my dancing do the talking." Praying he still remembered how, Kyler moonwalked into the waiting group of guys, who welcomed him with worshipping looks and smacks on the back. "We'll even concede song choice, right, men? Just to show how confident we are."

"Rookie move," Bree mouthed, before turning and jogging for the DJ booth. Kyler watched her go with his heart lodged somewhere behind his jugular. When he'd walked in, Bree had been sitting in the shadows alone and he'd hated it. Hated her being hidden, no one there to point out how amazing she was, just like he'd been unable to stand having her in the background in high school. Now that she was animated, glowing, satisfaction had been breathed into Kyler's veins, so heavy and real, he couldn't move without feeling it. Feeling *her*.

But…she preferred the background. Right? Isn't that why she'd ended their relationship? When he'd been accepted to the university, he'd been so positive she would get the same letter soon enough. They'd filled out those applications together, laying side by side on the floor of his bedroom, laptops open. Looking back now, he remembered Bree being so quiet while they'd written essays and answered questions. Months later, he'd found out why.

So now he was back in Bloomfield, back to his old tricks. He'd been in town less than one day and he'd already caused a scene outside the diner and pushed Bree into a dance off. What if the truth was just too painful for him to accept, even four years later? What if he simply wasn't the kind of man Bree wanted?

All those years ago on prom night, she'd made it clear she'd decided on a quiet life, far away from the noisy crowds that came along with him. Did he have a hope in hell of convincing her otherwise? What if he couldn't?

Bree slipped back to the front of her lady crew, shoulders thrown back in a cocky pose, but her smug expression disappeared when she locked eyes with Kyler. "You okay?"

He nodded once and turned away before Bree could see deeper, the way only she ever could. "All right, men. Which four among you is the bravest?"

One hand went up.

Kyler issued a quick prayer toward the ceiling. "I'm going to pass on some valuable information. You ready?"

"Yes, sir," they all answered, well-mannered country boys to the core.

"Those girls aren't waiting around for you to take initiative. They have a whole bunch of initiative all their own if they want to use it. But they'll appreciate a guy a lot more for trying. And does anyone know what happens when girls appreciate you?"

"Sex?"

"*No*." His genuine outrage made several of them laugh. "No. Not…well, fine. Yes. But kissing was the answer I was looking for. *Kissing.*" He made eye contact with every single one of them. "Except when it comes to Kira Justice. Leave her be and that's an order." He clapped his hands once. "Now, who's willing to make a fool out of themselves in the name of glory and potential kissing?"

Every single hand went up.

Unfortunately, that's when, "Run the World (Girls)," by Beyoncé crackled through the speakers.

Kyler disguised his curse with a laugh. "No backing out now."

The triumph on Bree's face when he turned back around was worth the awkward dances that followed. Smooth definitely couldn't be used to describe the jolting moves displayed by the men he'd sent into battle, but at least Kyler made good on his promise. The girls were definitely laughing as one by one, the four battles took place in the center of the basketball court, a clear winner each time.

With the song almost over, Bree and Kyler finally got their turn—and of course the fates had them competing in a tie breaker.

For all Bree's unwillingness to be the center of attention, she could move like nobody's business. In the midst of their competition, she'd forgotten all about being shy and Kyler thanked the dear Lord for that fact. The way she swaggered out to meet him at center court was nothing short of a miracle. Those gorgeous, long-legged strides had him growling low in his throat, looking her up and down when she stopped a mere inch away… And without a verbal agreement, they began circling one another, mean mugging the whole time. The laughter from either side was so loud it almost drowned out the music, and neither one of them could help the smiles they were battling.

"Ladies first," he drawled, sweeping his hand out in a wide

gesture. "Better make it count."

"Better watch and learn."

She brought the house down. There was no other way to put it. With a cocky grin on her face, she danced circles around him, taunting him and sticking her tongue out behind his back. Kyler was only guessing about that, but the crowd's reaction bolstered his theory. It took every ounce of his willpower not to pull her into a bear hug as she spun past, all graceful limbs and flushed pleasure.

God above, what a woman. The *only* woman.

If he broke during one of their challenges, though, Bree would never let him live it down, which was only one of the reasons he loved her. The need to win never stopped flowing in his blood and Bree's presence fired it up even more. Channeling that desire into football was his usual method of meeting that need, but hell, today it was dancing.

So as soon as it was Kyler's turn, he pulled out all the stops.

He twerked. And he twerked hard.

It was a tie.

Kyler reckoned the outcome of their challenge couldn't have been more perfect because it gave him an excuse to track Bree down as soon as possible to issue another one.

Chapter Five

"What do you mean, you never sent in your applications?" Kyler tugged on his bow tie like it was choking him, eventually throwing it down on the damp earth surrounding the creek. "We did them together. We...Bree, it was hours, just the two of us—"

"That's why I did them. I loved being with you." Tears blurred the sight of him. "The ones I actually sent in were for pre-vet programs closer to home. I can't leave my home. The business. My family."

He stared at Bree like she was speaking in a different language. "But we'd be together." His whisper turned into a shout. "I'm your home."

Bree's heart lurched. "This isn't easy for me. M-my mom—"

"Not easy for you?" He turned and paced away, attacking his hair with agitated fingers. "I'm leaving. I'm leaving and you won't be with me. We'll be apart. That's not how this was supposed to happen."

"It was always going to happen like this." She held tight to the lapels of the jacket he'd draped over her shoulders, positive it was the only thing keeping her glued together. She'd felt that way since earlier, when he'd arranged to have them dance together at prom, her heart twisting at yet another reminder of what she'd soon be giving up. "Right now, we're in this tiny town. But someday, Ky, someday you're going to be too big to fit inside of it anymore. That scares me. I'm scared of where you're headed."

"There's only us, Bree." He shook his head. "The rest is just noise."

As Bree had known it would be, choosing to remain in Bloomfield over going with the boy she loved was excruciating. She had to hold fast, though. Deep in her bones, there was a need to stay rooted. Right where she'd been standing since the walls threatened to crumble around her family once before. Holding them up was her job. She'd taken on the responsibility and wouldn't shirk that duty. Not now. Not ever. No matter how much it killed her. "I'm happy with what I have. I have to be." She tried to swallow the knife in her throat, but it only dug in deeper. "I'm sorry. I'm staying right here, right where I'm needed."

"No." He came forward, framing her face in his hands. "No."

"Yes—"

His kiss cut her off and for long moments, all she could do was sink into it. Let it pull her down. Ever since Kyler's star had started to rise, she'd let her reservations get lost in times like these. When she'd put off the inevitable in favor of his touch, his words. Their senior year was all but finished, though, and after dancing with him tonight, seeing their future playing out in his green eyes, she couldn't put it off any more.

Kyler groaned, his strong hands locking their hips together, rolling their lower bodies as he sunk hungry teeth into her bottom lip. God, if she let him pull her down to the soft earth and use their attraction as a bargaining chip, there was every chance he could persuade her from her decision. And she couldn't allow that.

"I'm sorry," Bree whispered, breaking free of his hold. "Good bye, Ky."

She could still feel his touch as she ran away along the creek bed, scalding tears coasting down her cheeks.

Bree's cell phone buzzed in her pocket for the fifth time in a row. Again, she ignored it, focusing instead on the wounded golden retriever she was attending. He lay on a ten-seat kitchen table, surrounded by his family, each of whom whispered comforting words and stroked some section of the nervous dog.

"Now, don't you worry," Bree murmured, smiling at the youngest member of the family, a six-year-old girl. "Bowser is one tough dog. That coyote only got a tiny nibble out of him. He's going to heal up just fine."

The little girl relaxed, smiling into her mother's hip, although she continued to eye the blood-dappled sheet beneath the dog with trepidation. Bree usually preferred to work in private when making house calls, but when it came to beloved family dogs, she made an exception. It was obvious they were providing much needed comfort for Bowser as Bree finished stitching and bandaging the bite mark on the dog's right front leg.

Moments like these, telling people their animal would recover, made the struggle through school worth every penny. Made it worth never feeling fully rested. She took pride in her work and the business her father had built. When her parents had moved to Bloomfield in the eighties and opened the practice, it had taken hard work to get it off the ground. They were not only the new folks in town, they were an interracial couple—her mother white, her father African-American—in a place where that hadn't been considered typical, meaning they'd faced a lot of curiosity and adversity early on.

While her father had worked triple time to prove his skill as a veterinarian, Bree's mother turned restless. Her father had confided in Bree later on that her mother found contentment hard to achieve. Always had. He didn't even fault her for it, which confused Bree to this day. A loving family, a town that had embraced them, a thriving business. What more had she needed?

Calls like this one were a reminder to Bree that she had everything she needed right here in Bloomfield. She had the community's trust, friends, family. Contentment. Her father did the inpatient work at the office so he wouldn't have to travel, which meant Bree rarely had the privilege of working with canines, most of her calls concerning horses and cattle. It was rare that she witnessed the love between family members and their pets up close. Which had to account for the little spark of yearning in her breast, right?

A family of her own was something Bree had stopped dreaming about without even realizing, it seemed. How long had it been since she'd pictured her own children racing around the yard after their puppy? School, work, and running the house had put those dreams on hold, but they were trickling back in now as she watched the father reach over and squeeze the little girl's shoulder.

Heat pressed against the back of Bree's eyelids.

Shit almighty. What was up with her today?

"Almost done here," Bree said. "Bowser is going to need lots of rest. I'm going to leave a prescription for painkillers to crush up in his food. And before I leave, we'll have to put a cone on him so he doesn't ruin his stitches." She smiled at the little girl. "I'm recommending lots of doggie treats for the next week. Doctor's orders."

"I can give him those," whispered the six-year-old.

"Good. I'm counting on you."

Bree cut the final thread and tied it tight before disinfecting the wound once more and wrapping the damaged leg with a bandage.

The cell phone went off in her pocket a sixth time.

Worried Kira needed her for something, Bree peeled off her gloves and excused herself under the guise of retrieving the cone from her truck. As soon as she closed the front door behind her, Bree plucked the phone out of her pocket, refusing to acknowledge the lick of excitement that slid up her spine at the possibility it could be Kyler. When she saw the name Heidi blinking on the screen instead, she flicked away the disappointment and braced herself.

"Hello?"

"Woman, this conversation needs to start with something better than a damn *hell*-o. It deserves a cymbal crash or a British accent. I don't know. But hello ain't cutting it."

Heidi lived for drama. In high school, she'd been the lead in every school play from *Wizard of Oz* to *Cats*. When the stage wasn't an option, she created her own titillating scenarios, playing matchmaker to her friends just so she could sit back and watch the fireworks. Underneath the lip stains and bleached white hair, though, Heidi had an overly-sensitive heart of gold. Which was why Bree considered the town's gym receptionist her best friend, even though they were polar opposites.

"Okay, I'll bite. Why is this conversation going to be so earth-shattering?"

"Oh no. You make me call you thirty-nine times, you're going to wait for the Tootsie Roll center, baby. Keep licking."

Bree snort-laughed. "You called me six times."

"Splitting hairs." Heidi hummed and Bree waited, knowing her friend wouldn't be able to hold out on sharing whatever gossip she was peddling for long. "Heard you danced all your business up on Kyler Tate last night."

Bree's jaw dropped down to her knees. "That better not be why you're calling me, Heidi. It was innocent fun. At a *church* dance."

"You fix those animals up better than you lie. That's what I know."

"Ooh. I'm fixing to *hang up*."

"You will *not*." A phone rang in the background and Heidi gave a long-suffering sigh. "Hold on, I've got another call."

"Don't—"

The line went silent and Bree stomped the remaining distance to her truck, going through the list of suspects of who might have ratted her out. Kira, most likely. Her little sister and Heidi were Facebook friends and Bree was pretty sure they messaged on the regular. After Kyler had walked Bree and a bouquet-toting Kira to the parking lot last night, pressing a polite, if lingering, kiss on Bree's cheek, her sister hadn't let up a single second. Were they back in love? Was Kyler a good kisser?

Hell yes, he was. Not that she'd be sharing that information with Kira or anyone else, for that matter. The man had a method of kissing that Bree always suspected had been specifically designed to turn her wild. At the start, Kyler played aggressor. But as soon as she got good and worked up, he let her take the lead, encouraging her with his hands, his tongue, his husky groans. Basically, he turned himself into her own personal playground.

Heidi's voice popped the daydream bubble over her head. "I'm back."

"Guhh." Bree shook herself free of kissing memories. "I-I don't have long. I'm putting a cone on a golden retriever, then I have another appointment."

"Fine, I'll stop torturing you. But I want the details of this alleged dirty dance with Kyler. *Grown-up* ones."

"Ha! I knew it was Kira who ratted."

Her best friend clucked her tongue. "Speaking of Mr. Tate…"

Bree paused in the act of removing the plastic cone from a supply bag on the passenger seat. Her lack of movement only made her pounding heart more noticeable. Since yesterday, when Kyler announced *pretty as you please* that he intended to take her for dinner, she'd been living on the edge of—what? Anticipation? Fear? Bree only knew her focus had been hijacked along with her common sense. Because some crazy part of her wanted to say yes.

Not that she would. Oh no. That dance with Kyler last night had proven one very troubling fact. She wasn't *quite* over him yet. Not her heart and not her body. Dinner would only make it worse. Make her…less than content.

"What *about* Kyler?" Bree asked, striving for casual.

"He's here in the gym," Heidi answered. "Working out like it's no big thing."

"It's not a big thing," Bree said automatically, already conjuring up an image of him in sweaty shorts. "Right?"

"Tell that to the string of admirers glued to the windows. A bunch of suction-cupped Baby on Board signs. You know the ones?" Heidi's chair creaked in the background. "That's what they look like, drooling over your man like that. Can you believe the nerve?"

"He's...he's not my man."

"So you don't mind if Karen Hawthorne asks him out?"

"What?" Bree's stomach plummeted. "When did Karen Hawthorne come into the picture?"

"Since now." Satisfaction weighed down Heidi's tone over successfully getting Bree's attention. "I can see that hen in the fox house from here. She's parked at the curb, fixing her mascara in the rearview. That's as good as confirmation in my book."

A pressure formed on top of Bree's lungs, pushing down. "So...she should go ahead and ask him." She tried to swallow, but her throat was as dry as the desert. "It's none of my business."

"No, I suppose not." Bree could hear Heidi's manicured fingernails tapping the reception desk. *Clack. Clack. Clack.* "Hell. You can't really blame the woman, can you? Kyler Tate, soon to be professional NFL receiver, rolls up into the local gym looking like something out of *Sports Illustrated*. He runs so fast and so long, he soaks his T-shirt right through with sweat. It's *so wet*, he has to take it off and—"

Bree dropped the cone, straightening in the truck's front seat. "Kyler...it's...he took his shirt off?"

"That's exactly what I said." Smug. Heidi was so smug. "Now, you know I have a man and I do *not* have a wandering eye, but Bree, when an unattached man walks into your town looking so mighty, so heavy with muscle, like he could grind a woman's vagina to *fine powder*, ladies start fixing their mascara. It's just the nature of the beast." She blew out at a breath. "Good thing he ain't your man, huh?"

"Stall her. I'll be there in ten."

"Consider it done."

Chapter Six

Nothing is ever going to be the same, is it?

Kyler hurried through his final repetition of bicep curls and replaced the weight on the rack. The tiny but functional gym was lined with floor-to-ceiling mirrors and every few seconds, a camera phone flash would go off, reflecting back at him. He pretended not to see them, but each one smarted. Home represented a place he could relax. Let his guard down. A place where no one would demand perfection from him. Maybe it couldn't be that way anymore.

He loved the people of Bloomfield. The saying "It takes a village to raise a child" applied directly to his home town. Growing up, he'd been lectured by the local florist about the importance of proper apologies. Been told to tuck in his shirt by every senior in town at least twice. And he'd gone along with the owners of Nelson's Diner to feed the less fortunate every year during the holidays. His greatest life lessons were wrapped up in this place.

But with camera flashes going off and people waiting outside for signatures, he suddenly felt like a stranger to everyone. Even…himself.

Lord, who *was* Kyler Tate anymore? Who would he be in Los Angeles? Would he be able to hold on to himself, his core, if coming home only fed him more of the same lack of reality?

Who was he kidding? The cameras might have bothered him once upon a time, but he'd grown accustomed to them. This was about Bree. Who would *Bree* become if he took her out of this place? Dance floors and halftime surprises were one thing, but if he loved Bree, would he be so intent on taking her to Los Angeles, knowing it could make her unhappy?

"Ky."

He lifted his head and saw Bree in the mirror behind him. On cue, his gut cinched inward, heat rippling outward from his belly. No other woman had ever elicited the smallest percentage of his body's reaction to Bree. Not ever. No one ever would, either, because his heart was connected to every part of him. His heart knew what it wanted and it wouldn't waver.

So he would give Bree a happy life. One way or another. *How* he would do so remained to be seen. He'd come to Bloomfield to convince her that the attention and notoriety wouldn't be so bad. That as long as they were together, the cameras would be irrelevant. At this very moment, he should be making light of their presence, hoping she would follow suit. Instead, he stood there and stared back at her, trying to telegraph every damning thought in his head.

I'm miserable. I hate the cameras because you hate them.

Here was the truth. Hiding from someone you love wasn't an option because all you *really* wanted was them to come find you.

Bree's eyes were soft, her head tilted. Kyler remembered that look from many an occasion. Sympathy shot through with steel. An expression singular to Bree and one an athlete like himself needed to be on the receiving end of frequently. It said "I understand, this sucks, but don't even *think* about wimping out on me."

He wasn't quite ready to put his game face back on, so he looked away. "You here for a workout?"

"It would seem so," Bree murmured, flashes going off behind her. "Hard to concentrate with all that ruckus going on outside, I bet."

"It's fine." Kyler turned, watching her chew that sweet lower lip. "I can go if you want some privacy."

"Since when do you care about that?"

She meant it as a joke, but the gravity of it wrapped around him like a giant squid. His mouth tried to issue a rejoinder, same as always, but it got stuck. Since when, indeed? Countless times since middle school, he'd dragged her into center stage, against her will. Now he was back trying to do it again.

"I…" Regret shone in Bree's eyes as she shifted. Kyler immediately surged forward to reassure her, but she danced out of his reach. "I have a better idea than you leaving. You see, Heidi knows how to sit and look pretty—"

"*I heard that!*"

Bree winced at her friend's distant shout but didn't halt her progress toward the windows. "She means well, that *sweet baby angel* Heidi, but if she'd only known about these..." Bree tugged on a cord and a blackout shade dropped down, covering one of the windows. "You might have been more comfortable."

One by one, his insanely beautiful ex-girlfriend lowered shades in front of each window, ducking her head to avoid the disappointed frowns from onlookers. Soon enough, the two of them were cocooned inside the tiny room, with only a bench press between them. The low beat of rap music matched the pulse drumming in his wrists, his neck. "Thank you."

"Welcome." For the first time since arriving, her gaze skittered down to his bare chest and Kyler watched closely, noticing her fingers curled into her palms. Her lips rolled inward. One of her shoulders twitched, like she wanted to shrug off whatever she was feeling, but her body wouldn't quite allow it. Her tells all played out in a matter of two seconds and Kyler wished he could rewatch it over and over for the rest of his life. Hiding their attraction to one another had always been impossible. "I see you've made yourself comfortable," she said finally, her voice throatier than before.

Suspicion had Kyler narrowing his eyes. "If you came down here for a workout, you're sure as hell not dressed for it."

"I work out in leggings all the time."

"You're wearing your doctor coat."

"I..." She cleared her throat. "Have a tank top underneath."

Kyler crossed his arms and waited, laughing under his breath as vexation flashed in her eyes. Bree's hesitation was brief, before she unbuttoned the white coat and shrugged it off her shoulders. What she revealed had Kyler's cock waking up with a vengeance, straining against the front of his shorts. "That's not a tank top."

"Sports bra, tank top. Same difference." Her hands fluttered in front of the expanse of bare stomach between the white bra and the waistband of her leggings, as if wanting to cover herself. "I was running late this morning."

Drawn to his counterpart by a force stronger than himself, Kyler skirted past the bench press and stopped in front of Bree. Taking a long inhale of her crisp morning dew scent and inwardly groaning at the effect it had, he slipped a finger beneath the strap of her bra, dragging the digit over the curve of her shoulder and down the slope of Bree's back. And he circled her, watching the rise of goosebumps appear on her neck. Her back and arms. When she shivered, her head dropping forward, there was nothing Kyler could do to resist the temptation of her nape. His mouth hovered over it, breathing, but she turned and evaded before he could taste her.

Foggy brown eyes raked him. "Kyler—"

"What really brought you down here?" His tone was so low, the music nearly swallowed up his question. "I know when you're telling lies, Bree Caroline."

Her chin firmed but her eyes danced away. *Goddamn.* He *loved* her like this. Guilty and indignant. It signaled that he'd won a battle, she wasn't happy about it and would compete twice as hard next time. That fire in her stoked his own like nothing else could. Not even football.

"Karen Hawthorne was out fixing her mascara in the rearview." Bree crossed her arms and lifted her chin. "Aren't you the one who said we should be friends? Yes, yes, you did. And I was just looking out for my friend." She sniffed. "She's a viper, that one. Tried to steal Heidi's man right out from under her nose."

Kyler had nineteen female cousins and they'd haunted his house while growing up, so he considered himself pretty adept at deciphering girl code. Clearly he'd overestimated himself. "What does mascara have to do with anything?"

She shook her head at Kyler like he was a simpleton. "It means she was fixing to ask you out."

"And you didn't like that idea." Satisfaction simmered in his gut. "Gotta say, I'm beginning to warm to this conversation."

"Well, cool off. I was just being friendly."

"I could eat you up in one bite in that outfit, supergirl."

Kyler dropped his gaze just in time to watch her stomach hollow, leaving a tiny gap between her smooth belly and the waistband of her leggings. His attention dragged higher and was rewarded with the hardening of her nipples, the anxious wetting of her lips. The girl needed a good, hard ride as bad as he did.

Unfortunately, she would die before admitting it, which meant a lot of finesse was required.

"Y'all, I'm going to—" Heidi popped her head around the corner, turning into the cat who caught the canary when she glimpsed Bree's attire. "I'm going to run out for an iced coffee, so I should be gone about twenty minutes. I'll be locking the door behind me, should that information be of any interest to you."

"It's not," Bree called.

"Thank you, Heidi," Kyler said at the same time.

Neither one of them moved as the lock clicked in the distance.

Chapter Seven

Shit. Almighty.

In high school, Kyler had been in great shape. Six pack, big shoulders, biceps for days, ample height without the awkwardness. The whole nine.

College had turned him from a prince into a god.

Bree went to church on Sundays, so she knew the comparison was blasphemous, but she'd ask for forgiveness later. Like when her brain cells were finished playing ping pong with her common sense. Which would not be happening with six foot four inches of brawn staring her in the face. Kyler had so many ledges, cuts, and bulges of muscle, Bree had the urge to strap on a harness and scale him like a rock climbing wall.

Too close. He was standing *way* too close. The smell of sweat and Nautica Blue climbed on board and got cozy. Lord, his calf muscles were the size of grapefruits. Those mesh shorts, riding so breathtakingly low on his pronounced hip bones, were doing exactly zero good at hiding just how *effective* her unplanned striptease had been. It hadn't been her aim to turn him on, but she definitely had. And now her own screams and moans from all those years ago were echoing in her ears like a taunt.

Kyler knew exactly how to use what lived inside his shorts. The memories of just how well were creating a weight in her tummy, pressing down, down, until wetness formed between her thighs. His parted lips and quick breaths said he knew it, too. "Don't let me keep you from your workout, Bree."

"Right," she rasped. Brushing past him, her arm grazed his

ridged chest, making him groan. Bree barely resisted doing the same.

He followed her through the maze of equipment, slowly, close enough that she could hear his breaths. Her inner walls clenched tight when he made a rough sound and without turning around, she knew he was admiring her backside. *God.* God, this was a very bad situation. Closed in the tiny gym with Kyler, no one there to interrupt or distract them, if he made a move, Bree wasn't sure she had the strength to decline. It wasn't merely the fact that she'd gone four years without sex. No. It was her chemistry with Kyler, specifically. They'd gone from daily wild, desperate encounters at the creek, in his truck, behind the school…to nothing. No contact.

Her hormones were demanding she fix the way she'd slighted them. And since they hadn't been this vocal since prom night, she couldn't deny that the yearning was all for Kyler. Dammit. This was very bad. She'd made so much progress moving on.

Hadn't she?

Bree stopped at the vertical knee raise, a machine designed to work the abdomen, turned, and climbed on. Right away, she realized she'd chosen the wrong machine. It was a well-known fact that lifting your knees up to your chest while suspended sparked a down low tickle, which only increased with repetition. Throw in the scenery— her bare-chested, sexy as a motherfucker, fresh from pumping iron, aroused ex-boyfriend—and the down low tickle threatened to become a riot of lust.

"I don't need an audience," Bree managed, executing her first lift.

Kyler fastened his gaze on her stomach, where she hoped a decent flex of muscle was taking place. "Maybe not, supergirl, but you demand one." His tone was deep, sending the pulse in her neck into a flutter. A fast one. "Where were you when Heidi called?"

"I don't know what you're talking—" Bree huffed a sigh. "You knew she was going to call me, didn't you?"

He appeared to be fighting a grin. "Didn't answer my question."

"A coyote got hold of a golden retriever named Bowser." That low thrum began between her legs, intense and weighted, but she kept raising her knees, because Kyler was watching, waiting for her to say uncle and quit early. "He's going to be fine after some rest and healing."

"I've never had a chance to see you work." He didn't look happy about it, but the brooding set of his brow only made him sexier. Lift. Lift. The dull throb between her legs turned sharp, urgent. "Let me. While I'm here."

While he's here. He's leaving. "If the chance arises."

"Fine enough. For now." His tongue slid from one corner of his lips to the other. "How are these leg raises treating you? Feeling a pull anywhere?"

"Uh-uh," she said too quickly. "Nope."

"Oh no?" The next time she raised her legs, Kyler caught her beneath both knees, his movement so lightning quick she sucked in a breath, her heart flying into a chaotic hammering pace. A wicked glint flashed in Kyler's eyes. Bree didn't have a chance to decipher it before he pushed her knees higher, all the way to her shoulders, squeezing all those sensitive, aroused muscles and starting a ringing in her ears. "How about now?"

"Uh…" She gave up pretending to breathe normally, her neck ceasing to support her head. "Ky, please…"

And then she felt it. Tiny bites along the insides of her thighs, branding her through the cotton leggings. Slow, precise, *just* enough pressure. Commanding her neck to play ball, Bree looked down to find Kyler's eyelids at half mast, his white teeth sinking in every couple inches, his own chest and stomach shuddering in and out, his nipples in tight points. At the sight, the walls of Bree's core constricted and released with enough force to send a rattling gasp flying from her mouth.

"*Kyler.*"

"Bree?"

"Just…"

"Yeah." His double grip beneath her knees vanished, but before her legs could fall, Kyler was inserting his hips to catch them. One arm snaked around the base of her spine, sliding her forward and out of the machine…and then there she was. Legs wrapped around her ex-boyfriend's waist, heart pounding, moisture pooled between her thighs, their mouths separated only by a matter of an inch.

"You wore that cologne on purpose," she breathed. "Admit it."

His grin flashed. "Guilty as charged and unrepentant as a sinner."

Her gasp only widened his smile. "Bragging about sinning now, are you, Kyler?"

"You say my name all shaken up and sexy like that when you want me to kiss your pretty mouth." Hunger made his tone sound like two knives sharpening each other. "I reckon nothing has changed."

With those vivid green eyes penetrating her defenses, Bree couldn't have lied to save her life. "Yes," she whispered, her voice catching at the feel of his erection full and proud against the seam of her leggings, the warm press of his abdomen muscles at her belly. "I- in the name of being friendly and all."

Kyler rolled his hips and Bree saw stars. "It's just good manners making your pussy wet, is that right?"

"Yes?"

"Hush up, Bree."

His mouth claimed Bree's at the same time one big hand found her bottom, pulling her close, grinding their lower bodies together. And so their first kiss after four years started with an identical groan born of frustration, before it spiraled straight into madness.

Kyler wasted no time taking on the role of aggressor, his tongue sliding in to mark its territory, licking over hers once, twice, three times, before twining around it, sucking with a desperate sound, licking more.

Sensation exploded in Bree's body...but also her mind. It was like turning on a Jumbotron in a dark stadium, waking up an entire sleeping crowd and having them erupt with a foot-stomping standing ovation. Heat pulsed between her thighs, in her nipples, the sensitive areas of her neck. As if she were being touched everywhere at once, her skin kneaded by fire.

Kyler's strong hand moved in punishing efficiency on her backside, gripping her flesh tight, hefting her up when she started to slip, growling every time she re-settled on his hardness. Teasing her with low-key upthrusts designed to drive her insane. Craving a loss of control from him, ready to sell her soul for friction, Bree's legs began to move involuntarily, up and down his hips, trying to get closer, climb higher, rubbing herself on Kyler's thick flesh in the process.

"*Jesus, Bree.*" His lips slanted open over hers, released a shuddering breath right against her mouth before diving back in with barely leashed intensity. "This is how it always used to start. 'Hug me, Kyler. Keep me warm.' Soon enough, you'd have a leg around me. Didn't take long before the other one followed, did it?" They both shook their heads no, causing their lips to graze together. "No, it didn't. Now open your eyes and keep them on me while you remind me of the rest."

Bree didn't realize her eyes were closed until Kyler's words shot them open. "We'd be at the creek, most times." A lusty haze wrapped around them. "And y-you'd wait for my say-so—"

"Soon as you flashed me those eyes—you know, you *know* the hot little teasing way you did it—then I'd get on top of you, wouldn't I? Pin you down like I couldn't help it." His groan made her nipples tighten painfully. "Shit, Bree. I could barely unzip my pants and shove up your skirt, you'd have me shaking so hard."

"I'd be shaking, too," she admitted huskily, wondering if it was possible to have an orgasm just from knowing how well Kyler remembered those nights at the creek. When they were so high on each other, nothing and no one else in the world existed. Kind of like right now?

The thought might have thrown off Bree, but Kyler's tongue danced back into her mouth with enough skill to muffle it. Her fingers tingled with the need to plow through his hair and Bree obliged them, savoring the hitch in his breath. She felt the shift of control, Kyler allowing her to play. He rocked back on his heels, hips angling out to give her a sexy perch while she charted the kiss, desire detonating along her spine as his hands rode up, up and around to her breasts.

"Tell me the rest of the story," Kyler rasped at her lips. "What would happen after I'd get your skirt shoved up to your belly button? After I got a good look at your tight pussy in the moonlight?"

Bree opened her mouth to answer or moan—she had no idea which—but the response stuck in her throat when Kyler lifted her sports bra, exposing her breasts. "*Kyler.*"

With a croaked curse, he sucked one bud into his mouth, his hands sliding down to span her waist, squeezing. And he didn't let up, mouthing the tip of her breast between his lips, flickering his tongue against it. Bree could do nothing but hold on to the strands of his hair and offer herself up.

She was so lost in the oncoming rumble of a climax, she sucked in a breath at the ragged sound of his voice. "Waiting on that story, Bree. My cock is aching like a son of a bitch from having your legs around me. You've given me the look. Now you're pinned underneath me with your panties off on the creek bed." His tongue curled around her left nipple before giving it a light bite. "What happens next?"

"You'd…" The words she was about to say made her tremble, right down to her throbbing center. "You'd push yourself inside of me."

As if he thought she wouldn't have the nerve to say it out loud, his body dipped and staggered forward a step. "Had to find a different spot every week because we'd wear the grass down to nothing. From fucking on top of it. Wouldn't we, Bree?"

Oh my God. She could feel the grass beneath her now, tearing away at the roots, Kyler's hips pumping, his voice straining near her ear. "Yes."

Kyler wound a fist in her hair and tugged, his face looming above hers. "You want me to push myself up inside you right now?"

Yes, yes, yes. So close. She was *so close*. There was a good reason she should say no, but her body was in the throes of arousal so painful, tears were prickling behind her eyelids. "I-I—"

With a massive sigh, Kyler stopped rolling his body, dropping his forehead down onto hers. "That's not a yes."

She searched his heated expression up close. "I just can't…shake the feeling you want more than this from me."

Until that moment, Bree hadn't acknowledged the little voice in the back of her head telling her Kyler wasn't operating like his usual self. That his behavior was suspicious. And at her words, his green gaze sharpened. "Dinner," he said after a long hesitation. "I want dinner." His right eyebrow lifted. "Unless you're scared."

Bree dropped her legs and shoved away from Kyler, not too proud to admit she was still *dangerously* turned on. So was he. Every single inch of him. But until she figured out his angle, no way was she taking any chances letting her guard down. "All right, Ky. I'll have dinner with you."

"Yeah?"

"Yeah. Tomorrow night at my house." She fluttered her

eyelashes. "My daddy will be so thrilled to see you."

Kyler narrowed his eyes, but not before she saw grudging approval drift across his face. It was a well-known fact that Bree's father was the one person in town Kyler had never won over. Probably because he'd been sneaking her out to the creek after dark since junior year and returning her home with grass stains. The fact that Bree was an active and eager participant wouldn't have mattered to Samuel Justice, though. No one was good enough for his girls and that, as they say, was that.

"I'll be there," Kyler said. "Your father still a Scotch drinker?"

"Now and again." She found her coat on the floor and put it on, determined to ignore the observance of Kyler's hungry eyes. "Bring whatever you like; it won't make a difference."

"Sounds like this calls for a bet."

Despite her better judgment, Bree's interest was piqued. "What did you have in mind?"

Kyler ambled toward her, looking like a big, sexy beast who'd had his meat dragged away before he could devour it. "If I win your daddy over this time around, you come down to the creek with me afterward."

Yearning and excitement braided together in her middle. "So your plan is to win him over, then lose favor just as fast?"

He smirked and held out his hand. "Do we have a bet?"

Again, the intuition that she was missing a piece of the bigger picture simmered in the back of her mind. But she'd never turned down a challenge from this man and wouldn't start now. She reached out and shook with Kyler, but before she could retrieve her hand, he snared her wrist. Dragged her right up against him.

"I would trade anything that happened on the field over the last four years..." He spoke in a rough whisper against her ear. "...to keep that kiss we just had from fading away. You hear me, Bree Caroline?"

Her heart rolled over and purred inside her chest. "Still a charmer, I see," Bree managed, easing past Kyler toward the exit just as Heidi returned. She muttered a hello and good-bye to her friend, prepared to leave. Before opening the door, she turned and glanced over her shoulder, finding Kyler staring after her in a way she recognized. Like she was a football about to be snapped. But his smile restored itself when he caught her looking.

Moments later, when Bree reached the sidewalk, a thought stopped her in her tracks. She'd called Kyler a charmer. As if sweet words were something that just rolled off his tongue in every direction. That wasn't true, though. It never had been.

He'd *only* ever been a charmer...for her.

Bree shook herself and kept walking. Time had changed everything and she needed to remember that. His charm wasn't reserved just for her anymore.

But a hazy intuition continued to gnaw at her.

Along with an army of angry, thwarted hormones.

Chapter Eight

Kyler leaned against the porch rail of his family home, staring out at the surrounding cornfields and really *seeing* them for the first time in his life. When he was a child, the Tate farm was a given. The immortal place he'd been born that would never change or be taken away. Last December, however, they'd had the notion of immortality torn away when the bank attempted to repossess the land on account of late mortgage payments.

Now the cornfields looked completely different. They were more elusive. Looking at them called to mind the passage of time, the people that came before him and would come after. As he'd gotten older, a tug of war had begun inside Kyler, the farm right at the center of the rope. Football could support the people and place he loved…but pursuing the sport professionally required his absence. Required him to grow and change in a place far away from Bloomfield. Maybe even meant he would return a different man some day.

The ink was finished drying on his contract with the Rage. He'd stood on the Draft Day stage and pledged loyalty to a team. A lot like the cornfields, continuing on in the sport seemed like a given.

But not so long ago, him and Bree being together forever had seemed like a given, too. Having the rug ripped out from beneath a man brought into perspective what was important. Was it coming too late to make a difference?

Kyler's mother pulled up in her station wagon, kicking up dust on the dirt driveway. When he caught her hooded glance through the windshield, common sense told him he was in for a lecture about something. In no rush to find out what it concerned, he jogged down the steps to help with the groceries, slinging all five tote bags onto one arm. "Who's all this food for?"

"It's for *you*, Kyler. You bottomless pit son of mine," his mother huffed. "You've been eating five full meals a day since you got here, or didn't you notice?"

He thought back over the last few days and admitted silently that most of his time had been spent at the refrigerator or stove. "It's all the working out making me hungry. Sorry about that." Holding the door open for his mother, he planted a kiss on her cheek as she passed, pleased when she flushed. "You don't have to worry about me tonight. I'm having dinner with the Justices."

"Don't I know it. The news is all over town."

There it is. Kyler dropped the tote bags onto the counter, feeling his optimism sink down to the pit of his stomach. Bree would hate being the subject of gossip. As if he needed his odds of winning her back to be any lower. "Shit. Don't tell me that."

"Watch your language. And when you go closing yourself into the gym and sharing dances with a woman, you can't expect anything less. Not in Bloomfield." She busied herself emptying her supermarket haul into various refrigerator compartments. "Sandy down at Kroger—you remember her, don't you?—she's taking wagers on whether or not Samuel Justice is going to poison your dinner."

Kyler paled. "Shit. Really?"

"*Language.* And no, I'm just softening the blow." She propped an elbow on the counter, looking downright gleeful. "The wager is whether or not the town football hero will take back up with its star animal doctor."

Oh, even *better.* He could only pray Bree hadn't been in town much since he'd seen her yesterday and she'd avoided the gossip. If she started to put together why he was in Bloomfield too soon, it could blow the whole plan to hell. "Did you take any action?"

"Of course not. That would be *dis*loyal."

"You bet against me, didn't you?"

His mother didn't even have the grace to look guilty. "Only because I'm bitter." A hand went to her hip. "Honestly, Kyler. Letting me think you're home for some TLC, when all the while you're trying to sweep a girl off her feet. And didn't even let me help you." She sniffed. "Not to mention, I could have lorded this information over everyone. Now *that* is unforgiveable."

Kyler laid his cheek on top of his mother's head. "Sorry, Mom. Didn't want to jinx myself."

Another longer sniff. "I'll forgive you if I get some details."

"There's not much to say." He blew out a laugh at his understatement of the century and slumped sideways against the kitchen counter. "I need her. I love her. She's mine and I'm hers. Her stubbornness is why I love her most of all, so I'm going about this in a language only she and I know."

His mother burst into tears.

"Dad," Kyler called.

They both laughed and Kyler handed her a napkin, tugging her into the crook of his arm.

"I knew she broke your heart," his mother sobbed. "I knew you weren't over her and I don't mind saying, I didn't want you to be. That girl is special."

Hearing its name called alongside Bree's, the organ in his chest gave a hard tug. "I bet you feel pretty terrible about betting against me now."

"Almost." Her laugh was watery. "What are you bringing to dinner tonight?"

"Scotch."

Her horrified gasp could be heard three counties away. "No son of mine is showing up to dinner with liquor like some kind of social deviant." She did a quick scan of the groceries. "Give me twenty minutes and I'll have you a pie."

"I'll try not to eat more than one or two slices on the way." He winked at her warning look. "Any more suggestions?"

"Plenty." She unearthed a rolling pin from the closest drawer. "But if you only listen to one bit of advice, make it this one."

Kyler lifted his eyebrows and waited.

"I didn't raise a punk. So stop holding back and tell that girl how you feel."

Forty-five minutes later, Kyler—feeling properly chastised—drove to the Justice house in his truck, an apple pie cooling on the passenger seat. Back in Cincinnati, his teammates had always found it odd that he never got nervous before a game. Chilled as ice, he would lean against his locker and wait for Coach Brooks to deliver his speech, not a single butterfly in his stomach.

Tonight? Different story.

Not only was Kyler determined to get Bree alone tonight, but hell, he just wanted Samuel Justice to trust him. Bree loved her father and respected his opinion, so Kyler wouldn't win Bree over without his approval. Not completely. Maybe if he'd worked harder all those years ago at gaining her father's respect, she wouldn't have cut him off at the knees on prom night, revealing she wouldn't be following him to college.

With the painful memory clogging his throat, Kyler pulled up in front of the Justice house and cut the engine on his truck. Balancing the pie in one hand, Kyler climbed out. But he stopped short when Samuel Justice straightened from behind the trunk of his old silver Buick, leather briefcase in hand, and leveled Kyler with a bored look.

"Explain yourself, son."

Kyler laughed. "So much for small talk." His mother's advice from earlier came back in a tinny rush. *Stop holding back.*

Kyler thought of the cornfields. The gentle sway of the green spread out before him. All the people who'd tended to them in years past, how much purpose and routine it would take to keep them growing for eternity. Purpose swelled inside him at having been given this moment to make something lasting, like those fields. If he did it right. If he stayed true to himself and didn't allow his stride to be broken. Just like they'd fought to keep the farm, he would fight to keep Bree.

Setting down the apple pie on the hood of his truck, Kyler straightened the collar of his good shirt. "What is it you'd like to know, Mr. Justice?"

"How it's possible you're eating dinner at my table when I thought myself well rid of you four years ago?"

"Mainly because I tricked Bree into issuing the invitation. But that's not what you're asking. You want to know why I'm back in Bloomfield, haunting your dining room." Kyler glanced toward the house and caught sight of Bree moving in the indoor glow, carrying a stack of plates. "I wanted to take her out somewhere nice, but I know now that would have been a mistake. This—you and me—is a road that needs crossing."

The older man folded his arms, the briefcase still dangling in his right hand. "Why is that?"

"Because four years gave me enough perspective to know I'm nothing without her." He didn't stop to acknowledge the other man's clear surprise. "I'm back in town to make your daughter my wife. My life won't ever be complete without her. I have to believe hers won't be complete without me, either. Just for my sanity." Inside, Bree turned to look at him through the window and his pulse started knocking around. "She's not going to make this easy. Neither are you. But all due respect, sir, this time around, I'm looking forward to the test."

* * * *

Lord have mercy.

Kyler walked into her house with a face full of determination. Soon as he crossed the threshold behind her father, he sent that fortitude flying in Bree's direction and she almost had to sit down.

They hadn't been in one another's company since yesterday at the gym and she'd been plagued by hot needles of lust stabbing her at the most inopportune moments. Especially right now with those green eyes riding over her like a roller coaster car, lighting her erogenous zones up with bolts of thunder.

She'd worn *two* bras to dinner. That's how responsive her body—most noticeably, her nipples—were in Kyler's presence. Well, sitting across from her father with nipples hard enough to poke an eye out wouldn't be appropriate, would it? Thank God for her foresight because they were already reminiscing about his mouth and tongue's treatment yesterday, sitting up and begging for more attention.

Is that what Kyler's determination was all about? Getting her down to the creek after dinner to revisit old memories? Granted, those memories didn't feel in the least bit old. On the contrary, they were so fresh, she could remember them in vivid detail. As if they'd lain together on the grass as recently as today.

Since their interlude in the gym, Bree had tried to put herself into a more practical mindset. Maybe she was overthinking this situation with Kyler. They were two consenting adults with off-the-freaking-charts chemistry. He was in town for a matter of days, offering what sounded like no-commitment sex. They liked and respected one another. Why couldn't she indulge and stop worrying about what it would mean if they hooked up?

She was still asking herself that question when Kyler set down his apple pie offering on the table and leaned in to kiss her cheek. "Supergirl."

"Ky." Even after Kyler pulled back, her face tingled where his lips had touched. "Don't try and pass that pie off as your own creation. I know a Jess Tate original when I see it."

A dimple showed at the corner of his mouth. "Official taste tester is a very important job. It often goes underappreciated."

"Speaking of, I'm surprised you didn't eat half on the drive over." Flirting. She was *flirting*. In her own dining room, for heaven's sake. "Are you finally learning to control yourself?"

His voice dropped, along with his gaze, where it lingered on her double-lifted breasts. "Leaning to control myself?" He made a low sound. "Just barely."

Bree's face heated. "Kyler Joseph Tate."

"Stop tempting me when your daddy is nearby." His grin and wink sent her blood to rushing. "I've got a bet to win."

"Right. The bet."

Something about the way she said it made Kyler's smile flatten, his eyes growing troubled. "Bree—"

"Get comfortable. Dinner's almost ready."

She escaped into the kitchen, hoping she hadn't shown her hand. It was ridiculous to feel hurt by Kyler being interested in her physically. He didn't have it in him to be disrespectful. Heck, he'd shown up on time with a pie to have dinner with her father and sister. But the floor of her stomach had dropped out, half with lust, half with…disappointment soon as he made his intentions clear.

"Let me help you."

Kyler's voice in the kitchen made her pulse jump. "I've got it under control."

He hummed on his way to the stove, picking up a spoon to begin stirring. "Tell me about your day."

Bree tried not to examine the soothing heat that settled over her shoulders like warm wool. "It was a slow one, actually. Well, wait. There was one interesting patient." She bit her bottom lip to capture a smile. "A bunny rabbit came in complaining of the hiccups."

Pleasure rippled in her chest when Kyler let out a bark of laughter. "Hopped right in on his own, did he?"

"You know what I mean. His owner brought him in." She bumped him with her hip. He bumped her back. "Turned out he'd gotten out of his cage and found a puddle of spilled bubbles the kids had left around. I laid him on his back, pushed on his little belly, and a big old double bubble came right out of his mouth."

Narrowed green eyes turned in her direction. "You're making this up."

"Figured it would be more interesting than my back-to-back neutering appointments." She laughed when Kyler winced and bent forward slightly at the waist. "Men. It gets you every time."

Kyler grumbled for a few seconds until something seemed to occur to him. "So you, uh…haven't been out and about in town much since yesterday?"

"Why?"

"Just making conversation."

"Uh-huh." Bree moved closer to him, going up on her tiptoes to examine his too-casual expression. "There something I should know about?"

Kyler seemed momentarily distracted by her proximity, his Adam's apple bobbing. "Sure is." With a flick of his wrist, he turned off the burner beneath the gravy. "There's a two-for-one sale on pickles at Kroger."

"Very funny."

"One tall tale deserves another, Bree Caroline." Suddenly serious, he turned toward her and propped a hip on the stove. "Now *really* tell me about your day. I want to hear about the steps you took. If something made you laugh. Whether or not you were happy or tired or sad during any of it."

The bottom that had dropped out of her stomach back in the dining room restored itself, lifting, lifting. Pressing against her heart. When she spoke, her voice was in a whisper, like they were sharing a big secret. "I snuck out of work at lunchtime and got a pedicure while I ate a giant chocolate chip cookie." Their smiles built at the very same rate, degree by degree. "But I didn't let my polish dry enough. I never do. So my big toes have smears."

"There you go bringing up those cute toes again," he murmured back. "Let me see it."

Before she could question herself, Bree toed off her ballet flat, presenting her right foot for Kyler's inspection. "Now you know my great shame."

"Tell me I'm the only one who knows it."

His request was packed with so much gravity, Bree grew short of breath. "You are."

Kyler nodded, then reached out to slip a stray curl behind her ear. "They're taking bets in town on whether or not your daddy is planning to poison me."

"I haven't decided yet," Samuel said behind them, letting the kitchen door slam.

Bree hopped backward, ramming her hip into an open cabinet. Kyler didn't even bother taking his attention off her. In front of her father, the level of intense focus in those green eyes felt downright inappropriate, but Bree couldn't deny the pleasure spreading in her middle.

"How do I sway the odds in my favor, sir?" He paused. "Of not being poisoned, that is."

Her father hesitated a moment, which was rare for a man who so often got straight to the point, his purpose clear. "Bree, I think Kira is calling for you upstairs."

"I don't hear—" She stopped mid-sentence, realizing her father wanted to be alone with Kyler. Why? It killed her not knowing, but her father was the one human being on this planet she didn't question. "I'll go see what she needs."

At the kitchen door she looked back at Kyler, a quick rhythm starting in the center of her chest when he nodded at her. As if to say, *consider the bet won.*

Chapter Nine

Kyler knew every bump of the road leading to the creek. He steered left and right to avoid them now, but didn't quite succeed in missing them completely. His mind was in two places at once. On the girl who sat in the passenger seat looking like a lamb on the way to slaughter. And on the conversation he'd had with Samuel before dinner started.

A beat passed as the kitchen door snapped shut behind Bree.

"You want to know how to swing the odds in your favor, Mr. Tate?"

They both knew the topic of discussion had nothing to do with poison and everything to do with Bree. "Yes, sir. More than anything."

Brown eyes, a masculine version of Bree's, scrutinized Kyler. "Tell me, when did Bree decide she wanted to be a veterinarian?"

The question threw him. Hard. He'd expected the man to inquire about his cumulative GPA, medical history, or political affiliation. Panic set in upon realizing he didn't have the answer. He was not going down easy now, though, so Kyler thought hard, remembering every peak and valley he'd traveled with Bree. The occasions she'd needed time to herself. Times she'd needed extra attention from him and he'd been desperate to give it. "When her mother left."

Grief shone briefly in the older man's eyes, followed by grudging approval. "Yes. And I advise you to consider why." He tapped a fist against his thigh. "I don't make decisions for my daughter. I raised her to do that herself." Samuel started toward the door and stopped. "She puts on a good show, but she hasn't been the same since you went away. Not even close." He sighed. "In regards to what you told me outside, I won't stand in your way of trying. But I have one more condition."

It took all his willpower not to deflate into a heap of relief. "Yes, sir?"

"Get a new tie. The one you wore on Draft Day was ugly as shit."

The laughter boomed out of Kyler. "Yes, sir." He pushed himself off the counter, joining Samuel at the door and pushing it open so he could pass through. "Maybe you can take me shopping. Sounds like you have an eye for fashion."

"Don't push it."

Kyler sat down at the table, shooting an open-mouthed Bree a wink.

So Kyler should consider the night a victory, shouldn't he? Over a decade after he'd begun dating Bree, he'd finally gained Mr. Justice's favor. Or at least his assurance he wouldn't prevent Kyler from *trying* to make Bree his wife. Real reassuring. But Kyler found himself focused instead on Samuel's advice to consider the timing of Bree's decision to become a veterinarian.

Following in her father's footsteps hadn't been her passion until Mrs. Justice walked out on them. Almost immediately, she'd started accompanying her father on house calls, spending more time at the local shelter, caring for animals. Only Kyler had never considered *why*. Why was her mother leaving the catalyst?

When she'd broken up with him at the very creek to which they were driving, he'd been too devastated to look for a deeper meaning. His sole focus had been escaping the hurt and learning to live with the huge chunk losing Bree had taken out of him. A chunk that would never be filled back in, no matter how hard he tried.

But with Bree's happiness at stake, Kyler needed to examine what really held her back from coming to Cincinnati with him. And he needed to do it fast.

His flight to Los Angeles left in three days.

With that chilling fact on a repetitive loop in his head, Kyler pulled the truck to a stop at the forest's edge, rolling down the window so they could hear the gentle babble of the creek. "Here's the thing, Bree. I want you. So bad that I've been crying a little every time I zip my jeans since coming home." He turned to find a bemused expression on her gorgeous face. "But I'll be damned before I hold you to a bet where sex is my prize. I was an asshole for letting you think I'd do that." He gripped the steering wheel tight, out of annoyance at himself. "We haven't spent any real time together in a while. I shouldn't have assumed you would give me the benefit of the doubt. So what we're going to do is sit here a spell and talk.

Tomorrow, if you decide to mess up the grass with me, I'll break the speed limit coming to pick you up. But I'm happier than I've been in goddamn years just looking at you, Bree. Just to ask you things and hear your answers."

Kyler forced himself to maintain eye contact. And not to look down at the *quick quick quick* way her tits were rising and falling.

"Why'd you have to go and say all that?" she finally whispered after what seemed like an hour. "I was prepared to lay on a guilt trip."

"Sorry, supergirl." He chuckled into the near-darkness. "Go on ahead. I want whatever you've got to lay on me."

"Kyler."

"What?"

"I want to mess up the grass with you."

Talk about crying. His dick stretched up and out from the root so fast, Kyler gritted his teeth with a curse. "Tomorrow, Bree," he managed, stars shooting in front of his eyes. "When it's clear you're not fulfilling your end of some stupid challenge."

Bree shook her head. "Our challenges aren't stupid; they're exactly what we both need." She blinked, as if the admission had surprised her, too. "Maybe we should have another one right now."

Hope waved its flag on the horizon, but he staunchly ignored it. "I'm listening, but I'm not making any promises."

"Let's start with a clean slate."

She turned her body, sliding her bent left knee up onto the seat. *Don't look for that sweet flash of panties. Don't do it.* "A clean slate," he rasped. "I'm with you so far."

"There was never a bet to win my father over." Bree scooted closer and Kyler held his breath. "How you accomplished that is still a mystery, but that explanation is for another time. Right now, we're getting a do-over." She unhooked his seatbelt, the zip-reel sound going straight through him. "Dare me to turn you down."

He caught her hand before it could settle on his chest. "You're not hearing me. I'm turning myself down on your behalf."

"Come on, Kyler. If you dare me to turn you down, I'll be obliged to do the opposite." She twisted her hand out of his grip, curling those long, graceful fingers of hers in his collar. "It's how we do things."

Christ, having Bree so close was mental damnation and salvation, all at once. She was crumbling his resistance little by little, but he didn't want her on a technicality. "That's not how we're doing things tonight." He brought their foreheads together, let his tongue slide out and meet with her lower lip. "No games, Bree. Say you need me."

With the ultimate challenge lying between them, brown eyes traced up to lock with his. "You're not making this easy, are you?"

"What's holding you back from saying it?"

Time slowed down, the watery bubbling of the creek fading out. "The worry that it might be true."

Kyler's heart went wild in his chest, hammering so fast his vision tripled. His hands shook. The light she'd blown out inside him flamed brighter than ever, a fireworks display inside his chest. Bree, however, looked like a frightened deer in a hunter's sights. She attempted to throw herself back toward the passenger side of the truck, but Kyler wasn't letting her go now. Oh no. She'd finally said what he'd known in his bones since day one, all the way back in middle school.

Their need went both ways. It was solid, immeasurable, and couldn't be weakened by absence or the passage of time.

"Get over here, Bree Caroline." Kyler grabbed her around the waist, hauling her back across the seat and out of the truck. She was in his arms before she could form a protest, but she certainly made a show of sputtering as he strode with her toward the creek. "Go on, then. Now that you've given me the truth, I'll let you complain a little. Right before I lick it straight out of your mouth."

"You..." she started in a shaky whisper. "Y-you're..."

"Sad. Happy. Horny. Miserable. Confident. Worried. Horny. Did I say that last one twice?" As soon as he reached the grassy bank surrounding the creek, Kyler dropped to his knees with Bree still cradled in his arms. And then she was on her back beneath him, twin reflections of the moon lighting up her eyes. "*You.* You make me everything on that fucking list."

"Oh yeah?" Baring her teeth, she took hold of either side of his shirt and ripped it straight down the middle, sending buttons flying in every direction. "If I make you so crazy, what do you want with me?"

"*Everything.*"

Chapter Ten

Shit.

Almighty.

The kiss Kyler dropped on Bree almost sent her into a blackout. A lust-driven, not-in-control-of-her-limbs, shot-into-another-dimension loss of awareness.

His teeth nipped around her lower lip, dragging it down, leaving her mouth vulnerable so he could lay claim. With his tongue. His lips. And Lord, did he ever. It was the kiss that wouldn't stop giving. Just a wet, writhing, slanting mating of mouths and at some point, Bree gave up on the act of breathing. If she died this way, she wouldn't even feel death creeping in because she was too busy being consumed by Kyler. His kiss was wild, frustrated, giving, desperate. She felt everything inside her expand in the presence of it, threatening to burst.

Bree's body must have acted out of self-preservation, pulling on the roots of Kyler's hair until he broke the kiss, allowing her to suck in deep, labored pulls of oxygen. His face was hard to see in the shadows, but worry for her made his eyes an intense green, his lips descending once more. But not for another kiss. No, he fit their mouths together and breathed. Breathed again.

"What is this?" Bree murmured, voice catching. "Some sexy version of CPR?"

His lips curved briefly against hers. "We should trademark it. I might be on to something." Once again, he gave her a slow dose of air and sensual languidness slithered through Bree's body. "Nah, I'm keeping it just for you."

Maybe it was the additional oxygen. Or maybe it was just the intimacy of the act itself. But her body stretched out and arched beneath Kyler's, her thighs opening and inviting him to drop down. To push. To pin. Her body was a begging mass of nerve endings screaming for an anchor. "*Kyler.*"

"Shh, I'm coming." Bracing one hand beside Bree's head, he gave her the full weight of his lower body, hissing when her warmth welcomed the thick flesh behind the zipper of his jeans. As if his body was operating on pure animal need, he thrust once, driving her a few inches up the creek embankment. "This what you're impatient for?"

"*Yes.* I…"

"Tell me, Bree. Tell me everything."

"Say you need me back."

Oh *God.* Where had *that* come from? Now it was a competition to see what would burst into flames first—her face or her body. It didn't help when Kyler stared down at her like she needed a straightjacket. "Bree, I'm a mess. I've been a mess since the last time we stood beside this creek. You want to know if I need you? Just look at me. All you ever have to do is look at me and you'll see it."

Bree used a mental machete to slash a pathway out of her head… And once she stood on the other side, it was like stumbling into a vivid, Technicolor dream. So much pent-up passion ran circles in Kyler's eyes, she couldn't believe she hadn't seen it before. At least not since he'd come home to visit. "Oh." She swallowed hard. "You *are* a mess."

He dropped his face into the crook of her neck and rolled those powerful hips, denim dragging over cotton, enticing the flesh beneath. "Heal me. Please."

Responsibility and a renewed wave of desire moved inside Bree. Following instinct, she urged Kyler to roll onto his back, leaving her straddling his lap. Now that she'd slipped into the land of Technicolor, her senses were so sharp, so attuned to this man, she heard his fingers digging into the earth, heard the *whap whap whap* of his heart.

Need her? This snapping connection between them went beyond need. And there was no denying it right now. Not with him in pain beneath her. Pain she was driven to relieve, the urge to do so stronger than anything she could remember. Her own desire more than matched Kyler's, swelling with every passing moment.

Bree gathered the hem of her dress and whipped off the garment, turning slippery between her thighs when Kyler groaned, his hips lifting and falling beneath her. A raring engine. Glorying in his hunger, Bree unhooked the front of her bra, removing it in a slow tease. But she stopped short when Kyler's eyebrows drew together. "How come you took off your bra, but you've still got one on?"

"Oh th-that." She got busy unhooking the second bra. "Would you believe it was an honest mistake?"

His lips jumped at one corner. "Nope."

"I didn't want my hard nipples showing at dinner. You happy?"

"Blissful." Her exposed breasts got rid of the grin on his face. "Bree Caroline, you are the most beautiful woman on the goddamn planet."

Bree's pulse thudded in her temples, the base of her neck, between her legs. If she basked too long in Kyler's devouring gaze, surely she would explode, so she slipped back on his thighs, her fingers working to unzip his pants. She couldn't stop herself from stealing glances at him, though, his huge, chiseled body lying there in the grass, waiting to give pleasure.

By the time she finally held his thick shaft in her hand, Kyler's breath had grown labored, sweat beginning to dapple his heaving chest. "You've still got those little red panties on, Bree. Come on up here so I can get them off."

Urgency pumping in her veins, she stroked Kyler, struggling to come up with a plan that didn't involve her climbing off him, because that would suck. The only plan she was interested in was seating herself on that hard part of him and riding him until they were both mindless. "I think...I think I can slide them down."

"Uh-uh. You know what I want." He crooked a finger at her. "We both know I won't go in smooth without giving you a good licking first. So come on up here and get it. Want your gorgeous thighs around my face."

Kyler didn't give her a chance to follow his instructions, grabbing her by the hips and hauling her up, up, until the material of her panties was stretched just above his mouth. Bree fell forward, planting her palms on the grass, whimpering when Kyler's warm breath heated the sensitive insides of her thighs. The sound of the creek rushed in her ears, interrupted only by the sounds of cotton ripping, a guttural groan. Lips met her damp flesh almost immediately and Kyler's hands returned to her hips only to press them down, meeting the most sensitive part of her with the flat of his tongue. Rubbing it there.

"Oh, that's *oh...*" The summer evening dew on the grass made Bree's knees slip wider. *That* and the fact that they were trembling out of control. "I'm not going to make it. I'm going to..."

Apparently Kyler wasn't listening, because he continued to mete out torture, massaging her hips and buttocks in his calloused hands, slipping his tongue up and back through her folds, teasing her nub endlessly until Bree's cheek was grinding against the soft ground, her hips rolling toward the only thing that could end the pain. Every delicate and neglected muscle south of her belly button began to converge in on itself, constricting, stealing the breath right out of her lungs. But just as she bit down on her bottom lip and readied herself to field the orgasm of the century, she heard the sound of foil ripping. Then in one hasty, hungry move, Kyler used his grip on Bree's hips to lift her up, repositioning her on his lap.

"Need you, Bree. *Need you.*"

His hand shifted between her thighs, brushing her flesh, and she let out a sob. The head of his erection met her entrance and they locked eyes, Kyler's the definition of starvation. Enough to humble Bree, start a rhythm in her chest she wasn't sure would ever stop. "Need you, Kyler."

Bracing her hands on his chest, Bree filled herself with Kyler's hard length, gasping from the pressure. The incredible, mind-blowing pressure. She let her gaze sweep over the straining cords of his neck, the shuddering lift and fall of his stomach, the desperate grip spanning her waist. *Everything is right where it's supposed to be*, said a voice in the back of her mind.

Not even the sky falling could have prevented her from moving in that moment. From twisting her hips back, lifting to the plump head of his shaft, and rolling back down. A dance that was somehow singular to them and old as time, all at once. That first downward grind had Kyler throwing his head back and releasing a satisfied shout. Which was when Bree remembered why they'd always found it necessary to drive out to the creek to make love.

"We never did this quietly, did we?"

Kyler's voice sounded just as unnatural as hers when he responded. "A man can't stay silent when he's wrapped up in something so tight." His thumb rubbed over her clitoris, side to side. "Christ, I thought my mind had exaggerated how good you feel, Bree. How good *we* feel. It's taking everything I got not to flip you over and *ram* myself—" He cut himself off with gritted teeth, eyes closing. "No, I'm going to make this last. I want this to go on forever. You sitting there, full of my inches, thighs dancing around like you can barely handle them."

"Forever might be a stretch if you keep talking like that," she managed on a shaky inhale, her hips bucking involuntarily.

"Ride it, Bree," he gritted, levering his hips up for a long, slow grind. "Been too damn long since I came with my cock inside you and not just imagining it there."

Her pulse stuttered. "Did you imagine it a lot?"

"*Every. Time.*"

Something worrisome tugged on Bree's subconscious, but she could only focus on the pressure mounting inside of her. The incessant quickening that built higher every time she snapped her hips, Kyler's thickness pumping in and out of her wet heat. The base of him grazed her clitoris every time she moved, but Kyler—who she'd often suspected knew her body better than she did—pressed down on the small of her back, creating an angle that made her climax loom like an inferno.

"Oh my God." She let out a broken sob. "*Yes.*"

"There's my girl now. Who knows what you like?" His thumb joined the base of his erection in stroking the sensitive spot, his eyes glittering up at her in the darkness. Encouraging her to come apart, to take what she needed. "Spent the best hours of my life learning your needs, making sure you'd always finish first. Got my girl's slippery-wet pussy memorized, don't I?"

When his hips started giving quick upward thrusts, his thumb moving in a blur, Bree dug her fingernails into Kyler's pectorals and screamed, the pleasure reaching into her belly pulling everything *tight, tight, tight.*

Releasing.

Kyler shoved up deep and Bree pressed down, working as a team without exchanging a single word to give her the longest peak, and it went on and on until her voice started to go hoarse from calling his name. Her legs clamped around Kyler's hips like he was the only raft in a storm. In a way he was because Bree swore she'd been struck by lightning.

"Missed you clinging to me most of all, didn't I?" Kyler said through gritted teeth. "Only time I know you won't run off is when I'm giving you a good fucking. You stay put for that, don't you?"

Without giving her a chance to recover, without giving her the sweet kisses and reassurances of their youth, Kyler turned them a final time, settling Bree on her hands and knees in the grass. Bree stared out into the moonlit trees as Kyler dragged his hot open mouth up her spine and buried his face in her neck, sounding like a man who'd just swum from the bottom of the ocean without an oxygen tank.

One of his knees slid in between her thighs, prying them wide. That hard, heavy part of him filled her in a rough shove. And, groaning into her shoulder, one hand fisted in her hair, he fucked her into next week.

"Slide your ass up my stomach. I've got a few more inches to give you." His answering curse was followed by her name, and satisfaction flowed hot in her blood, dizzying her. "Dammit, Bree, that's so fucking good. Now push, push back...*Jesus*. You have no idea what you do to me. What you've *always* done. *No idea*."

She started to slide forward in the grass, but he jerked her back with a forearm beneath her hips. "Oh God," she whimpered. "*Harder*."

"There it is." His growl sent shockwaves through her blood. "There's our magic word. My harder's a little different this time around, though. You want it?"

"*Yes*."

The impact of his lower body spurring into a ruthless pace made Bree suck in a ragged breath, her flesh quickening around him. Her vision started to glaze with another oncoming wave of pleasure, teeth beginning to chatter in her mouth. Behind her was not the boy who'd spent countless hours in that very spot learning her body, teaching her about his. No, this was Kyler Tate the *man*. A rough, demanding man that couldn't achieve release without *her* and that very thought alone, coupled with his groans, spurred her into another mind-blanking orgasm.

"Kyler. *Kyler.*"

"So sweet. You're so fucking sweet and snug, Bree, shaking around me. I can't hold it back anymore. Too long. It's been too long." His husky ramble hitched in her ear, followed by a long moan, the broken pumping of his hips. Those strong arms banded around her, supporting her, but also crushing her up into his body. One final thrust and they both went down into the grass, Kyler's arms breaking her fall as he shuddered through his peak. "Bree," he breathed finally, his body going limp, laying partially on top of her. "My girl."

It took a few minutes for the fog to part. Bree almost wished it wouldn't, wished they could go on lying there together all night, not thinking about a single thing. Except for the fact that they'd surely just raised the bar on sex between humans. Because holy damn. She was going to feel it for a week and she didn't even mind.

Her heart wouldn't let her rest, though. No, it walked right upstairs to her brain and knocked on the door, tapping its foot until it was acknowledged.

At some point during the night, she'd forgotten all about what was bothering her. Kyler was leaving in a matter of days. Which made tonight nothing more than a hookup. A pit stop on his way to Los Angeles. And while Bree wished she was the kind of woman who could appreciate sex for sex's sake... The increased discomfort in her sternum was making it painfully obvious that sex with Kyler had never, ever, just been about sex. Although, that wasn't the case for Kyler, was it?

You broke my heart. I went away and healed it up. Now we're going to be friends.

Just friends. A visit with an old flame.

For him, anyway. In the blink of an eye, Bree was right back where she'd started the day Kyler left for Cincinnati. Alone. Missing him so bad she could barely perform basic functions like walking or tying her shoes. No way to fix the ache and remain true to what she loved. Who she was. Her options were even more limited this time around because tonight was purely physical for Kyler.

"All right, supergirl. Smoke is about to come out of your ears."

He dropped a kiss onto her nape, bundled her closer. "Tell me what's wrong."

"I thought, um…" Her voice was doing that super high-pitched thing that always betrayed her when she got overwrought. "I thought I would be okay with just, like, hooking up, but it turns out I'm not. Not okay with being your hookup."

Kyler tensed up behind her. *Jerk*. He was probably regretting bringing her down to the creek in the first place, thinking she'd gone all psycho ex-girlfriend on him. Wanting more when he no longer did.

That distressing thought had Bree attempting to scramble out of Kyler's arms, but he held on tight. "How dare you get weird on me, Kyler Joseph? I'm not asking you to go steady. I'm just…I'm *just*…" To Bree's horror, tears pricked the back of her eyelids, lost the battle to stay contained, and slipped down her cheeks. "Maybe I could have handled this kind of thing better with someone else—"

"What the hell are you talking about, *someone else*?"

"Maybe it wouldn't have felt this *awful* afterward," she shouted back, finally succeeding in breaking free, reaching out to snag her dress. Oh God, she had to get home. Something was wrong with her. Her foundation felt like it was cracking straight down the middle. "You were honest with me, so I-I guess I shouldn't be mad. But this doesn't feel like us. We hook up a-and then you leave? This doesn't feel like the us we used to be. I'd rather remember us like we were."

Dress pulled on, Bree finally turned toward Kyler and saw his face. He stood a few yards away, breathtaking and bare-chested in the moonlight, his boxers pulled back into place. His face was paler than the orb lighting the forest, but when he saw her tears, devastation rippled over his features.

"This is what I get for holding back," he whispered.

Chapter Eleven

At what point in his life would he realize his mother was always right? The possible repercussions of what he'd just done socked Kyler in the stomach, one after the other, as if he were standing in front of a fast pitch machine without a bat.

"Bree, please." He took a step forward and she retreated, increasing his panic. "Please don't cry."

"This is what you get for holding back. What does that mean?"

Kyler dropped his head into his hands. Where the hell did he begin? "I can't get my thoughts together when you're crying."

"Try harder."

He rasped a sound. Shit, the more he concentrated, the worse his reality became. He'd been deceptive. Maybe he'd considered playing it close to the vest necessary to his plan, but sleeping with Bree when he hadn't been honest? That behavior was inexcusable and now... Now the love of his life thought the worst. Thought he'd brought her to this place that held so many memories just to get his rocks off. Well, he could clear that nonsense right up.

Unfortunately, the truth could send Bree jumping into the creek, doing a freestyle stroke to get away from him. Too bad. He'd landed himself in that same creek with no paddle and now he owed her an explanation. God, he'd sell his soul right now to stop her tears.

Without taking his gaze off Bree longer than necessary, Kyler stooped down to retrieve his shirt, pulling it on. First off, if she ran, he didn't want to chase her naked. Second, a man ought to have his nipples covered when a woman's claws came out. "I'm asking you to take what you know about me, Bree. Take what you *know* and apply it to this situation."

Bree's swiped at her damp eyes. "I don't understand."

"Think. Think about senior year when the fall carnival came to town. You remember that?" Her nod was hesitant. "I emailed the director two months in advance asking him to let us in an hour before everyone else on opening day. I emailed him and made phone calls until he caved. All because you loved the Ferris wheel and I wanted you to be the first one to take a ride. You remember that?"

She crossed her arms. "Are you trying to buy yourself points here?"

"No, I'm trying to remind you that I'm a planner." He took another step in her direction, thankful when she stayed put. "Think, Bree. Do you really believe I would come to Bloomfield unannounced, show up at the dance, and risk being poisoned by your daddy…just to hook up with you? Not that touching you, kissing you again, wouldn't be worth all that work and a lot more, supergirl, but you know me better than that." Tension was beginning to creep into her frame, so Kyler took that final step to bring them toe to toe. "You know I want more with you, Bree Caroline. You know I want it all. And I'm not going to stop until I get it."

A little puff of air passed through her lips, thoughts zigzagging behind her eyes. "I—what?" Her swallow sounded more like a *thunk*. "You said you went away and healed."

"That was the biggest lie I told you." Of their own accord, his hands slipped around her upper arms and held fast. "You broke my heart. And it's *still broken*." Saying the truth out loud after keeping it penned up for so long started flames licking inside his blood, sending gray smoke whirling inside his head. "I've loved you as far back as my memory reaches. I will *never* fucking stop. I came to town for one damn reason, Bree. So I could leave here with my wife. You."

"Kyler," she breathed, her cheeks growing more and more damp, every tear doing its best to slay him. "That's…crazy. We haven't been together in four years."

Holding back or being delicate was out the window. Cinder and ash and truth poured out of him, scorching him on the way out. "And yet I've been faithful. My hands are meant for you alone and I haven't laid them on a single other person." He held them up, palms out, as if the proof was visible. "Tell me you haven't been faithful right back, so I can kiss your lying mouth."

When she didn't respond, Kyler had his answer and relief melted in his gut.

"You're *my* girl. You always have been." His voice shook. "That's why you run and hide every time I come to town, because your heart wouldn't let you forget it."

He watched as she desperately searched for a defense. "You didn't exactly come find me, either."

"I wasn't ready, Bree. I was still angry. At you for cutting me off. At myself for not being good and smart enough to keep you." She made a sound and looked away. "Now I'm only angry over how much time has passed. I forgive us both. But I can't make it without you. I got called to the stage on Draft Day and all I could think about was you. How none of it meant shit unless you were standing beside me."

It made him want to tear out his hair, the disbelief she turned on him. "This is my home, Kyler. Nothing has changed. I won't leave it or my family."

"Well, *you're* my home and I won't leave you behind, either." He shook her a little, knocking tears free of their perch on her eyelashes. "There are some things I missed last time we stood in this spot. You've got reasons for not wanting to give up this life to start a new one with me, the way we planned. I'm going to learn every one of those reasons." Kyler braced himself. "But right now, I just need you to tell me you still love me. Tell me you never stopped."

The war that went on inside Bree was beautiful. She sobbed and blinked through it, words being formed and discarded on her kiss-swollen lips. "You know I hate surprises, Ky. You can't just come here and *spring* this on me. E-expect me to tell you what you want to hear. If I'd known you wanted to get back together... If you'd told me the truth—"

"We wouldn't be standing here. So I can't regret it." Forcing himself to breathe through the agony and disappointment, Kyler used the hem of his shirt to wipe her cheeks. "Only thing I regret is making you cry."

"I feel like I'm hurting you all over again." She batted his hands away, wrapping her arms around her middle. "Why are you doing this?"

"You're hurting, too." Banking the urge to hold her and refuse to let go, he pointed back to the spot where they'd made love. "That feeling you got afterward? The one that said me leaving was wrong? That's fate trying to tell you something, Bree. I'm begging you to listen."

"I won't leave," she whispered.

His heart twisted. "Look me in the eye, Bree Caroline." He stepped closer so she wouldn't have a choice, her head falling back to maintain his gaze. "I won't leave this town without you."

Knowing Bree as long as he had, Kyler knew when she'd gone her maximum number of rounds. No decisions or resolutions were going to be made tonight, or even tomorrow, because his girl was a thinker. A brooder. After the shit he'd been pulling all week, Kyler reckoned he owed her some stewing time, much as staying away from her would be pure, punishing torture.

"Come on, supergirl." He kissed her forehead. "I'll drive you home."

He'd waited four years. He'd wait a hundred more.

* * * *

Bree snapped her supply bag shut and took a deep breath.

Two days was long enough to be holed up in the house.

Who was she kidding? It hadn't been *nearly* long enough. She was still reeling from Kyler's confession and that wouldn't be changing any time soon.

He still loved her.

He'd been faithful.

He wasn't leaving Bloomfield without her.

Bree from the past was somewhere laughing like a lunatic, because Bree of the present had broken the cardinal rule when it came to Kyler Tate. She'd let her guard down. Growing comfortable in the past had led to sunrise Ferris wheel rides, gifts left inside her locker, taps on her window at night.

Growing up, a lot of people had underestimated Kyler. He looked the part of a man who was treated to surprises and pleasure from *others*. A man who had things handed to him. Not the other way around. But the gorgeous football god had never failed to amaze her.

Somehow she'd forgotten—and once and for all been knocked straight back onto her ass.

Grateful for the silent house, Bree sat down on the bench in the entryway, applying pressure to the center of her chest. She felt winded. Every time she got a burst of energy, she would think of Kyler's pleading eyes, his familiar face outlined by the night sky, and she would ache. *Ache.* Almost like she'd suppressed the misery for four years and was only now allowing it to manifest.

She looked across the hall at the family portrait hanging there. Her mother sat at the forefront, Samuel's hands on her shoulders, Bree at her side, Kira on her knee. There was a distant look in the woman's eye, as if she'd been dreaming about some far-off place. Tahiti, Berlin…Los Angeles. Every time Bree passed the picture, she forced herself to look at it. Used it as a reminder to be satisfied with what she'd been given. In Bloomfield with her family, she was happy. Content.

There was nothing more to it.

When she stood up, bag in hand, the uncomfortable throbbing remained in her chest, but she ignored it, pushing out the front door.

Kyler stood on the porch, his eyes weighed down with dark circles.

"Bree," he said, his voice a husky scrape.

Her heart picked up into a gallop. "Ky."

They stood there for a full minute, listening to the rain fall softly on the eaves above. Lord, Kyler had been right about one thing. She'd avoided him every time he came to Bloomfield because the sight of him affected her like nothing else could. Her mouth dried up, her pulse creating a racket. Now that she knew he still loved her, it took all of her willpower to keep her knees from buckling. The power of his emotions was so thick, reaching out and curling around her.

But what about her own? Had she spent so long convincing herself she was getting over him that she'd succeeded?

Her heart didn't seem to think so. Not in the slightest.

Bree thought of the picture hanging in the entryway and squared her shoulders. "I'm sorry. I haven't changed my mind."

The wattage of his gaze dimmed, but he nodded. "Where are you headed?"

"House call."

"Mind if I come with?"

"I certainly do." She took the umbrella out of her bag, opening it. "It wouldn't be very professional of me to show up with an audience."

"Doubt anyone in Bloomfield would mind."

"The appointment isn't in Bloomfield."

Bree recognized her mistake when Kyler's brows slashed inward. "Where?"

Schooling her features, she breezed past him down the stairs. "Hashtown."

Kyler was hot on her heels. "This wouldn't happen to be the trainer that keeps asking you out, is it?" He slapped a hand on the driver's side door to keep her from opening it. She gasped when he aligned their bodies from behind, pressing her up against the car. His mouth found a sensitive spot on her neck and stayed there, his warm breath coasting into her hair, down the collar of her T-shirt. "You wouldn't want to drive me stark raving mad like that, would you, Bree?"

"Not on purpose," she whispered. "There's a mare about to foal. The horse trusts me and I want to be there."

"Have some *mercy* on me," he enunciated. "And let me come *with* you."

"Fine," she said, his urgency cutting through her reservations. "Yes. Okay."

When he took away the heat of his body, the weight of it, Bree no longer felt tethered to the ground. After taking a moment to compose herself, she turned to find Kyler growing increasingly soaked by the rain, droplets running down his face and bare arms, the white T-shirt he wore clinging to his muscular chest. A chest that started a rapid rise and fall when he caught her looking. "What other mercies can I earn from you today?" Kyler rasped. "If you've already forgotten how I beg for that mercy, my tongue is dying to show you."

When he came close once more and stopped a mere inch away, her nipples tingled, making her wish she'd worn a second bra again. Especially when his gaze swept down and made blatant promises to the traitors. "Kyler—"

"Shhh." He dropped his head down and grazed wet, masculine lips over hers, sending her ovaries into chaos. One hand rose to bury in the hair at her nape, tilting her head to one side. Then, slowly, he raked that hot, open mouth up the side of her neck. "Just let me soak you up."

"Soak me up," she repeated, her nerve endings going wild.

He hummed in the affirmative, letting their hips meet and press so she could feel his thick need against her belly. "Soak you up." His tongue traced a path up to her ear, creating an answering tug between her legs. "Hell, just *soak* you. In both of us. I'm full to aching. Don't tell me you aren't after that reminder of what we've been going without."

Bree almost succumbed and let Kyler have her, right there against the truck, because hell yes, she'd been replaying their night at the creek on mental repeat. Now wasn't the time, though. Not while they were smack dab inside a gray area with no resolution in sight. Furthermore, didn't she have a job to do in Hashtown? An important one? "I-if you're going to come with me, there's no touching." His jaw tightened until she thought it might shatter, but after a few seconds he stepped back, lifting his hands in surrender. Buried beneath his hunger, there was a hint of that boyish chagrin from her best memories and Bree was hit with a wave of nostalgia so strong, it made her knees tremble. She knew this man so well. Knew him right down to the very core. Always had. "I want to be your friend, Ky. Like you said outside the diner, on your first day back." She shook her head. "I'm sorry I hid from you."

Surprise flickered in his expression, but Bree could tell it was nowhere close to what he wanted to hear. "I'm sorry, too." His throat worked a moment, before he circled to the passenger side of her truck and climbed in, watching her through the rain dappled glass.

This was going to be a long afternoon.

Chapter Twelve

Being jealous was a first.

In the past, Kyler had always been possessive in the sense that he enjoyed letting people know the following: Bree belonged to him, he made her happy, and no one else need apply. But Bree never once gave him cause to be actively jealous and vice versa. A pretty rare feat among high school students. Kyler was damn grateful now that they'd been the exception to the rule because it meant Bree trusting his word without question when he said he'd been faithful.

Bree hadn't dated, either, so there was no reason to feel edgy and irritable. He didn't like the fact that she'd been asked out at all, though. Kind of felt like his tonsils were being yanked out with pliers. Not a nice sensation.

Hell, it didn't surprise him one bit that another man had taken notice of Bree. Big, beautiful bedroom eyes and a mouth that could snap out a comeback faster than lightning tended to get attention. Throw in that fluid, sexy way she walked, her grace, her intelligence? Kyler should count himself lucky someone else hadn't gotten the notion to propose to her while he was in Cincinnati.

Realizing his fingers were digging into the meat of his thighs, Kyler forced himself to rein in the green monster.

"This is a bad idea," Bree muttered, casting him a speculative look from the driver's seat. "You're an animal skin toga away from turning into a caveman."

"You want to see me in leopard print." He winked at her. "Hint taken."

Bree's laugh tinkled like jostled bells. "You're forgetting I already have."

The memory came back to him in a series of sounds and blurry pictures. "Valentine's Day. That's right." Wrapping paper tearing. Bree squealing as he tickled her ribs, the present resting on the floor beside them. "You always were creative when it came to giving gifts."

"I knew I couldn't beat you at being thoughtful, so I went for cheap laughs instead." Turning the truck off the road, she bit her lip. "You still have those leopard print boxers?"

"I have everything you've ever given me."

Her eyelids fell, silence filling the car for long moments. "I lived in fear of my father finding those boxers before I could give them to you." A small smile formed on her mouth. "Afterward, I lost sleep wondering if your mama would find them. You promised me to hand-wash them in the sink, so she wouldn't."

Kyler scratched his chin and braced for impact. "About that…"

Bree gasped, jerking the wheel of the truck. "Kyler Joseph Tate."

"I accidentally put them in the laundry basket once. Came home to find them neatly folded on my pillow." He shook his head. "My mom has a weird sense of humor."

"How am I ever going to look her in the eye again?"

An image of Bree and his mother sitting side by side at a dinner table made him yearn so hard, he had to take a few seconds to breathe. "You ever bump into my mother around town?"

"Don't think I'm letting the subject slide."

"Wouldn't dream of it, supergirl."

She sent him some hefty side-eye, but softened when Kyler pasted on his most contrite expression. "Once in a while at Nelson's. She's usually there with friends having coffee and pie." A beat passed. "She always asks me if I'm seeing anyone."

"And you always say, 'No, ma'am. Just textbooks and the backs of my eyelids.'"

Bree stretched her fingers on the steering wheel. "Should have known she was asking for you."

"Got the full report every Sunday." They traded a turbulent glance. "You want to know what really got it in my head, Bree? That I needed to come get you back?"

"I, um…" The pulse fluttered at the base of her neck, her body shifting in the driver's seat. "I don't know, I—"

"While you decide, I'll get started. How about that?" Kyler looked straight out the windshield toward the approaching farm, but in his mind's eye, he saw a man standing on his family's porch, cornfields spread out behind him. "You remember back in December when we almost lost the farm?"

She took one hand off the steering wheel and placed it over her heart. "Thank God you didn't."

"Yeah." Kyler swallowed the tightness in his throat. "Coach Brooks's girlfriend, Peggy—she's his wife now—came up with the fundraiser to satisfy the debt we owed to the bank. Well, it turned out Peggy and Brooks dated on the sly once upon a time. And while they were in Bloomfield, he was working on getting Peggy back. Failing pretty hard at it, best I could tell."

He laughed under his breath at the memory of his coach, living legend Elliott "Kingmaker" Brooks asking for dating advice on his porch.

"So I told him to take her to Marengo Cave." Kyler couldn't stop himself from grinning. "You remember when we went there?"

"I remember the bats."

"That can't be the *only* thing you remember." Taking a chance, Kyler reached across the console and laid a hand on Bree's thigh, groaning inwardly when the muscles twitched beneath his palm. "If I recall correctly, that was one of those times you couldn't keep these babies from cinching up around my waist."

With trembling fingers, Bree cranked the air conditioner, giving him an evil look when he chuckled. "I was scared of having my blood sucked out."

"All part of my diabolical plan." Giving her thigh one final squeeze, Kyler took his hand back. "I told my coach about you and he said something that stuck. Stuck harder than I realized at the time. 'Imagine you have one more day to fix everything…before she never thinks about you again.'" A chill moved through him and it had nothing to do with the air conditioner. "Scared the shit out of me, Bree. Still does. I didn't know how much until I was drafted."

She pulled the truck to a stop outside a freshly painted barn, her hand falling limp after turning off the ignition. "There's nothing that could stop me thinking about you. Our pasts are twined too closely together for that."

"You could say the same about our futures."

Her breath caught and the moment slowed down, Bree turning soft eyes on him, rain pattering on the truck's roof. In that space of time, he saw past her defenses. Saw they were weakening. And for the first time since coming back to Bloomfield, he reckoned he might have a chance.

"Kyler."

"I know I'm pushing, but I'm running short on time, Bree." Instinct screamed at him to drag her into his lap, to kiss the reservations and doubts out of her mind, but now wasn't the time. If he moved forward before she caught up, he'd ultimately lose ground, and that was out of the question.

His flight was scheduled for tomorrow afternoon.

The sound of the barn door sliding open had both of them looking out the windshield. A man who looked to be in his mid-twenties strode out through the opening, a cowboy hat shielding his head against the rain. His smile was wide when it searched out Bree in the truck, but it dimmed when he saw Kyler. *Good.*

"Behave yourself, Kyler Joseph, or I'll take a bite out of you."

"Promise?"

Color deepening on her cheeks, Bree collected her bag and climbed out of the truck, waving at the approaching fuck-face. "Hey, Mitch. How's the patient?"

"Mitch," Kyler snorted, then went to join them outside.

Kyler's competitive side could be fierce when the situation called for it. During his final year at Cincinnati, he'd been one of the three team captains, putting him at centerfield for the coin toss. No matter how often football purists waxed poetic about sportsmanship, that strut down the fifty-yard line to size up the opposing team's captains called for intimidation. Always had. While some of his teammates liked to crack their necks or bash their shoulder pads, Kyler chose to stand real still and make eye contact with each opposing player, looking for chinks in their armor. If he were the bragging sort, he'd call it damned effective.

This situation with Mitch wasn't a competition, though. He wasn't trying to be the bigger, more intimidating man. If he handled his jealousy by acting like a territorial dick, Bree would shut down on him faster than he could spit. So while the green monster hummed and shook inside him, begging to be appeased, Kyler forced himself to ignore it and remember one thing.

A life with him in Los Angeles was Bree's choice. Not his. He'd laid his cards on the table, bared his feelings, and the next move belonged to her. All he could do at this point was surprise her. And God knew, he loved doing that.

"Good to meet you, Mitch. Kyler Tate." He put his hand out. "Hope you don't mind me tagging along to watch Bree work."

Mitch's eyebrows hitched up—hell, the trainer almost looked disappointed in him being friendly—but he shook with Kyler nonetheless. "No, uh…that's fine." He tilted his head. "Kyler Tate, you say? Why does that ring a bell?"

"I don't know. Maybe it'll come to you."

The trainer scrutinized him another few seconds before shrugging. "Well, let's get out of the rain, shall we?"

Kyler gave Mitch what he hoped was a winning smile. "Great idea. Thanks."

When the other man turned for the barn—shoulders slumped a good deal more than before—Kyler found a mixture of suspicion and amusement on Bree's pretty face. "You see something interesting over here, supergirl?"

"When exactly am I going to get a handle on you?"

He checked the urge to throw an arm around Bree's shoulders, draw her up against his side. "Guess we'll have to wait and see."

They stopped at the entrance to one of the stalls. Inside, a brown horse with patches of white lay down, muscles tense. If Kyler didn't see it with his own eyes, he wouldn't have believed that the mare sighed in relief when it spotted Bree. She murmured something to the animal but made no move to approach, seeming to communicate from ten feet away.

"Her name is Flo-Rida."

He smiled "Like the rapper?"

"Yeah." She leaned into him and pointed at the horse's behind. "But also because she has a white patch in the shape of Florida. The owner's teenage son named her."

"Give that kid a medal."

Mitch cleared his throat behind them, reminding Kyler they weren't alone.

"Looks like you have everything under control for now," Mitch said. "I'm heading out for a bit. Call my number if you need anything."

Ignoring Kyler's grumble over her speaking with another man on the phone, Bree turned to Mitch and nodded. "Will do. Thank you."

If Kyler wasn't mistaken, Mitch looked a little dejected over not being asked to stay, so Kyler took some pity on him. "Wait up, Mitch." He jogged over and met the trainer at the barn entrance. "You mentioned my name ringing a bell. If that's on account of me playing football for Cincinnati and—"

Mitch snapped his fingers. "That's it. Hol-ee shit." He smacked a hand against his outer thigh. "You're playing for the Rage next season."

"Right." Kyler winked over at a dumbstruck Bree, who was probably going nuts not being able to hear their conversation. "I have a line on Bearcats tickets if you're ever up for a drive."

A few minutes later, Kyler's number was programmed into the trainer's phone and Kyler had to admit, not succumbing to jealousy had been harder than evading a tackle, but twice as satisfying.

Returning to Bree at the stall entrance, he leaned down to talk beside her ear. "Aren't you going to go in?"

She turned sparkling, excited eyes on him. "Not unless I'm needed." The backs of their hands brushed together and Kyler's belly tightened up like a drum. Not only because her touch never failed to have an effect, but her love for the animal, for her job, was contagious. "Foals are born naturally. They're cleaned by their mothers afterward and the bonding process begins. I try to stay out of it, only helping if there's a complication."

"Does that happen a lot?" Kyler asked, just to keep her talking in that rushing, euphoric way.

"I wouldn't say a lot. But nature needs a push once in a while." Her excited smile stopped his breath. "That's where I come in."

You want to take her away from this?

Ten gallons of cement coated Kyler's shoulders, hardening immediately. Bree was watching him closely, though, so he forced a casual demeanor. "You were right. The horse does trust you. I could see it." A million thoughts raced in his head, but one stood out brighter than all others. "Dammit, Bree. I'm so proud of you."

"I'm proud of you, too," she whispered, her brows drawing together at whatever she read on his face. "Kyler?"

Who was he kidding? He'd never been able to hide anything for long from Bree. A fact he'd completely forgotten in the face of seeing how much she thrived in this environment. An environment that might as well be a million miles from Los Angeles.

She started to speak again, but the mare made a distressed sound and stood on shaky legs, sending Bree rushing into the stall.

Chapter Thirteen

Bree's hands were steady, but her adrenaline pumped hot.

Above her, the mare made a long, guttural sound of distress. "Only one of the foal's feet is showing," she explained to Kyler, her voice thick. "We need to stand Flo-Rida up and walk her around. That should hopefully reposition the foal. If it doesn't, I'll have to do it myself."

Without missing a beat, Kyler rubbed his hands together. "Okay. Stand her up and walk around. Let's do this, supergirl."

I'm still in love with him.

Freaking obviously.

Who *wouldn't* love this man? Especially—*God*—when he loved her with so much conviction and patience and persistence. After four years of no communication. He'd signed a multimillion-dollar contract to play professional football. Fame, idolization, and freedom were at his disposal. Yet here was Kyler Tate, same exact man he'd always been—with the addition of some extra drool-worthy muscles—ready to help her deliver a foal on a rainy day in a barn. No questions asked. Because it was what she needed.

It was time, however, that she stopped denying what she needed *most.* That she'd never *stopped* needing. Kyler.

Lord knew she was a stubborn woman and always had been. Kyler was her equal in that way. They'd both spent their separation operating in unique ways. Kyler had bided his time while Bree lived in denial. Had she really believed that someday she would magically get over Kyler? What a farce. Until she took her final breath on this earth, his face would be the first she pictured when someone uttered the word love in her presence. He was her first love and down in the pit of her soul, she'd known he would be her last.

Tucking away the truth for later, Bree blew out a deep breath and stood. After unhooking the bridle from where it hung on the wall, she took care sliding it over the agitated mare's head, whispering comfort to her as she cinched and secured it. With some urging, she led Flo-Rida toward the stall exit, Kyler holding the mare steady on the other side.

"My dad used to be in charge during foaling time. Without him here, the waiting still makes me anxious," Bree murmured. "Talk to me about something."

"I'm going to hook Mitch up with Bearcats tickets," Kyler answered immediately, *shhing* the horse when she made a low whinny. "Despite his name being Mitch."

A chuckle burst free of Bree's lips. "What's wrong with the name Mitch?"

"Nothing. It's perfect. It's exactly what I would name the man I had to battle for your favor."

"But you didn't battle him," she pointed out.

He winked at her over the top of the mare's head. "Didn't I?"

Right there, less than three feet away, was the only person in the world who always managed to make her laugh, grow exasperated, and be surprised, all at the same time. "Where are you going to live in Los Angeles?"

The question slipped out without warning, but Kyler showed no reaction apart from his grip creaking on the reins. "They put us in a hotel for training camp. It gives us time to find a place to call home." He slid her a glance. "I don't know what this life is going to bring, Bree. I could be traded after a few years. Find myself down in Dallas or up in New York. So I figured while…we're in California, we should live by the ocean. Someplace small that makes the change not seem so huge. Two bedrooms, a giant bathtub. A big, floppy dog sleeping on the end of our bed."

A wrench fell in her stomach. "Low blow."

His mouth ticked up at the corner, hope flaring in his green eyes. "I've had some nervous energy on my hands over the last couple days waiting for you to have a good think, so I've been looking at apartments." A beat passed. "I don't know if you still have the same plans, supergirl, but if you wanted to attend a four-year veterinary school, Western University is only a short drive away."

"My plans haven't changed." The wings of fear and excitement tickled her throat, battling one another. "You looked into all that for me?"

"Made sure there was a diner within walking distance of the apartment, too. I know that's how you like to get your coffee."

Her knees wobbled. "Never really got into Starbucks."

"I know."

"Something so formal about ordering coffee off a menu," she whispered under her breath, just to fill the charged silence. "Whipped cream on coffee doesn't seem like it should be an everyday thing."

They reached the wall of the barn and gently turned the mare around, Bree running a hand down her flank. "In the off-season, we could come back to Bloomfield," Kyler continued, his tone low, bordering on urgent. "Whatever you want."

"What about what you want?"

"I want *us*," he rasped. "I'll build everything else around that. That has been my plan since age thirteen. It just got delayed."

"Kyler. This is crazy." The slow pace of their walk was a stark contrast to Bree's rapid heartbeat. The gravity that continued to consume and release her, wrecking her balance. "Can we really ever come back, though? All the attention that follows you around..." She shook her head. "Before college, it was town pride. Now it's curiosity and people standing outside the gym or crowding you to death in Nelson's—"

"I'll keep it away from you." Threads of determination stitched themselves together in Kyler's voice. "No more dragging you out into the open, Bree. I've learned my lesson."

"You can't stop being yourself, Ky. I wouldn't want you to stop."

"Where does that leave me?" he whispered to himself.

Bree ached to take a leap, but impulsive decisions were never how she'd worked. Time and pro/con lists, testing the waters. That's how she operated. Once upon a time, Kyler had been her listening ear. Her sounding board. So while she wanted desperately to leap into his arms, kiss his mouth, and agree to California, she wasn't quite ready. Not without laying some things to rest in her mind.

They reached the stall and Bree guided Flo-Rida back down onto the pallet, observing for long minutes while the mare labored. When she saw both legs emerge, confirming the foal had been repositioned during their walk, Bree fell back on her butt with a sigh of relief, remaining there under the false assumption her heart rate would slow now that the danger had passed. But it didn't.

"Talk to me," Kyler said, threading his fingers through her curls. "Tell me what's holding you back. Tell me what you didn't say on prom night."

"My family needs me," she breathed. "I belong here. In Bloomfield."

"There's more."

Bree looked up to find Kyler watching her from beneath hooded eyelids, seeing straight through to her center. "I've never stopped aching over hurting you. It was the worst night of my life."

"Mine, too." Mouth in a grim line, Kyler scooped Bree up and carried her from the stall. "Talk to me."

She shoved his shoulder, but he didn't budge. "I'm getting there."

Just outside the stall, he set her down, backing her up against the wooden partition. Intensity radiated from every inch of his rock-wall body. "I'll just wait here and be patient. Sound good?"

A laugh shuddered out of her, but it held little humor. Spiked wheels turned in her belly, digging in and getting stuck. "My mother left when we needed her." Words she'd never said out loud poured free, through the cracks of a smashed dam. "She wanted more. I'm afraid to admit I want more, too. Even to myself."

The tension lines around Kyler's mouth softened. "It isn't more, Bree. It's *different*."

"It's *more*. It's California, money and fame and all the things *she* wanted. I'm betraying my family by accepting them, by wanting them, aren't I?"

"I could tell you no, but you're the one who has to believe it."

"That's annoyingly logical." She dropped her forehead onto his chest. "My father would never say it out loud, but I know he feels like a failure for not making her happy. I can't be his instant replay."

Kyler sighed hard, pressing kisses into her hair. "He gave you *this*. Being a vet. As much as I'll bust my ass to make you happy, this will always be something that's yours. And his. You'll never stop sharing it with him, no matter where you are. Los Angeles or Bloomfield."

"It won't be the same." She looked around the barn and thought of her clients. The animals. Familiar faces. Her routine. And the ground shook beneath her at the thought of leaving it all behind. But the idea of Kyler going to Los Angeles without her? It wasn't just tremors beneath her feet. It was a ten on the seismograph. "I can't—"

From the stall came a long, guttural sound, following by the rustling of the ground, the pallet stuffing. Bree and Kyler moved to the opening of the stall, peeking around the edge to find a newborn foal being licked by his mother, tail to head. No matter how many times she witnessed the miracles of her profession, these moments never failed to amaze her. She cupped a hand around her mouth, laughing into it with pure joy.

But when she turned to Kyler to capture his reaction, to store it away in her heart, he was watching her instead. And for once, she couldn't read his expression.

Chapter Fourteen

What if the best way to make Bree happy...was to leave her?

Walk away from her, remembering this moment of total rapture on her face? And just admitting that he'd failed, so that she could succeed.

There were so many snapshots in his memory of Bree as a girl, smiling up at him, just like this, usually when they were alone and he did something goofy. Or when they'd reached the very top of that Ferris wheel, that misty fall morning a million years ago, sunlight breaking through the clouds to kiss her face.

"Ky?"

This wasn't Bree the girl, though. Now she was a woman and she'd found a way to make herself happy, all by herself. She was the same Bree, with new, amazing differences. Changes she'd carved into her heart, without him there to witness it.

When she said his name again, it was a short punctuation, her mouth snapping shut afterward. "Ky."

She reached up with both hands, smoothing fingers over his eyebrows, looking almost frustrated as she searched his face. That was a first. He'd never been capable of mystifying her, nor had he ever tried. He cleared his throat, determined to reassure her, but he stopped himself. What would he say? His world seemed determined to break apart and the only thing keeping it together was Bree's touch exploring his features, tracing down the grooves of his cheeks, sliding up into his hair.

More. Whatever would happen tomorrow, he needed more of Bree now. Needed to hold on tight while time seemed to rush around them, unable to be controlled.

"Say something," she whispered. And it was the fear in her eyes that compelled him forward. The need to rid her of it.

"Everything is going to be fine," he murmured, grasping her wrists, holding her warm palms against his face. "I understand now, Bree."

"Y-you understand—"

His mouth stopped Bree's question, his tongue savoring her jagged gasp. Color exploded in his mind, splattering on the backs of his eyelids in patterns. God, the taste of her was a fucking work of art. Her gasp, the way she tilted her tits up. None of it could be helped. Just the music they made together.

There was some reservation in her kiss, the stroke of her tongue hesitant against the insistence of his. So Kyler used his grip on her curls to tilt her head, branding her mouth with hot slants of lips and hunger, reminding her nothing took precedence over the need they shared. It was alive, sliding warm and liquid down from their belly buttons. Preparing them. His head might be on fire with regret and worry, but nothing burned hotter than they did. It was the definite he needed right now.

Bree caved to his urgency, tension leaving her neck, making it fall to one side. Kyler took advantage of the opening, racing his open lips up the smooth column, clamping the lobe of her ear between his teeth. At the very same time, he fit his erection into the notch of her thighs, ramming her lower body against the partition. "Where?"

"Where?" Bree gasped. "Where what?"

"Focus." Those legs snapped around his hips like they'd been painted on, tearing a groan from his throat. "Where in this barn can I fill up the pussy I was born to satisfy? Give me an answer, supergirl. Going to take off my jeans and wear you instead."

Rain pounded on the barn's roof. Thunder rolled. Lightning struck and lit up the space with white light. Or maybe it was all taking place in her eyes. Kyler couldn't tell. Only knew if he didn't bury himself inside his woman, if he didn't plead for pleasure from her body with his own, he might not survive to the next minute. "H'um…there?" She jerked a thumb over her shoulder at nowhere in particular, never taking her gaze off his mouth. "Thereabouts."

Kyler's laugh was rife with pain and starvation, but he marched in the direction she'd indicated, entering the first empty stall and pinning her sexy, giving body up against the far wall. They were covered by darkness, except for the occasional burst of lightning, making Kyler's groping hands seem like an act of nature. Hell, they were. His God-given humanity was in total control now, feeding on his woman. As though her kisses, the welcome of her body, could sustain him until the world ceased.

"Need to get your shorts and panties off," he muttered huskily, cupping his hands beneath her knees. Raising them and grinding down against her center until she cried out. "Can't let you unwrap these sick legs just yet, though. Ride my dick, Bree. Break me. Tease me. Give me an excuse to be rough."

Her position didn't give her much room to move, but Christ almighty, she worked with what she had. Reaching between their heaving bodies, she lifted the hem of her T-shirt, displaying her silk-cupped tits. Then her hips started circling in a rhythm designed to kill a man. Her fingernails sunk into his shoulders through the material of his shirt, her pussy dragging over his pulsing inches in a torturous dance that left Kyler sucking in deep gulps of breath. Running the tip of his tongue over the hills of her cleavage, leaving a trail in his wake, Kyler took her ass in both hands, moving her in the pattern she'd started, shattering his control one grind at a time.

But when she blinked those bedroom eyes up at him and flexed her thighs, whispering, "There's your excuse," Kyler lost his grip on reality.

Growling low in his throat, he shoved her legs down, tearing aside the cups of her bra with bared teeth. With one of her nipples sucked into his mouth, he unzipped her shorts and wrenched them down, along with her panties, grunting an unspoken command to kick them off. As soon as she was bare from the waist down, Bree dropped her right hand from his shoulder and freed his cock in a few frantic movements.

"Now, now, now, Ky. Please."

His middle finger slipped through her folds, finding her dripping wet, and his dick jerked up against his abdomen, making his teeth clench on a moan. Insistent hunger clawed at the walls of his stomach, weighing down his balls like hot, liquid metal. Taking his hurting inches in one hand, he positioned himself against Bree's tight entrance and filled her in one bone-rattling thrust. His mouth clamped over hers just in time to catch her scream of his name, and he swallowed it, savoring the way it vibrated on the way down.

"Just once I'd love to be between these thighs in a fucking bed, Bree. You have any idea what I would give for that?" He pulled out and drove deep, consuming another one of her screams, reveling in the pain of her nails breaking skin through his T-shirt. "My fucking soul. I would hand it right over."

"Oh my God." Her eyes were blind, words pushed out from between her teeth, her thighs tight and trembling around his waist. "Doesn't matter where. Feels so good. Kyler, *don't stop.*"

"It *matters.*" He ground their foreheads together, beginning to pump in earnest, one forceful drive after the other. "Where I fuck the love of my life matters. I want to buy sheets together, bring them home, and lick you until they're drenched. I don't want time limits or worrying if we'll get caught. I'm a goddamn man and I want my woman beside me when I sleep, Bree."

"I picture you beside me sometimes." The treasure blew out of her in a rush and unglued him, deconstructed him into tiny pieces. He could only absorb the impact as she planted kisses on his face, rubbing circles onto his chest with the heels of her hands, down his back. "When I'm nervous or I have a big surgery the next day, I think of you lying beside me, telling me it'll be all right. That afterward, it'll just be you and me."

"Bree," he croaked, pressure pushing inward on his skull. "Fuck, Bree. I almost died from missing you."

"I'm sorry. I'm *sorry.*"

There it was. Those two words were the answer he'd come to Bloomfield afraid to hear, weren't they? She couldn't come with him. Taking her to Los Angeles would dim the beautiful glow inside her, and he wouldn't be responsible for that. No way in hell. Kyler wouldn't fault her for it, though. Being angry at Bree never lasted because the love smashed it. Always would.

The call of his body to give her satisfaction rose to a fever pitch, moving his hips in greedy drives. Jesus, he'd always been twice Bree's size, but he'd grown broader, more solid, and she bounced off the hard surface of his body now with loud, moist slaps, her legs spread for his cock. She tossed her head back and gave hot, little whimpers every time her tits jiggled with the force of his thrusts. And Lord help him, he adored every gorgeous inch of her. Knowing her glow came from the inside made her twice as beautiful. His open mouth planted itself over hers, stealing her exhales and filling his lungs with them. "You'll always be mine, won't you?"

"Same as you'll always be mine."

Tongue twining with hers, he used his grip on her ass to hold her steady for a final series of drives, committing the increased shaking of her thighs to memory. The way she sucked in a gasp and held it, her brown eyes darkening, chin dropping. His cock throbbed, on the verge of release, but he held fast and waited, waited, for her to go hurtling past the finish line, her head falling back and slamming against the wall, muscles tensing and shuddering. "Oh…my God. *Kyler.*"

"Bree. *I love you.* My girl. *Always* mine."

He kissed her though the end of her storm and the beginning of his.

And when it was over, everything in his world had been rearranged.

Chapter Fifteen

"You can't be here. How did you get this address?" Raised male voices cut through the lethargic haze of Bree's mind. She sat up and looked around at the darkened interior of the truck, moonlight spilling across the dashboard. Eleven-thirty said the clock. No wonder she was exhausted. After two restless nights, the foal's birth, and Kyler taking her in the barn, fatigue had hit her like a two-by-four. The last thing she remembered was Kyler snagging the keys and telling her to catch some z's. "This is my girlfriend's house. She—you need to leave. Now, please."

Bree forced her heavy eyelids to widen and found Kyler outside the truck. He continued to shift left and right, blocking her view of the man he argued with. Argued with…in her driveway?

Her fingers went to the door handle, curling around it, but she recoiled when a bright light cut through the night and blinded her. The man held a camera.

"Training camp starts next week and the Rage has been chosen for a documentary. This is just preliminary stuff," said the stranger. "Couldn't hunt you down at your parents' house and someone in town was kind enough to direct me here. Your girlfriend, you say?"

Again, the light crept over Kyler's shoulder, so intrusive and stark. Bree covered her face and scooted toward the driver's side, climbing out, but remaining hidden behind the truck. "Ky?"

"Bree, go on inside. It's going to be all right." Kyler spoke without turning to look at her. His back and shoulder muscles strained beneath his white T-shirt, hands balled in fists, his posture daring the man to raise his camera one more time. Her suspicion was confirmed a moment later when he gritted out, "Lift that camera and you'll never find all the pieces."

A low whistle came from the stranger. "I get it, man. You're protective. Must be serious, then. How long have you been dating? How do you think she'll manage while you're on the road? Any plans for a family?"

"*Bree.*"

Surprisingly, her instinct wasn't to run. The spotlight usually sent her tearing off to the closest parking lot. But fleeing didn't even occur to her in that moment. No, leaving Kyler to handle the situation alone felt wrong. Her instinct demanded she go to him, pull him inside. Let the jerk cameraman take whatever pictures he wanted. They weren't doing anything wrong. They were two people who loved one another. Why should they hide themselves away?

How would she handle Kyler going on the road? They'd survived *four years*. Mere days would be child's play. She almost had the urge to laugh.

There was nothing funny about Kyler's demeanor, though. And she was far too fatigued to fight this battle tonight. They didn't *need* to fight any battle but their own, and tomorrow would be soon enough. Los Angeles was light years away and she still needed to examine the move from every angle. Kyler would understand. He would be patient, as always. They would figure out what came next in their life together when she could keep her eyes open.

"Come inside," she called. "Come with me."

Finally he turned, a wealth of turbulence in his eyes. So much undisguised emotion, her stomach began to churn. "I'll handle this. You go in."

She shook her head. "No."

"Please, Bree. This is your home." Then quieter, "I did this."

"If you're not gone in thirty seconds, I'm calling the police." Bree lifted her chin and made a little shooing motion toward the cameraman. "I'm counting."

Kyler stood there with his back turned to her long after the red sedan disappeared down the driveway. With exhaustion weighing heavy on her shoulders, both of them locked inside the darkness, she felt as if she were in a dream. Nothing seemed real. Not the cameraman, not the new, shimmering image in her mind of a home on the beach, a floppy dog on the bed. Definitely not the new confidence and strength in her bones, possibly ready to embrace change. None of it.

"Kyler," she whispered, going up behind him, laying kisses along the breadth of his shoulders. "Tuck me in?"

Turning, he made a gruff noise and led her inside by the hand. Her father had left the front door unlocked, but after what happened, she reasoned they should be cautious. Kyler watched as she turned the bolt with a pained expression, obviously still upset over the scene in the driveway. "Hey, I don't think he'll be back." She tugged him down the hallway toward her bedroom, keeping her voice to a whisper. "Once he discovers the cast of characters in Bloomfield, he won't need a sound bite from me. They'll keep him entertained."

Bree didn't bother turning on the light in her bedroom. She simply kicked off her shoes, dropped her jean shorts, and curled into a fetal position on the bed. It wasn't until sleep started to descend like a heavy metal curtain did she realize Kyler still stood just inside the door, silent and still as a statue.

"Where's my kiss?" Bree murmured, turning onto her back.

He moved so fast, she'd barely managed to suck in a breath before Kyler planted his hands on the mattress, caging her in...and delivered a knock-out blow courtesy of his mouth. There was something about the kiss that snagged her memory, but she was too consumed to place it. Her limbs turned to jelly, her fingers grappling with the bedspread. The insides of her thighs began to itch, greedy for his hips to settle between them, but he broke contact before it could happen.

"Sleep, supergirl," he said huskily, planting his lips on her forehead. "Everything will look better in the morning."

A tingle on the back of Bree's neck commanded her to go after him, but it took too long for her legs to move. His tall, reliable form disappeared through the doorway, the outline of him lingering and renewing the notion she was dreaming. And then there was nothing.

* * * *

Bree woke up smiling. She'd had the *best* dream. One she'd had many times in the past, but not recently. Not since Kyler left. And now she knew why.

She was supposed to be with him. Wherever he went.

Sitting up in bed, her heart was bursting with certainty from the remnants of her dream. Kyler standing on a green lawn, sunlight catching on the stubble adorning his chin and cheeks. Behind him, a house, modest and loved. A flannel shirt was tucked crookedly into the waistband of Kyler's jeans because he'd been wrestling with their two boys and a big, clumsy dog. Footballs, dog toys, and bikes laying haphazardly every few feet on the grass.

This image, one she'd had a thousand times, had never been more vivid. Never more real. She could smell the chimney smoke in the air, feel the love in Kyler's eyes as they reached her across the yard.

Bree gasped out loud at the impact of it. She needed to go see him now. Spending even one night apart seemed ridiculous all of a sudden. Or maybe it always had. She didn't know. Didn't know, but they would sort through everything together as soon as they were in the same room. Being away from him was causing this horrible ache. One that made her hands flutter over the spot, a lump sticking in her throat.

When her gaze landed on the bedside clock, Bree knew why. It was past one o'clock in the afternoon. Kyler's flight left for Los Angeles today.

Bree's blood chilled as memories from last night began to trickle in. The cameraman in the driveway. *I did this*, Kyler had said. Then…then that kiss. The familiarity of it.

Because he'd only ever given her a kiss like that once before. To say good-bye when she ended things on prom night.

"No. No. He wouldn't leave yet." Bree's feet twisted in the sheet on the way out of bed, almost knocking her to the floor. In a daze, she went to the bathroom and brushed her teeth, not seeing herself in the mirror. Seeing nothing except Kyler's unreadable expression last night in the barn.

Everything is going to be fine. I understand now.

He understood what? Why…why she couldn't go with him? Why she needed to stay? That's what they'd been talking about, right? Los Angeles. Bree's mother. All the cons on the list of why Bree couldn't go with him. But none of the pros.

None of the reasons why she *could*.

Her bloodless fingers dropped the toothbrush in the sink, fear slicing straight up her middle.

He'd left.

Last night, he'd been saying good-bye.

Cymbals crashed in Bree's head, balance deserting her as she ran back into her bedroom. Blood beat in her temples, her lungs scraped raw from dragging in jagged breaths. She pulled on the jean shorts still resting on the floor, shoved her feet into galoshes, and ran for the house's front door. Rainclouds covered the sun, shrouding the house in gloom, moisture pouring down the windows.

She turned in a circle, trying to gather her bearings, but it didn't work. Various images of Kyler cycled one by one through her consciousness. Dancing. Speaking to her outside the diner, casual ease forced into his voice. How could she have missed his determination? Had she been blind? Kyler across from her at the dinner table, driving beside her, walking the mare.

"Oh, please." Bree grabbed her stomach and jogged toward the door. "Oh God, please."

If he'd already left, changing Kyler's mind would be a feat equivalent to turning back time. Convincing him she wanted—*needed*—to come along would be impossible if she let the deadline of his flight pass. The man did what he thought was best for her. Never failed. And she'd stupidly given him every reason to leave, to set her free.

I don't want to be free of him. Being free of Kyler is the real prison.

Just before Bree reached the door, something stopped her in her tracks. The family portrait—which included her mother—that had been hanging since she was a child...had been replaced. The new photograph featured her father, her sister, and herself. Just the three of them.

It was the look in her own eye that captured Bree's attention. It wasn't far off and disconnected, the way her mother's had been. No. She was present, looking down at Kira lovingly, her hand resting over Samuel's where it lay on her shoulder.

A light went on behind her. "You could be a million miles away and we'd still feel you here. With us." Her father's voice came from the dining room, strong and steady. Full of affection. "You're not abandoning us, Bree. You never could."

She pressed the back of her hand over her mouth for a beat. "I abandoned him, though, didn't I? Now I'm too late."

"You're underestimating him." Her father's long-suffering sigh turned Bree around. "I wouldn't say that unless I meant it."

"I know." She pointed an accusing finger at her father but didn't have the strength to keep her arm up. "You love him, too."

"Don't push it." With a wink, he jerked his head toward the door. "Go."

Bree rushed out into the rain without an umbrella, going straight for her truck. She pulled down the sun visor and the keys dropped into her lap, where Kyler had apparently left them. Such a simple gesture, but it made a sob rise in Bree's throat as she gunned the truck in reverse down the driveway. Before turning onto the street, she caught sight of a red sedan parked on the main road. In the driver's seat, a man watched her with a cautious smile.

An idea formed. But it would only work if Kyler hadn't left.

And an awful pit in her stomach yawned wide, telling her...he had.

* * * *

Bree's worst fear was confirmed when she pulled up in front of Kyler's home.

There wasn't a vehicle in sight.

Not his truck, not his daddy's. His mother's station wagon was gone, too.

Were they seeing him off at the airport? Was Kyler already on the way home, his plane nothing but a speck in the air on its way to Los Angeles?

She climbed out of the truck on shaky legs, her galoshes sinking into the mud, making her slip forward. The red sedan pulled up behind her in the driveway, the cameraman stepping out with plastic already positioned over his head and the camera. A look of sympathy skittered across his face before he hid it.

God, she could very well have brought this man along to witness her humiliation. She was too late. Had to be. Why would Kyler wait around for someone who'd doubted what they had together? Over and over. She wouldn't even blame him if he'd given up and left.

Rain coasted down Bree's cheeks as she walked slowly for the front door. Each footstep sank into the mud, as though God was trying to inform her this was a fool's mission. The cameraman's footsteps echoed hers, *glopping* every couple seconds in the mud. A slow-moving funeral procession.

Finally, she'd climbed the steps and stood outside the door. Her knock sounded so hollow, ringing back at her from inside the empty house. The rain began falling heavier, pounding the ground around the Tate house, thunder rolling far off in the distance.

Still, she knocked again, harder. "Kyler?"

The camera light went on behind her, reflecting in the brass doorknob, but Bree no longer cared about having an audience for her worst moment. No, there had always been far more at stake with Kyler than stupid cameras could ever capture. She would welcome hundreds of them in her face as long as Kyler held her at the end of the day, issuing challenges in her ear. Calling her—

"Supergirl?"

For a second, Bree thought it was her imagination conjuring Kyler's voice. She whipped around toward the cameraman, but he was no longer pointing his device at her. No, the light shined on Kyler where he stood at the base of the steps, rain pouring down his head, dripping off his chin.

He was the most incredible, most beautiful sight she'd ever seen. Relief caught her so hard in the belly, she slumped back against the door, pinned there by the miracle she'd been given.

Kyler shot up the steps, concern etched on his beloved face. "Bree? What's wrong?" He turned wild eyes on the cameraman, who wisely backed up but kept filming. "Don't worry, I'm going to take care of this. It won't happen again—"

"No. No, he's... I asked him to come." Her hands trembled as she swiped at the rain in her face. "Oh God, I-I thought you'd left. I thought you'd *left*."

Bree didn't realize she'd slid down the door into a sitting position until Kyler went to his knees, crawling toward her. "Hey." He cupped her face in two warm hands, his green eyes blazing. "I told you, Bree. I said it and you heard me. I'm not leaving without you."

"But your flight—"

"I missed it." His gaze moved over her face, catching on her eyelids, stray curls, her nose, mouth. "Your home is here. This is where you're happy—"

"No, wait—"

"So I'm staying." He shook her and repeated himself. "I'm staying. That's how this was always going to work if you didn't decide to come, supergirl. You just weren't hearing me all the way."

For the next few moments, the sound of rain falling and her tortured heartbeat was all she could hear. "You were going to give it up for me?"

"Not were. Am." His thumbs skated over her lips. "None of it means a damn thing without you, Bree. I'm getting a little tired of saying it and not having you believe me."

"So stop." Lord, she couldn't get her breath. This man. He was one and the same with her dreams. "Stop saying it. Because it means something to me." She desperately tried to gather her thoughts. "I dreamed of you last night. Sons. We had sons. A yard and a dog. And you loved me. I could feel how much you loved me, clear across the yard." Her voice fell to a whisper. "Clear from Cincinnati."

Kyler's eyes turned glassy, his breath escaping in a giant rush. "Damn right I love you."

"California is the first step in that journey. We're going to take it together. I *want* to, Kyler. I don't want to stay here and wonder what we could have seen and done. Our *own* life. All the things that'll steer it. The directions we'll take." Tears mixed with rain on her cheeks. "I want to go with you."

He stayed very still, but hope livened his features. "Do you mean that?"

Bree was still nodding when he launched himself at her, wrapping her in a bear hug and hauling her onto his lap. They fell back onto the porch in the glow of the camera, still wrapped up in each other's arms. "Christ. I thought I was imagining you standing on this porch, Bree."

She clung to his neck. "Where were you?"

"Walking through the cornfields. Deciding on my next move with you."

Her heart tripled its tempo. "What did you come up with?"

"I got as far as another dance off..." They both stopped to laugh, Kyler rubbing their noses together. "But I decided to go for broke and propose instead." His hand went to his pocket, coming back with a simple antique engagement ring between two fingers. His expression turned serious, even in the wake of Bree's gulping cry of his name. "I was going to refuse to take no for an answer. In case you're wondering, that part hasn't changed."

"Ask me," Bree murmured, framing his face with her hands.

"Be my wife, supergirl. Let me love you from across the yard."

"Yes."

A slow clap started from the base of the steps. Clearly having forgotten about their audience, Bree and Kyler both turned to look to find the cameraman flipping off the light and lowering his device. "Congratulations." He turned away and started toward his car. "And good luck next season."

"Who needs luck when I've got Bree Justice?" Kyler blew her mind with a slow, drugging kiss, his mouth hot and uncompromising. "Why did you bring him along?"

"To show you I'm going to be okay. There's just you and me, Ky." She licked into his mouth and moaned when he shifted his hips. "The rest is just noise," she gasped.

"Come for a walk in the cornfields with me."

"In the rain?"

That challenging expression she knew so well made Bree's heart float up, up into the clouds. "Scared?"

"Scared?" She shook her head. "No. I'll go anywhere with you."

Minutes later, they disappeared into the stalks, eternity stretching out around them and in front of them.

Epilogue

Kyler had expected attention and cameras. He hadn't planned on national interest in his and Bree's relationship. Only this time, *she'd* been the one dragging *him* into the spotlight. And boy, did she appear to be reveling in the turnabout.

During their first week in Los Angeles, Kyler and his fiancée had been recognized on the street by well-wishers, media, and Rage fans everywhere they went, thanks to the viral video of his proposal. The first time they'd been approached and asked for a picture, he'd gone tense, but Bree didn't so much as flinch, flashing her beautiful smile at the cameras he'd once dreaded.

Signing the lease on their apartment and enrolling Bree in the veterinary medicine program at Western University was the first order of business, before Kyler fell into the full-throttle hell of training camp. Every morning, Bree sent him off with a sleepy kiss and each night he crawled into bed beside her, pushing textbooks and binders out of the way before pulling her into his arms and passing out.

Yes, they finally had a damn bed. Since they'd forgone putting down expensive roots in California right away, they'd splurged on the most extravagant bed Kyler could find, tricking it out with soft sheets and feather pillows. The only trouble with their first shared bed was getting out of it. And on their mutual days off, they didn't even bother trying, only emerging from the bedroom for food. Or to take a walk on the beach, which stretched out from the end of their block, straight through to forever, a lot like the cornfields they often missed.

Bree's fall semester coincided with football season, so those days were few and far between, but they only treasured them more. No amount of time or difficulty could touch them. Commitment was in the way they looked at one another. Not a damn thing, especially some days apart, could test their bond. It was airtight.

Today was Kyler's first regular season game. Walking out onto the field, a flashback to high school hit him. Bree up in the stands, red-faced over the way everyone stared at her when his name was announced. The ooohs and kissing noises. High school stuff.

This stadium full of thousands of roaring fans? *Not* high school stuff. Truth be told, Kyler lost his ever-loving cool envisioning Bree in the center of it all. Recognizable. Alone, despite the team security that escorted the players' family members. His hands clenched in the leather gloves, his gaze searching uselessly through the writhing crowd for her face.

She's there. You're going home to her. Relax.

Easier said than done.

Taking a deep breath, Kyler prepared to put his helmet back on when a sign caught his eye, just even with the fifty-yard line, about four rows back.

It said, "Supergirl," and had an arrow pointing downward, at the only person who could calm him down in that moment. Bree.

Relief and love rocked him back on his heels. Especially when Bree stood and Kyler saw that she wore his jersey. She blew him a kiss and turned around... And on the back, above his number— instead of Tate—the name read, "Superguy."

Leave it to Bree to make him feel invincible.

And that day, he was. And *every* day, they were.

THE END

* * * *

Also from 1001 Dark Nights and Tessa Bailey, discover Rough Rhythm.

About Tessa Bailey

Tessa Bailey is originally from Carlsbad, California. The day after high school graduation, she packed her yearbook, ripped jeans and laptop, driving cross-country to New York City in under four days. Her most valuable life experiences were learned thereafter while waitressing at K-Dees, a Manhattan pub owned by her uncle. Inside those four walls, she met her husband, best friend and discovered the magic of classic rock, managing to put herself through Kingsborough Community College and the English program at Pace University at the same time. Several stunted attempts to enter the work force as a journalist followed, but romance writing continued to demand her attention. She now lives in Long Island, New York with her husband of ten years and five-year-old daughter. Although she is severely sleep-deprived, she is incredibly happy to be living her dream of writing about people falling in love.

Also By Tessa Bailey

Discover More Tessa Bailey

ROUGH RHYTHM
By Tessa Bailey

God help the woman I take home tonight.

Band manager James Brandon never expected to find the elusive satisfaction he'd been chasing, let alone stumble upon it in some sleezy Hollywood meat market. Yet the girl's quiet pride spoke to him from across the bar, louder than a shout. Troubled, hungry and homeless, she'd placed her trust in him. But after losing the grip on his dark desires that one fateful night, James has spent the last four years atoning for letting her down.

This time I'll finally crack him.

Rock band drummer Lita Regina has had enough of James's guilt. She wants the explosive man she met that night in Hollywood. The man who held nothing back and took no prisoners—save Lita. And she'll stop at nothing to revive him. Even if it means throwing herself into peril at every turn, just to get a reaction from her stoic manager. But when Lita takes her quest one step too far, James disappears from her life, thinking his absence will keep her safe.

Now it's up to Lita to bring James back…and ignite an inferno of passion in the process.

Reader Advisory: *ROUGH RHYTHM* contains fantasies of nonconsensual sex, acted upon by consenting characters. Readers with sensitivity to portrayals of nonconsensual sex should be advised.

Too Hard to Forget
Romancing the Clarksons, Book 3
by Tessa Bailey
Now Available

This time, *she's* calling the shots.

Peggy Clarkson is returning to her alma mater with one goal in mind: confront Elliott Brooks, the man who ruined her for all others, and remind him of what he's been missing. Even after three years, seeing him again is like a punch in the gut, but Peggy's determined to stick to her plan. Maybe then, once she has the upper hand, she'll finally be able to move on.

In the years since Peggy left Cincinnati, Elliott has kept his focus on football. No distractions and no complications. But when Peggy walks back onto his practice field and into his life, he knows she could unravel everything in his carefully controlled world. Because the girl who was hard to forget is now a woman *impossible* to resist.

* * * *

Peggy couldn't pinpoint what drew her toward the tunnel. The football game was going to start in just fifteen minutes, and she was supposed to be leading the Bearcat cheerleading squad's warm-ups. But just like always, she was aware of his absence. On the field, pacing the sideline, terse instructions being delivered into his headset, while eagle eyes watched the team stretch and prepare. And in the same way she never failed to sense him nearby, his absence was having the opposite effect now. Instead of feeling hot and full, her stomach was cold and empty.

Pompoms in hand, Peggy walked on the balls of her feet down the silent, airless hall leading to the football team's locker room. She had no authorization to be there but couldn't ignore the pull. She'd find him back there. The man who watched her as if she were the Promised Land one moment, hell the next.

Elliott Brooks. Head coach of the Bearcats. Two-time recipient of the Coach of the Year award. Uncompromising hard ass known for demanding perfection not only from his team, but himself. Devout Catholic. They called him the Kingmaker, because so many of his players had gone on to be first round NFL draft picks. That man. The one who visited her bed nightly.

Well. In her dreams, anyway. In real life, they'd never exchanged a single word. Their long, secretive glances were a language all their own, though. When cheerleading and football practices intersected, his burning coal eyes moved over her like a brush fire.

What are you looking at? *His gaze seemed to ask. But in the same glance, she could read the contradicting subtext.* Don't you *dare* look at anyone on this field but me.

Give me one good reason, *she would blink back, cocking a hip.*

And he would. Commanding the field with a whip crack command, stalking the sidelines like a predatory creature, seeing all, commenting only when strictly necessary. Those eyes would sneak back to her, though. Without fail. Their message would read, I'm a man among boys. There's your reason.

Or she'd imagined everything and the telepathic communication was in her head alone. A scary possibility…and one she couldn't bring herself to believe. Was it finally time to find out?

The crowd's excitement followed Peggy down the long tunnel, fading the closer she came to the locker room. That's when she heard the heavy, measured breaths. The forceful clearing of a man's throat.

His throat.

Before she could second-guess her sanity, Peggy stepped into the off-limits room, dropping her pompoms and slamming back against the wall under the weight of his attention. It snapped against her skin like an open hand. God, he was gorgeous, even in his sudden fury. Hard bodied, golden from the sun and righteously male, all stubbled and tall and full of might. The muscles of her abdomen squeezed—squeezed—along with her thighs as he stormed over, his words being directed at her for the very first time.

"What the hell do you think you're doing here?"

Don't lose your nerve now. Years. She'd been watching him for years. Since she'd entered the university as a freshman. Watched his triumphs from afar. And the horrible tragedy, still so recent. So fresh. "You should be on the field."

Elliott's crack of masculine laugher held no humor. "And you thought it was your job to come get me, cheerleader?"

So condescending. But accompanied by his raking glance down her thighs and belly…she couldn't help but be turned on by it. She loved him addressing her at all. Finally. "Yeah. I did. Everyone else is probably too scared of you."

Dark eyes narrowing, he stepped closer. So close, she almost whimpered, the fantasies having taken such a deep hold, her longing was on a hair-trigger. "Well, you were wrong. It's not your job. So pick up your sparkly bullshit and move *out."*

"They're called pompoms and I'll leave when I'm good and ready." With an incredulous expression, Elliott started to move away, telling Peggy she needed to work fast. Toward what goal? She'd come with no plan. Had never expected to actually speak to this man in her life. "I've seen you watching me."

He froze, a muscle leaping in his cheek. "You were mistaken."

"No. I wasn't. I'm not." She wet her lips, gaining confidence when his eyes followed the movement and she saw the hunger. The same hunger she'd watched grow, even while he begrudged it, over the course of the last few months. Since the tragedy. "You don't have to feel ashamed about it. Not now."

His fists planted on either side of her head with a bash, shaking the lockers, then his face hovered mere inches away. "What would you know about shame?"

Wetness rushed between Peggy's thighs as his apples and mint scent took hold of her throat like a giant metal hook. "I know the last six months were awful for you. They would be so hard for anyone. But especially you, because you carry everyone on your back. The whole school lives for Saturdays. If you'll win or lose." His brow furrowed, his scrutiny so intense, she wondered how her legs kept from giving out. They must have moved closer without realizing, because the tips of Peggy's breasts grazed Elliott's chest and he groaned. A harsh, guttural sound that might as well have been a symphony, it was so welcome to her ears.

"You…" His throat flexed. "You don't know anything about me, Peggy."

Her pulse went haywire. The wordless communication hadn't been imaginary. Those hard eyes really had *been speaking to her. It was the way he said* Peggy. *As though he'd tested her name on his tongue a million times. "You know   my   name."*

Hunted

An Eternal Guardians Novella
By Elisabeth Naughton

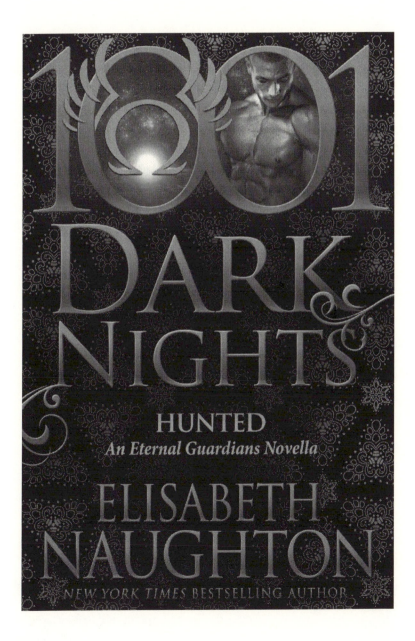

"From the deepest desires often comes the deadliest hate."

—Socrates

Chapter One

One thing Erebus could say for the Sirens—they sure made their trainees feel special. So special they couldn't even refer to them by name when they crashed and burned and Zeus decided it was time to hunt them down and snuff them out.

Not that Erebus cared all that much. He knew his place. He was a minor god in service to Zeus only because Hades had lost him in a bet to the King of the Gods. He didn't particularly enjoy serving, but it was better than the alternative: being decimated altogether like his kinsfolk or spending eternity suffering in the pits of Tartarus. While he'd been spared the same fate as his family thousands of years ago, his time in servitude to Hades in the Underworld had shown him just what happens to prisoners in Tartarus—at both the hands of Hades and Tartarus's most famous prisoner: Krónos—and he had no desire to get stuck in that living hell as an inmate himself.

A flash of blonde hair to his left caught his attention as he ran through the dark forest. His target—Trainee #429745—was close, but then he knew that already. His god powers were strongest in darkness, and his hearing, smell, even sight were amplified when night disadvantaged other hunters. He could hear her labored breaths echoing in his ears, could smell the lemony scent of her skin in his nostrils, but seeing the flash of long blonde hair had surprised him.

He hadn't looked at her picture before he'd left Olympus for this hunt. He'd memorized her trainee number, read through her file and made mental notes of her trainers' mostly average comments about her hand-to-hand combat and warfare skills. Had questioned the stupid guards she'd overpowered at the gates of Olympus when she'd fled, and who were now suffering their own just fates. And he'd located the portal she'd used outside the gates to cross into this forest in the human realm. But he'd purposefully not looked at her image.

Putting a face to a number gave his prey a human quality he didn't need to concern himself with. His orders from Zeus were clear: "*She failed her last Siren test and ran. Hunt her down and bring her back to me.*" It was not Erebus's place to question Zeus's command. The King of the Gods could have ordered Erebus to kill the trainee— which he'd done in the past and would do again when called upon *because it was his duty*—but Zeus hadn't. That made Erebus's job this time a helluva lot easier, and for that he was thankful.

But that flash of blonde...

He'd seen it somewhere before. Or hair like it. Not a white blonde. Not a honey blonde. Not even a multicolored blonde like many of the Sirens sported on Olympus. This hair had been a golden blonde so bright it had looked like a gilded waterfall in the darkness of the forest when she'd whipped past him through the trees.

Not important.

What she looked like had no impact on his current assignment. Clearing his mind, he shifted direction and picked up his speed, heading toward the flash of blonde he'd seen. Her labored breaths grew louder. Her scent stronger. Ahead, that golden blonde flashed again, whipping behind her as she turned to look into the dark forest at her back then angled forward again and ran faster.

Leaves and pine needles slapped him in the face. The forest floor was damp and soft beneath his boots. She wasn't particularly fast for a nymph, but she zigzagged around trees and brush quite a bit, changing direction so much it was hard to anticipate her next move. He'd researched this forest in preparation for this hunt, though, and he had a good idea where she was headed. Instead of chasing her maze of steps, he shifted to his right and ran at an angle away from her.

He calculated distance and speed in his mind. The ground rose and fell in the mountainous terrain. Somewhere above, an owl hooted and the whir of bat wings echoed like background music to his steps. When he'd run far enough, he cut back to his left. The terrain gave way to a small clearing between the mountains. Just as he predicted, she came tearing down the hillside to his left and emerged from the trees, that blonde hair a blur around her face as she repeatedly glanced over her shoulder to check his position.

Victory flared hot in his veins. He increased his speed and shot into the clearing at her right. Her surprised gasp met his ears when she spotted him, but she didn't have time to react. Lowering his shoulder, he slammed into her, knocking her off her feet to fly through the air ten yards before hitting the meadow grasses with a grunt.

He slowed his steps as he approached and looked down. She groaned and rolled onto her side away from him in the grass. That oddly familiar golden hair covered her face, triggering a sense of déjà vu, but he ignored it. He ignored everything except what he was here to do.

His pulse slowed now that he'd captured his prey. "Your fun's over now, nymph." Leaning forward, he reached for her arm. "On your feet."

His hand closed around her biceps. She still wore the typical training attire: knee-high kick-ass boots, slim black stretch pants that molded to her muscular legs, and a fitted black tank that showcased her curves and plump breasts. Heat from her bare skin burned into his palm as he wrapped his hand around her upper arm, but she didn't immediately climb to her feet, which irritated him. And something about her scent... It was warm and familiar, like a summer breeze blowing through a lemon grove at dusk.

Like a lemon grove at dusk? He gave his head a swift shake, knowing the hours he'd spent hunting her were catching up with him. Fuck him. He was the god of darkness. It was in his DNA to be moody and short-tempered, not romantic and idealistic. The sooner he got this insolent nymph back to Olympus, the sooner he could catch a few hours of shut-eye to recharge his dwindling energy reserves. He might be a god, but he still had needs. And after he dumped Trainee #429745 in Zeus's lap, he needed to gear himself up to instruct the newest class of Siren recruits. The ones who were even more inept than the last set Zeus had sent him.

He was tired, grouchy, and in need of a little R and R before he had to deal with more bratty Siren trainees who thought they were all the shit. The fact this one was causing him so much trouble didn't do a thing to ease his perpetual bad mood.

"I said your fun is over, nymph." He jerked on her arm.

A blur of golden hair whipped in front of him, and he saw the briefest flash of silver in that blur. But he had no time to react. Hot metal pierced the flesh of his upper arm and stabbed deep before his brain clued in to what the silver meant.

Pain ripped through his arm. His hand reflexively released her, and he jerked back. The recruit yanked the blade of a dagger free from his arm, lurched to her feet, and faced him with both malice and fury in her brilliant blue eyes. "Wrong, asshole. I say when it's over."

Her features registered the instant she found her footing, and in a flash he realized where he'd seen that unique blonde hair before, where he'd smelled that exotic, hypnotic scent.

During her one-on-one training sessions.

During their highly specialized time alone together.

During her extremely erotic, immensely pleasurable seduction sessions, directed by him.

Seraphine. Sera. *His* Sera. He'd been her seduction trainer twelve—no, eighteen months ago.

He blinked, barely believing what he was seeing. She looked different from what he remembered. Every other time he'd been near her she'd been dolled up with sexy makeup, her hair perfectly styled, her voluptuous body wrapped in whatever arousing attire he'd picked out for her. Now she looked more like a warrior than a Barbie doll, but he still recognized her. Knew not just from her scent and that unique hair, but from the way his blood heated and rushed straight into his groin as a rash of memories of her wicked hands, her sinful mouth and tight body consuming his flooded his mind.

All nymphs were easy to train in the Siren ways of seduction, but this one had been a natural. She'd been able to suck and fuck better than any other recruit he'd worked with in his last hundred years serving Zeus as a Siren trainer, and that was saying a lot, considering Zeus handpicked the females he wanted in his Siren Order from across every race and realm.

The pain in his arm faded from his mind. In her familiar eyes he saw a flash of recognition that pushed him a step closer and caused him to reach out for her. But just as his fingers grazed her skin, she kicked out with her leg and nailed him in the side of his head with the toe of her kick-ass boot.

The force of the blow knocked him off his feet and set him flailing toward the grassy meadow. Pain spiraled up his spine as he hit the hard earth and grunted. Opening his eyes, he blinked several times, shocked that she'd gotten the jump on him. Blonde hair flashed in his line of sight once more, followed by the icy glare of her crystal blue eyes as she leaned over him with her blade held high.

And holy shit, that was hot. Hotter than he ever remembered her being.

"If you think this is fun, *god*," she said in a low voice, "then you're more useless than I thought."

Oh, but this was fun. Staring up into her challenging gaze was more entertainment than he'd had in months—no, years. And anticipating what the little vixen would do next didn't just fuel the flames already rising inside him; it made him hard as stone.

* * * *

Of all the hunters she'd expected Zeus to send after her, Erebus had been the last.

Sera probably should have struck while he was down, but something had held her back. She'd told herself it was because he was a minor god, which meant he was immortal. Any further attack on her part wouldn't kill him, only enrage him, and she didn't want to tangle with the god of darkness out here in the dark. So instead she'd decided to take advantage of his shocked expression and ran. But that niggling voice in the back of her whispered that wasn't the real reason she'd held back.

She shook the voice away as she pushed her legs harder through the dark forest. Erebus was nothing to her now but one of Zeus's henchmen. She didn't care what her stupid heart had once felt for him. She only cared about putting as much distance between her and the asshole as she could now.

Her muscles burned as she darted around trees and brush, over downed logs and across a narrow stream. He would chase her, she knew. He would probably catch her. Her only hope at this point was to make sure he didn't catch her with *it*.

A searing pain tightened her lungs as she slowed her steps in the darkness and scanned the forest. Dried leaves and fallen twigs crunched under her boots as she searched for something—anything—that would help her. Panic spread through every cell, and she started to run again, squinting to see, hoping—

Her boots skidded to a stop when she spotted the decaying log lying across the forest floor ten yards to her right. Rushing in that direction, she dropped to her knees near the base and felt around, searching for any kind of hole. The instant she found one, she silently rejoiced, pulled the medallion from her pocket, and shoved it deep into the log where no one would accidentally find it.

Pounding footsteps echoed through the silent forest at her back. Her adrenaline surged.

She lurched to her feet and tore off to her left, zigzagging around trees and brush. The medallion didn't look like much—a coin slightly smaller than the palm of her hand, stamped with the imprint of Heracles and surrounded by the traditional Greek key design. Even if some hapless person did manage to find it in that log, she hoped it would be so covered in dirt and grime that they wouldn't know what it was. But Erebus absolutely could not find it because one look and he would know. He'd know the power a person could wield with it, and she knew without a doubt he'd take it right back to Zeus.

Her heart pounded, feeling as if it had taken up permanent residence in her throat. Sweat slicked her skin even though the fall night was cool and damp. She ran harder, faster, intent on getting as far from that log as possible. She couldn't go to the half-breed ruins now as she'd planned. She couldn't risk Erebus following her there. Couldn't risk his interfering with her only chance to contact her friend Elysia in Argolea.

Something hard slammed into her from the side, knocking the air out of her lungs and the thoughts from her mind. She grunted as her body sailed to the right and smacked against the hard earth. A groan tore from her throat. Pain spiraled through every cell in her body, and her vision wavered.

She rolled to her side. Groaned. Tried to get up. Tried to find her feet so she could run. But he was on her before she could even push up on her hands.

His big body straddled hers, and he dropped to his knees, his massive tree-trunk-like thighs pressing against her ribs. She lashed out with her hands to claw him off her but he captured her wrists easily and pinned them to the ground over her head. "Enough!"

Hearing his voice so close colored everything in red. She kicked out with her legs and thrashed from side to side, trying to throw him off, but he was too strong. Her hair whipped across her face as she fought harder, not wanting to hear his deep voice, now wanting to feel his hard body against hers, not wanting *him* ever again.

He squeezed his thighs so tight against her ribs, she gasped, and his fingertips dug into the skin of her wrists until pain shot straight to her brain, slowing her fight. "I said *enough*, nymph."

Breathing hard, she glared up at him through wisps of sweaty hair, hating that he was here now. Hating even more that he was just as handsome and enticing as he'd been a year and a half ago when she'd seen him across the Siren training field for the first time. Jet black hair, dark eyes, mahogany skin, and a body that was an almost seven-foot wall of solid muscle.

She knew those muscles intimately. Had traced them with her hands and fingertips and tongue during their steamy sessions when he'd been her seduction trainer. Only for her it hadn't just been seduction. Because of those erotic nights and the things he'd made her feel, he'd ruined her ability to think about or even look at another guy without remembering his whispered words against her overheated flesh and the way he'd been able to make her melt with just one carnal look. And then he'd cast her aside as if she'd never meant a single thing to him at all.

Which she hadn't, she realized as she glared up at his narrowed black-as-night eyes. He hadn't even used her damn name when he'd ordered her to stop fighting. Knowing him, he probably didn't even recognize her.

And why would he? He'd fucked hundreds, probably thousands of trainees in his time serving Zeus as one of the Sirens' trainers. She'd been nothing special to him. She'd just been the stupid nymph who'd foolishly believed every bullshit lie the gods—him included—had fed her.

Fury coiled tight in her veins, and her chest rose and fell with her quick breaths, but she didn't fight. Didn't look away either. He might have caught her, but he didn't have the medallion. And the second he loosened his grip, she'd be gone.

"That's better," he said, his voice losing that edge of rage she'd heard when he'd pinned her to the ground. "I've spent the last twenty-four hours tracking you, and I'm tired."

She didn't buy that for a second. Not that he hadn't spent that amount of time tracking her—he was a god known for hunting down Zeus's most menacing foes—but that he was tired. He was a fucking *god*. Gods didn't get tired. They were Energizer bunnies raring to go at the slightest provocation, as she'd learned multiple times when he'd fucked her until she'd passed out.

He lifted his weight off her and hauled her to her feet with one hand wrapped tight around her biceps. "Get up."

She stumbled. Gasped as he jerked her up and against the hard wall of his chest. Tried to push away. But he kept her close so she was forced to inhale his natural badass scent of snapdragon skull flowers, leather, and hints of cognac.

He glanced around the dark forest as if searching for something. Or someone.

With his hand still wrapped tightly around her upper arm, he turned to the left and hauled her with him. "This way."

His legs were way longer than hers, and she had to hustle her steps to keep up so she didn't trip and fall. And as she did, she couldn't help but wonder why he hadn't searched her for the medallion. And why she wasn't already dead.

She wasn't stupid enough to ask those questions, but she wasn't exactly upset over that fact, either. Since he hadn't killed her, it meant she still had a chance. Her mind spun with every step, her eyes scanning the darkness for something—anything—that would offer the opportunity to flee.

They reached the top of the rise, and he slowed his steps. Light was already rising on the eastern horizon, just enough for her to see the massive lake surrounding a small island housing some kind of crumbling structure far below. "There it is."

"There what is?" she mumbled, glancing around the dark forest and the steep mountains that rose out of the crystal blue water.

"Where we're going."

He pulled her with him down the hillside toward the lake.

"Wait." She grunted as her boot hit a rock, and she stumbled, hoping he wasn't taking her where she suddenly thought he was taking her. "Where *are* we going?"

"Somewhere we can be alone."

His hand tightened around her arm, and his gaze drifted down to her. But this time when he looked at her, his eyes were no longer enraged. They glowed with an erotic light. One she recognized well. One that sent a new kind of fear and anger swimming in her veins.

"I've got plans for you, Seraphine. Big, hard, very wicked plans."

Shit, she was right. And the fact he'd used her name meant she was in serious trouble because this male knew her every weakness.

Unless some kind of miracle happened in the next few minutes, there was no way she could hold out against what he had planned next.

Chapter Two

Motherfucker, he was hard.

Not just from the feel of her hot little body plastered to his side as he hauled her down the mountainside, but from the way she'd very nearly kicked his ass out there in the trees.

Darkness closed around him as he dragged her into a cave that opened to a series of tunnels, which provided passage beneath the lake to the island beyond—a darkness that only made his dick throb harder. Darkness turned him on. Danger made him hard. This minx's reactions and the way she was still trying to fight him made him absolutely ache with the need to take her and tame her and show her who was really in control. Especially when he remembered how responsive she'd been during their training sessions and how easy it had been to drag her into all the dark, dirty filth that got him off.

"I want to know where you're taking me," she said as he pulled her around switchbacks in the tunnel, her breath heavy at his side, her skin so hot against his he was starting to sweat.

He didn't owe her an explanation. She was lucky he hadn't decided to kill her after the way she'd lashed out. Or taken her to Zeus already. The second he'd recognized her he'd decided not to do either, though. Not because she didn't deserve one or both but because he had his own plans for her. Plans that didn't include the King of the fucking Gods, at least not yet.

Eventually he knew Zeus would want her back for punishment, which could include anything from having her reassigned as a servant or handmaiden or even a sex slave. And though Erebus wasn't wild about any of those options—especially the last, unless she was *his* sex slave—he knew he had time. Time to have his own fun before his life-long obligations to Olympus drew him back.

Hell, he deserved some fun after the years he'd spent in servitude, didn't he? As far as he was concerned, he deserved more than a little fun simply because he had to deal with Zeus's incompetent Siren trainees on a daily fucking basis.

"I'm taking you to the half-breed ruins," he said, tugging her around another corner in the dark, deciding he didn't want her completely defiant. Oh, he enjoyed an adrenaline-amping fight now and then, but it was so much more enjoyable when he could coax a female's reluctance into cries of sensual pleasure. With Sera's nymphomaniac tendencies, he knew it wouldn't take much persuading.

"No one's there," she argued. "The half-breed ruins have been empty for twenty-some years."

Exactly. No one was there. No one could hear her screams from inside its walls. No one would even know a minor god had gone off the grid there with a cheeky little nymph who made him so hard he hurt.

She tugged against this grip. "Erebus, please. This is a bad id—"

It was the *please* that brought him around. Or maybe it was the way she said his name. He wasn't sure which, but something in her voice made him whip back and push her up against the cold rock wall.

She gasped as he moved in close at her front. Blood rushed straight into his cock at the reaction, making him even harder. He knew he shouldn't tease her, that he was only tormenting himself by doing so, but he didn't care. She was like a drug making him high, making him want. And it had been so long since he'd wanted anything purely for himself, he couldn't seem to force himself to stop.

"I like it when you beg, Seraphine." He leaned in close and traced the line of her ear with the tip of his nose. She trembled, which shot his blood even higher. "I love it when you beg me. Do you remember when I had you tied to that bed in the training center, when you begged me to fill you, to fuck you, to make you come?"

Her throat worked in the darkness as she swallowed, and her hands landed against his chest. Hands that were warm and soft and so much more than he remembered. He wanted them on his skin. Wanted to feel them wrap around his cock. Wanted her to draw him toward all her warm, wet heat all over again as she pushed him over on that bed, as she straddled his hips, as she rode him to a blistering climax that had been better than any he'd had in a thousand years.

She didn't answer, but the way her breath sped up, the way her hands curled into the fabric of his shirt and didn't push him away told him she was already acquiescing.

A smile curled his lips as he lowered his face to her neck and breathed hot over her scintillating skin. "I remember, *oraios*. I remember the way your fingers clawed at my back after I released your bindings and you screamed for me to give you more." He drew in a deep whiff of her rich, citrusy scent. A scent that was so intoxicating it had made him wild on Olympus anytime she was near and still haunted his dreams to this day. "I remember the way you flipped me to my back, the way you scored your nails down my chest until you drew blood, the way you made *me* scream."

She groaned, a sound that caused his erection to twitch against his fly and him to rock against the wicked heat of her lower body.

She bit down hard on her lip. Her fingers curled tighter in his shirt as she fought what he knew was her own growing desire to press back against him. But instead of giving in to her needs as he wanted, she whispered, "Why are you doing this to me?"

He drew back just enough so he could see her face. It was pitch black in the tunnel, so dark he knew she couldn't see his face, but one look was all it took to see she wasn't peering up at him. Her eyes were tightly shut, her face scrunched as if in pain. But not the same pain of lust and desire swirling like a vortex inside him—this was another kind of agony. An emotional torment he didn't understand and which dimmed his craving until it was a manageable ache instead of a burning demand.

He eased back a step, putting space between them, and released her arm. As cool air swept over his body, he watched her eyes flutter open. Watched her head turn and her gaze narrow as she tried to see him. Watched that silky blonde hair he'd enjoyed fisting flutter over her slim shoulders.

His heart hammered against his ribs, and his blood was still up from a hunger that hadn't been satisfied. But the heartache he'd seen in her features moments ago continued to resonate inside him, keeping him from touching her again.

Conflicting thoughts raced through his mind. She was a nymph, a Siren recruit, Zeus's *property*, so he shouldn't care what she was feeling besides lust. But he did. As his heart continued to beat in long, steady thumps, he realized he cared more than he liked. Even now, when all he wanted to do was strap her down and ravage her until they both screamed, he cared. Because his desires where she was concerned were rooted firmly in pleasure, not pain. He wasn't a sadist, regardless of his darkness. He wasn't Hades. He wasn't even Zeus. And even though he'd fucked hundreds of Siren recruits, all in the name of training, he remembered now what it was about Sera that had resonated so strongly with him then.

She had been different. She hadn't just wanted sex, as so many of the other recruits did the moment they saw him. She'd wanted to talk. She'd spent time getting to know him. As they'd lain in bed together after her sessions, she'd made him smile with tales of the recruits' antics in the barracks and on the field. At times she'd even made him laugh, as she had when she'd tried to bind him to that bed and hadn't been able to tie a knot that would hold.

In the long, lonely years of his life, for brief flickering moments, she'd been a light to his darkness. A breath of fresh air. An oasis in the middle of a desert whose grains of sand were nothing but years of servitude to the gods. And he wanted *that* nymph back. He wanted to see her smile. He wanted to hear her laugh. He wanted her wild and willing and begging and *his*. The way she'd been his before she'd been wrenched from his grasp and he'd been reassigned to another recruit.

The force of that want was strong. So strong he turned away from her, swiped a hand down his face to cool himself down, then reached for her arm again—but only when he knew he wouldn't give in and try to force her to want him back.

"Come on," he said, pulling her away from the wall, this time tugging gently. "We're almost there."

Confusion pulled her brows together. He saw it from the corner of his eye.

And he knew she was wondering why he'd stopped his advances and what he had planned next.

He frowned because...he was suddenly wondering that too. His so-called plans had just changed. Oh, he still wanted her, still intended to have her, but the ways in which he would get there were now swirling in his mind. Along with just what he needed to do to remind her just how much she'd wanted him long ago.

How much the woman he'd awakened inside her years ago still wanted him now.

* * * *

Sera was unnerved. Unnerved and confused and more aroused than she wanted to admit.

That moment in the caves, when Erebus had pressed all his succulent heat against her and whispered those dark and naughty things in her ear, echoed in her mind, replaying like a silent video set on repeat. He was a highly sexual beast. She'd seen that on Olympus. She'd felt it moments ago in the caves. And she knew exactly why he'd dragged her into these ruins and what he intended to do to her.

She knew and she hated him for it.

She knew, and she trembled with anticipation over when it would happen.

The half-breed colony had once occupied an abandoned castle on an island in the middle of a glacial lake. As Erebus drew her into the structure and up several flights of stairs, she'd realized that the tunnel he'd pulled her into had led to the island. Walls were blackened and burned. The ceiling was open and missing in places from some kind of fire, but the rock of the castle remained, as did several floors that had been built out of stone. Now, after twenty-odd years left abandoned, plants and vines had crept into the space, making the ruins their home.

Erebus ignored the main floor with the broken wide windows that looked out over the early morning light rising above the lake and dragged her to an upper room. To what she recognized had once been a bedroom suite but was now scattered with broken furniture, dirt, and dried leaves.

She swallowed hard when she spotted the enormous bed, the old, worn mattress covered in a layer of dirt and slashed in the middle, stuffing falling out to mix with the debris on the floor. Though she tried not to be turned on by the presence of that bed, heat built in her veins and her treacherous body tingled to life.

Her whole body tensed as he tugged her toward the bed, but instead of tossing her onto that dingy mattress and having his way with her as she expected, he backed her up against one of the four posts. "Put your arms down at your sides."

Her heart beat faster. Some instinct deep inside warned her not to obey, but she did as he said, not wanting to do anything to set him off. He was twice her size, the epitome of darkness as she'd seen when he'd attacked her in the forest, and she was a nymph who hadn't completed her Siren training and who was currently without weapons. But that wasn't the only reason she'd acquiesced, she knew. The other reason was because her lascivious body liked his touch. Her traitorous mind craved his commands. And that submissive part of her lineage—the part straight from her nymph heritage—yearned to please him as she had eighteen months ago on Olympus when he'd been her seduction trainer and she'd done every dirty, erotic thing he'd demanded.

Anger welled inside her as she watched him pull a length of thin rope—rope that didn't look like it was strong enough to hold a cat, let alone a person—from somewhere in his pocket. Anger and disgust with her own body. He hadn't once looked at her since they'd left the darkness of the tunnels. Wasn't looking at her now as he wrapped the rope around her torso and the bedpost several times. Didn't even glance at her face when he tied it off at her back and finally stepped away.

He'd ignited a slow-burning fire inside her with his words in the tunnel, and now he was letting that fire smolder. Tormenting her in a new and torturous way.

He moved to the far side of the bed, and she heard the sounds of fabric rustling, then the bedpost shook at her back. Excitement surged inside her. An excitement she didn't like. Knowing he was distracted, she shifted her shoulders and tried to move, but the rope held her tight, and she realized belatedly that the rope had to be charmed by some kind of otherworldly force.

Of course it was. He was a freakin' god, after all. Had she honestly thought escaping would be easy?

He stepped around her with a pile of filthy sheets and moved toward the door without another word.

Confusion drew her brows together. "Hey," she called as he reached the threshold. "Where are you going?"

He didn't answer. Just turned the corner and disappeared.

Panic pushed in. She didn't like being confined. Strapped down and ravished was one thing. Bound and deserted was something altogether different. "You can't leave me like this!"

The only response that met her ears was the sound of his boot steps fading down the stone corridor.

Alone, she heaved out a sigh. He'd be back. He hadn't dragged her all the way to these ruins to abandon her. While she knew she should be thankful he wasn't tormenting her with his hands and lips and sinful body as he'd done in the caves, part of her couldn't help be disappointed. Yes, she hated him for so easily ditching her on Olympus all those months ago, but she couldn't deny that sex with him had been earth shattering. Just the memory of how he could seduce without even touching made her whole body tremble. And the things he could do with that mouth...

Her skin grew hot. She cleared her throat to fight her body's natural response to him. Instead of thinking about hot, sweaty, satisfying sex, she needed to stay focused on why she was here. Why she'd been out in that forest in the first place. Not for herself, but to set right a wrong that been done a hundred years ago and to prevent what had happened to her world from happening to someone else's.

She glanced over the suite, searching for any kind of escape route. This room had avoided the fire that had charred other parts of the castle. A dark fireplace fronted a ratty couch, what used to be a side chair, and an old coffee table. The door on the far wall looked as if it might open to a bathroom, but she couldn't see inside to be sure. Peering over her shoulder, she caught the movement of gauzy white curtains, frayed and hanging in front of what looked to still be solid windows. Beyond, the rising light of morning told her the view was from several stories up, and unless she planned to jump to her death, her only way out was the main door Erebus had left through.

She frowned and looked back to the fireplace. At least she wasn't going to freeze to death when the chill of night swept back over the castle. But even that was a small comfort as minutes turned to an hour and still there was no sign of her captor.

Where had he gone? What was he doing? He'd said he had

something big, hard, and very wicked planned for her. She'd felt that big, hard, wicked bulge in the caves and knew he'd been close to giving it to her there. But now, when she was bound, and—thanks to her licentious body—aching for the same damn thing, he was nowhere to be found.

She struggled against her bonds, but soon decided all she was doing was exhausting herself. As daylight warmed the room, the last few hours—the last few days caught up with her, and her muscles grew limp.

It had all started when she'd heard rumors in her training class of the Sirens' recent discovery of a medallion with special properties. Something about the location of the discovery had seemed oddly familiar, and she'd gone to the Hall of Sirens during her free time to research. Little had she known that research would trigger her memories—memories that had been blocked by the Sirens when she'd been handpicked by Zeus to train with his elite female warriors. And that those memories would reveal a deception so great, she was sure only the gods could conceive of something so heinous.

In retrospect, she probably shouldn't have confronted Athena, the leader of the Sirens. That had been a bad idea and had led to Sera being tossed in the Pit—a black hole in the ground on Olympus where Sirens were often punished—for a week. At least she hadn't told Athena she'd regained her memories. Doing so would have resulted in her immediate death. But it had made her realize that everything she'd been told from the moment she'd arrived on Olympus was a lie. When she'd emerged from that black hole of despair, she'd pretended to step back in line, but behind the scenes she'd plotted her revenge.

Of course, that revenge had landed her here—in this cold castle in the middle of nowhere, wondering where the hell Erebus had gone and when the heck he was coming back.

She heaved out another sigh and glanced up and around the room. No wonder she was tired. She'd barely slept in the last two weeks, and her adrenaline was rapidly crashing. As much as she didn't want to encourage Erebus and his nefarious plans, she wished he'd tied her to the mattress before he'd left so she could sleep. Wished he'd had the sense to tie her lower to the post so at least she was sitting and could rest her weary legs.

Her eyes grew heavy, and her head drooped. Thoughts of Erebus and the sensual way he'd held her against the cave wall in the dark swirled in her mind. Whatever he had planned, she knew she would endure it. Just as she knew she'd likely enjoy it. The key would be making sure she found a way to escape as soon as his body was sated and he dropped his guard. Because staying, and ultimately letting him haul her back to Olympus, was not an option.

She hadn't sacrificed her future to fail now. Too much depended on her success. Erebus might be the master of seduction, but she wasn't going to let her treacherous heart fall for him again. She was going to escape.

Or, the Fates help her, she'd die trying.

Chapter Three

Erebus took his time finding somewhat clean sheets and blankets. While the castle hadn't been used in years and a good portion of it was in ruins, he'd been surprised at how much was still useable.

The sheets, blankets, and even a few pillows he'd discovered in the back of a cupboard on an upper floor. In the bowels of the castle, he'd found a gas-powered generator and enough fuel to supply the north wing, where he'd left Sera, with lights and running water. Firewood was easy to locate—there was plenty of wood thanks to destroyed furnishings—and a quick trip down to the lake provided him with berries and fish he'd be able to cook for dinner.

Thoughts of Sera flittered through his mind as he finally headed back up to her room several hours later. Wicked, hot, erotic thoughts he had to tamp down because he didn't want her to see them on his face as soon as he walked in. He'd save overwhelming her like that for later. Sure, Zeus might be pissed it was taking him so long to track the little nymph down, but he didn't care. He'd take her back to Olympus soon enough. Tonight was for him—and her too. After all, there was no telling what Zeus's punishment would entail. It could be her last chance for fun for a good long time.

Unless he plans to execute her. Then it's her last chance for fun ever...

His brow wrinkled as he moved up the stairs. The last time Zeus had executed a recruit it had been for something much more sinister than simply failing the Sirens' tests. Over the last twenty to thirty years that Erebus could remember, recruits who failed a checkpoint were reassigned to various jobs. Of course, none of those recruits had run, he realized.

Would Zeus consider running grounds for execution?

His head said no—after all, she was a quick learner, bright, and highly erotic. Even though he didn't like the idea, Erebus could easily see her being reassigned as a pleasure slave to any one of the gods. But his gut... His gut said yes, Zeus would see her going AWOL as prime reason to execute her, if for no other reason than to make an example of her to other recruits who might be considering the same thing.

He needed to find out why she'd run. Peppering her with questions would likely dampen the seductive mood he wanted to set, but perhaps if he knew why she'd taken off he could come up with a way to help her. Or, at the very least, maybe it would give him an idea how he could put in a good word for her with the King of the Gods.

Afternoon light shone into the room as he stepped under the doorjamb, but the first thing he spotted was Sera hanging limply from her bonds, her head forward, her golden hair covering every inch of her face. Panic pushed him across the room in two steps. He set his bundle down and grasped both sides of her face, lifting so he could see her eyes. "Sera?"

She grunted. Her eyelids fluttered. And in a moment of clarity he realized she wasn't dead, just asleep.

The pressure in his chest eased. Yes, he'd been away from her most of the day, but it was unusual for a Siren—even a recruit—to drop her defenses enough to sleep when she was in a hostile situation, which he knew she considered this to be. Carefully, so he didn't wake her, he lowered her head once more and watched as that mass of blonde covered her features all over again.

Had the instructors on Olympus worked her so hard she wasn't sleeping? He managed most of the Siren instructors and knew their schedules. Granted, he'd been immersed with a new class the last few months and up to his ears with newbies who didn't have a clue, but Sera's class—almost two years into their training—should have been well adjusted to the physical demands of the Sirens by now.

Something didn't add up. With questions swirling in his mind, he went to work remaking the bed. He'd flipped the mattress before he'd left, and the underside wasn't nearly as disgusting as the top had been. When he was done, he threw the covers back, carefully untied Sera from the bedpost, and hefted her into his arms.

She weighed practically nothing, and that erotic scent of citrus and vanilla floated around him once more, as enticing as anything had ever been. Her head lolled against his shoulder as he moved and laid her on the fresh sheets. This time her eyes didn't even flitter. The second her body hit the mattress, her head lolled against the pillow and a soft snore echoed from her lips.

It took every ounce of strength he had to tug off her boots and nothing else. To pull the covers up around her shoulders and *not* climb into that big bed with her. But he was determined to make this good for both of them, and there were things he needed to do first for that to happen. For a moment he considered tying her wrists to the headboard, but then dismissed the idea. She was dead to the world right now, and from here on out he didn't plan to leave her alone. Which meant there was no reason to bind her—unless of course she asked to be bound.

That thought shot a burst of wicked heat all through his body, which lingered as he used the broken wood in the room to build a fire, then found a broom in a nearby closet and went about sweeping the floor of dust and debris. In an upstairs kitchen area, he'd found candles, a frying pan, plastic plates, utensils, wine glasses, and even an old bottle of wine. He had no idea if the wine was still any good, but he figured anything to help set the mood—and relax her enough to get her talking—was a plus.

The sheets rustled on the bed behind him just as he was finishing cooking the fish. One glance over his shoulder at her confused expression told him she was shocked at what he'd done.

He smirked. "Good morning, sleepy head." He pulled the frying pan from the heat and slid the two trout he'd caught onto the plates. "Or should I say good evening." Pushing to his feet, he grabbed two forks and the plates and crossed toward the bed, where she eyed him like he'd grown a horn right in the middle of his forehead. "Here."

"What is that?"

"Dinner."

"Why?"

"Because it's rude to eat in front of someone." He pushed the plate closer to her hand. "Take it."

She glanced from the plate up to him, and he didn't miss the skepticism in her blue eyes.

He frowned. "It's not poisoned. If I wanted to kill you I'd have done so already."

The expression on her flawless face said she wasn't so sure of that, but she hesitantly took the plate and lowered it to her lap, carefully watching him as he walked back to the club chair he'd hauled in from another room and sat.

Her gaze skipped around the room while he started eating, and from the corner of his eye he caught the surprise in her features at what he'd done while she'd been asleep. She glanced at the bedpost where she'd been tied, then chanced a look over her shoulder at the wood headboard. "Why am I no longer restrained?"

Heat rolled through him all over again. He cut another piece of fish and stabbed it with his fork. "Do you want to be restrained? If so, I can easily play along."

Her gaze narrowed to a glare. Several moments passed where all she did was glower at him while he ate. Then slowly, she set her untouched plate on the far side of the bed, then threw back the covers.

He leaned back in his seat, eyeing her warily as she pushed to her feet. "Where do you think you're going?"

"I need to use the restroom."

His stomach tightened at the bite in her words.

She rounded the bed and scowled deeper when she spotted him standing with the plate in his hand. "Unless you want my bladder to explode, of course. In which case I could just sit here and we could wait for it to happen. Then you could clean up the mess. Which will it be?"

Her tongue had definitely sharpened in the time she'd been away from him and with the Sirens, a fact he didn't like. Part of what he'd been most drawn to eighteen months ago was how sweet she'd been.

He eyed her boots where he'd left them by the side of the bed. Even if she did bolt, she wouldn't get far in bare feet. He stepped back and held his arm out toward the bathroom door. "Be my guest."

She huffed and stepped past him.

"But, Sera..."

She paused when she reached the darkened bathroom doorway but didn't turn to face him. A fact that for some reason only heightened his desire for her.

"When you come back out," he said calmly, "we're going to talk about the real reason you were running. And then we're going to finish what we started in the tunnels."

* * * *

"We're going to talk about the real reason you were running..."

Erebus's words pounded in Sera's brain as she closed the bathroom door and leaned back against the solid wood. But it was the second part of his command that made her heart thump even harder. *"...then we're going to finish what we started."*

There was no way she was finishing anything with him. She'd seen what he'd done to the room out there and knew he was maneuvering her just where he wanted her. Her entire body was already vibrating with the need to feel his touch. She knew if she let him that close she'd melt under the weight of his erotic commands. But more than that, just the fact he'd said anything about the "real reason" she was running was a giant red flag telling her she needed to get as far from the minor god as possible. Because if she melted the way he wanted her to, she didn't trust herself not to accidentally let the truth slip out. And the second he discovered she'd stolen the medallion from Zeus, any sexy mood he'd had toward her would turn to malice.

Her fingers shook as she hit the lock on the bathroom door, then darted toward the window. It hadn't been opened in over twenty years and she had to grit her teeth and pry up on the wood until her fingertips turned white. It finally gave, and she breathed easier as she pushed it up an inch, but as the crack of old wood separating echoed through the bathroom, her anxiety shot through the roof, and she froze.

She listened, waiting to see if he'd heard it. When nothing but the sound of her own heart pounding met her ears, she let go of the window, rushed to the sink, flipped on the water to drown out any more noise, then moved back to her one shot at freedom.

Her fingertips burned, and the muscles in her arms ached as she forced the window higher. When it was open far enough for her to crawl through, she pulled herself out and onto the small rock ledge that ran the length of this wing of the ruins.

Wind whipped her hair around her face. Dusk was just settling in, shrouding everything in an eerie gray light, but she could still make out the waves of the lake crashing against rocks three stories below. And glancing up, she spotted another four stories above her and spires that reached for the darkening sky.

It had once been an amazing castle. Still could be with a little work. Though she wasn't sure why it had been completely abandoned after the inhabitants had obviously beaten back their invaders, she told herself that wasn't her concern. Her only concern now was getting away from Erebus, retrieving the medallion she'd hidden in the woods, and taking it somewhere Zeus and the Olympians could never find it.

Her stomach tightened as she leaned back against the wall and used her hands to help guide her to her right. The ledge was only six inches wide, and more than once her bare feet stumbled over chipped and broken sections. When she reached another closed window, she slid down the wall until she was crouched on the ledge, reached over and tried to pull the window up. Like the one in her bathroom, though, it was sealed tight. There was no way she could pry it open from out here, not without falling to her death in the process.

She kept going. Her pulse thumped hard and loud in her ears as she moved faster, hoping and praying that Erebus wouldn't suddenly realize she'd been gone too long and appear on the ledge beside her.

Three windows down from the one she'd exited, she finally came to one that was broken, the glass jagged and half-covering the opening. Victory pulsed in her veins. Without shoes or long sleeves, she had nothing to shield herself from the glass, but she figured a few cuts were a small price to pay for freedom.

She positioned herself in front of the broken window, turned sideways, and gripped the casing on both sides to steady herself. Then she held her breath and shoved the knee of her pants through the rest of the glass.

A burn spread across her knee and thigh. She knew she'd torn her pants, was fairly certain she'd cut her leg, but she didn't stop to look. Gritting her teeth against the pain, she knocked the rest of the glass away, then carefully lowered herself into what looked to be a sitting room for another suite.

The room grew darker with every passing second, but somehow she managed to avoid stepping on shards of glass with her bare feet. Pulse racing, she rushed to the door, pulled it open a crack, and peered out into the dim hallway.

Nothing moved. No sound met her ears. A golden glow to her right indicated the door to the room Erebus had taken her to was still open, the fire and candles continuing to burn bright.

She couldn't go that way. Couldn't risk his seeing her. She glanced to her left. This castle was huge. There had to be a back set of stairs that led to the main level.

Deciding that was her best bet, she crept out into the hallway and moved as quietly as she could, stepping over debris littering the space. Something moved in the shadows ahead. Her heart rate spiked again, and she stilled. But when no sound met her ears and nothing else moved, she realized it had to have been some kind of small animal, not Erebus, as she'd feared.

She didn't know how long he'd wait before checking the bathroom to see what was taking her so long. Reaching a set of back stairs, she hustled down as quickly as she could. At the main level, she looked around, trying to remember which way they'd come. The castle was surrounded by a lake. Her only hope for escape was to backtrack through the tunnels.

She pushed her legs into a jog, searching for the stairs that led down. Just remembering those tunnels made her think of the way Erebus had backed her up against the rock wall in the dark, how he'd made her whole body tremble with just a few simple words. He'd always been able to do that to her, and she hated him for that. Hated him even more because her stupid heart was still hung up on the minor god who clearly didn't feel anything for her besides lust. She'd been nothing to him but another recruit he could use to get his rocks off. He was still trying to use her for that, evidenced by the seduction scene he'd set up in that room upstairs. She was a complete fool for ever thinking he'd cared for her. An even bigger fool for falling for him when she'd known better.

Disgusted with herself all over again, she found the stairs and hustled to the lowest level. Once there, she stepped over debris in what looked as if it had once been an anteroom, and moved out into the darkened tunnel.

Her pulse jackknifed. The tunnel was pitch black. When Erebus had first led her into the caves, the cool air moving across her skin from different angles had made her think there were other tunnels jutting off from the main route. Without a light she could be lost down here for weeks. She needed to go back into the ruins. Needed to find a candle of some kind so she could see where she was going. She turned back toward the ruins. The stairs she'd just come down creaked, causing her to freeze.

"Sera!"

Erebus's voice sent her heart straight into her throat. This time there was no hint of seduction in his voice. Only rage.

Knowing she didn't have time to find a light, she whipped back toward the darkness of the tunnel, swallowed her fear, and pushed her legs forward. Rocks and debris dug into the soles of her feet, but she ignored the pain. All she could do was hold her hands out in front of her so she wouldn't slam face-first into a wall. All that mattered now was ignoring everything except the instinct echoing in her head to *run*.

* * * *

When Erebus reached the main cavern, he used his heightened sight to search the darkness for Sera. Several tunnels veered off from the main route. She could be in any of them, and though he could see well in the dark, he couldn't see around twists and turns and through solid rock.

He stilled and focused on his enhanced hearing. The sound of heavy breaths and the rustle of cloth echoed from the tunnel to his right.

He darted in that direction, not even questioning if it was her. It *was* her. It had to be her. No one else was down here in these blasted caves.

The tunnel curved to the right, then left. He pushed his legs harder, racing around the corners without slowing. This wasn't the same tunnel they'd used to enter the ruins, and he had no idea how she was moving so fast. It was pitch black and he doubted she had any kind of light. She was being spurred on by pure panic. Panic, he sensed, that had little to do with him and what he wanted to do to her upstairs in that bedroom and everything to do with what Zeus wanted from her.

Zeus's intentions swirled in his head as he zigzagged through the cave, ducking under low-hanging rocks. The King of the Gods was nothing if not secretive. If he wanted to terminate Sera for running, he could have ordered Erebus to simply find her and kill her. But he hadn't. And her panicked reaction now told Erebus there was more going on here than met the eye. More than what he'd been told on Olympus. Way more.

He passed a small opening that looked like it led to a new tunnel. Something moved in the darkness, and he slowed his steps, wondering if she'd shifted direction and was trying to hide. Bracing one hand on the rocks above, he leaned down to peer through the archway, but saw only more rock. He listened for the sound of her rapid breaths, the beat of her heart, the rustle of fabric that told him she was in there. The cave was silent. Silent but for a faint clicking noise he was sure did not come from her.

To his right, a flutter of blonde hair caught his attention and then was gone. Ignoring the animal he'd stumbled across, he tore after her. The sound of her labored breaths met his ears along with the thump of her footfalls on the uneven rocks and the roar of blood rushing through her veins.

His adrenaline surged. He ran faster. And heard the unmistakable sounds of rushing water.

Motherfucker...

Running water meant some kind of underground river. Since he couldn't see any puddles in this cavern, that meant the underground river was below them, accessible through a hole or fracture in the floor ahead. And he'd bet his position as a trainer with the Sirens that she didn't know what she was about to run straight into.

Blonde hair flashed ahead of him again. The roar of the water grew louder. He was gaining on her, but not fast enough to stop her. "Sera!"

Whipped around to look back at him. Gasped. Stumbled when she realized he was closer than she'd thought. A panicked look crossed her features as she twisted away and burst forward.

The roar of the river grew louder. He reached out to grab her. His fingertips brushed the ends of her silky blonde hair.

Then she slipped through his fingers and her scream rose up around him.

Chapter Four

Erebus skidded to a stop at the edge of the sinkhole and stared down at the rushing river thirty yards below. Sera's scream was drowned out by a splash of water that echoed in his ears.

His heart lurched into his throat as he used his enhanced sight to scan the river for any sign of her. *Come on, come on, come on...*

The surface of the water broke twenty yards from where she'd gone in, and a gasp echoed up to him.

He didn't pause to consider what could be in the river below. Just stepped off the cliff and fell feet first into the frigid liquid. Water bubbled above his head. Something green and totally out of place flashed in the corner of his vision, but he didn't have time to see what it was. Instinct urged him up toward the surface.

His head popped out and he sucked in air, treading water as he turned and searched for her. The current was strong, quickly sweeping him downstream. He whipped right and left, scanning the darkness. The sound of labored breaths met his ears. He twisted back around and squinted. Then spotted her clinging to a boulder, fifteen feet away on the edge of the river.

Relief overwhelmed him, forcing air into his one-size-too-small lungs. He swam toward her, but the swift current slammed his body against the boulder she clung to before he could stop it from happening.

He grunted. Pain shot up his spine. Ignoring it, he worked his way around the rock to her side, then wrapped an arm around her shivering body and drew her against him. *"Agápi?* Talk to me."

Her eyes were closed. She sagged against the rock. Water

dripped from her hair over her face. She opened her mouth to answer but no sound came out. And when her arm slipped from the boulder and slumped into the water, he realized she was losing consciousness. He grasped her before the current could whisk her away.

"Shit. Stay with me." He tugged her with him as he climbed out of the water and hauled her up onto the rocky ledge.

Blood dripped down her temple. Her head lolled to the side. Before he even let go of her, she started to shake, not just a shivering shudder of muscles, but full on tremors that told him she was going into shock.

Nymphs weren't immortal, not like the gods—not like him. Her race had been blessed with a long life-span—over five hundred years in most cases—but her body was still fragile and she could definitely die from injuries and hypothermia. Moving quickly, he tugged off his shirt and pants, then went to work stripping her of her clothing. Once she was dressed in nothing but her bra and panties, he pulled her onto his lap so her slim body was pressed up against his chest and he could close his arms and legs around her. As he leaned back against the rock wall for support, he grasped his wet T-shirt and held it against the wound on her head to slow the blood flow.

"You're okay, Sera. I've got you. I'm going to get you out of here."

Long minutes passed where she continued to tremble, and it felt as if his heart had taken up permanent residency in his throat. But slowly, as the heat of his body seeped into hers, her shakes slowly subsided, and she relaxed against him. He took that as a good sign. Lifting the shirt from her wound, he breathed easier when he saw the blood flow had lessened. She was going to have a nice-sized goose egg, but swelling outward from the impact was better than swelling inside the brain, and he knew that was an even better sign.

His pulse inched down. Glancing at her familiar face resting against his shoulder, he brushed a lock of wet hair back from her cheek, and as he did something warm and sweet slid through his chest. An emotion he hadn't felt before. A yearning that wasn't just sexual.

The feeling was so strong, so foreign, it threw him off kilter. He didn't *have* emotions. He was a god who'd learned long ago that emotions were dangerous. And yet... Somehow he recognized the feelings taking up space inside him now had been spawned by fear. Not fear that she was going to drop to her death and that he was going to miss out on the rough, hot sex he'd been envisioning since the moment he'd recognized her in the woods, but fear that something bad would happen to her. That he'd never see her again. That he would lose her.

Sweat broke out along his forehead, and an odd tingle started in his chest. He told himself it was her heat making him feel weird. Not denial. Not anything else. But even that didn't sound right, and he had no idea what the hell he was supposed to do next.

"Sera." The word was a whisper, a plea, a demand. "Sera, wake up and look at me." He needed to see her eyes. Needed her to explain what was happening to him. Needed to know if she felt it too.

She didn't move. He knew she was breathing. Knew she wasn't in any real danger. But the danger to him was suddenly all he could focus on. "*Agápi*. Open your eyes. Look at me, baby."

She sighed and snuggled closer. But the reaction didn't fire him up and make him ache to take her as he expected. It brought a calm over him that was more unsettling than the fear he'd felt before.

He didn't know what was happening. This female was doing something to him he didn't understand. He needed to get her back upstairs and into a bed. Needed to give her time to rest before he decided whether he was going to go ahead with his seduction plan or haul her back to Zeus without touching her. And he needed to think. Because the only thing he knew for sure at the moment was that he wasn't ready to let her go. And he had no idea what that meant or how it was going to impact his service to Zeus.

You can't take her back to Zeus...

The thought circled in his mind, unwilling to disappear. He glanced back down at her again, wondering just what the hell was really going on and why Zeus wanted her so bad.

"It's female," a raspy voice said in the darkness.

Erebus's head came up, and his adrenaline surged all over again.

"We haven't had us a female in forever," another low voice answered.

He squinted through the darkness, searching for the source of the voices, and spotted two sets of beady eyes peering out from behind a large boulder. Two sets of gnarled fingers wrapped around the stone. Two sets of claws, digging into the rock.

Fuck me.

Kobaloi. The gnome-dwarves who mined and protected Hades's invisibility ore. Erebus's gaze shot back to the river, and he easily picked out the spots of green glowing from the bottom of the riverbed that he'd noticed when the water had rushed over his head, but which he'd ignored because he'd been so intent on getting to Sera.

His jaw clenched down hard at his stupidity. The green glow was the ore, the therillium that powered Hades's invisibility cap. No wonder this colony was now fucking empty. Because Hades had discovered it sat right over his precious ore. The kobaloi clearly had free run of the ruins. He'd sensed another creature in the tunnels with him when he'd been chasing Sera. While they weren't particularly dangerous in small clusters, they often congregated in hordes. And while he knew he could fight off two or three or even ten, a thousand gnome-dwarves with razor-sharp teeth and knife-like claws could spell imminent doom for Sera.

He pushed to his feet, hefted her in his arms, and held her close to the protection of his body. Oblivious to the sudden threat in front of them, she sighed again, hooked an arm around his neck, but otherwise didn't wake.

"It's not just a female," Erebus declared in a deep voice, hoping it would scare the shit out of the scavengers and make them scurry. "And you do not want to mess with me."

A hiss echoed in the darkness, followed by a rapid clicking sound. "Erebus," a voice growled. "His scent was masked by the female."

Yeah, you better cower, dumbass.

"Hades wants him back," the other murmured. "This will bring us great reward."

The cavern filled with hundreds of rapid clicks, telling Erebus there weren't just two or three kobaloi hiding behind those rocks, there was an entire horde.

His adrenaline went sky-high. Stepping back toward the river, Erebus glanced up at the ceiling toward the hole Sera had fallen through. Options, strategies, possibilities ignited in his mind.

"We'll take him to our lord," a voice growled, closer this time but still hidden behind the stones. "And then the female will be ours."

Fuck that. Erebus tightened his arms around Sera. She was his. And this time no one was taking her from him.

* * * *

Sera was in a dream. A hot, sweltering fantasy that was extremely arousing.

She opened her eyes, blinked several times against the warm glow, and tried to focus. A fire burned across the room, which made zero sense since the last thing she remembered was darkness, running, and the bitter bite of frigid water.

She glanced down at her hands and spotted the comforter wrapped around her body. Rolling to her side, she realized she was in a bed. A comfy, soft, soothing bed that seemed to cocoon her in safety. And at her back? Something solid, warm, and muscular that felt incredibly tempting.

She rolled to her side, then stilled when she spotted Erebus lying on his side facing her, sharing space on her pillow. His dark eyes were closed, his shirtless torso relaxed, and his arm was entirely too possessive wrapped around her waist, holding her against him.

The beat of her heart turned to rapid fire in her ears, pounding blood through her veins. She'd been running. He'd been chasing her. Not because he'd wanted her as he'd led her to believe when he'd pressed all his succulent heat against her in the caves on their trek to these ruins, but because Zeus wanted her back so he could get his slimy hands on the medallion.

Panic condensed between her ribs. She needed to get up. She needed to run. He was asleep. Now was her chance to escape.

She rolled to her opposite side as quietly as she could. Lifted her head from the pillow. Reached out one hand and gripped the sheet a foot away to pull herself across the mattress.

His arm immediately tightened around her waist, and he tugged her backside into firm contact with his hips. "Should be sleeping, *agápi.*"

She froze. *Agápi?* My love? She *had* to be hallucinating. No way he would ever call her that.

Her pulse roared in her ears, but she knew she was stuck at least until he drifted back to sleep. Trying not to do anything to wake him further, she breathed deep and worked puzzle pieces around in her mind to figure out what the heck he was doing.

Where was she? Why was he in bed beside her? And why the heck couldn't she remember what had happened?

Pain lit off behind her skull, and she lifted a hand to rub at the spot, only to realize a bandage covered part of her forehead near her hairline on the right side.

The arm across her waist lifted, and he gently tugged her hand back to the mattress. "Let that heal. It'll be better in the morning."

A flash of something green flickered in her memory. She remembered hitting a rock. Remembered...voices.

"What did you do to me?" Her voice didn't sound like her own. And her accusation clearly wasn't threatening because he only wrapped his arm tighter around her waist, pulling her even tighter against him.

"Rescued you," he said in a sleepy and sexy-as-hell voice.

Holy gods. Stop thinking he's sexy. That will only make things worse.

"From what?" she asked, ignoring how warm and perfect he felt pressed up against her back.

"Kobaloi. Shouldn't run off without me, *agápi*. All kinds of bad shit out there trying to take you from me."

Gnome-dwarves? Her eyes widened.

Okay, she was seriously dreaming because gnome-dwarves weren't even real. And he'd called her *agápi* again, which made zero sense, especially when he claimed things were trying to take her from him. *He'd* been the one to toss *her* aside on Olympus, not the other way around. If he'd wanted to hold on to her, he'd had plenty of opportunity long before this.

He sighed and pressed his face into her hair. His warm breath tickled the hairs on her neck and sent a shiver straight down her spine. A shiver that felt way too damn good. "Sleep, Seraphine. You wore me out. Need to rest before you get all feisty with me again."

Feisty? He thought she was feisty? Another shiver rushed down her spine, only this one wasn't because of his sexy breath but because his words had sounded like a compliment.

Logic told her to get up. To climb out of this bed. To run while his defenses were down and she had a chance. But her head was already drifting, her limbs heavy, her body too warm and comfortable to move. And his heat at her back was exactly what she'd been missing for so damn long, part of her just didn't want to go.

Not even if leaving meant saving the world.

* * * *

The second time Sera woke, she knew she wasn't in a dream. Her head was clear, her limbs still heavy and sore, but there was a realness to the room as she glanced around, a recognition that told her she was back in the suite at the half-breed ruins where Erebus had taken her.

Slowly, she pushed to sitting and slid the covers back. She was dressed in a black tank and cotton pajama bottoms he must have found in another room. They were old and musty, but surprisingly soft. The fire smoldered, but the curtains on the wide windows were pushed back to let late afternoon sunlight spill across the floor.

The last time she'd awoken—if she could call that being awake—she was sure it had been night. She didn't know if a day or more had passed since then, but when she lifted a hand to her forehead, the bandage she faintly remembered Erebus telling her not to touch was gone and a thin, one-inch long scab ran along her hairline. She pressed all around the scab, trying to recall what had happened. The skin was tender but not swollen, but she couldn't remember anything other than running, darkness, and falling.

Falling...

Pressure condensed beneath her ribs. Before she could figure out why though, footsteps sounded to her right. She looked in that direction just as Erebus appeared in the doorway carrying something flat in his big hands.

"You're awake. Good. I won't have to wake you." He rounded the bed, balancing whatever he was holding in one hand, and reached for the pillow at her back. "Lean forward."

Sera's stomach tightened. She had no idea what he was doing, but she couldn't find the words to ask because something kept spinning in her head. A word. Spoken in his voice. Repeated several times. Something that started with a...

The word was on the tip of her mind but wouldn't formulate into something solid she could reach. Had he said it when he'd been chasing her? Had she imagined it in her dream?

"There, you're good. Lean back."

One glance over her shoulder told her he'd fluffed her pillow against the wooden headboard and added another. Confused, she glanced up at him, then stared down as he set a tray of food on her lap.

It was some kind of soup, hot and steamy. Basil and rosemary drifted to her nose, and her stomach rumbled as if on cue.

Erebus chuckled and stepped away from the bed, stopping to use the poker to move the embers in the fireplace. "Sorry there's no bread. Baking is not my specialty."

Sera had absolutely no clue what was going on or what his end game was here, but she was suddenly too hungry to care. When was the last time she'd eaten? Before she'd stolen the medallion. Before running from Olympus. Long before she'd been tackled by Erebus in that meadow.

She reached for the spoon, ladled a bite of the warm broth, and realized there were carrots, celery, noodles, and some kind of white meat in the soup. Bringing it to her lips, she sipped slowly, in case it was too hot. The broth was warm, not scalding, and it stimulated her salivary glands. She took a big bite and moaned before she could stop herself.

Erebus glanced over his shoulder and grinned. And even though she was looking down at the soup, she caught the mesmerizing smile and the way it brightened his entire face, transforming him from devil-may-care to absolutely irresistible.

"Guess it's safe to say you like that." He turned back to the fire and added another log to the flames.

Sera's brow wrinkled. She wasn't sure what she liked. She wasn't sure of anything at the moment except that she was hungrier than she'd ever been.

She finished off the soup, and when there was nothing left but a spoonful of broth she couldn't quite scoop up, she set her spoon down, lifted the bowl in her hands, and poured what was left into her mouth.

It wasn't until she set the bowl down and used the napkin that she realized Erebus was standing at the end of her bed. His hands were tucked into the pockets of his jeans, his head tipped to the side, and he was watching her with a very amused expression. Not one smoldering with heat like she remembered from before, but one that was rooted in something else. Some kind of tenderness she didn't understand.

Erebus? Tender? Those were two words that definitely did *not* go together.

Nerves bounced around in her stomach as she lowered her napkin to the tray. He was her captor, nothing more. She needed to stop looking at him like some kind of hero—*because he isn't.*

Ag... Agi...Aga... Shit. Whatever word he'd said in that husky sex-god voice of his kept pinging around in her brain, unwilling to leave her memory. Or fantasy, or...hell, she didn't know what now.

She cleared her throat, working for nonchalant when she felt anything but. "So what did you do to me?" Her fingers drifted to her forehead again, and she felt the edge of the scab, knowing without a doubt that whatever had happened was totally his fault. "And how much time has passed since you did it?"

Instead of growing angry, as she expected, the corner of his lips curled. "You've been asleep for two days. You had a concussion. Hit your head pretty hard when you fell into an open cavern in the tunnels and tumbled into an underground river."

His words shot hazy memories through her mind. She remembered climbing out of the bathroom window, rushing down to the tunnels beneath the ruins, running in the dark. She remembered his voice calling her name. She remembered him chasing her. She remembered air whooshing past her face, something ice cold cocooning her body, then...absolutely nothing.

She'd fallen into a river. Knocked herself unconscious. Gotten a concussion. And he'd rescued her?

He must have read the confusion on her face because that amusement twisted his lips even higher. "You look surprised."

That he'd rescued her and *didn't* look like he was about to jump her bones? Hell yeah, she was surprised.

His expression took on a serious note. "There are kobaloi in the tunnels beneath us. I barricaded the door into the ruins, but I'm fairly sure I trapped a few in the castle with us, ones that were skulking around in here unnoticed. You don't need to worry, though. I lit fires in every fireplace from here to the kitchen, and I'll keep them all going. Kobaloi don't like flames. They'll keep their distance. Plus, they won't risk coming out where they could get caught in sunlight."

That didn't exactly put her at ease. She racked her brain for what she'd learned about kobaloi on Olympus. The gnome-dwarves were thought to be a fable, but if Erebus had seen them, that meant they were real. Her brow wrinkled. "All the tales I've heard about kobaloi claimed they congregate near therillium."

"Hades's invisibility ore. Yep. Those tales were correct. It's beneath us." He looked up and around the bedroom suite. "There's no telling how long this colony existed without Hades even realizing the half-breeds were perched right on top of his precious ore. Kind of fitting, don't you think? A way for the half-breeds to stick it to the god-king of the Underworld."

The fact he found amusement in that unsettled her. Erebus was a minor god *from* the Underworld. He'd served Hades for a thousand years before being lost in a bet to Zeus. There'd been a time—when she'd been so enamored by him during her seduction training—that she'd convinced herself he wasn't the epitome of darkness she eventually realized he truly was. But why would something created from darkness seem happy to know his true master—Hades—had been duped?

She couldn't come up with a logical answer. And that damn word...*agi, aga, agap*... It wouldn't leave her stupid brain. The only thing that remotely made sense was that this story about the kobaloi was just that...a story. A ploy to convince her she was safer *with* him than without him.

She knew how to take care of herself, dammit. She didn't need him.

Except...

The way her chest tightened when she looked up at him told her she *was* safe with him. Way safer than she'd been in years. And that didn't just unsettle her, it completely unnerved her.

Hands suddenly shaking, she moved the tray to the far side of the bed, tugged the covers up to her chest, and leaned back into the pillows. Her instincts screamed to get up, to retreat into the bathroom, to escape again, but her muscles wouldn't listen. Yes, she felt better than the last time she'd awoken—and now she was almost sure that hadn't been a dream. But she wasn't anywhere near a hundred percent, and if she ran like this, he'd easily catch her. Which meant she needed to rest. To think. To plot. And act on that planning later.

She closed her eyes, not because she was anywhere near falling asleep again but because she couldn't keep looking at him, not when she had no clue what was really happening and why he was being so damn nice. "Thank you for the chicken noodle soup. I don't know where you found the ingredients but it was very good. I'm just more tired than I guess I realized."

Liar.

Okay, why did she feel guilty about lying to him now?

"You're welcome." A shuffling sound echoed from the far side of the bed, and the mattress jostled, just enough to tell her he'd picked up the tray. Footsteps faded as he crossed the room, and she exhaled, thankful he was leaving. "It wasn't chicken, though. It was rabbit."

Oh great. On top of all the other stuff in her head, now she'd be thinking of boiled bunnies the rest of the night and that old movie she'd watched when she'd been with the half-breeds in Russia. The American one about the guy who'd had the affair with the psycho woman who tormented his family.

"I'll let you get some sleep," Erebus said. "When you wake later you can tell me what test you failed on Olympus."

"I didn't fail a test on Olympus."

"You didn't?" His footsteps silenced. "Zeus said you failed your last benchmark."

Her eyes popped open wide. And in a rush of understanding she realized that Zeus had lied to him about why he wanted her back and that she'd just given herself away.

Shit.

Shiiiiiiit.

Stay calm, Sera. If you accidentally spill the real reason you escaped Olympus and what you left with, you're as good as dead. Forget about how nice he's been to you tonight. Forget about that stupid imagined emotion in his eyes.

His loyalty is to Zeus, the king of fucking everything, not you.

"Fail?" Her heartbeat whirred in her ears, but somehow she found the strength to close her eyes and breathe deep, feigning exhaustion. Rolling to her side away from him, she tucked her hands up by her face and added, "I thought you said fell. My balance improved quite a lot on the training field after you moved on to a new class of recruits."

Silence met her ears, but she knew he was still there. Staring at her back. Wondering what the hell she was hiding. Her pulse raced even faster.

Stay calm...

"Can we talk about the Sirens and my failures later?" She faked a yawn and forced her muscles to relax so it looked as if she were about to drift to sleep. "I'm really tired again."

Still no response from him. But seconds later the sound of his receding footsteps drifted to her ears.

She lay still a long time after he'd left, listening, waiting, afraid if she looked he'd still be there. But when she finally rolled to her back and peered toward the doorway, it was empty.

She threw back the covers and lurched to her feet. The room swayed, but she grasped the post at the foot of the bed and waited until her blood pressure regulated. When she felt steady, she scanned the room, searching for her clothes.

They were gone. He'd taken them, probably to prevent her from running again. Her boots were missing too.

Dammit.

Her heart raced with indecision but she decided it didn't matter. All that mattered was getting away from him before he learned the truth.

She bolted for the open door and headed for the back stairs she'd used before to escape. And hoped like hell *this time* she chose the right tunnel to freedom.

Chapter Five

Sera was hiding something.

Erebus didn't know what, but he was now convinced the story Zeus had fed him about why she'd escaped Olympus was total shit.

"I didn't fail on Olympus."

The way she'd said that, off the cuff, as if she'd been shocked he'd even assume such a thing, kept circling in his head as he sat in what used to be the main gathering room of the castle. He'd dragged the chair in from another room and set it in front of the fire. Staring into the flames as he swirled an ancient glass of brandy—the bottle another treasure he'd found in storage—he thought back to the Sera he remembered from those early days with the Sirens.

Before she'd been assigned to him for seduction training, Sera had pretty much sucked at marksmanship, agility, hand-to-hand combat, and warfare strategy. She'd been at the bottom of the class in almost every category. But by the time she'd moved on from his seduction training, she'd already been steadily improving in all the areas of the field. He'd told himself a well-satisfied Siren made a better warrior, but the truth had little to do with him. A confident Siren made a much better warrior, and he'd watched her confidence grow over the months they'd been together, not just in their steamy seduction sessions, but out on the field as well.

Which was why when Zeus had pulled him aside only days ago and told him he had an AWOL Siren, Erebus hadn't once considered it could possibly be Sera. By the time she'd moved on to the second phase of training and he'd been assigned to a new set of recruits, he'd been sure she'd adapt to every one of her training routines and pass each of her upcoming benchmarks. And remembering back to the way she'd almost kicked his ass out in the woods when he'd been hunting her proved she could hold her own. Shit, the way she'd scaled the side of this freakin' castle and very nearly escaped from him down there in those tunnels proved she wasn't just confident as hell but completely capable.

She was definitely hiding something. And he was determined to find out just what that something was.

Creaking floorboards echoed from the hallway. His head came up, and he looked into the darkened corridor. Night had spread over the lake and ruins, and although he'd checked the barrier he'd erected where the tunnels opened to the ruins, that didn't mean there weren't kobaloi hiding in the shadows inside the castle, now looking for a way to get back into the tunnels where they were safe.

Another floorboard creaked, the sound pushing him to his feet. Setting his half-empty glass on a side table he'd dragged in along with the chair, he quietly moved toward the dark hall. A shadow moved, heading slowly toward the stairs that led down to the tunnels. A shadow that was definitely not small enough to be kobaloi.

Amusement spread through him. Amusement and challenge, and a tiny bit of disbelief that she was trying this *again*.

As a god, he could flash in any realm. He wasn't limited by laws of physics or solid walls, like mortals. Gathering his energy just as he'd done when he'd flashed Sera out of that cavern and away from that horde of kobaloi, he envisioned the top step of those stairs and appeared directly in front of her before she could take that first step down.

"Going somewhere?" he asked.

Sera gasped and scrambled back. "Erebus." She pressed a shaky hand to her chest. "Y-you scared me."

"Uh huh." He didn't buy that for a minute. "You were looking for me, I assume."

Panic flashed in her eyes, and she took another giant step back, the pajama bottoms he'd dressed her in pooling around her bare feet. "I... Well, yes. I didn't know where you'd gone."

Liar...

He moved up the step, eyes locked on her, and stepped forward. "I was sitting in the main room. In front of the fire. You couldn't have missed me."

She scrambled back another step, glanced over her shoulder toward the glow from the fireplace, then quickly looked back, only this time the panic was stronger in her sweet blue eyes. "Oh, I... I heard a sound. I didn't even look in the main room. I just assumed you were downstairs."

Two days ago, if she'd fed him this line of B.S., it would have enraged him. Now all it did was entertain him, because even when she knew she was caught red-handed, she still wasn't backing down.

He had to admire her for that. Had to admire that even after escaping Olympus, nearly falling to her death, and suffering a concussion, she was still willing to take on a god. A minor god, albeit, but a god who was still a hundred times more powerful than her.

"Since you're out of bed," he said, drawing closer, "you must be feeling better."

"Better?" She inched backward until her spine hit the wall. Pressing her hands into the stone behind her, she sidestepped to her left, toward the glow of the main room. "I-I wouldn't say better, per se. Just...worried."

Worried? About him? He wished she was, but considering she looked like a cornered animal at the moment, he was calling bullshit. "Well, for what I have planned I don't really need you better, just able to stand upright."

Her eyes widened. "What you have planned?"

Was that excitement he heard in her voice? Oh, he definitely liked that.

He braced a hand against the wall over her shoulder and leaned toward her seductive heat. She immediately tensed, but didn't try to move away. And he liked that even better. "Why do you think I nursed you back to health? So we could finish what we started the other day."

She sucked in a breath and held completely still as he pressed his face into all her silky hair. "You don't mean—"

"I mean exactly that, female." He bent at the knees and hefted her over his shoulder. Holding her tight, he ignored the yelp that passed over her lips and headed straight for the main staircase. "We have unfinished business, and now that you're well enough, we're going to get back to it."

Her hands landed against his back. Warm and small and so damn enticing. She tried to push herself upright, but he held on tighter, keeping her immobile as he carried her up the steps.

"B—but," she sputtered. "I have a concussion!"

"Then I guess you should have stayed in bed."

A warm glow emanated from the fireplace in her room, bathing the corridor in an eerie orange light. Dropping her to her feet in front of the same corner bedpost he'd tied her to originally, he reached for the charmed rope that was still wrapped around the wood and pressed her back. "Hold still."

"Erebus, you can't do this!"

She struggled but was no match for his strength. Satisfied she wasn't going anywhere, he stepped back, perched his hands on his hips, and eyed her carefully. "This looks very familiar. Though this time I'm going to do more than just leave you alone to plot your escape."

Her eyes shot daggers into his as he grabbed a chair, dragged it in front of her, turned it around, and straddled the seat. Resting his forearms on the back, he watched as she struggled to break free, smirked at the way her long, silky blonde hair fell over her eyes and the delicate skin of her face, and smiled as she grew more outraged by the second.

"We can do this the easy way or we can do this the hard way, Sera, but know this, you're not getting away from me until I'm ready to let you go. And I have no intention of letting you go until you give me what I want."

She glared hard in his direction. "I'm not giving you anything. If you want it, you're going to have to try to take it from me."

Excitement pulsed inside him because that was exactly the answer he'd hoped for. After twiddling his thumbs the last two days, waiting for her to heal and regain her strength, he was more than ready for some fun. He could have gone back to Olympus during that time and checked in with Zeus to let the King of the Gods know he was still looking for the nymph, but he didn't want to risk giving Zeus a reason to reassign him and send another hunter after Sera. Plus, if memory served, fun with Sera was hotter than anything Erubus had experienced before or since her, and he wasn't about to let anyone else near her.

Grinning, he pushed up off the chair. "I guess we're doing this the hard way then. Good thing that was my first choice." He crossed the room, reached for a pair of scissors he'd found in a dresser drawer downstairs, then moved back to stand in front of her. "Okay, nymph, where should we start?"

Her eyes zeroed in on the scissors and grew so wide the whites could be seen all around her sexy blue irises. "W-what are you planning to do with those?"

"Get you naked, of course." He reached for the hem of her shirt. "Top or bottom, *agápi?* Where we begin is all up to you."

* * * *

The statement—the implication—should have enraged Sera. Only it didn't. It didn't because all Sera could focus on was that one word...*agápi*. The same word she'd heard him utter in her dream, when she'd been groggy and wounded and he'd been lying in the bed beside her, holding her close as if she were...precious.

Precious.

Her.

To a minor god who didn't give a shit about anyone or anything. *Agápi*...

Holy hell. The ancient endearment registered, and her breath caught in her throat. He *had* called her "my love" in the tunnels. He was calling her "my love" now too.

He tipped his head, and a mischievous smile curled his lips. "You look confused."

She wasn't confused. She was way the hell freaked out. He'd never called her *agápi* when he'd been fucking her senseless on Olympus. Why the hell was he using *that* word on her now?

Her mouth was so dry she wasn't sure she could form words, but somehow she mumbled, "W-why are you doing this?"

"Because nothing else seems to grab your attention. All you want to do is run."

She glared down at the ropes, then back up at him. "Well, I obviously can't run now, can I?"

"No, you definitely can't." His heated gaze swept over her chest where the ropes bound her to the post above and below her breasts, causing them to push out even more. "Though I can't complain. I like you like this."

Using the scissors, he sliced into the bottom of her tank. Cool air washed over her belly as he pulled the hem of her tank away from her skin and cut through the thin material.

Her pulse shot straight up. "Erebus. Stop."

"Hold still, *agápi*. I don't want to accidentally cut you."

He snipped again, and with every swish of the scissors tingles shot across her skin. Tingles that weren't all laced with fear. Even as he came dangerously close to nicking her flesh, her blood heated and an excitement she knew she shouldn't be feeling flared in her veins.

He pulled the scissors away, then tugged the bottom four inches of her tank free all the way around, leaving her stomach exposed to his view beneath the bottom rope holding her in place.

"Mm." He set the scissors on the seat of his chair and skimmed his gaze over her exposed flesh. "You've been working out, *agápi*." Drawing close once more, he brushed the back of his knuckles down the center of her abs. "I like this line right here."

She sucked in a breath. Tried to move back from his touch. Knew she couldn't get away from him. Knew also that part of her didn't even want to try.

Dammit, *this* was why she needed to run. Because the son of a bitch wasn't going to force her. He was going to seduce her, just as he'd done on Olympus. And her traitorous body would enjoy every single moment of it, even knowing when it was all over that he was going to haul her ass back to Zeus and abandon her.

"Please don't," she whispered.

His knuckle grazed the sensitive skin just beneath her belly button, sending tiny electrical arcs straight between her legs. "Please don't what?"

"Don't touch me like that," she managed, but the words were so soft even she had trouble hearing them, and there was no heat behind them. Just a quivering, aching need.

His hand stilled, and his head lifted. Holding her breath, she chanced a look up, and in the silence as their eyes held and nothing but the crackle of the fire sounded in the room, she had absolutely no idea what he was thinking.

There'd been a time when she'd been so head over heels in love with him on Olympus that she'd thought she knew what went on in that gorgeous head of his. That she could predict his reactions. Then she'd discovered he'd barely thought about her at all outside that farce of a bedroom where he'd screwed her blind in the training center, and every one of her beliefs had changed.

That realization had hurt, but it hurt more now because, even though she'd told herself she'd gotten over him, one gaze deep into his eyes here in this room and she knew she'd never be over him. It didn't matter what he had planned. It didn't matter what he did to her next. It didn't even matter that he was going to turn her over to Zeus when he'd had his fill of her. All that mattered was that she was a fool for ever thinking someone like him could love her back. At his core, regardless of what he'd done to "save" her, he was immortal. A god. As selfish as the Olympians. As emotionally void as Hades himself. As deserving of love as that bastard Zeus.

"Go on," she whispered, looking away, resigning herself to something she ached to feel, didn't really want, but knew she wasn't about to fight. "Just get on with it already."

"Okay," he said just as softly. "Since you asked so nicely."

She tensed, anticipating his touch on her breasts or between her legs, but it didn't come. Instead, he lifted the strip of black fabric he'd cut from her tank and used it to cover her eyes.

With swift movements, he tied the fabric behind her head so all she saw was darkness. "Where I want to start, *agápi*, is with the truth. You didn't fail any benchmark test with the Sirens, did you? You ran from Zeus for another reason. Before I untie you from this post and give you what we both want, you're going to tell me why."

Give you what we both want... The words echoed in her head and were so arousing, she suddenly wanted his hands everywhere she'd just told herself she didn't want them.

She waited for him to say more. Waited for him to cut away more of her clothing. Waited for that touch that would make her melt in ways she'd hate herself for later, but it still never came.

Neither did his voice. The only sound she heard was the squeak of leather.

"Erebus?"

"Right here. Waiting."

His voice was feet away. Lower than her ears. As if he were

sitting in that chair again, watching her.

Without her sight, her other senses heightened. Everywhere the rope bit into her, her flesh heated, aching for more contact. The gentle push and pull of his breath sounded over the crackle of the fire—steady and even, not fast like hers, as if he had all the time in the world to sit and wait. And his scent—that hypnotic blend of leather and cognac and skull flowers—filled her nostrils, making her light headed in ways she didn't expect.

What the hell was he doing now? Making her suffer so she'd *beg* for his touch?

She clenched her jaw. "Erebus, what's going on?"

A shuffle sounded, like a boot scraping the floor, and heat flared in her veins all over again. She braced herself for the feel of his fingers against her skin—all but *ached* for it—but the touch never came.

"Erebus?"

"I heard you, *agápi*." His voice was still coming from that damn chair. The bastard *was* making her suffer. "But I'm still waiting for you to tell me what I want to hear."

Shock rippled through her. Shock and disbelief that he wasn't seducing her, wasn't taking her as she'd expected him to do.

The muscles in her stomach quivered, and between her legs—though she couldn't believe she was reacting this way—her sex grew heavy and tingly. "Erebus, take this blindfold off me."

"Why?"

"Because I don't like it."

Another scrape of his boot across the floor. "And I don't like you avoiding my questions. Tell me why you ran, and why Zeus is so pissed."

Holy hell, he was going to sit there and stare at her until she gave him what he wanted. And dammit, why was that suddenly a worse kind of torture than his seducing her?

Because you want him to seduce you. You're envisioning it now. You're getting all hot and bothered just thinking about it.

Dear gods, she was. Damn her nymph bloodline. Damn her body's natural reaction to sexual taunting.

"Come on, *agápi*. Give me what I want, and I'll give you what you need."

Her sex tightened at the sound of his deep voice caressing that term of endearment, and she ached to have his hands caress her hypersensitive flesh in the same way.

"I'm a very patient god, you know." His chair squeaked again. "I could watch you all night. All day tomorrow if that's what it takes. And the day after that and the day after that. I do love watching you."

Her stomach clenched, and against what was left of the black tank, her nipples pebbled with the thought of his heated, needy eyes roving over every inch of her.

She swallowed hard, knowing he'd do exactly what he threatened. Knowing just as surely that it would make her absolutely throb with need.

"*Agáááápi...*"

He drew the word out until she wanted to scream.

"Fine," she blurted out. "You win, okay? I ran because I found out Zeus is a sonofabitch."

He chuckled. "That's not exactly news."

Anger burned inside her. Anger that she was about to tell him anything when she should just keep her mouth shut.

But maybe if she gave him a little information it would encourage him to untie her from this stupid post. And with any luck, when that happened, she'd be strong enough to squash this growing desire for a god who'd always been her greatest weakness.

"You want to know why I ran?" she said. "I ran because I remembered. I remembered everything the Sirens wiped from my memory when they kidnapped me and brought me to Olympus. I remembered that Zeus murdered my parents, that he destroyed my home, and that he wiped out my entire race. All because he's an asshole who doesn't give a shit about anyone but himself. And I ran because I wasn't about to stay another second in a realm with a god who hunts women down like dogs and gets a sick thrill out of turning them into his brainless Siren bimbos."

She drew a deep breath. "Now, are you happy?"

Chapter Six

No, he wasn't happy.

Erebus stared in shock at Sera, blindfolded and tied to the corner post of the bed. Firelight flickered over the smooth skin of her belly and the gentle features that made her look more like an angel than a warrior. But it wasn't her sexy-as-hell body or even her looks that held him entranced right now. It was her words.

"Zeus destroyed your people?" he asked. "Who were your people?"

She pursed her lips, every muscle in her body tight. And for a heartbeat he was sure she wasn't going to answer. Then she said, "Atlanteans. I'm from Atlantis."

No fucking way...

"I thought you were a nymph."

"I am," she said with a frown. "Don't you know anything about genealogy? Atlanteans are descended from water nymphs."

Holy shit...

"My father was the first knight of the queen's guard," she went on when he didn't respond, still clearly perturbed. "My mother was a handmaiden in the queen's castle. When my father discovered that the queen of Atlantis was having an affair with Zeus, he warned her Zeus would tire of her eventually and that the affair would not end well. She ignored him. My father was worried about Zeus's intentions regarding the queen, so to keep his loved ones safe, he smuggled me and my mother out of Atlantis and into the human realm. Half-breeds from the Russian Misos colony took us in. My father was duty bound to return to the queen's guard and couldn't stay with us, but it was only a few months later that we got word his fear had come true. In a fit of rage, Zeus destroyed Atlantis and all who dwelt there, including the queen and my father. Not long after that, Zeus's Sirens showed up looking for us. They slaughtered my mother and many of the half-breeds who tried to protect her. The leader of the colony managed to hide me away during the attack, but I spent the rest of my childhood knowing I was the last of a race that had been nothing but collateral damage to the King of the Gods."

Erebus's heart rate slowly increased as he listened to Sera's story, and though disbelief churned in his brain, he was already racing back over everything he'd ever heard about the utopian society of Atlantis. He knew Zeus'd had a hard-on for the Atlantean queen and her realm. He also knew that the queen had strung him along, giving him just enough to appease him—in this case, as Sera had pointed out, her body—but that she'd refused to give him what he really wanted, which was the entirety of her realm to command and corrupt.

"How did you remember all that?" he asked. "Every Siren recruit has her memory wiped before her training begins."

Her shoulders stiffened. It was a very subtle reaction, but he caught it. And he didn't have a clue what it meant.

"I don't exactly know," she said, a touch of her anger gone. "I just know that I overheard Athena and another Siren talking about Atlantis one day in the mess hall. Their discussion about the Atlantean queen triggered something in my memory. As soon as my training was finished that day, I rushed to the Hall of Sirens and researched everything I could about Atlantis. And the more I read, the faster the memories rushed back."

Humans thought the utopian society of Atlantis was a myth. Those who believed it had actually been real thought it had been destroyed thousands of years ago. But Erebus knew the truth. Atlantis had been a thriving, advanced, self-contained realm hidden in plain sight in the human world, and it had continued to exist as recently as a hundred years ago. Atlantis had only fallen to destruction very near the time Hades lost Erebus in that bet that had plucked Erebus from the Underworld and dropped him on Olympus.

His hands grew damp against the back of the chair, and he pushed to his feet. "If what you say is true, it means you're not a twenty-three-year-old nymph Zeus randomly chose for his Siren

Order."

"No. I'm not." Her jaw tightened again. "I'm a hundred and fourteen years old. After about eighty years with the half-breeds and no repeat attack from Zeus's Sirens, the leaders of the colony figured Zeus didn't know about me. They decided it was safe for me to leave their walls. Even though I'd lived as one of them, I'd never felt as if I belonged there. And part of me wanted to leave. To live near the ocean, as my people had for thousands of years. I ventured out across Europe and finally settled on an island off the coast of Italy. I taught music to children. I built a life of my own surrounded by humans who had no idea who or what I really was. And I met a man who made me feel safe. But that safety was fleeting because Zeus found me there. He was screwing some human on that island and spotted me walking on the beach one day. His Sirens killed the human I'd been living with, destroyed my music studio, and wiped my memories. And then they took me to Olympus and told me I was a twenty-year-old nymph with no family who should be grateful she'd been chosen for the Siren Order. But there was no randomness to my being there. Zeus knew exactly what I was. He knew who I was. And instead of just killing me like he did my mother and the rest of our people, that sick fuck got off knowing he'd turned me into the very thing that had destroyed my entire world."

Pressure built in Erebus's chest. Pressure and warmth and an emotion he'd felt in the tunnels below this castle only days ago but hadn't understood. A feeling he knew now wasn't just sexual. It was rooted in a connection he never could have predicted that bound them together.

She tensed as he moved toward her, hearing or sensing him, he didn't care which. And when he lifted his hand to her soft cheek and tipped her face up, she sucked in a surprised breath.

But it didn't deter him. Heat flared in his belly. Heat and life. Without hesitating, without asking, he lowered his mouth to hers and kissed her.

She froze. Didn't kiss him back. Didn't even move. But he felt the jump in her pulse against his skin, and he heard the tiny moan she tried to stifle echo in his ears like fireworks.

He didn't demand more. Didn't coax her mouth open to deepen the kiss. Just let go of her jaw as he softly skimmed his lips against hers again and untied the blindfold from her the back of her head then tugged the ropes free at her back.

He half expected her to push away as soon as she was free, but she didn't. She lifted her hands to his chest and broke their kiss, drawing back just far enough to peer up at him with confusion and heat in her cerulean eyes. Eyes that were the same color as the seas around her homeland.

And filled with so much damn heat his blood pounded straight into his groin.

"W-why are you kissing me?"

"Because I didn't know." He lifted his hand back to her face and caressed her silky cheek. "Because I now understand. We're the same, you and I. The last of our people. I thought the reason I couldn't get you out of my head was because you were just better at seduction than any of the other recruits I'd trained. But I know now that wasn't the truth. The truth is that my soul recognized yours long ago, Sera. I was just too blind to see what was in front of me."

The lines in her forehead deepened and were so damn adorable he couldn't stop himself from pressing his lips against them and inhaling her sweet lemony scent.

"I'm older than Krónos," he confessed, moving to her temple. "I'm a primordial deity, spawned from Chaos."

Against his chest, she gasped. "Th-that makes you nearly five thousand years old."

"Older." Gods, he liked the sound of that gasp. Couldn't wait to hear it when she was in the throes of ecstasy. "I existed for many years before Gaia and Uranus created the Titans."

He shifted his fingers to the soft skin of her nape and gently massaged, part of him still unable to believe all that she'd told him, another part shocked he hadn't recognized their connection sooner. "The primordial deities had no idea the Titans were power hungry, thus they had no defense against the Titans when they were stripped of their human forms. My father, my siblings, they all ceased to exist as I had known them. But me... Krónos kept me as I was because he wanted my darkness. He wanted to use it to control the other Titans. And he did for a very long time. Until his own children overthrew him."

She drew back once more and gazed up at him. Questions still swirled in her hypnotic eyes, but he also saw awe. An awe that electrified him.

"I don't remember my life with my family," he said. "Just like Athena does with the Sirens, Krónos stripped my memories so I would never question my servitude to him. Then he bound any powers I had that were stronger than his. Unlike you, though, I'll never regain those memories. What I know of my past came from Hades. After Zeus, Hades, and Poseidon overthrew Krónos, Hades kept me for himself. I was duty bound to serve him in the Underworld. He's the one who told me of my past. And he made certain to point out how lucky I was to still be alive. But he didn't do so to educate me. He did it so I would never be inclined to release Krónos from his prison in Tartarus, and so that I would never fall victim to Krónos's lies and deception."

Her mouth fell open, but it was the empathy he saw swirling in her spellbinding eyes that cut right to the heart of him.

He dragged his fingers back to her face and gently traced the sleek line of her jaw, mesmerized by her all over again because he never thought he'd ever meet anyone in the long years of his life who knew what it was like to be alone. "What Zeus did to you was wrong. What he did to your people was wrong. I know what it's like to lose everyone and to be the last of your line. If I had known about your past..." His gaze dropped from her eyes to her lips. "If I had known, things would have been different. I never would have let you be hunted. After all you've been through, *agápi*, you deserve to be cherished and protected. Because you're special. Precious. You are the epitome of rare and irreplaceable and unique, and I won't ever let anyone hurt you again. I'll do whatever I have to do to keep you safe. I vow this to you here and now."

Shock rippled through her eyes, and then those eyes darkened to a warm deep blue just before she lifted to her toes and pressed her mouth to his.

He opened to her kiss. Slid his fingers into her hair and stroked his tongue against hers. Drew her scent and taste and essence deep into his soul. Into a place he hadn't known existed until this moment. Into the very core of who he was and wanted to be.

And as her hands slid up and around his neck and she tipped her head to kiss him deeper, he promised himself that no matter what

Zeus or any of the other ruling gods wanted, this time he wasn't letting her go.

* * * *

She shouldn't be kissing him. She knew she shouldn't be kissing him. But Sera couldn't make herself stop.

He tasted like darkness, like sin, like seduction and salvation. And though she knew there was a chance he could be lying to her, that he'd just made up that entire story to coax her into bed, something inside her believed him. Something in her heart went out to him. Something in her soul latched on to his and was unwilling to let go.

He wasn't the emotionally closed-off minor god she'd convinced herself these last eighteen months he really was. He was the male she'd fallen for all those nights ago on Olympus. The one who'd been able to ignite passion in her with just one look. The one who'd been able to melt her with a single touch. The one whose words had echoed in her head for months and months after he'd left her bed.

Agápi...

She was wrong. She *had* heard him say that to her on Olympus. In the dead of night—on their *last* night—when she'd been drifting to sleep and he'd been wrapped around her like a warm blanket. She remembered it now. Remembered it like it was yesterday. Couldn't believe she'd ever forgotten.

She kissed him harder. Pulled her body flush against his so there was no space left between them. And groaned at the thick, heavy pressure of his arousal growing larger against the bare skin of her belly.

"Sera..." He turned her away from the bedpost. Nipped at her bottom lip. Kissed her cheek, her jaw, and breathed hot over the sensitive skin behind her ear as he maneuvered her to the side of the bed. "Sweet, stubborn, sassy Seraphine."

Emotions closed her throat. Made her desperate to touch him, everywhere. She grasped the T-shirt he wore, drew back from his lips, and wrenched the garment over his head. He did the same to her tank, then reached for her face and pulled her mouth back to his, all the while groaning as her bare breasts grazed his chest.

Her nipples hardened. Electricity arced between her breasts and into her sex. He wrapped an arm around her waist and lifted her up onto the mattress, then knelt over her and claimed her mouth. Claimed what was left of her resistance as well.

It was wrong. She knew it was wrong. She'd only told him a fraction of the truth and was sure if he discovered the rest he wouldn't be frantic to take her and taste her and have her at all. But she couldn't stop. She didn't want to think about the consequences. Didn't want to think about Zeus or Hades or what anyone else wanted. She only cared about this. About him. About holding on to the absolute pleasure only he'd ever been able to draw from her and giving it back to him tenfold while she could.

She arched up to meet him, licked into his mouth, and opened her legs so he could press that heavenly erection right where she wanted it most. A groan slid from her lips as he rocked against her core, but all she could hear in her ears was the word *more*.

Her hands slid down his chiseled abs and found the button of his jeans. She flicked it free, then slipped her fingers beneath his waistband to graze the carved vee of his hipbones. He groaned into her mouth, pulled his arm from around her waist, and closed his hand over her right breast. Pain and pleasure shot from the spot and arced straight between her legs, causing her to rock against his length and tremble with primal need.

"Oh, *agápi*." He trailed a path of fire from her lips to her jaw, down her throat and across her collarbone. "You feel so good. So much better than I remember."

Her heart fluttered, a reaction she warned herself she needed to contain. She could feel. She could enjoy. She could give and even take. But she was not going to fall in love with him again. She couldn't and still survive.

Wrapping one leg around his hip, she rolled him to his back on the mattress. Surprise registered in his sinful eyes as she climbed over him and straddled his hips, lowering the heat of her pelvis against his already straining cock. A surprise that quickly morphed into eager anticipation.

Her palms landed against his chest. She pushed her weight back and ground herself against his groin. His eyes darkened, and between the layers of fabric between them, she felt the pulse of his need right where she wanted it most.

"Is this what you remember?" She trailed her fingers to his nipples and gently squeezed the dark tips.

"Oh yes." He rocked up to meet her downward thrust. His hands shifted to her hips as she teased and rolled his nipple, and his fingers slid beneath the waistband of her thin cotton pajama bottoms. "Keep doing that, *agápi*."

She had no intention of stopping.

Her skin was shades lighter than his, ivory where his was obsidian, and she loved the contrast. "What else do you remember?" she asked, moving to torment his other nipple, continuing to rock and grind and rub against his swollen erection.

"I remember your mouth, *agápi*. Devouring me."

The husky sound of his voice, the rolling heat filling his eyes, it all coalesced inside her to make her absolutely ravenous. Before he could push her pajama bottoms down her ass, she lowered her mouth to his nipple and laved her tongue all around the pebbled tip.

He groaned, lifted his big hands to sift into her hair, and arched up against her. "More."

She moved to his other nipple, licked and laved, then scraped her teeth over the sensitive tip. He hissed in a breath and flexed his hands, trying to pull her mouth back to his, but she easily slid from his grip and trailed her lips lower, across his carved abs, over his belly button, and down to lick the soft skin just above the open waistband of his jeans.

His stomach caved in. She shifted back, pushed his legs open with her knees, and climbed between them so she could grasp his waistband and tug his jeans down his thick thighs.

His cock sprang up, hard and thick and proud. Her gaze shot right to it, and her mouth watered as she tugged his pants the rest of the way off, dropped them on the floor, then climbed back onto the mattress to take her first sinful taste.

Her tongue brushed the flared underside of the head, and he groaned deep in his throat, his heated eyes watching her every movement. "Oh, yes, *agápi*. Do that again."

She licked all around the head, savoring the taste of him, then closed her lips around him and sucked.

This time, his groan was a mix of pleasure and pain, and when his fingers threaded into her hair and tightened, she took the hint. She drew him deep, wiggling the flat of her tongue along the underside until he breached the opening to her throat.

"Fuck, yes, Sera." His big hands helped drag her head back so the tip of his cock almost slipped free of her lips. Then he flexed his hips and thrust deep all over again. "Suck, just like that."

She remembered exactly what he liked and gave him precisely what he wanted. Used her tongue to drive him wild. And while he fucked her mouth with long, deep, penetrating strokes, she relaxed her throat and trailed one hand down to scrape her fingernails against his balls.

Pure pleasure tightened his features. Her breasts grew heavy as she watched him. Her sex throbbed, and the erotic sounds of pleasure he made as he used her mouth filled her ears, making her ache to bring him to a blistering climax so she could taste his release on her tongue. She sucked, licked, took him deep again and again and let him use her however he wanted. His fingertips tightened against her skull, and she felt his cock swell in her mouth. His thrusts grew faster, deeper. Relaxing her gag reflex, she gave herself over to his desire and let him breach her throat. And when he grunted and plunged in even harder, she swallowed all around the head, knowing it would send him right over the edge.

His whole body shook, and he grunted through his release. She didn't let up, continuing to suck and lick and swallow until there was nothing left. When his hands finally released her and his massive body relaxed against the mattress, she slowly worked her way back up his length, flicked her tongue around the head one last time until he twitched, then released him.

A satisfied smile curled her lips as she took in the thin layer of sweat all over his body and the way he lay completely wrecked beneath her.

She'd done that. She'd made him absolutely limp. He might have taught her a thing or two about seduction on Olympus, but she'd always been able to rock his world right out from under him. Right from the first night they'd spent together.

"Is that what you remember?" She squeezed his thigh and breathed hot against his still engorged cock.

Something else she remembered. He was a god. He didn't need

any down time. Which she'd never been more thankful for than she was right at that moment.

His eyes drifted open and locked on her still kneeling between his legs. Eyes that were glossy from his orgasm but not nearly satisfied. "That's a good start, *agápi*."

Heat flashed in his sinful eyes just before he sat up, grasped her shoulders, and dragged her up his body so he could devour her mouth. She groaned, sucked on his tongue, reached for him. But before she could straddle his hips, he lurched out from under her, slid to her back, and pushed her to her belly.

She grunted as her face pressed against the mattress. In one swift move, he stripped the pajama bottoms from her legs then pushed her to her knees. "Ass up, *oraios*." When she tried to push up on her hands, he placed one big palm between her shoulder blades to hold her down. "*Only* your sweet ass."

Excitement swirled inside her when he used the ancient word for beautiful. And between her thighs, which he was already pushing apart with his knees, her pussy trembled.

Long, thick, torturous fingers slid along her swollen flesh, and he groaned. "Oh, you naughty nymph. You're already wet and dripping. Let's see what I can do about that."

She didn't know what he had planned, but when the bed bounced, that excitement inside her flared even hotter. Then she felt the flat of his tongue flicking over her clit and sliding through her heat, and all she could do was press her forehead into the sheet and groan.

Yes, yes, yes... That was exactly what she wanted. She rocked back, loving every moment of his attention. Decadent pleasure teased every nerve ending. He licked her again and again, until she was thrusting against his tongue and desperate to feel him slide inside her aching sheath. With one hand she squeezed her breast. With the other she gripped the blanket above her head and simply held on. The orgasm she'd been so close to feeling since the moment he'd dragged her into this room barreled toward her at light speed, and the instant he drew her clit between his lips and suckled, it consumed her like a fireball engulfing everything in its path.

Her whole body shuddered, and her knees gave out so she landed on her belly on the bed. But even before her powerful climax faded, he was pulling her hips up with his hands, pushing his knees between her legs, and brushing his monster erection right where she needed it most.

"Don't pass out on me, *agápi*. Not yet. We're not finished."

The head of his cock stretched her pussy so wide it was a mixture of pleasure and pain she'd only ever felt with him. A groan rumbled from her throat, one that was rooted in both ecstasy because of the way he made her feel and relief that with him she never had to have that awkward discussion about safe sex. Otherworldly beings—her included—were immune to human viruses and diseases. And thanks to her long life span, she was only fertile once every couple of years. She knew the signs when her fertility was active—as did he, being a god—and thankfully it was nowhere close now.

She tightened around him, trying to drag him deeper into her slick channel. Felt his fingers digging into her hips, felt the rough scratch of his leg hair brushing the backs of her thighs. And then he was there, shoving in so deep all she could do was gasp and curl the fingers of both hands into the blanket while she hung on for the ride.

"Fuck, Sera..." He drew back, shoved in even harder, and moaned. "So tight. So good." He slid back out once more, then thrust home all over again. "I forgot how hot and perfect you were."

Every time he drew almost all the way out, her sex contracted to hold him in, and each time he thrust deep, the head of his cock slammed against her G-spot and sent tiny electrical arcs all through her body. Her eyes slid closed. Her mouth fell open as he fucked into her again and again. She spread her knees and pushed back against every thrust, wanting more, wanting everything, wanting to pull him with her into mind-numbing ecstasy.

He leaned forward so the hard plane of his chest brushed her back, wrapped one arm around her waist, then slid his fingers into her wetness and flicked her clit in time with his thrusts. "Tell me how much you like this, *agápi*."

"So much." She arched her back so he could drive even deeper, so he could hit that perfect spot even harder. "Oh, god, so, so much."

"I am your god, Sera. Don't you forget it." His thrusts picked up speed until he was pistoning into her and the edges of her vision turned black. "Don't you forget it, baby."

Another orgasm, this one even bigger than the last, steamrolled straight for her.

"Oh yes, *oraios*. Squeeze me. Just like that. Don't let up. I'm going to make you come. I'm going to make you come so hard you'll never want anyone but me."

Her mouth dropped open in a silent scream, and just before her climax hit she had one thought.

She didn't want anyone but him. She hadn't wanted anyone else since the moment she'd tasted him eighteen months before. And she knew she'd never want anyone after him, even when this night was just a memory.

The orgasm consumed her, making her whole body jerk and quiver. A scream registered in her ears. Her scream. But all she could feel was blinding ecstasy.

Her cries of ecstasy faded and were drowned out by his grunt of satisfaction and a low growl as he said, "That's it. That's it right there, *agápi*. Fuck yes, that's exactly what I've been missing."

She wasn't sure when he came. When she finally tore her eyes open, all she knew was that she was flat against the mattress on her belly and that Erebus lay across her back, his rapid heartbeat pounding into her spine.

Every single muscle in her body was limp, her skin slicked with sweat, her brain completely wrecked. His heavy weight pressing into her made it painful to draw air, but she loved it. Loved the feel of him against her, around her, *inside* her. And even though it made her weak, even though she knew fucking him into exhaustion wasn't physically or emotionally smart, she didn't care. He was right. She'd missed this. And holy hell, as soon as she regained even a fraction of her strength, she wanted to do it all over again.

He slid off her back so she could breathe but didn't roll away from her. Though his heavenly erection was no longer inside her, she felt it lying semi-hard against the back of her thigh as he draped his leg over hers. Just the thought of rousing that magnificent beast back to attention made her pussy twitch with need all over again.

He pushed her hair to one side and trailed his fingers down her sweaty spine. "Are you still alive, gorgeous?"

Groaning, she turned her face toward his and found his mouth temptingly close. So close she could feel the heat of his breath across her swollen lips. "Barely."

A smile cut across his dark face, making him look absolutely beautiful in the low firelight. "That's the way I like you. Completely ruined from my touch."

"It's not just from your touch." She pulled her arm from beneath her, shifted it to her back so her fingertips grazed his hip, then closed her hand around his length, wet and slick from her body where it lay across her. "It's from what you can do with this magical monster."

His eyes darkened as she used her moisture to stroke him base to tip until he was hard and hot and ready all over again.

He groaned low in his throat, then the hand on her spine grasped the back of her head and dragged her mouth to his. And as he kissed her, he rolled her to her back and climbed over her.

Oh yes. That was exactly what she wanted. For however long she could have it.

She opened to his kiss, to his touch, to his every want and desire. Knew she couldn't hold back. Knew she'd never been able to. His big hands cradled her head. His body pressed her back into the mattress. His glorious cock settled between her legs and teased her aching sex.

She wound her arms around his shoulders and held on, but instead of thrusting deep like she expected, he drew back from her mouth and stilled his taunting movements between her legs.

His eyes held hers, hot and insistent and filled with so much emotion her chest tightened. "I'm not letting you go, Sera."

She inhaled slowly, fighting the feelings coursing through her chest. They were the words she'd longed to hear for ages, but they'd come too late to make a difference in her life. Focusing on his lips so he couldn't see what was going on inside her, she said, "I'm not yours to keep."

"Yes, you are," he whispered. "You always were. And this time I'm going to prove it to you."

He lowered and took her mouth just as his cock took possession of her body, and she gave him both without question. Gave him everything even as tears burned her eyes because he was right.

She was his. She'd been his from their first touch on Olympus. She'd always be his and forever curse the fact she'd finally gotten exactly what she'd always wanted but that fate still wasn't on her side.

Because the truth would come out, and the moment Erebus discovered what she'd stolen from the King of the Gods, he'd have no choice but to haul her back to Olympus.

He thought he had free will, but he didn't. He was a servant to the ruling gods. No matter how much she loved him, she would never again be a pawn in any of their games.

Chapter Seven

Erebus was warm and content and more relaxed than he'd ever been.

The fire crackled in the fireplace as he dozed with Sera beside him in the big bed. She'd fallen right to sleep after he'd brought her to a fourth blistering climax—or maybe he'd been the one to drift to sleep; he wasn't sure. Regardless, now, as he drifted in that space between sleep and consciousness with her heat warming the coldest places inside him, thoughts echoed in his mind. Thoughts he hadn't considered until this very moment.

His draw to Sera—not just here but eighteen months ago on Olympus—made so much sense now. She was from Atlantis, the enlightened race, the golden utopian realm, and he was from darkness. She was everything he wasn't—light instead of dark, selfless instead of selfish, resourceful instead of resigned. She balanced him in ways no one he'd encountered before her ever could. And he knew with her, he could lift himself to a place he'd never been able to reach on his own.

He wasn't giving her up. He didn't care what the Sirens said. He didn't care what Zeus wanted. He needed her, and he'd do whatever it took to keep her with him.

He rolled toward her, reached across the space between them to draw her back against his body, and faltered when his hand met nothing but cold sheets and blankets. Tearing his eyes open, he lifted his head and looked across the bed, surprised to see her side empty.

He pushed up to sitting and glanced across the room illuminated only by the dying fire toward the darkened bathroom. His pulse picked up speed, and he quickly climbed out of bed, telling himself the whole time she was in there, only the room was empty when he reached it.

Panic shot through his chest, chilling all those places that had warmed because of her. One look at the closed window told him she hadn't gone out that way. Turning back into the room, he spotted the open bedroom door, and reality hit him hard in the chest.

She hadn't run. She'd walked right out of this room. And he'd been too blinded by pleasure to stop her.

His fingers shook as he dressed. He didn't know how long she'd been gone, but he had to find her. Why the fuck would she run? They'd reconnected tonight. He'd seen it in her eyes, felt it in that space that hurt like a motherfucker in his chest right this moment. She was his. She knew she was his. What had spooked her into running when he knew she'd felt everything he had?

Zeus.

Fear stabbed like a knife straight through his heart, stilling his feet on the stairs.

Zeus could scare the fuck out of her and make her run. If the King of the Gods had been privy to what they'd done, if Zeus had any idea what Erebus was planning, he could have shown up here. He could have threatened Sera. He could have taken her.

He pushed his legs into a sprint and shot down to the tunnels. His enhanced sense of sight scanned the main corridors for any sign of her but he already knew she wasn't in any of them. She was gone. She was outside the ruins. All he could do was hope and pray he got to her before Zeus took her back to Olympus.

The forest was dark and damp when he raced out of the tunnels and stilled in the silence to search for her. He couldn't see her through the thick trees, but faintly he picked up the crashing of brush. Picked up racing heartbeats. Recognized heavy breaths and pounding footfalls.

Most were animals. He sensed elk not far away. A raccoon was in a tree a quarter mile to his left. And a cougar roamed the hillside to his right. But there was no sign of Sera.

He closed his eyes and focused on her, able to find her now because of his connection to her. Tuning in to his hearing, he searched the area for the familiar sounds of her breathing, the memorable scent of her skin. And located her a mile up the mountain to his right, not far from that cougar.

Using his god senses to zero in on her position, he flashed to that spot, muscles tight and ready to step between her and the King of the Gods. Except when he appeared at her back there was no sign of Zeus. No sign of anyone else but her. And she wasn't running away as he'd expected. She was crouched on the ground with her hand inside an old, decaying log.

"Come on," she muttered with no clue he was behind her. "I know you're in here."

Erebus had no idea what she was doing, but something about the scene, about her hair shining almost silver in the moonlight set the hairs on his nape straight to attention.

"There you are." She exhaled what he recognized as a relieved breath and pulled something out of the log. He tilted his head to see over her shoulder and watched as she brushed dirt from a palm-sized silver coin.

"What are you doing, Sera?"

She jerked to her feet and whipped around to face him. Wide-eyed, she closed her fist tightly around the coin, hiding it from view. "Erebus. I—you scared me."

"I see that." He didn't like the guilty look on her face or where his thoughts were going at the moment. "Tell me you have a good reason for running this time. Right out of my bed when I thought you'd enjoyed that as much as I had."

"I..."

Warning signals fired off in his head when she couldn't even formulate a simple answer, and that darkness inside surged right to the forefront. Warning signals that screamed she hadn't felt any of the shit he had in that room tonight. "Start talking, Sera, before I come up with scenarios you don't like."

She swallowed hard and pulled whatever was in her hand against her chest. Her feet shuffled backward, and fear replaced the guilt in her eyes. The only thing that stopped her from bolting was the log at her heels that slowed her movement.

Before she could step back and over it, he grasped her wrist, pulled it away from her chest, and pried her fingers open. She yelped and tried to push his hand away, but he blocked her and stared down at the silver coin that was no bigger than her palm and stamped with an image of Heracles surrounded by the traditional Greek key design.

"I've seen this before," he said in a slow voice, lifting it so he could turn it in the moonlight.

"Erebus... Don't."

"This is the Medallion of Heracles. The key that opens the doors of Argolea, the realm of the ancient heroes, to any being who possesses it." His brow lowered in disbelief as he glanced back at her. "Where did you get this?"

She swallowed hard, and her gaze shot to the medallion still in his hand. "Just...give it back. Please."

Something didn't make sense. What the hell was she doing with the key to Argolea? He'd heard of its existence when he'd been with Hades, but it had been lost for years.

His jaw tightened. "Start fucking talking, Sera, because I can't think of a single reason why you, the last surviving Atlantean, would have this key. Unless you stole it from someone and plan to sell it to the highest bidder."

"Okay, just listen. And don't do anything rash until I tell you everything, okay?" She lifted her hands in what he knew was a pleading move, but it did little to settle the darkness inside him. "I did steal it. From Zeus. That's why he sent you after me. Not because I failed any of the Siren tests, but because I took the key so he couldn't use it."

His eyes flew wide. Not just because of what she'd done but because he hadn't known the King of the Gods had come into possession of the key. Zeus despised the Argoleans and could do serious damage with this key. He bet Zeus also wouldn't think twice about doing serious damage to the person who stole it from him.

"You know the story about the creation of Argolea, right?" she said quickly. "How Zeus created the realm of Argolea for his son Heracles to keep Heracles and his descendants safe from Hera's wrath? When Zeus created Argolea, he created a border that was impenetrable to the Olympians. He thought that would protect Heracles and all the others. And it did, but it also prevented Zeus from crossing into Argolea whenever he wanted. To get around that, Zeus had Hephaestus forge a special key, that medallion in your hand. It grants the bearer of the medallion the ability to cross into

Argolea, regardless of race. For hundreds, thousands of years, Zeus had no reason to use the key so he kept it hidden. And the place he chose to hide it was in the one realm he knew Hera had no interest in visiting: Atlantis."

She wrung her hands together and glanced at the medallion. "He gave it to the queen of Atlantis to hold in safe keeping. It was hidden in my realm for ages, long before I or my parents were born. Zeus kept close tabs on it by seducing each and every queen so he could retrieve it whenever he wanted. But he made a mistake with the last queen. She sensed Zeus would one day use it for evil purposes, so she gave it to my father, and she told him to hide it in the human realm, someplace Zeus could never find it. And he did. He sent it with me and my mother to that half-breed colony in Russia. But Zeus discovered the queen's deception. That's why he destroyed Atlantis. That's why he murdered my father and sent the Sirens to murder me and my mother. So he could get his precious key back and get rid of anyone who knew what had happened to it."

Erebus's gaze strayed to the medallion between his fingertips. It looked like a coin, but even he could feel the power vibrating inside the small metal disk. And he knew if Zeus caught wind he had it, the King of the Gods would do to him what his father Krónos had done to Erebus's ancestors.

"Don't you understand?" Sera said. "Zeus is looking for the water element. He needs only that to complete the Orb of Krónos, the circular disk that holds all four classic elements and has the power to start the war to end all wars. He stole the Orb from the Argoleans. It already holds the three other elements—air, fire, and earth. Zeus is convinced Prometheus, who created the Orb, hid the water element in Argolea, where the Olympians cannot cross, and Zeus is frantic to get into that realm and find the last element."

She stepped toward him. "Erebus, if Zeus does that, if he finds the water element, he'll be able to release the Titans from Tartarus. He'll be able to command Krónos to wield all his evil powers for *his* purposes. And if he can do that, he'll control every realm—Olympus, the Underworld, the oceans, Argolea, and even the human world. No one and nothing will ever be able to stop him."

Understanding swirled in Erebus's mind. And visions of Zeus wielding unlimited power burst like fireworks behind his eyes.

"Erebus." Her soft fingers landed against his forearm, squeezed, gently. "If Zeus does that, he won't just destroy the other realms as he did Atlantis. He'll bring about death and destruction in ways even Hades cannot comprehend."

She was right. With this key, Zeus had almost everything he could ever want. And every race would be enslaved to him...exactly as Erebus had been enslaved to the Titans and Olympians since his family had been stripped of their human forms.

"If what you say is true and Zeus had this, then why didn't he use it immediately? And how did you even know Zeus had it?"

She exhaled a slow breath. "Remember I told you that I overheard Athena talking to one of the Sirens in the mess hall? That was true. But they weren't just talking about Atlantis. They were talking about this key. The Sirens have been searching for it ever since he annihilated Atlantis and discovered it was missing. He figured my father must have hidden it with me and he was right. It was at that Russian half-breed colony. They were protecting it. When I left there, I thought it would be safe. I never thought his Sirens would find it. That's what I overheard them talking about on Olympus. Something about the half-breeds registered as familiar, and after I left the mess hall that night, I went to the Hall of Sirens to look it up. That's when my memories came back. That was the trigger for me. I remembered everything then. Everything I told you about hiding with the half-breeds for eighty years and Zeus eventually finding me on that island off Italy was true. I just didn't tell you about this key."

His gaze shifted to her face, cast in the shadows of the trees, and he searched her eyes for lies. But he only saw truth. A truth that made his spine tingle. "Why? Why did you keep this secret?"

She swallowed again and glanced at the medallion. He could tell she was itching to take it back but knew she wasn't fast enough or strong enough to wrestle it from his grasp. "I-I wanted to tell you. I did." Her gaze shot back to his. "But you work for Zeus. And you were sent to bring me back to him."

Disbelief churned in his gut, a disbelief rooted in the knowledge that she didn't trust him. "You think I want Zeus to have this kind of power?"

"Don't you?"

His jaw clenched down hard. "Are you seriously asking me that question?"

"I—"

"I'm nothing but a fucking slave to Zeus. That's all I've ever been to the Titans or the Olympians. That's all I *will* ever be."

Her shoulders sagged, and relief filled her eyes as her fingers tightened around his arm. "Then we have to make sure he never gets his hands on it."

She was right, and yet he didn't like the fact she hadn't trusted him. Even after everything he'd seen in her eyes and the connection he'd felt with her, she still saw him as the personification of darkness. To her, he would likely *always* be only darkness because he came from Chaos and had served the three gods she considered the big evils: Krónos, Hades, and Zeus.

Motherfucker. Stupidity echoed through every cell in his body. He was good for a hot and dangerous fuck now and then but not for the truth.

"Why hasn't Zeus used this already?" he demanded.

"I'm not sure. I don't think he's able to. There's magic in it. Magic that is not from Olympus but from witchcraft. I remember my father and the queen discussing it. They thought Hephaestus had Hecate cast a spell over it that prevented Zeus from using it. From what I could gather, Hecate never wanted him to be able to use it either, so she cursed it. But it was only a matter of time before he broke that curse. Which is why I had to get it away from him."

That made sense. But before he could say so, another thought hit him. One he definitely didn't like. "And just how did you get this from Zeus?"

Her face flushed a gentle shade of pink, and for the first time since she'd started this plea to draw him to her side, she dropped her hand from his forearm. "Well, ah, I located its likely position on Olympus by following Athena, and then, well, I, um..." She scratched the back of her head and glanced down at the ground beneath her bare feet. "I overpowered the guards protecting it."

His gaze narrowed on her nervous features. She'd said *guards*. Not Sirens. "Overpowered them," he repeated slowly. "How?"

"With my Siren skills."

A vibration lit off low in his gut. "Which Siren skill?"

She bit her lip, seemed to debate her answer, then finally said, "Seduction."

Oh, no godsdamn way... "You fucked them?"

Her irate gaze shot up to his. "I didn't fuck them. I just distracted them with seduction skills *you* taught me. Then I immobilized them with the hand-to-hand combat I'd learned, and I stole the medallion. Isn't that what Sirens are supposed to do?"

Yes. But not *his* Siren. He didn't care that she hadn't actually fucked those guards. He didn't like the thought of her using her seduction skills on anyone but him. Which he knew was completely hypocritical considering all the Siren trainees he'd fucked during his time on Olympus, but he didn't care. They hadn't meant a thing to him. She meant everything.

He closed his fist around the medallion and swept his other arm around her waist, yanking her tight against his body. She gasped and braced her hands at his chest, but didn't try to push away.

"You're not seducing anyone else, *agápi*. Got that?"

Her fingertips curled into his T-shirt. "Does that mean you're not taking me back to Olympus?"

"That's exactly what it means. You're mine."

"And what about you? Does that 'mine' thing work both ways?"

"Absolutely."

Something softened in her eyes. Something he wanted to believe was trust, but a niggling voice in the back of his head whispered it wasn't. "And the medallion?"

"Zeus can't have it."

The tension in her muscles eased where he held her. "We have to take it to Argolea. It's the only place where it will be safe. You remember Elysia, right? The Siren trainee who escaped Olympus with Damon?"

Damon had been one of the Siren trainers Erebus had worked with. He'd always liked the mortal and had been oddly disappointed when he'd learned the guy was really an Argonaut who'd been duped by Zeus and that he wasn't coming back. "Isn't Elysia's the Argolean princess Damon broke out of the Siren compound?"

"Yes. She's in Argolea with him. But his name is really Cerek. They're our way in. They'll know what to do with the key and how to keep it safe from Zeus. That's why I came here, to the half-breed colony, because I thought maybe there would be a way to signal the Argonauts from here. They allied with the half-breeds for many years before that colony was destroyed."

Erebus knew all about the Argonauts. Do-gooders Hades—and Zeus—had bitched about in his presence on more than one occasion. "I know how to signal them."

"You do?"

The excitement in her voice didn't thrill him. He didn't want her around any so-called heroes who might try to take her away from him, but he knew in the center of his gut that they weren't getting back to any sort of seduction until they got rid of this medallion. "Yes, but I'm not about to call them unless you agree to one thing."

Unease filled her blue eyes. "And what's that one thing?"

He leaned close to her lips and breathed hot over her mouth. "That you promise to stop fucking running from me. I am not the one you have to fear. I'm the one who's going to save you."

* * * *

"I'm the one who's going to save you..."

Erebus's words in that damp forest echoed in her head as they crossed the portal into Argolea. She didn't need him to save her. Didn't need anyone to save her. She'd been on her own long enough to know how to save herself.

And yet, something inside her recognized that he *wanted* to be the one to save her. Which was a totally new experience for her and left her completely uneasy.

No one had ever cared enough to want to save her...no one but her parents. Sure, the half-breeds had kept her hidden and safe from Zeus's Sirens for eighty years, but not because they'd cared for *her*. They'd done that simply because they didn't want Zeus to have the key to Argolea, and quite possibly because they'd been afraid she might reveal their location and put them all in danger if they didn't protect her. She'd had to beg and plead her case to finally get them to agree to let her leave the confines of the colony, and even then they hadn't been thrilled with the decision.

That unease turned to a burst of guilt when she thought of the Sirens finding the Russian half-breed colony and destroying it, but at least she knew that hadn't been her fault. She'd never told the Sirens a word about the half-breeds' location. Now that she had her memory back, she was sure of it.

Erebus released her hand as their feet hit solid ground in the protected realm of the ancient heroes. Getting to Argolea had been a heck of a lot easier than she'd thought. Erebus, being a minor god, knew more about the key than she'd assumed. He'd flashed them to a mountaintop in Northern Greece and led her to a cave that looked as ordinary as any other she'd ever seen. He'd explained that the cave was actually the tomb of Heracles, and just inside there had been a small circular indentation that was the exact size of the medallion she'd stolen from Zeus. Anyone who didn't know what it was for would have easily overlooked it, but when Erebus slid the medallion into the slot, a flash of light erupted around them and the portal to Argolea opened.

Four guards dressed in armor and carrying long spears rushed toward the raised dais where they appeared. Behind them, the portal lights slowly faded until there was only an ancient stone arch above them.

Sera stiffened, but Erebus slipped the medallion into his pocket and immediately stepped in front of her, shielding her as he held up his hands in a nonthreatening way. "Careful, boys. Pretty sure you don't want to do that."

The guards' eyes flew wide. They clearly recognized he was a god, even if they didn't know which one. As a unit, they crouched down in fighter stances, their spears held out menacingly in front of them, and shouted to each other with rapid words Sera didn't catch. Another guard, one who must have heard the commotion, came running from another room, saw Sera and Erebus on the dais surrounded by spears, and sprinted toward a different archway flanked by columns.

"I don't think we're as welcome here as you thought we'd be," Erebus muttered under his breath.

"They're not used to people just appearing through the portal unannounced." Pressing a hand against his forearm, she stepped around him.

"Sera—"

"We're not here to cause any harm," Sera said to the guards, ignoring Erebus's warning. He might think he needed to save her, but he was the threat to these people, not her, and this time she was the one who was going to do the saving. "I'm a friend to your princess. Princess Elysia."

The guards exchanged confused glances, and Sera knew she had to get them to understand if they were going to believe her. "We trained together on Olympus."

The guards shouted again and shoved their spears forward. Sera's adrenaline shot up as they jerked toward her, and she yelped and stumbled back into Erebus.

His arms closed around her as he pulled her against him and moved back three steps. "Not a great idea to mention Olympus," he hissed in her ear.

He was right. She hadn't thought that one through. Her mind spun with options. She didn't want to take the key back to the human realm, where Zeus could possibly find them, but she didn't see another option at this point. Living was better than being skewered two steps into this realm. "Can you use the medallion to open the portal again so we can get out of here?"

"I'm not sure." He let go of her with one arm and reached for the medallion in his pocket. "I don't know how it works on this side. If I can't, we might have to make a run for i—"

"Holy Hera," a voice exclaimed from across the room. A voice Sera vaguely recognized.

Footsteps echoed, and Sera looked toward the arched doorway, where a very familiar face peered up at them.

"Damon," Erebus said in surprise, seeing the muscular blond male as well.

For the first time since they'd stepped into this realm, Sera breathed easier. "No, not Damon. Not anymore. He's Cerek." Her gaze dropped to his marked forearms, visible where his long-sleeved gray T-shirt was pushed up to his elbows, the ancient Greek text that identified him as one of the chosen warriors of the great heroes visible in this realm.

Cerek moved into the middle of the room, his eyes filled with confusion and disbelief. "Erebus? Is that you? Why—? When—? How the heck did you get—"

A horde of footfalls filled the room, and Sera glanced from

Cerek to the other massive males rushing up behind him, each sporting the same holy shit expressions and the very same markings that identified them as Argonauts.

"Yeah, it's me," Erebus said, releasing Sera and moving up to her side. "And I'm not here to cause any trouble, so you can tell your guards to relax."

"Stand down," Cerek said to the guards. "The Argonauts will handle this."

The guards looked less than thrilled, but they did as Cerek commanded and cautiously moved back to their posts, though Sera noticed their attention never left Erebus and they watched every single movement he made.

The Argonauts fanned out around Cerek, murmuring words to each other Sera couldn't hear. Still clearly in shock, Cerek climbed the steps of the dais until he stood in front of them. "I don't understand what you're doing here. Or how the heck you even got here."

"It's a long story." Erebus reached for Sera's hand and glanced down at her at his side. "You remember Sera, don't you? She was in the same training class as Elysia."

Cerek's gaze slid Sera's way for the first time, and recognition flared in his brown eyes, but they were still laced with a helluva lot of confusion. "Yeah," he said slowly, glancing back to Erebus. "Though I'm not quite sure what you're doing here with a Siren."

Sera's back went up. "I'm not—"

"She's not a threat either," Erebus said, cutting her off as he squeezed her hand, telling her without words to let him handle it.

She closed her mouth and let him take the lead, but frustration surged inside her that he didn't think she was capable enough to deal with an Argonaut. As sweet as it was that he thought she needed him to save her—which was still not exactly something she'd ever expected from him—she didn't like being brushed aside as if she were fragile and incapable.

"But she is the reason we're here," Erebus went on, clearly oblivious to what was going on in her head. "And when you hear what she did for you and your realm and everyone in the human world as well, I think you're going to be pretty damn impressed. Just as I was."

Cerek looked down at her, expectantly awaiting an explanation, and from the corner of her eye she spotted Erebus gazing down at her as well. But she couldn't think of any words to fill the awkward silence because all she could focus on were Erebus's last words.

"Well then," Cerek finally said, sensing she wasn't going to speak. "I can't wait to hear what you did. I'm sure Elysia would like to hear it as well. She's back at the castle."

The Argonaut was still talking. Sera could hear him speaking over his shoulder to the Argonauts and introducing them to Erebus, but she didn't catch his words. She was too hung up on what Erebus had said.

He'd been impressed? By her? By what she'd done for this realm and the human world? He hadn't seemed impressed in that forest. He hadn't seemed anything but ticked she'd left his bed, then frustrated he'd been dragged into this mess. The god of darkness was all about seduction and control and domination when he wasn't in Zeus's presence, so his being impressed by anything other than sex when he was with her seemed completely out of character.

Somehow she found the strength to glance up at him. Voices continued to echo around her, but she didn't hear them. And when her eyes met his, she didn't see irritation or darkness or even a hint of that domination—sexual or otherwise—in his dark eyes. She saw awe.

An awe that told her he hadn't lied when he'd said he felt a connection between them. An awe that completely rocked the ground right out from under her feet.

Chapter Eight

After two days in the protected realm of the heroes, Erebus could see why Zeus was so hot to get his ass here.

It wasn't Utopia, at least not the kind written about in fantasy novels. The country had its fair share of problems, which included political strife and class delineations, along with a little bigotry and misogyny thrown in—mostly spurred on by the aging male Council members who technically advised the monarchy but who Erebus had learned were secretly scheming to overthrow their queen.

But if a person could look past all that? Yeah. Erebus could see exactly what was so special about this place. Soaring mountains, a vast ocean, an ancient city with massive marble buildings and spires that reached to the sky. Not to mention the people. Everyone he'd come in contact with since arriving in this realm had been real. Not the fake, ass-kissing opportunists who lurked around every corner on Olympus. Sure, some of them weren't thrilled he was here—like the Council members and a few of the city's inhabitants who'd seen his size and stature and immediately assumed he was evil. But the others—like the queen and the leader of the Argonauts and Cerek's mate Elysia, and hell, everyone in the damn castle—had welcomed him with open arms once they realized just what he and Sera had brought them.

His gaze drifted to Sera walking twenty yards ahead of him in the trees as they headed toward the Kyrenia settlement far outside the walls of the capital city of Tiyrns. He watched as Sera glanced toward Elysia at her side, smiled at something the female said, then linked her arm with Elysia's and lifted her face toward the sunshine.

Next to Erebus, Cerek droned on about the Misos ruins where Erebus had caught up with Sera, but Erebus barely listened. He'd barely been listening for the last hour as Cerek and Elysia had shown them around Tiyrns and the major points of interest in the realm. His focus was locked solidly on Sera and the twinkle in her eye as she laughed at something Elysia said. At the way she smiled. At how relaxed she seemed now in this realm where Zeus couldn't follow them.

Gods, she was stunning, her blonde hair picking up the light filtering through the trees in a way that made it almost sparkle. The way her pale skin glowed in the sunlight. The way her lips were so plump and perfect and soft he ached to kiss them and lick them and devour them as he'd devoured her last night.

Tingles rushed from his chest to his belly, and memories lit off in his mind—meeting with the Argonauts and the queen to discuss the key he and Sera had brought them. Being shocked not only at the way they'd all accepted him, but also offered him a place to stay. Elysia taking them to a suite in the castle that night, and the way Sera had launched herself into his arms as soon as the outer door closed and they were finally alone.

Oh yeah, last night she'd smiled. Except then her smile had been laced with heat and need and a passion only he could sate. He was definitely planning a repeat performance as soon as they were alone again, but tonight he wanted more. Tonight he wanted to make sure she knew that she was his and that no matter what the queen decided to do with the key, she would still be his.

"After Hades joined forces with Zagreus and they attacked the Misos colony," Cerek said as they emerged from the trees and crossed into a field with knee-high, undulating wheat, "the colonists were transferred here." He pointed across the vast field toward a city wall made of stone and wood. "That's Kyrenia. It used to be a witch settlement, but now it's home to witches, Misos, and any others looking for life outside Tiyrns."

There were no marble spires. No towering white columns. No castle gleaming in the sunlight, but Erebus figured that was the point. Not everyone wanted to live in a giant city. Hell, not even him. Fancy wasn't his style. That was part of the reason he'd enjoyed the times Zeus loaned him to the Sirens and he could get out of the stuffy temples on Olympus. As nice as the Argolean queen's castle was in Tiyrns, someplace like Kyrenia was a lot more his style.

"Are there other villages in the realm?" he asked, wondering where Sera would prefer to live. She'd pretty much been a refugee her whole life. He had a hard time envisioning her settled in Tiyrns for long.

"Yes." Cerek swiped at a stalk of wheat and plucked it from the ground. "Smaller ones in the mountains. Kyrenia is the closest to the capital, and the most aligned with the monarchy. The queen is committed to protecting it from Council interference."

Ah yes, the infamous Council of Elders. Those old, bigoted men who wanted this realm to revert back to its patriarchal ways as it had been before their exalted King Leonidas had passed and his headstrong daughter Isadora assumed the crown and started making changes that promoted equality. How dare she?

"How many live here?"

"Thousands," Cerek said. "The population grows every day."

That was a lot of people fleeing from the confines of the Council. "And what kind of protection does the monarchy provide them so the Council doesn't exert authority?"

"Not a lot," Elysia answered from ahead. She and Sera had both stopped and stood looking back at them as they approached. "The monarchy doesn't need to provide protection because they have Nick."

Erebus's belly warmed all over again as his gaze locked with Sera's and he saw the spark of hunger in her eyes. A hunger he couldn't wait to feed.

"And who is Nick?" he asked, unable to look away from her brilliant blue eyes.

"A god." At Sera's side, Elysia smirked. "One stronger than you."

Erebus's feet stilled as they reached the females, and he finally tore his gaze from Sera and looked toward Cerek for confirmation. "Another god? In this realm?"

Cerek nodded and slung an arm over Elysia's shoulder. "Krónos's bastard son. He's the half-breed leader, and he and his mate Cynna manage the settlement. He's also as strong as Zeus and Poseidon and Hades, and we've got him on our side."

"With you," Elysia said, "we now have three gods on our side."

The "*we*" in the princess's statement hit him hard. Right in the center of his chest. He'd never been part of any "we." Even though he served the ruling gods, he'd never aligned himself with them. Serving wasn't his choice; it was his duty.

The thought spun in his head as he glanced from Elysia back to Cerek. "Sorry, did she say three?"

"We also have Prometheus," Cerek supplied, "though he's kind of a recluse and doesn't show his face all that often. He and Circe have a place up in the mountains. He tends to keep to himself, but he's been known to help out now and then when we need him."

Holy shit. A Titan and one of the most powerful witches in the cosmos were also both hiding in this realm. Erebus remembered vividly how pissed Zeus had been when Prometheus had broken free of his chains and the temper tantrum that had followed when Prometheus had then broken Circe out of her prison high on Mt. Olympus. He just hadn't realized they'd both come here, to Argolea.

"See," Sera said softly at his side, sliding her arm around his and leaning all her sultry heat against him. "You're not the only immortal being who finally saw the light and decided to side with the good guys."

Erebus's heart pounded hard as his gaze dropped to the nymph at his side. Was that what he'd done? Betrayed the ruling gods and declared himself a rebel like the Argonauts? Sided with the enemy?

It was, he realized as his pulse beat faster. By coming here and not delivering Sera back to Zeus, he was basically saying "fuck you" to the gods and making himself a target to be hunted for all eternity.

Sera, Elysia, and Cerek continued to chat around him but he couldn't focus on their words. All he could focus on was the fact that staying in this realm wasn't an option. Yes, he was immortal, but even immortal beings could be punished for disobeying orders. He'd served Hades in the Underworld for thousands of years. He knew what kind of penance awaited him if Zeus decided to turn him over to the god-king of the Underworld as a prisoner. But that wasn't his biggest fear. His biggest fear was suffering the same fate as the other primordial deities who'd been banished from this world when the Titans had come into power. To be stripped of his human form and cast into nothingness. To remain conscious of all that happened around him but forever be unable to react, to breathe, to live.

That wasn't something he was willing to risk. He liked living too damn much.

His hands grew damp. He needed to get the hell out of this realm. To return to Olympus before anyone realized what he'd done. He still had time to fix this. He could tell Zeus he hadn't found Sera. He could say he'd heard she'd crossed into Argolea before he'd been able to locate her. Now that the key was safe with the queen, Zeus couldn't follow Sera here. He couldn't take the key. Sera was safe. The key was safe. There was no reason not to return to his duty.

And yet...

His gaze strayed to Sera at his side. She smiled at something Elysia said, then glanced up at him. And as their eyes met and held and his pulse slowly regulated, his chest filled with a warmth that burned everything else to ashes in his mind, and he realized... He didn't want to go back to Olympus.

He didn't want to leave her. For the first time in his long-ass life, he had something of his very own. Something not linked to duty and service and what the gods wanted, but something pure and special and his. He didn't want to let that go. He didn't want to walk away from her and forget the way he felt right now. He wanted this. He wanted her. He wanted a chance to finally—and maybe for the first time ever—truly *live*.

Sera's brow slowly wrinkled, and a worried look crept into her eyes. "Are you all right?"

His heart beat strong, steady, thumping pulses against his ribs. But they didn't hurt. They felt good. Spreading heat and life through his veins to give him strength. A strength that told him this decision—choosing *her*—was the right one.

"Yeah." Unable to stop himself, he slid a hand under all that gorgeous hair of hers, grazed her nape with his fingertips, and tugged her mouth toward his. "Yeah, *agápi*. I'm perfect."

Her lips were soft and sweet where they brushed his, but not nearly enough. And as she slid her arms around his waist and kissed him back, all he could think about was getting her back into that suite where they could be alone, where he could pin her to the mattress and make her his all over again.

"*Skata*," Cerek said at his side. "Uh, guys? We've got a

problem."

Irritated by the interruption, Erebus lifted his head to tell the Argonaut to mind his own business but froze when he spotted the four females standing on the edge of the forest fifty yards away.

All four were decked out in fighting gear. All four looked like something straight off the pages of a *Victoria's Secret* magazine. And all four were staring at him kissing Sera across the field with wide, shocked eyes.

Those weren't trainees. Those were the real deal.

Sirens.

In Argolea.

Fuck.

Sera glanced over her shoulder and gasped. At Erebus's side, the unmistakable *shiiiing* of Cerek's blade being drawn echoed in the air.

"Get back to the castle," Cerek said, pushing past Elysia. "Tell the queen they're here."

"How the hell did they get here?" Erebus asked, pushing Sera to his back. His adrenaline surged as he watched the Sirens bolt back into the trees.

"Probably through the moving portals." Cerek pulled two more blades from his hips, these daggers not nearly as long as the parazonium he'd unsheathed moments before—the ancient Greek blade all Argonauts carried—but big enough to do some major damage. He handed the daggers to Erebus. "They're manned by the witches. While this realm is blocked to the Olympians, it's not to Zeus's warriors. The Sirens monitor where the moving portals open and close in the human realm and have jumped through before."

Grasping Elysia at the arm, Cerek pressed a hard kiss to his mate's lips. "Go. Get back to the castle. Tell the queen. We can't let them reach the portal. If they do, Zeus will know Erebus and Sera are here."

A worried look passed over Elysia's face, but she whispered, "I will." Cerek glanced at Erebus and nodded toward the trees, then took off at a run.

Elysia reached for Sera's hand. "Come on."

Erebus was just about to follow Cerek when Sera said, "No. I can fight." She struggled out of Elysia's grip and looked up at him. "You need me. We can't let even one of them make it through the portal."

He did need her. He needed her to live. Now that he'd decided he was staying here with her, he didn't want her in any situation where she could get hurt. But he was smart enough to know if he tried to convince her of that right now, they'd never catch up with those Sirens before it was too late.

His pulse raced with both fear and worry as he grasped her at the waist and pulled her tight against him. And when his lips met hers in a fierce kiss, he knew if he lost her now, just when he'd finally found her, it would ruin him for all eternity.

He drew back and met her gaze, hoping she saw with her eyes what he couldn't say in his words. "Stay with us and don't do anything stupid. I didn't betray the gods so I could be stuck here in this realm alone."

She took one of the daggers from his hand and grinned. "Not a chance, *omorfos*. And don't worry. I'm a lot better with a blade than I was when you were my trainer."

She slipped out of his arm and ran after Cerek.

Holy hell. He sure the hell hoped so because if Zeus found out they'd brought the key to Argolea, he'd unleash everything he could on this realm even if he couldn't cross into it himself.

* * * *

"There were four," Cerek said to the queen as he stood in the middle of her office in the castle of Tiyrns. "We took all four down before they reached the portal, but odds are good more will be coming when Zeus realizes these four aren't returning."

From her spot where she stood leaning against the wall with her arms crossed, Sera glanced from face to face at the people in the room. After stopping the Sirens from crossing the portal, she, Erebus, and Cerek had returned to the castle to update the queen and the Argonauts. She was sweaty and dirty from the fight, but her blood was still up, and more than anything she was still vibrating from the reality she'd played a part in killing four of Zeus's Sirens. Sirens who'd once been her trainers even if they'd never been her friends.

At her side, Erebus leaned toward her ear and whispered, "Are you okay?"

She shifted her feet and in a low voice answered, "Yeah," but she didn't look at him. Because she wasn't okay. Not really.

It was true—those Sirens had invaded this realm and instigated that fight, and from the first it had been clear that they were not going to allow anyone to take them prisoner. But still, knowing there'd been no other choice and living with the fallout from that choice were two completely different things.

A heavy weight pressed down on her chest. There was absolutely no going back to Olympus for her now. No going back to the Sirens. But she'd already accepted that the second she'd stolen the key to Argolea. Now all she could do was hope that no one in this realm was hurt because of what she'd done.

The queen pursed her lips. "The Sirens slaughtered the inhabitants of the witch's tent city when they kidnapped Elysia eighteen months ago. Brute force was warranted here to prevent another massacre. If Zeus cries foul, we make that clear. He doesn't know we have the key; therefore we had just cause to protect our realm. You did the right thing, Cerek." She looked toward the leader of the Argonauts. "What are our options at this point, Theron?"

Theron crossed his meaty arms across his broad chest. "Just cause or not, Zeus will retaliate. He already thinks Sera and the key are here."

"Zeus will send more Sirens," the tall Argonaut at the queen's side said, the one Sera was pretty sure was Elysia's father. "He's convinced Prometheus hid the water element in Argolea, and he wants the key so he can get into our realm, find the last element, and complete the Orb of Krónos. He won't stop until he has the key, which means no one here is safe until that key is destroyed."

"It always comes back to those damn elements," the queen said on a sigh.

Sera knew from Elysia that no one—not even Prometheus—was sure where the water element had landed after he'd scattered the four basic elements across the realms. Water was the most fluid of all the elements, and over the thousands of years since Prometheus's imprisonment for not choosing Zeus's side against the Olympians' war with the Titans, the water element had moved and morphed and changed location. It could be here in Argolea, but it could just as easily be hiding in plain sight in the human realm.

Regardless, if Zeus suspected the key was in Argolea, he would send as many Sirens as it took to get it back. And once he had it, he would sweep into this realm and destroy everything until he either found that element or annihilated the realm, exactly as he'd done to Atlantis.

Warmth radiated against Sera's lower back, interrupting her thoughts. Warmth and a soft, kneading pressure where Erebus rubbed his fingers gently along her spine.

For a moment, while the queen and the Argonauts discussed the situation, she zoned out and focused on that one spot. On how good his hand felt, how relaxing his touch was, and just how much she liked that he was here now—even on what had turned out to be a pretty shitty day.

His spicy scent surrounded her, and without even thinking, she leaned her head against his strong chest and just let his touch and scent and comforting presence calm her. Against the top of her head, she felt his lips press a kiss to her hair, and then he shifted her in front of him so she could lean back against his chest and those big, tempting hands were massaging the stress from her shoulders.

Oh, heavens... She could get so used to this. Her eyes slid closed, and she drew one deep breath, followed by another. And as the heat of his body seeped into her back and warmed the last cold spaces inside her, all kinds of visions about how he could relax her in their room filled her mind, making her anxious to get him alone.

When he pulled her back against him, she wiggled her ass against his lap, feeling his erection spring to life. She bit her lip to hold back a groan.

"Naughty little nymph," Erebus whispered near her ear. "I think they've got this handled on their own. Why don't we go back to our room and get cleaned up? Then I can handle you."

A wide smile spread across her lips, and heat exploded in her veins. She glanced over her shoulder at him and lifted her brow. "I'm up for that."

"No, *agápi*." He flexed his hips, and she felt his impressive arousal against her backside. "I'm the one who's going to be up."

Yes, yes, yes... Frantic to feel just that and more, she reached for his hand and pulled him with her as she stepped away from the wall.

"I'm telling you," the long-haired Argonaut who always wore the gloves said to the queen as Sera and Erebus drew closer to the group on their way toward the door and utter bliss. "That's the only way. In Phlegethon."

Erebus's hand slipped free of Sera's, and when she turned, she realized he'd stopped near the group. A perplexed expression crossed his face as he looked at the long-haired Argonaut. "What about Phlegethon?"

Sera frowned at the interruption and tried to pull him back to her, but he was like solid stone and wouldn't move.

The queen glanced up at him, looking absolutely tiny surrounded by the Argonauts and a god. "The key was forged by Hephaestus and is charmed by the powers of Olympus. The only way to make sure no one can ever use it again is to destroy it. And the only way to do that is to cast it into the river of fire in the Underworld. Phlegethon is the only heat strong enough to melt Hephaestus's weaponry."

Erebus looked from the queen to each of the Argonauts. "How do you know this?"

She nodded toward the long-haired Argonaut. "Because of Titus."

When Erebus's confused gaze swung Titus's way, Titus said, "I'm a descendant of Odysseus."

The Argonaut Sera had heard the others call Orpheus crossed his arms over his chest with a frown and leaned back against the queen's desk. "Don't question it, Erebus. Titus's forefather blessed him with enhanced knowledge about tons of ancient shit. He's right on this. He's always right. And it's getting really fucking irritating."

Titus cast Orpheus a smug grin but it faded when he glanced back at the group. "Someone has to take the key into the Underworld and toss it in Phlegethon." He looked back at Orpheus and lifted his brows. "O? You're the only one of us who's been there—besides Gryphon, of course, and I think it's pretty safe to say he's not volunteering to go back there anytime soon."

Orpheus huffed. "So because I was there once I get the job? Screw you, Rapunzel."

Titus chuckled.

The queen brushed her blonde hair back from her face and rubbed her forehead, looking like she had a massive headache.

"Before we start talking about who should take the key into the Underworld, let's talk about how we even get there. Orpheus, you said the cave you and Skyla used to access the Underworld was destroyed when you left there with Gryphon. Who else knows how to get there?"

"Prometheus," Theron answered.

"Yes, but there's no guarantee we can even find Prometheus right now," the queen said with a frown. "He and Circe have been exploring the Aegis Mountains, searching for any sign of the water element. He could be on the other side of Argolea right now."

"Even Natasa isn't sure where he is at the moment," Titus said.

Sera was still trying to piece together who was related to whom in this realm, but she remembered Elysia telling her that Titus's mate Natasa was Prometheus's daughter. She wasn't sure how that was possible, since Prometheus had only been freed from Zeus's chains a handful of years ago and Natasa was older than that, but at the moment she was too focused on the key and this conversation to try to figure it out.

"There is someone right here who would know," Orpheus said.

All eyes turned toward Erebus.

Of course. Erebus. Sera's brow lifted as she looked up at him.

But instead of the gentle, helpful friend he'd been to Cerek and the others since they'd arrived in this realm, his stiff posture, hard jaw, and narrowed gaze skipping from face to face told her he wasn't feeling the least bit friendly at the moment.

"I brought you the key," Erebus said in a low voice.

"*We* brought you the key," Sera corrected, confused about the reason he looked ready to pound someone into the floor.

Erebus glanced down at her and nodded, then glared back at the group. "We brought you the key. What you do with it from here is up to you. I'm not getting involved with that."

Surprise shot through Sera. He wasn't here to help them? She thought that was *exactly* why he was here. It sure as hell was the reason she was here.

"No one's asking you to take it to the Underworld," the queen said.

"Though actually..." the leader of the Argonauts started.

"Actually, that's not a bad idea," Orpheus finished for Theron, uncrossing his arms and focusing on Erebus. "It's the perfect way to get around the prophecy."

"What prophecy?" Sera asked, her gaze swinging to Orpheus.

"The one that says he who destroys the key will be trapped in the Underworld for all eternity." Titus rested his gloved hands on his hips and looked at her. "That's why your ancient queen in Atlantis didn't just destroy the damn thing as soon as Zeus gave it to her. It's why none of your queens did. Because in order to destroy it, someone has to offer up a sacrifice. In this case, that sacrifice is being stuck in the Underworld after you do the deed."

Erebus's whole body stiffened. And, okay, yeah, if that was the case, Sera could see why he wouldn't be thrilled to help them with this.

"But Erebus isn't mortal," Orpheus pointed out. "He wouldn't get stuck there."

Oh....true. Sera's brow lifted once more.

"According to who?" Titus tossed back. "The prophecy says nothing regarding mortality."

"Maybe not," Orpheus countered. "But he already served Hades in the Underworld. He wouldn't be tortured there like any of us. And I'm betting he wouldn't even be stuck there. I guarantee Zeus charmed that thing with some special back door loophole which prevents it from impacting an immortal. We all know how Zeus loves back doors."

That was true as well. Sera was all too aware of how much the gods loved fucking with mortals but were reluctant to do anything to harm each other.

"Titus?" the queen asked.

Titus rubbed a hand across his jaw and considered for a moment. "It's possible. It's highly likely, actually. Zeus wouldn't risk bringing harm to an immortal because doing so could cause the other gods to join forces and rise up against him. He definitely doesn't want a repeat of the Titanomachy with him on the losing side. For once, O's logic is sound." When Orpheus frowned and flipped him the bird, Titus grinned, then looked back at the queen and added, "Though I can't confirm for sure. That part isn't in any of my enhanced knowledge. But if it's true then, yeah. Erebus would be the logical choice. Especially since he can cloak himself in darkness to slip into the Underworld unnoticed. If Prometheus or even Nick were to try to destroy the key, Hades would spot them immediately."

The queen looked toward Erebus with an expectant expression. And slowly, one by one, each of the Argonauts in the room did as well. "I know it's a lot to ask," the queen said. "But you're the only one who can do this without repercussions."

Sera's gaze followed, and hope gathered in her belly. But it shattered like a glass against the floor when she saw the slice of steel that was his jaw beneath his skin. The one that told her loud and clear he wasn't thrilled to be the center of attention. And that he had no intention of doing anything to help those in this realm. Her included.

"I'm not going to the Underworld," Erebus said in a low voice. "Not for you or anyone."

He left the room without another word.

The Argonauts quietly whispered about what was up with him and why he wasn't willing to help them when he'd so easily turned his back on Zeus, but Sera barely listened. All she could focus on was the reality swirling like a vortex in her head.

He hadn't come here to help anyone but himself. As soon as he'd held the medallion in his hand, he'd known what it was. He'd known what it protected from the gods. And he'd seen his way out. A way to hide from Zeus and do whatever—and whomever—he wanted out from under the control of the gods.

She shouldn't be surprised. He was, after all, the personification of darkness. And darkness, as everyone knew, was immoral and selfish and absent of any kind of light that illuminated the soul.

Chapter Nine

The door crashed against the wall as Erebus shoved it open and stalked into the suite he'd shared with Sera last night, trying like hell to calm the roaring vibration still buzzing inside him.

Of course they'd all assume he was the perfect one to sacrifice eternity for them. He was the god of darkness. He probably liked the Underworld, right?

They could all piss off as far as he was concerned.

The door to the suite slammed shut, and footsteps sounded across the floor before coming to a stop at Erebus's back. He didn't need to look to see that Sera had followed him. He could smell her lemony scent and all but feel her own anger seeping from her.

The vibrations slowly lessened. Knowing she was just as outraged as him eased his rage.

"When were you going to tell me your plan?" she said at his back.

Confused, not just by the question but by the bite in her voice, he turned to look at her.

But her eyes weren't the compassionate eyes he'd hoped for. These were like blue ice chips, cold and staring at him as if she were looking at a stranger.

"Excuse me?"

"You heard me. You never cared about helping these people. You only came here with me because you saw it as an opportunity to get away from Zeus. To take a break from your duties and fuck me for a while. But now that you know the Argoleans are going to destroy the key, that changes things, doesn't it? Are you planning to take it back to Zeus tonight?"

His eyes widened in disbelief. "*What?*"

"You heard me." Fire flared in her eyes but it didn't warm that icy chill brewing in their cold blue depths. "I can't believe I was so stupid when it came to you. You duped me once before, and you're doing it again right now."

He couldn't believe she thought so little of him. He couldn't believe that after everything he'd done for her, she could even ask such a question.

He reacted before he could stop himself. Crossing the distance between them in two strides, he grasped her by the arm. "You're right, nymph. That's *exactly* why I came here. I serve Zeus. I must be the same selfish asshole he is, right? Why else would I bother?"

Her chest rose and fell with her heavy breaths, and a whisper of doubt crept into her eyes. "Let go of my arm."

Something dark burned inside him. Something dangerous he knew he needed to stop but couldn't seem to tamp down.

"Why?" He moved a step closer, using his size to tower over her. "You knew why I came here. You said it yourself. I came here to fuck you. And you didn't put up any sort of fight to stop me. In fact, ten minutes ago, if you'd been wearing a skirt, you'd have let me fuck you right there in that office in front of the Argonauts. So why don't I do that one last time before I leave? I want it. I know you want it too; otherwise you wouldn't be here."

Her eyes widened as he pressed her up against the wall. She lifted her hands to his biceps and pushed, but she wasn't strong enough to budge him. "If you even think about raping me—"

"Rape you? Oh, *oraios*. In sixty seconds you'll be begging for me to fuck you blind."

"In your dreams."

Anger swelled inside him. Anger and a burning desire to make her pay. "Since I'm going back to Zeus, dreams are the only thing I'll have left of you, so I might as well get as much as I can right now."

He lowered his face to the hollow in her neck and drew in a deep whiff of her scent. Lemon and vanilla and something that made him fucking high. "Gods, you smell good." He bit down on the tender flesh—not gently, not hard—and she whimpered, which was exactly what he wanted. "Taste even better."

Her fingers dug into his biceps, but he ignored the pain and kicked her legs apart so he could press himself against her heat. Then he licked the spot he'd just bitten and sucked until her cry of protest turned into a groan of desire.

The sound supercharged his blood and made the darkness inside rush right to the surface of his control. She thought he would rape her? She thought he'd still side with Zeus? He'd been sure she was the one person in the cosmos who understood him, but now he knew the truth. She was just like the gods, using him for her own selfish needs, then discarding him when she had what she wanted, casting him aside as if he were nothing.

He rocked against her and lifted one hand to squeeze the soft mass of her breast. "Tell me you don't want this, *agápi*."

She swallowed hard, pushed against his arms again, but not with the force of before, and against him he felt her muscles already relaxing. Felt her body giving in to the heat of his and melting beneath him. "I-I don't."

"You lie." He lifted his head and closed his mouth over hers. Her fingers fisted in his T-shirt, and she grunted as his tongue swept into her mouth, demanding and unforgiving. But she didn't try to push him away, and as he stroked her tongue and pressed his hard body into hers against the wall, she tugged on his shirt and pulled him closer.

That's it. Just a little more...

He slid one hand over her side and across her lower back, then down to squeeze the soft right globe of her ass. She moaned into his mouth and lifted her leg, hooking it around his hip so his cock could press against her clit. Her hands swept up to his face, then she tipped her head and kissed him deeper, rocking her hot little body against his until he was hard and achy and ready to explode. Until he knew he had her right where he wanted her.

He trailed a line of hot, wet kisses from the corner of her mouth to her jaw and then to the sensitive skin behind her ear. "Tell me you want me, Sera."

"Oh gods." She grasped his face again, pulled his mouth back to hers, and kissed him.

"Tell me," he breathed against her lips, squeezing her ass with every press of his groin against hers. "Tell me and I'll give you exactly what you deserve."

"Erebus." She drew back from his mouth, nipped his bottom lip, swept her tongue over the spot and suckled until he groaned. "Yes, I want you. Take me."

Primal need pumped hot inside him, but he wasn't about to let it free. Not with her. Not ever again.

He jerked back from her mouth, let go of her with his hands, and moved away so cool air rushed across her overheated body. "Not even sixty seconds. You're a predictable little nymphomaniac. I should have seen how manipulative you really were from the start. Zeus did pick you himself, after all."

He moved for the door. At his back he heard her gasp of shock and disbelief, but he ignored it, wanting only to get as far from her as possible. To get out of this castle and out of this fucking realm before all that darkness inside him burst free and made him do something he knew he'd regret later.

Inches from the entry hall of the suite, his foot hooked something hard, and his weight went out from under him. He hit the carpet with a grunt. Before he could process what he'd tripped over, strong hands flipped him to his back, and the sexy little nymph who'd tormented his body and consumed his thoughts these last few days climbed over him.

She slapped her hands against the carpet near his head and glared down at him. "You're not leaving."

"The hell I'm not."

He shifted his hands to her waist and lifted his torso to shove her off him, but she dropped her weight onto his hips and wrapped her legs around his waist as he sat up, locking her in place against his hard, aching cock.

She leaned in to breathe hot against his ear. "You're not leaving because we're not done here." Her teeth sank into his lobe, then she traced her wicked tongue around the rim of his ear. "You said you were going to fuck me blind." Against his straining erection, she rocked her steamy sex until he saw stars. "Fuck me, Erebus. Fuck me, now."

The darkness inside him burst free. He didn't know what game she was playing but he was past the point of caring. Past the point of thinking. Past the point of stopping.

A growl echoed in the room, one he knew came from him as he pushed her to her back on the carpet, then drew away long enough to rip the pants from her legs. She gasped but didn't miss a beat, wrenching the shirt over her head and throwing it off to her side with jerky movements.

His blood roared in his ears as he flipped her to her belly. She grunted and pushed up on her hands and knees. Blonde hair spilled across her bare spine and tickled his frantic fingers as he unhooked the white lace bra and pushed it down her arms. She helped him by wriggling out of the garment, then groaned as he ripped the panties from her hips and the sound of tearing fabric filled the room.

With one hand, he unhooked the button at his waistband. With the other, he swept his fingers between her legs and across her hot, steaming flesh. Kicking her knees wider with his, he growled, "Is this what you want?"

She rocked back against his hand so his fingers swirled over her slick clit. "Oh yes... More."

He drew his fingers down, to her opening, then thrust up inside with two. "This?"

"*Yeeees...*" She dropped her head forward and moaned, then rocked her hips back, fucking his fingers with long, deep strokes. "Gods, that's good. But I want more. Give me more."

Fire roared inside him. Fire and a blazing need he couldn't ignore, one that shoved aside the darkness until the only thing he knew was this moment.

He yanked his fingers from her body, and flipped her to her back again. She grunted and reached for him as he reached inside his waistband to free his erection. "You want more? You want this?"

"Oh, yes..." She hooked her legs around his waist and lifted her hips, her hot, tight channel finding the tip of his cock until she sucked him in a fraction of an inch.

Every nerve ending in his body flared in that one spot. "Say it," he growled.

"I want your cock. I want you. Fuck me. Fuck me, Erebu—"

He claimed her mouth at the same time he slammed himself inside her. His name erupted on a scream that only shot his blood higher.

He drew out until she whimpered, then drove deep again,

grunting at the way her sheath contracted around him as he kissed her.

"Is this what you wanted?" He breathed hot over her lips. Bracing one hand on the floor, he used the other to hold her head still while he shoved deep again and again, fucking her with hard, long strokes that made her whole body shudder.

"Yes, yes..." Her fingertips dug into his shoulders.

She was leaving bruises, he was sure, but he didn't care. All he could focus on was thrusting deeper, faster, proving to her that he wasn't at all what she thought.

"Don't stop," she rasped. "Gods, don't stop..."

He couldn't. He was too far gone.

Shifting his weight to his knees, he grasped both of her legs and shoved them forward, then drove even deeper. "Say you like fucking me," he growled.

Her eyes slid closed. "I do. Gods, I do."

A frenzy rose up in his mind. One that told him to prove to her she wasn't at all what she thought either. "Say you're a dirty nymph who likes to be fucked by the gods."

"No." She tossed her head from side to side and her channel grew impossibly tight around him. "Just by you. Only you. Ah, gods, Erebus. Don't stop. Please don't stop."

Electricity raced down his spine and gathered in his balls. He plunged into her harder, unable to do anything but what she demanded, hating that she was still manipulating him, even now. "Say it," he growled, his fingers tightening around her knees where he held her open to him. "Say you're a manipulative little slut who uses sex to get what she wants."

Her eyes shot open, and before he realized what she was doing, she jerked her legs from his hold, pushed her hands against the floor and shot forward so her legs were around his waist, her chest was plastered to his, and her arms were locked tight around his shoulders.

Her slick and tempting pussy clenched around his length as she lifted and lowered herself on his lap. "I'm not," she breathed against his lips as his hands settled at her hips. "I didn't. I only want you. I've only ever wanted you."

She pressed her mouth to his and kissed him, and as her tongue swept into his mouth and she groaned, he felt her climax claim her, and the feeling was so tight, so right, so seductive, it triggered his.

Grunting, he pushed her to the carpet and gave himself over to her kiss, to her body, to everything she was and the ecstasy she could give him.

When he was spent, when all he could do was twitch and groan, he pulled free of her slick core and pushed up on one hand to gaze down at her sexy, sated features covered in a thin layer of sweat.

His chest grew tight, so tight he knew it was way past time he left.

He braced his hands on the carpet and started to push up. Her legs hooked around his hips, preventing him from pulling free of her body, and then her hands were at his shoulders, pulling him back down to her.

"Uh uh." She tugged him back against all her tantalizing heat and stared up at him with eyes that were a soft, relaxed blue and lacked any of the anger he'd seen there before. "I said I'm not through with you, and I meant it."

His own anger had eased now that he'd released some stress, but he didn't want to do anything to trigger it again. "Sera." He reached up to pry her arms from his neck. "This has run its course."

She tightened her hold. "Not even close."

Frustrated, desperate now to leave, he frowned down at her. "I'm not going to stay here when—"

"I was wrong. I shouldn't have jumped to conclusions. I was just..." She bit her lip, looking sexy and nervous and innocent all at the same time. "I was scared, okay? I fell for you a year and a half ago during my training sessions. I fell hard, and when our sessions were over, you moved on to a new trainee as if I hadn't even existed. That hurt me."

A little of his frustration waned. He braced a hand on the floor near her head. "I didn't have a choice in that."

"I know, I just... It still hurt. And when I heard you in there with the Argonauts, I thought... Well, I thought you were getting ready to move on again. I lashed out because I'm weak."

He frowned. "You're spirited and frustrating and sexy as hell, but you're not weak."

One corner of her mouth curled.

He sighed, liking the way she fit against him way too much.

Knowing it was going to be a major problem for him when he left here. "I wasn't saying no to them because I wanted to leave you. I said no because I have no interest in returning to the Underworld, even for just a visit. I spent thousands of years there doing shit work for Hades. As soon as I step in that realm he'll try to find a way to keep me, prophecy or no prophecy, whether I use my cloak of darkness or not. Life on Olympus serving Zeus wasn't a helluva lot better than it was serving Hades, but at least on Olympus I was away from all that misery and death. I can't go back there."

"I know. I'm sorry. I should have realized that. I wasn't thinking. Please forgive me."

He wanted to believe her, but he was still unsure what was truth. He only knew one truth he should have told her before. "For what it's worth, I had to put you behind me at the Siren training compound. I couldn't get emotionally involved with you then. It would have meant the end for both of us. But I didn't forget about you. I never forgot about you."

"You didn't even know who I was when you tackled me in the forest."

"I knew who you were as soon as I saw you. As soon as I touched you. How could I forget the one person in the world who ever made me feel alive?"

Her eyes went all soft and dreamy, and before he realized it he grew hard inside her once more.

"And what about now?" she asked, her words distracting him from how tight and wet she was around him. "We're not in danger anymore and you're free to make your own choices here in Argolea. Do you still want me? Because I want you. I wasn't lying when I said I'm yours. I want only to be yours, Erebus. Now and always."

His heart skipped a beat. But he was still worried. Especially if she would only ever see him as a servant to the gods. "That depends on your friends in the other room. The only thing they want me for is to sacrifice myself for some prophecy I know nothing about. They won't let me stay in this realm now that I've said no."

"Then we'll go somewhere else."

When he looked away, she tugged him down to her, so his chest was pressed up against her gorgeous breasts and her mouth was a breath away from his lips. And around his cock, she clenched her muscles until it was all he could do to keep giving in to the pleasure and thrusting hard and deep all over again.

"I don't care what they want, Erebus. I mean, yes, I want them to be safe. I don't want any other realm to suffer what Atlantis did, and I was willing to help them if I could, but not if it means losing you. They have the key. We brought it to them. Whatever they do with it now is up to them, not us. All I want is you. I want the future we couldn't have before." She clenched even tighter, drawing a groan from his throat. "I love you, Erebus."

His lungs felt as if they'd completely closed off. And for a moment, he didn't breathe. Just stared down into her soft blue eyes, trying to see the lie, the manipulation, the contrary truth she was keeping hidden. But he didn't see any of those things. He saw her. Her innocence when they'd first met on Olympus. He saw the fire inside her when she'd run from him at that half-breed colony. And he saw love. The kind of love he'd always hoped for but never thought was possible.

His mouth was dry as cotton when his lips parted, and the words stuck in his throat. "I..."

She pressed her lips against his. "Say you want the same. Say it, you dirty, dark, sexy god. Say you love me just as much. I know you do. I knew it the moment you pushed me up against the wall and I saw how much I'd hurt you." She kissed him softly again, lifted her hips and flexed around his aching cock. "I'm sorry. I'm so sorry for that. Stay with me. Stay and let me make it up to you. I need you. Not for your powers or what you can do. I need you simply because I love you and want you in my life."

Something in his chest warmed and swelled until it felt like he might crack open wide. Lifting his hands to her face, he drew back from her mouth and brushed the soft locks from her intoxicating eyes. "Oh, Sera. You're the only one who's ever said that to me."

"I'm the only one who's ever going to love you like this." She did that wicked rocking again that made him nearly see stars. "Promise you won't leave me."

He couldn't. Not anymore.

He captured her mouth with a searing kiss he felt everywhere, and when she groaned and kissed him back, the last of his doubt faded into the darkness.

He rolled to his back, tugging her on top of him. Brushing the hair back from her face, he drew his mouth back a fraction of an inch and said, "Since you asked so nicely, I'll stay. But only on one condition."

She grinned down at him. "Anything."

"Show me how much you love me, *agápi*. Make me believe it."

"I can do that." Her lips curled in a wicked smile, and she braced her hands on his chest and began to move. "I can happily spend the rest of my days doing that."

Oh, fuck yes...

She lowered and took his mouth, and as he kissed her back, he knew this time what she said was true. He also knew that he would easily be as happy letting her prove it to him for however long they were together.

He just hoped it was more than a few days. Because now that he'd betrayed Zeus and said no to the Argoleans, they'd soon have to leave this protected realm. And there weren't many places left in the world where he could hide from the Olympians and keep her safe.

Chapter Ten

Sera stretched and opened her eyes. The room was still dark, which meant morning hadn't hit yet. Snuggling back into her pillow, she closed her eyes and reached her foot back, searching for Erebus's heat behind her.

Her muscles were sore and exhausted from hours of pleasuring him, and she knew she needed a little longer to rest and recharge her batteries, but she was already thinking up ways to pleasure him all over again. And as soon as he curled up against her back again—the same way he had when he'd wrung the last orgasm from her body and finally let her drift to sleep—she knew she wouldn't be able to stop herself from doing just that.

Her foot passed over the cold sheet, and she moved it farther back, still searching for him. Rolling to her other side, she reached out her hand, but found nothing but cold sheets and an empty bed.

She lifted her head and peered around the dark and silent room. "Erebus?"

No answering voice called out to her. Nothing but silence met her ears.

A knock sounded at the suite's outer door, and she jumped. Pushing up to sitting, she captured the sheet at her breasts and held her breath as she listened, afraid she might have imagined the sound. Another knock echoed through the suite.

She exhaled and threw back the covers. It had to be him. He must have been hungry and gotten up to find something in the kitchen. They'd skipped dinner. Neither had wanted to venture out of their room. She wasn't sure if the outer door automatically locked when it closed, but she guessed it had and that he'd forgotten to take a key.

The knock sounded again.

"Hold on," she called, searching the floor for Erebus's T-shirt. She couldn't find it. Frowning, she grabbed her pajama bottoms and a cotton tank from the bottom dresser drawer and tugged both on as she moved into the living room.

Her stomach rumbled as she moved into the dark entryway. She hoped he was bringing back a feast because she was suddenly ravenous.

"I hope you brought enough to share," she said as she yanked the door open, "because I'm starv—"

Her words died as she looked into Elysia's brown eyes. "Lys, what are you doing here this late? Is everything okay?"

"No, everything's not okay." Dressed in her own pink cotton PJs, her hair pulled back in a messy tail, Elysia glanced past Sera and into the suite. "Is Erebus with you?"

Alarm bells sounded in Sera's mind. "No. I think he went down to the kitchen to get something to eat. Why? What's wrong?"

Elysia's jaw hardened. "What time did he leave?"

Those bells shrilled louder. "I don't know. I was asleep. Why? What's happened?"

Elysia reached for her hand. "A lot. You'd better come with me."

Elysia wouldn't say more than that the queen wanted to see Sera, and Sera's anxiety inched up the closer they drew to the queen's office.

What was going on? Were they kicking her and Erebus out of the realm right now? In the middle of the night? That didn't make sense, but neither did Elysia coming to her room at two a.m. acting cryptic and weird.

The queen's office was filled with more testosterone than Sera could handle. All the Argonauts turned to look at her as she entered, each one decked out not in pajamas like her and Elysia, but in thick leather pants, long-sleeved shirts, boots, and straps and gear she immediately recognized as warrior attire.

"There she is." The leader of the Argonauts stalked up to her and pinned her with a hard glare. "When was the last time you saw your god?"

"Erebus? I-I don't know." She looked from face to face, wondering what was going on. "A few hours ago, I guess. I was asleep when he left."

"So he was with you tonight?" the blond Argonaut to the leader's right asked, his silver eyes focused and expectant. "What time did you fall asleep?"

Why were they asking her these questions? She looked to Elysia at her side for help, suddenly feeling like a prisoner being interrogated.

Elysia patted her shoulder. "It's all right. Just answer them truthfully."

Truthfully...

She glanced back at the blond guardian, the one she was pretty sure was named Zander. "Eleven thirty, I guess. I don't know for sure though. Why? What's happened?"

"I'll tell you what's happened." The queen stepped out from behind the tall Argonaut—Demetrius—and wove through the sea of massive bodies before stopping in front of Sera. "Erebus is gone, and so is the key."

No.

Disbelief churned inside Sera. That couldn't be true. She wouldn't believe it. "He went to the kitchen to get food fo—"

"He's not in the kitchen," the queen said, interrupting her. "He's not anywhere in the castle. Maelea, Gryphon's mate, has the ability to sense energy shifts. We had her use her gift to scan outward from the castle, to see if he's hiding somewhere within the realm. Cerek said he was asking about Kyrenia and any settlements in the Aegis Mountains. But Maelea found no sign of him. He left Argolea, Sera. And it's no coincidence the key is missing now too. There's only one place we can figure he would go. To Olympus. To give the key you stole back to his master Zeus."

Pain slashed through Sera's chest, and her mouth fell open. She couldn't believe it. She didn't *want* to believe it. But even she couldn't deny it looked bad. He'd stormed out of this office only hours ago, seething with anger because the Argoleans were talking about destroying the key. She knew he didn't want to go back to the Underworld. She remembered the rage in his eyes when those Sirens had spotted him in this realm. If he was scared Zeus already knew he was here, if he thought his only chance for survival was to return the key to Zeus, would he do it?

Doubts, questions, fear vibrated in her chest and made her pulse race like wildfire. He'd told her he hated serving the gods. She knew that was true. But he'd also told her about his family, how the Titans had stripped the primordial deities of their human forms and cast them into nothingness, and she knew he'd do anything to prevent that from happening to him.

Voices echoed around her but she couldn't make herself listen to the words. Her head spun with memories of Erebus on Olympus, here in their suite, in that half-breed settlement just before they'd made love.

"If I had known about your past, things would have been different. I never would have let you be hunted. After all you've been through, agápi, *you deserve to be cherished and protected. Because you're special. Precious. You are the epitome of rare and irreplaceable and unique, and I won't ever let anyone hurt you again. I'll do whatever I have to do to keep you safe. I vow this to you here and now."*

Her stomach tightened as the words circled in her head. He hadn't said he loved her tonight, but she'd felt it. She'd felt every ounce of his love, and remembering his words from the half-breed colony, she knew they were true. He'd do anything to keep her safe. Even the very thing he'd told her he wouldn't do.

She glanced over the faces in front of her, over the Argonauts arguing about what they needed to do next. And in the center of her chest, her heart beat hard and fast, not from fear or heartache, but with love.

A love that told her exactly where Erebus had gone, and why he'd taken the key.

* * * *

The fiery river of Phlegethon snapped and sizzled as Erebus drew close under the cloak of darkness he'd cast. The heat was unbearable, the gasses and fumes from the river singeing the hairs on his forearms, the air so oppressive this deep in the Underworld he wanted to gag.

Swiping the sweat from his brow, he moved from sand to

blackened rock. He'd told himself he'd never venture into the Underworld again. Vowed nothing and no one could lure him back. Yet here he was, all because of a female. One who'd awed him with her ability to love. One who'd mesmerized him with the strength and light inside her. One who'd made him feel alive...so alive he knew she was worth sacrificing everything for so she could live.

His fingers closed around the medallion in his palm as he stepped around a charred boulder. He knew in his heart this was the right thing to do; he just really hoped like hell those Argonauts were right when they'd said the prophecy wouldn't apply to an immortal. Because he didn't want to get stuck down here. He wanted to get back to Sera, wanted to slide between those sheets, wanted to show her just how much he loved her with his hands and mouth and body.

A chuckle echoed at his back. One that pushed thoughts of Sera from his mind and brought his feet to a stop.

But it was the darkness lifting all around him that shot his adrenaline sky high.

"Well, well, well," a familiar voice said in the eerie red light. "This is a surprise. A very good surprise."

Slowly, Erebus turned and stared into Hades's face. The god was just as tall as Erebus remembered—seven feet of muscle and brawn—and he had the same angular jaw line, the same dark hair, the same soulless black eyes Erebus remembered from over a hundred years ago when Hades had been his master. But then, being immortal, he never changed.

"I would say you're busted, but I think we both already know that, don't we?" Hades nodded at Erebus's closed fist. "You came to use my river, I see."

Erebus was careful not to show any kind of reaction. He knew how Hades fed off emotional outbursts. "Don't try to stop me."

"Oh, I wouldn't dare." Clasping his hands at his back, Hades moved to his right and glanced toward the swirling river of fire. "Destroy it. I've no use for the key to Argolea. I don't need it." His dark eyes sparked. "Because I'm not an Olympian."

Erebus had forgotten that. Although Hades was technically the eldest son of Krónos and Rhea and brother to the Olympians Zeus and Poseidon, he himself was not considered an Olympian—all because Zeus, the ruler of Olympus, had denied Hades a temple within his realm.

"Personally," Hades said while Erebus's thoughts spiraled with options on how to get out of this one, "I'm just thrilled you're back." He laughed, a dark, menacing sound. "I thought I was going to have to find a way to scheme you out from under Zeus's thumb, but here you are. In my realm, all by your own choosing." He lifted his dark brows and nodded toward Phlegethon. "Go on. Destroy it. I'll not try to stop you. I'm tickled you had the balls to screw Zeus over on this." He winked. "Though I'm sure screwing his Sirens was a hell of a lot more fun."

For the first time since he'd been caught, Erebus's pulse raced. Hades didn't know about Sera, did he? He was doing this to keep her safe. He had to be careful not to show emotion or let Hades know what she meant to him. The last thing he wanted was the god-king of the Underworld crossing into Argolea to hurt her.

Without answering, he turned toward the river.

"I just wish I could see Zeus's face when he realizes his precious key is gone for good." Hades chuckled again. "Oh, to be privy to *that* temper tantrum." He sighed. "I guess I'll just have to console myself with the knowledge that my favorite primordial deity is back in my realm, ready to serve me for all eternity."

Erebus's steps stopped feet from the fiery river.

"Let me guess: you didn't realize destroying the key would trap you in the Underworld? That's the best part." Hades snapped his fingers. "See, there's this prophecy Zeus made up when he ordered Hephaestus to forge the key. 'He who destroys the key will be imprisoned in the realm from whence it was destroyed.' That's here. *My* realm."

Erebus glanced over his shoulder. "I'm immortal, though. And I no longer serve you. I serve Zeus."

"Not from where I'm standing, you don't. From where I'm standing it looks like you've gone rogue. I suppose I could turn you over to my brother for punishment, if, that is, you decide not to serve me."

They both knew what kind of punishment Hades was referring to. Erebus's palms began to sweat.

"Regardless," Hades said, blinking away the terrorizing look. "Zeus didn't care if the destroyer of the key was mortal or immortal.

And neither do I. Once you throw that key in Phlegethon, consider yourself done with Zeus for good. You'll be mine for all eternity. So get on with it. Throw it in the fire so we can move on to more important things."

Hades's soulless black eyes burned with an unnatural light, and as Erebus looked back at the fiery river, the totality of his life stretched before him.

He'd never fought, not even at the beginning when his family had been dissolved into nothing and he'd been handed over to Krónos. He'd served one god after another, for thousands of years, never challenging their rules, never questioning the things they ordered him to do, no matter how mundane or vile. He hadn't even thought to defy Zeus and the Sirens when they'd taken Sera from him on Olympus and forced him to train yet another faceless recruit in the ways of seduction.

He opened his palm. Stared down at the medallion and the imprint of Heracles. There weren't many things in his life he could be proud of, but this...protecting Sera from Zeus's retaliation and preventing another realm from the destruction her realm had faced...this he could be proud of. *This* was worth the sacrifice. She was worth sacrificing everything for.

His pulse slowed. His fingers curled around the medallion. It was warm not from the power inside it, but from him. From what was inside him.

Closing his eyes, he drew a deep breath and tugged his arm back. Before he could hurl it into the fiery river, a growl echoed at his back, followed by Hades's hissed words.

"No-good meddling Argonauts."

Erebus glanced over his shoulder, his eyes growing wide when he spotted three, four—no, seven Argonauts fanning out around Hades.

"Nice try, Guardians," Hades sneered. "But the god of darkness is mine. And none of you are strong enough to challenge me for him."

"None of them might be," a voice called from the back of the group. "But we are."

Two men—no, not men, gods, Erebus realized—stepped in front of the group. One was older, with dark hair and fine lines fanning out from his eyes. Strength radiated from his strong body and an aura that marked him as a Titan. The Titan Prometheus, Erebus realized with wide eyes.

His gaze strayed to the other god, the one leveling his amber gaze on Hades and smirking. Power emanated from his muscular body as well, but this power was directly linked to Krónos. Even across the distance Erebus could feel that power snapping and sizzling and just waiting to be freed, and in a rush Erebus remembered what Cerek had told him about the other god in Argolea when they'd been on their tour.

"Surprise, *adelfos*," Nick said.

For a moment, Hades stood completely still, then another growl built in his throat, one that grew in strength and intensity until it was a roar all across the land. He lifted his hands out wide. The ground shook. Rocks split apart, and the dirt cracked opened, shooting steam high in the air.

The shaking knocked Erebus off his feet. The medallion flew from his hand and ricocheted off a boulder. He scrambled up just as a seven-foot, ugly-ass daemon that looked like something straight out of a nightmare, crawled out of the hole and bared razor-sharp fangs at the Argonauts.

"Devour them," Hades cried.

All around the Argonauts, daemons climbed out of the ground and charged.

A massive battle broke out. Weapons clanged and fists slammed into bone. Voices echoed through the eerie red light and over the barren land, and Erebus knew he needed to join them, to fight with the Argonauts, but he had to find the key first. He had to destroy it before one of those daemons decided to keep it or Hades realized he could trade it to Zeus for something more valuable.

He streaked across the ground, kicking up blackened dirt and rocks, searching for the shiny medallion in the dead soil. Motherfucker, why couldn't he find it? It had hit the ground right here. It had to be close. He dropped to his knees, swept his hands through the dirt and rocks, searching. Knew it had to be somewhere—

There! From the corner of his eye he spotted a shiny object catching the firelight from the river. He skidded across the ground and scooped it up. Dirt and grime stuck to his skin, but when he brushed his finger across the surface of the object, the dull image of Heracles shone up at him.

He rushed back to the edge of the fiery river, drew his arm back, ready to throw it into the fires. Just before he could release it, a burning pain stabbed into his thigh and knocked him off his feet.

The medallion flew from his grip and smacked against the dirt. He hit the ground on his butt and grunted from the impact. His hands flew to his leg, and in total disbelief he focused on the arrow sticking out of his thigh, his blood gushing around the wound to stain his jeans a deep shade of red.

Footsteps sounded close. He lifted his head to see who had hit him, and his eyes widened when he saw Sera—*his* Sera, decked out in the same tight black fighting gear she'd worn on Olympus with the Sirens—stalking toward him with a bow in one hand.

"I'm sorry." She knelt at his side and pressed a kiss to his lips. "But I can't let you do this."

Confused, he reached for her, but she moved away before he could grasp her. Her slender fingers scooped the medallion from the ground.

He didn't know what was happening. He didn't know why she was here. He didn't know—

Every thought came to a shuddering stop when she stepped toward Phlegethon and drew her arm back.

"No! Sera!" He struggled to his feet. Tried to go after her. Tried to stop her. The second he put weight on his injured leg, though, his leg buckled and he hit the dirt face first.

He sputtered, coughed, spit the grimy black dirt from his mouth and lifted his head. Then watched in horror as she swept her arm forward and released, sending the medallion flying toward the fiery river.

"No..." Pain sliced through his chest. A blinding, burning pain that drowned out everything else—the sounds of the battle at his back, the burn of the arrow stabbing into his leg, the all-powerful gods wrestling for cosmic power only yards away. All he could see and hear and feel was what she'd just done.

His vision blurred as she drew close. He struggled to his side, pushed himself to sitting, and grabbed hold of her as soon as she knelt close. His dirty hands streaked up into her soft hair, and he pulled her mouth down to his, kissing her again and again, afraid to let go of her. Afraid of what would happen next.

"What did you do? How could you do that?" He pulled her onto his lap, not caring about his leg or what was happening around them. Not caring about anything but her. He kissed her again. "You stupid nymph. Why would you do that? Don't you know what that means?"

Her lips curled against his. "I know exactly what it means."

She drew away, and though he wanted only to pull her back, she pushed to her feet where he couldn't grab her.

"Do you want me to tell him, Hades? Or would you like to be the one to enlighten him?"

Erebus stared up at her gorgeous face, confused by the words she was speaking. To his left, he heard Hades growl, "Scheming Argonauts."

Blinking, Erebus looked across the barren ground toward the Argonauts and the two gods surrounding Hades. All around them, dead daemons littered the ground.

"Enlighten me about what?" Erebus asked, more confused than ever. "What the fuck is going on?"

Sera knelt at his side and placed a warm hand on his shoulder. "The prophecy said '*He* who destroys the key shall be imprisoned in the realm from whence it was destroyed.'"

She didn't elaborate, which only frustrated him more. "Yeah? So, we already know that." He reached for her hand. "I'm not letting him keep you."

She smiled and squeezed his fingers. "You don't have to, because he can't keep me. Isn't that right, Hades?"

Her gaze lifted. To Erebus's left, Hades growled low in his throat but didn't make any move to imprison her.

"I don't understand," Erebus said.

Sera ran her fingers over his jaw and grinned. "I am not a he."

Erebus stared into her gentle eyes, still trying to make sense of everything, when one of the Argonauts called out, "Duh. She's a *she*, dude. And a pretty clever one at that."

Holy shit. Hope filled Erebus's chest like sweet, sweet air. "So he can't—"

"Nope." Sera's smile widened. "I told you you were mine, silly god. I meant it."

He sucked in a breath as she leaned down to kiss him, and when their lips met, he felt the love she'd showered on him push aside all the emptiness inside him.

"You are defeated for now, Hades," Nick declared in a loud voice, causing both Erebus and Sera to look toward the god. "Tuck your tail and run back to your lair before Prometheus and I decide to punish you for this little stunt."

A growl echoed, then in a swirl of black smoke, Hades poofed away from Phlegethon.

Drawing Erebus's face back to hers, Sera gently kissed his lips. "Sorry about shooting you in the leg. It was the only way I could stop you from throwing the medallion in the river." Her eyes narrowed. "But running out on me in the middle of the night was not a smart thing to do."

"What can I say? I learned all about running from this really hot nymph I was once assigned to for seduction training."

Her lips curled. "Good answer, *omorfos*."

He tugged her down onto his lap and held her close. "I love you, *agápi*."

"I know. Which is the only reason I'm not going to make you suffer. Beg, moan, cry out in pleasure...absolutely, yes. But no more suffering. Never again."

He smiled, thinking that sounded just about perfect right now.

Someone cleared his throat. From the group to their left, another voice said, "Um, any chance you two can do that back in Argolea, away from torment and death and the ruler of this realm who would be more than happy to come back here and try to kick our asses again?"

Sera smiled.

Erebus chuckled.

Neither looked toward the group.

"What do you say, *agápi*? Want to start forever with me in the blessed realm of the heroes?"

She bit her lip in a nervous, sexy, adorable way. "Your forever and my forever aren't exactly the same. I'm not immortal like you. I may live for hundreds of years, but eventually, my time will come."

His heart squeezed tight because he didn't want to think about that. He searched her eyes, searching for something to say, for a solution he couldn't find.

"Not exactly," someone said before he could come up with anything.

Sera glanced over her shoulder where Nick was walking toward them.

"What do you mean?" Erebus asked, looking toward the god.

"My mate is Argolean," Nick answered, stopping not far away. "Her lifespan is the same as an Atlantean. And Gryphon's Argolean, whereas his mate is immortal. The Fates aren't going to let any of us suffer alone. When the mortal mate's time come, the choice to stay or go with them to the other side rests with the immortal mate."

Erebus glanced at Sera then back to Nick. "I don't see a Fate here offering us that option."

"Pretty sure the Fates steer clear of the Underworld." Nick winked. "But trust me, after the sacrifice you both made not just for Argolea but for the entire world, once we get home, I'm fairly certain one will be waiting for you. And if she's not, I'll find her and make sure she offers you the same deal. You deserve it after everything you've done us."

Hope bloomed inside Erebus, and he looked back to Sera. "*Agápi?* What do you think about forever in the realm of the heroes now?"

A wide smile spread across Sera's gorgeous face. "I think it sounds perfect. But only if you'll be my hero."

"Baby, I'm the only hero you'll ever need."

She slid her arms around his neck and lifted her mouth to his. "Damn right you are."

* * * *

Also from 1001 Dark Nights and Elisabeth Naughton, discover Ravaged, Unchained, and Surrender.

Eternal Guardians Lexicon

adelfos. Brother

agapi. Term of endearment; my love.

Argolea. Realm established by Zeus for the blessed heroes and their descendants

Argonauts. Eternal guardian warriors who protect Argolea. In every generation, one from the original seven bloodlines (Heracles, Achilles, Jason, Odysseus, Perseus, Theseus, and Bellerophon) is chosen to continue the guardian tradition.

Council of Elders. Lords of Argolea who advise the king

daemons. Beasts who were once human, recruited from the Fields of Asphodel (purgatory) by Atalanta to join her army.

Fates. Three goddesses who control the thread of life for all mortals from birth until death

Isles of the Blessed. Heaven

Misos. Half-human/half-Argolean race that lives hidden among humans

Olympians. Current ruling gods of the Greek pantheon, led by Zeus; meddle in human life

omorfos. Handsome

oraios. Beautiful

Orb of Krónos. Four-chambered disk that, when filled with the four classic elements—earth, wind, fire, and water—has the power to release the Titans from Tartarus

parazonium. Ancient Greek sword all Argonauts carry.

Siren Order. Zeus's elite band of personal warriors. Commanded by Athena

skata. Swearword

Tartarus. Realm of the Underworld similar to hell

therillium. Invisibility ore, sought after by all the gods

Titans. The ruling gods before the Olympians

Titanomachy. The war between the Olympians and the Titans, which resulted in Krónos being cast into Tartarus and the Olympians becoming the ruling gods.

About Elisabeth Naughton

Before topping multiple bestseller lists--including those of the New York Times, USA Today, and the Wall Street Journal--Elisabeth Naughton taught middle school science. A voracious reader, she soon discovered she had a knack for creating stories with a chemistry of their own. The spark turned into a flame, and Naughton now writes full-time. Besides topping bestseller lists, her books have been nominated for some of the industry's most prestigious awards, such as the RITA® and Golden Heart Awards from Romance Writers of America, the Australian Romance Reader Awards, and the Golden Leaf Award. When not dreaming up new stories, Naughton can be found spending time with her husband and three children in their western Oregon home. Learn more at www.ElisabethNaughton.com.

Also By Elisabeth Naughton

Eternal Guardians
(paranormal romance)
MARKED
ENTWINED
TEMPTED
ENRAPTURED
ENSLAVED
BOUND
TWISTED
RAVAGED
AWAKENED
UNCHAINED

Firebrand Series
(paranormal romance)
BOUND TO SEDUCTION
SLAVE TO PASSION
POSSESSED BY DESIRE

Against All Odds Series
(romantic suspense)
WAIT FOR ME
HOLD ON TO ME
MELT FOR ME

Aegis Series
(romantic suspense)
FIRST EXPOSURE
SINFUL SURRENDER
EXTREME MEASURES
LETHAL CONSEQUENCES
FATAL PURSUIT

Deadly Secrets Series
(romantic suspense)
REPRESSED
GONE

Stolen Series
(romantic suspense)
STOLEN FURY
STOLEN HEAT
STOLEN SEDUCTION
STOLEN CHANCES

Discover More Elisabeth Naughton

Surrender
A House of Sin Novella
By Elisabeth Naughton

The leaders of my House want her dead.

The men I've secretly aligned myself with want her punished for screwing up their coup.

I've been sent by both to deal with her, but one look at the feisty redhead and I've got plans of my own.

Before I carry out anyone else's orders, she's going to give me what I want. And only when I'm satisfied will I decide if she lives or dies.

Depending, of course, on just how easily she surrenders...

* * * *

Ravaged
An Eternal Guardians Novella
By Elisabeth Naughton

Ari — Once an Eternal Guardian, now he's nothing but a rogue mercenary with one singular focus: revenge. His guardian brothers all think he's dead, but he is very much alive in the human realm, chipping away at Zeus's Sirens every chance he can, reveling in his brutality and anonymity. Until, that is, he abducts the wrong female and his identity is finally exposed. It will take more than the Eternal Guardians, more even than the gods to rein Ari in after everything he's done. It may just take the courage of one woman willing to stand up to a warrior who's become a savage.

* * * *

Unchained
An Eternal Guardians Novella
By Elisabeth Naughton

PROMETHEUS – One of the keenest Titans to ever walk the earth. Until, that is, his weakness for the human race resulted in his imprisonment.

For thousands of years, Prometheus's only certainty was his daily torture at Zeus's hand. Now, unchained by the Eternal Guardians, he spends his days in solitude, trying to forget the past. He's vowed no allegiance in the war between mortal and immortal, but when a beautiful maiden seeks him out and begs for his help, he's once again powerless to say no. Soon, Prometheus is drawn into the very conflict he swore to avoid, and, to save the maiden's life, he must choose sides. But she has a secret of her own, and if Prometheus doesn't discover what she's hiding in time, the world won't simply find itself embroiled in a battle between good and evil, it will fall in total domination to Prometheus's greatest enemy.

Gone

(Deadly Secrets)
By Elisabeth Naughton
Now Available

Three years ago, Alec McClane and Raegan Devereaux lived every parent's worst nightmare: their one-year-old daughter, Emma, was abducted from a park when Alec turned his back for just a moment. Emma was never found, and presumed dead. The crushing trauma, plus Alec's unbearable guilt, ended the couple's marriage.

Now a four-year-old girl matching Emma's profile is found wandering a local park. Alec and Raegan are heartbroken to discover she's not their daughter but are newly motivated to find closure…and each secretly feels desperate to be in the other's presence again.

Alec suspects his vengeful biological father is behind Emma's disappearance. But as Raegan investigates other abductions in the area, she sees a pattern—and begins to wonder if Emma's kidnapping is actually linked to something more sinister.

As Alec and Raegan race to uncover the truth, a long-burning spark rekindles into smoldering passion, and they realize they need each other now more than ever.

* * * *

She should have listened.

Raegan stepped out of the hospital room, rubbed a shaky hand against her forehead, and drew in a deep breath, desperate to settle her racing pulse. Nothing helped. It felt as if a jackhammer was chipping away at what was left of her heart, the pain nearly as intense as the day Emma had gone missing.

She pressed her hand to her chest and focused on breathing. He'd tried to warn her. Alec had tried to keep her from rushing into that room and getting hurt all over again, but she hadn't listened. He might have decimated her once, but he still cared. If he didn't, he wouldn't have waited for her here at the hospital. He would have left as soon as he realized the girl in that room wasn't their missing daughter.

"Excuse me, miss?" The officer outside the door stepped toward her. "Are you okay?"

Tears burned Raegan's eyes. Tears of pain, of frustration, of trampled hope, but she blinked them back, breathed deeply, and pulled herself together. "Yes," she managed. "I'm fine."

She turned away and swiped at her eyes. One look and Raegan had known the girl wasn't Emma. Her hair had been too dark, her eyes too round, and she'd been missing the small, strawberry birthmark on the outer edge of her right eye that Emma had been born with. Raegan had known not to get her hopes up. Had known the chances were slim, but she'd hoped anyway. And she'd go on hoping regardless of what Bickam or Alec said. Because hope was all she had left these days.

Be tough. You can get through this.

Lifting her head, she drew a deep breath and smoothed her blouse over her slacks. She was no worse off than she'd been this morning, right? This didn't have to wreck her. She wouldn't let it.

She turned away from the officer and headed back down the hall toward the lobby, her heels clicking along the tile floor like an ominous warning. Her pulse was still too high, but as soon as she got back to the office and dove into her work, she'd be fine. Maybe she'd even cut out early and get a drink before she had to meet Jeremy and his friends for dinner.

Her footsteps fumbled when she spotted Alec sitting on a chair midway down the corridor, massaging his forehead as if he had a whopper of a tension headache. And her treacherous heart squeezed tight, thumping a bruising rhythm against her ribs as she stared at him.

They'd been divorced nearly three years, but every inch of her body still responded to him as if they'd just met. Her skin heated, her mouth watered, and a low tingle spread through her belly and inched its way downward until her knees were literally shaking.

He stopped his vigorous rubbing and lifted his head. And when his sky-blue eyes caught hers and held, that heat in her skin combusted.

He pushed to his feet, watching her carefully. Swallowing hard, she forced her legs forward and told herself not to get worked up. This was Alec. The man who'd told her their marriage was a mistake. The one who'd trampled all over her heart. The one who'd left her alone and broken when she'd needed him most.

"You okay?" he asked quietly.

Dammit, she wanted to hate him but couldn't. He'd been as broken as her when Emma had gone missing. He'd simply dealt with it in a very different way. One that now—years later—she'd accepted but would never understand.

"Yeah," she managed, slipping her hands into the pockets of her trench coat because she didn't know what to do with them. "I'm fine."

He nodded, but she could see in his eyes that he didn't believe her. And she found herself wanting to lean into him for comfort. Found herself wanting to scream at him for being here when she was emotionally wrecked and physically drained. Found herself wishing so many things between them could be different.

Nothing was different, though. This was her reality: a missing child, a failed marriage, and a life left tattered and crumbling around her when all she was trying to do was move on.

He slid his hands into the front pockets of his worn jeans, the movement pulling at the black Henley over his strong shoulders. A low pulse beat through her belly as she studied him. He was just as gorgeous as he'd always been—blond hair, a lean, muscular body he obviously still took care of—but the years had aged him in ways no thirty-two-year-old should be aged. Fine lines that hadn't been there before creased his temple, and she could see a hint of gray in the blond scruff covering his jaw. Dark circles marred the soft skin beneath his lashes, telling her he hadn't slept much recently, and worry churned in her belly at the thought he was drinking again. But one look at his clear blue eyes told her he'd exorcised that demon from his life, at least. The guilt, though, she still saw swirling in their cerulean depths.

She hated that she still loved him. Hated that she wanted to comfort him the way he'd never let her comfort him. Hated especially that even after all the misery and heartache and time apart, he was still the one. The one who made her heart beat faster and her palms sweat. The one who could rock her world with just one look. The one who would forever ruin all other men for her from now until the end of time.

Eyes On You
A BLASPHEMY NOVELLA
By Laura Kaye

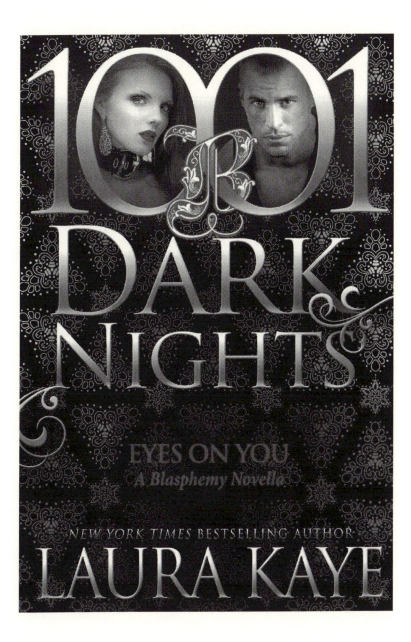

1001
DARK
NIGHTS

EYES ON YOU
A Blasphemy Novella

NEW YORK TIMES BESTSELLING AUTHOR
LAURA KAYE

Acknowledgments from the Author

Some books take you by surprise, and *Eyes on You* was definitely one. Of necessity, it came out in a rush of words, but I couldn't have slowed it down if I tried. Wolf and Liv just leapt onto the page, surprising and exciting me and making me laugh (and sometimes blush). And I have Liz Berry to thank for the opportunity to make that happen. 1001 Dark Nights is such an amazing and special project to be a part of, and I'm honored that I get to share stories I love through it. Thanks Liz and Jillian Stein for all you do to support and encourage and be there for me – it means the world.

Thanks also to KP Simmon who was there every step of the way, taking the heat off so I could focus on those fast and furious words. And thanks to my amazing critique partner, Christi Barth, for reading right behind me and making me shine as you always do. I appreciate having such amazingly supportive women in my life.

Thanks also to my Heroes and my Reader Girls, who give me motivation and encouragement even when they don't know they're doing it. And thanks, as always, to my readers, who take my characters in to their hearts and allow me to tell their stories again and again. ~LK

To everyone searching for that feeling of being deeply and intensely alive, listen closely to yourself, for no one knows you better.

"There is a voice inside which speaks and says, *'This is the real me!'*"
~ William James, American psychologist and philosopher

Chapter 1

Things that would be better than being on this date, Liv Foster thought as she stared across the high-boy bar table at her so-called perfect match, Jerry. *A popcorn kernel stuck between my teeth…finding a snake in my car…a pelvic exam…* She took a sip of her Prosecco, hoping the bubbles would make her feel better as the guy continued to complain about the hour-long wait for a table.

"…This really is unacceptable. I mean, it's not even that busy in here," he said, running his hand over his short black hair. He was attractive enough, although it was clear that the picture on his online dating profile was at least ten years old. Maybe more. She'd thought they were a few years apart in age, but she suspected it was more like ten or fifteen. "I just hate incompetence, don't you?"

Liv eyeballed the guy. You know, the one who hadn't bothered to make a reservation at a swanky new restaurant located in a hotel just two blocks from the baseball stadium on a Friday night before a Baltimore Orioles game. It took everything she had not to roll her eyes. "Yeah, I really do."

He huffed out a breath and shook his head, then started stretching and turning in his seat like he was looking for their waitress. In the thirty minutes they'd already waited, the two of them had apparently exhausted every small talk conversation of which he was capable. Jobs—she was a florist and he was an architect. The weather—sure had been a hot summer! Siblings—neither had any, so that was a short topic. Prior relationships—Liv hadn't offered any gory details—though she had them in spades, whereas she almost felt like she knew Jerry's ex, Angela, personally.

"So, what are you going to order?" Jerry asked.

Liv tilted her head. "Uh, well, I don't know yet. I haven't seen their menu."

He pulled a face. "I don't use menus."

"You...what? How does that work?" she asked with a little laugh. Was he joking? She honestly couldn't tell.

He shrugged. "I don't use menus."

In her mind's eye, she pictured her childhood golden retriever, Howie, tilting his head. Then tilting it even more. She was seriously channeling some Howie just then. "But...how do you know what you want to order?"

He waved a hand around at the restaurant as if it were self-evident. "It's a steakhouse. They have steak."

"Oh. Uh. Right." The waitress's appearance saved Liv from trying to come up with a better response. Right in that moment, she thought she *almost* would've given anything to turn back time to when she and Caleb were still happy. When they were looking forward to their wedding, their honeymoon, and their life together beyond all the celebrations. But she was beyond wishing for something that could never be—especially when she deserved so much better. Besides, too much of what she'd thought she'd had with Caleb hadn't been real, had it? And she never wanted to go back to that. Not ever again.

But, man. Jerry. Jerry was too freaking real. And Liv was still deserving better. But she was stuck on this ride at least until she'd choked down the last bite of her steak.

"Can I get you another round of drinks?" their waitress asked.

"Can we just eat here in the bar?" Jerry asked. "This wait is ridiculous."

"Oh, sure. Of course," the young woman said, pasting on a smile. Working in customer service, Liv knew what it took to deal with assholes like Jerry. And being three years single and back on the dating market, she was starting to know what it was like to date them, too. "I'll grab you menus."

He put a hand on the woman's arm. "That won't be necessary. We don't need menus. I'll just order for us."

Liv wondered if her expression appeared as stunned as the waitress's, especially when the woman stepped out of Jerry's grasp and looked at Liv as if to ask if this was okay.

No. Definitely, totally not okay. "Actually," Liv said, trying to keep her irritation in check. Because dang if breaking that *be nice* habit wasn't hard as heck. "I—"

"I'll have the ten-ounce Kobe filet mignon and she'll have the six-ounce Kobe filet. Both medium well with loaded baked potatoes and asparagus." He stared at the waitress.

The waitress shook her head. "I'm sorry, sir, we don't have Kobe beef. We have an excellent local provider of American beef, and we have Wagyu."

"That's okay," Liv said. "I prefer ribeye anyway. Medium *rare*."

"Ribeye is too fatty," Jerry said, looking at her like she was a child who'd disappointed him before his gaze returned to the hapless woman standing beside their table. "And I'd like to speak to your manager. Because what kind of steakhouse doesn't have Kobe beef?"

"I'll get her for you right away," the woman said, nearly running from them. Liv couldn't blame her.

The silence that followed was thick with tension, and Liv almost couldn't decide if she'd hallucinated what'd happened or if this first date was truly just that bad. Jerry wouldn't make eye contact and, instead, peered down at his cell phone beneath the table. So she took the opportunity to survey the diners sitting at the horseshoe-shaped bar near them in the hopes she'd see someone, *anyone*, she knew. *God, please give me a way to escape Mr. I Don't Use Menus.* But God had clearly forsaken her, because the party of three women having a girls' night out were strangers. As were the various groupings of men, some of whom wore Orioles gear and watched the pre-game commentary on the captioned television screens above the bar. An elderly man she didn't know sat alone nearest to their high-boy table nursing a glass of bourbon, and two seats down from him...sat the hottest man Liv had ever seen.

And that was her impression just from seeing him in profile.

He had dark blond hair and a chiseled jaw, and even sitting, it was clear that he was tall. Seriously broad shoulders filled out a dark green button-down shirt, and big hands gripped a glass of water. Now God was just being mean. Because someone was going to get to be with that man tonight while she was stuck here with Jerry of the I Don't Use Menus clan. As she watched, *not*-Jerry pressed his cell phone to his ear and began talking in tones too low for her to hear.

On a sigh, Liv returned her attention to Jerry. Not that it mattered, because his gaze remained fixed on his phone. She drained the rest of her Prosecco and wished someone would bring her the bottle. That wouldn't be too awkward for a first date, right? *Right?*

"How are you folks this evening?" a new woman asked as she stepped to their table. "I'm Ms. Sanderson, the manager."

"Well, Ms. Sanderson, we've been better," Jerry said, launching right into a tirade. "We wanted the Kobe filets."

The manager produced two menus from behind her back like she'd been hiding a present. "I'm happy to recommend some other—"

Jerry blocked the large leather folio from hitting the table. "I don't use menus."

It took Ms. Sanderson a moment to recover, but you could hardly blame her. She glanced at Liv like Liv might impose some sanity on the situation, but the sanity ship seemed to have sailed on this date. "Well, sir, that's really the best way to see what we serve—"

You don't say, Liv thought, pressing her fingers to her lips to smother the smile that threatened.

"Why are you making this so hard?" Jerry asked. "It's a steakhouse. I want your best steak."

"Very good," the manager said with a seemingly sincere smile. "We have several cuts of Wagyu. If you haven't had it before, I highly recommend it."

Red streaks climbed up Jerry's throat and face. "Wagyu is ridiculously expensive, and this is only a first date," he huffed.

"You know what?" Liv said, pushing her chair back before she'd really thought about it. "Whatever you order for me will be fine. I just need to use the restroom."

She'd never run from a restaurant table so fast in her life. Now the question was whether she could run from the restaurant itself. Or, at least, how long she could hide in the bathroom. Or, possibly, whether she ever had to come out at all.

* * * *

Wolf Henrikson watched the sexy stranger flee her table like it was the Titanic and the bathroom was the last available lifeboat. And he couldn't say that he blamed her. He hadn't been trying to eavesdrop on the couple's conversation; it was only that every time the man spoke to anyone from the restaurant's staff, he shouted like he wanted to make the scene he was in fact making.

What the hell was the cute brunette doing with such an asshole anyway? The few times he'd looked around to see if his dinner companion had arrived, he'd noticed the woman sitting not too far away—and she'd made him do a double take every time. Between her glossy chocolate waves, the bright red paint on her bow-tie lips, and the vintage-style red dress with the plunging neckline and the full knee-length skirt, she had the sex appeal of a pinup girl. He couldn't help wondering if she wore garters and thigh-highs beneath that skirt.

Wolf almost regretted that he no longer had any reason to stay at the bar because the scene playing out at the nearby table was like a train wreck he couldn't stop watching. And, oh, he *did* enjoy watching. People were just so fucking interesting, even when they were off their damn rockers.

But the prospective submissive he'd been planning to meet—in public, at her request—had just called to let him know she'd gotten cold feet. He respected the honesty. The BDSM lifestyle wasn't for everyone, and it wasn't something he recommended anyone explore frivolously. But the change in plans left him at loose ends.

Actually, that feeling was a constant presence in his blood these days. Restlessness. Boredom. Dissatisfaction without really being able to pinpoint why.

In anticipation of the meeting, he'd only had water, but he dropped a few dollars on the bar anyway, then pushed off the stool and made for the restrooms at the back. Blasphemy would be hopping soon, and even though he wasn't scheduled to work a shift, he could no doubt find a willing partner to play with there. Though he was one of the twelve Master Dominants and a one-twelfth owner of the city's most exclusive BDSM club, Wolf's particular kink didn't require all the equipment and special rooms that some did. Really, voyeurism and exhibitionism could be enjoyed anywhere. Which was kinda the point.

As long as he could watch, or knew others were watching, or was with someone who got off on being watched, he was all kinds of good.

Or, at least, he used to be. Something had been missing for him in all of it lately, leaving him wondering whether his role in Blasphemy still made the most sense—for him and his partners. A number of the other Masters had found women to love and to collar, and even to marry. They were committed to the club because it was central to their lives and their relationships. For years, being a part of the scene there had been important to Wolf, giving him a safe place to play and meet likeminded women. But lately, he wasn't getting the same thrill, the same satisfaction out of it. And it left him feeling like a bit of a fraud. Because the Masters of Blasphemy should be all in. The club and its patrons deserved no less.

On a distracted sigh, Wolf stepped into the narrow hallway that led to the restrooms and nearly bowled someone over. "Damn, I'm sorry," he said, grasping the woman's arms to keep from knocking her down. Momentum made it so that he nearly flattened her against the wall, and he got a lungful of a flowery scent from her hair. He prepared for the smackdown his carelessness deserved, but instead what he got was laughter. Full-on, deep belly, throw-your-head-back laughter.

From the sexy pinup girl with the atrocious taste in dinner partners.

"Just…just…an accident," she gasped between bouts of laughter she tried but failed to restrain. "That full body contact with you…will probably end up being the highlight of my night. *Trust me.*"

Wolf grinned as he took in her meaning. He wasn't sure which he appreciated more—her humor, her easy-going nature, or the compliment. Or that dress. Because seeing it up close, *damn.* The V-neckline emphasized the swells of her breasts, and the full, flaring skirt emphasized a narrow waist over satisfyingly full hips.

"That bad?" he asked.

"Oh, mister. The worst. Like, the God's honest worst. And my friend can't rescue me." She rolled her eyes. "So clearly she's fired and I need to hire a new bestie first thing Monday morning."

His grin grew. "From what I overheard, I think you're fully within your rights."

She chuckled. "I didn't even know *not* using menus was a thing. I mean, who does that?"

"Literally no one does that," he said, enjoying her playful

manner. She had an interesting face, expressive and a little dramatic. He wondered what she looked like when—

Nope. He couldn't let himself finish that thought. Not unless he wanted her to see exactly how much she appealed to him. And given how her night was going, he doubted that.

"Right? Just my luck. I'm gonna have to cancel my matchmaking service, too. Clearly." She sagged a little against the brick wall, almost like he'd pinned her there. Or commanded her to hold her position. Trying to rein in his lust for her, he dropped his gaze to the floor, but her calves were like artwork perched on a ridiculously sexy pair of strappy black heels with satin ribbon that tied at the ankles.

Wolf's mind exploded with ideas of things he'd do to her—or have her do for him—if they'd come to this place together. If she'd been into the same things he was. If she was his. He licked his lips and shook the thoughts away. He didn't often play with people outside Blasphemy because voyeurism and BDSM were more than most vanilla people could deal with. Admittedly, telling someone that you wanted to fuck them in public where other people could see didn't easily create a good first impression.

"Sounds like your Monday is going to be busy," he managed.

She chuckled. "I think you're right." She heaved a sigh. "Well, thanks for making my night a little better."

He tilted his head and considered, and then the words were out of his mouth before he'd decided if they were a good idea. "I could save you, if you wanted."

"Aw," she said, peering up at him with striking, bright turquoise eyes. "That's the sweetest thing anyone has said to me in a really long damn time. But I guess it would be rude."

"Yeah?" he said, a surprised at how disappointed he was. But her openness and honesty in this short conversation piqued his interest and made him wonder what *else* she might be open to.

"Yeah," she said, also sounding more than a little disappointed.

Which officially intrigued Wolf, because she was interested even if she thought she shouldn't be, given the disastrous date waiting for her. So he held out his hand and threw her a lifeline anyway. Given how he'd been feeling lately, what did he have to lose? "I'm Wolf. I'll be at the bar. Change your mind, just give me a signal."

Her eyes went wide as she slid her hand into his. "Liv. Olivia.

And I...don't know what to say."

Wolf leaned down until he could look her eye to eye. Testing her. Observing her. Commanding her. "Say 'thank you, Wolf.'"

When the words finally came, they were a little breathless. "Thank you, Wolf." But she remained pinned to the wall.

Breathing in her floral scent, he waited a moment before he said or did another thing, just to see what she'd do. And all she did was keep her eyes on him. Which was exactly what he'd wanted. Finally, he gave her a wink and then a single nod toward the bar. Only then did she move. With one longing, last glance back, she left the hallway.

And hello, excitement...

Which was the moment Wolf knew he wasn't leaving this restaurant without her.

Chapter 2

It was quite possible that Liv had never been so turned on in her life. She had no idea how she'd peeled herself off that wall, because she wanted nothing more than to stay there. The brightest green eyes she'd ever seen staring at her. Pinning her. Looking like they quite possibly wanted to devour her.

Wolf. It was a crazy name, but holy wow, did it seem to fit. Because something about the way he looked at her made her feel like he was the hunter and she was the prey.

Actually, she was the one who must be crazy. Because *that* feeling should've scared her. Instead, it gave her post-disastrous-date plans that involved her rabbit and her favorite porn scene about a woman who gets taken by a stranger on a subway while everyone around them watches. And there was more than a little likelihood that Liv would be imagining Wolf as the seducer—and her as the seduced—while she watched.

Hating her urge to be nice even when people didn't deserve it, she slid back onto her bar stool and tried to smile at Jerry, but that was hard when he started gloating about how his rudeness had gotten them an offer for free dessert. Liv's hips proved that she could eat the heck out of some dessert, but she'd had her heart set on steak-and-go, so no way did she want to stick around for another course with this guy. At least another glass of Prosecco had been delivered in her absence.

"That's great," she managed, her gaze straying over her date's shoulder to where Wolf was settling onto his bar stool again. He didn't look at her, but somehow she knew that he was aware of her.

Keeping tabs on her, even. Would he really rescue her from this date if she gave him a signal? And what would that signal be? Maybe she could wave her white linen napkin like a general surrendering a battle. That thought finally made her smile. The way the bubbly was going to her head helped, too.

Before long, the manager was personally delivering their steaks to the table. The freaking filet mignon, after all. Fine. Whatever.

"Will there be anything else right now?" Ms. Sanderson asked.

"I'll let you know," Jerry said.

Sighing, Liv gave the woman an apologetic smile. "No, thank you." At her wit's end, she finally dropped the niceties. "You know, Jerry, you catch more bees with honey. It's hardly fair to treat a restaurant's staff poorly because they don't serve food they shouldn't be expected to serve because it isn't even on the menu."

He shook his head and shrugged. "You never get what you don't ask for." He pointed his fork at her. "Remember that."

She was still processing his insufferable arrogance when he did something even more astonishing. He reached across the expanse of pressed white linen with his fork and knife…and began cutting her steak.

Liv reared back in her chair, her jaw dropping. "What in the *world* are you doing?"

His gaze rose to meet hers, even while he cut her filet into bite-sized pieces. "I like taking care of little girls," he said, a tendril of heat slipping into his eyes.

Oh, nope. Nopenopenope. A thousand, million times, nope.

She shoved up out of her chair, and the napkin tumbled from her lap to the floor.

As stunned as she was, she wasn't sure which happened first—Jerry asking where she was going or Wolf appearing at her side.

"God, Liv. It really is you," Wolf said. "I worried I'd never see you again."

Liv blinked, swallowed, and played along as she stared up at that handsome Nordic face, all dark-blond and sharp-jawed good looks. "Wolf. Wow. I can't believe it's you."

He stepped closer. "I see you're in the middle of something here…"

"Yes, she is," Jerry said. "If you'll excuse us."

Wolf ignored him. "...but after the way we last parted, I promised myself if I ever saw you again, I wasn't going to let you get away twice."

Liv was nearly breathless. Was he role-playing or talking about their brief encounter? Either way, her response was the same. "I don't want you to let me get away."

She felt out of her element, outside the bounds of propriety, out of control. She had no idea what she was doing here, what she was maybe getting into with this man who was, except for an intense five-minute conversation, a total stranger. She had *no idea*...except that her head said *How could it be worse than my date?* And her instincts said *Go with Wolf, go with Wolf, go with Wolf.* And her body said *And climb him while you're at it.*

"Damn, I hoped you'd say that," Wolf said, green eyes flashing. And then he took her into his arms and kissed her. Right there. In the middle of the bar of a fancy steakhouse. In front of Jerry, who was babbling in outrage that Liv couldn't hear.

Because Wolf dominated every other sense. His hard chest crushing her breasts and his big hands cupping her jaw and sliding into her hair. His cool tongue licking across her lips. His shower-clean scent adding to the Prosecco to make her head swim. Liv stood frozen and still for long seconds, not because she didn't like the kiss, but because she *did*. Oh, man, she really freaking did.

And not just the kiss, though it was by itself the best kiss she'd ever had. It was that Wolf was kissing her where everyone could see him doing it. It was that Jerry's rising volume was drawing even more eyes to them. It was that people were *watching*.

Liv thought about that porn scene she'd been planning to enjoy, and suddenly she felt like she was living it. And she didn't think she'd ever been more turned on in her entire life. Everything tingled as if her nervous system had been plugged in for the very first time. Her nipples puckered so hard they almost ached. Adrenaline had her nearly trembling. And she got wet between her legs. Wet enough that her panties were damp, too.

By the time Wolf released her, she could've fallen to her knees. That was how hard he'd rocked her world. Instead, she just said, "Yes, please."

Something flared in his gaze that she couldn't name, and Wolf grasped her hand and her purse in a show of possession that made her wetter. He led her away from the table, away from where Jerry gawped and sputtered. Liv was too stunned to even give him a parting piece of her mind.

They passed their original waitress near the entrance that led out to the hotel's lobby. "Give me a minute, Wolf?" Liv said, gesturing for her purse.

He halted immediately and passed her the bag.

Unzipping her wallet, she grabbed some bills and pressed them into the woman's hand. "I'm really, really sorry for the way he treated you. And that I didn't put a stop to it sooner."

The waitress shook her head. "Thank you, but I'm just glad you got away. That looked like the date from hell. We've all been in the back debating if we should rescue you."

"I've got that covered," Wolf said, his voice deep, gravelly, sexy.

The other woman grinned up at him. "I see that." She gave Liv an approving wink. "I hope your night gets better from here."

Glancing up at Wolf, Liv strongly suspected it would. Exactly what that might mean, however, she wasn't yet sure. "Yours, too," she said.

Wolf took her hand again and led her to a private nook in the hotel's lobby, shrouded in mood lighting and pulsing with the slow beat of a seductive, electronic song. For a long moment, he just stared at her, like he was debating, and then he stepped closer and got all up in her space. "I liked kissing you."

Liv released a shaky breath. "I liked it, too." Good God, what an understatement.

"I liked kissing you in public," he said.

She shuddered as if his words had been a physical caress. "I liked being kissed…in public."

"Did you now? Well then I wonder, sweet Olivia, what else you might like?"

In public. He hadn't said those words again, but she heard them anyway.

Tell him, Liv. See where it goes. What do you have to lose?

She felt a whole lot like she was standing on the edge of a cliff— a cliff she'd been peering over for a long, long time. She'd known for years that public displays of affection turned her on. She'd become aware forever ago that the idea of being caught, being *seen* having sex or being seduced was her favorite fantasy. She had plenty of experience with the fact that nothing got her off faster than imagining that fantasy, too.

But one thing held her back from jumping off that cliff with Wolf. Her ex's words still rang in her ear from the night she'd revealed her fantasies to the man she'd thought she could trust most in the world. And not just revealed them, but also asked him to make them come to life. Just once.

Geez, Liv. Fantasies are just that. I'm a partner. You're coming up for partner. If we got caught, it would ruin our reputations. And since when is normal *sex not enough for you?*

As if her wanting to try out a fantasy *wasn't* normal. As if *she* wasn't normal.

Three years had passed since they'd split, and Liv was ninety-five percent over that relationship. But Caleb's judgmental, dismissive tone about *this* still stuck with her.

"Where did you go just now?" Wolf asked.

"I'm sorry," she said, reflexively.

"Don't be," he said. "Just tell me what you want. You want to have a drink with me? I want that, too. You want dinner, because you didn't really touch yours? I'll get you that ribeye or anything else you want. You want me to kiss you again, I will. In a damn heartbeat."

Just tell me what you want.

It had been a long time since someone wanted nothing more than to please her. The fact that it was this beautiful man wanting to do so was more than a little heady.

"And what if…" Her heart hammered so hard her voice got breathy. "What if I wanted something more than kissing?"

* * * *

Wolf's big hands slid into Liv's hair, and he crowded her body with his until she was forced to tilt her head way back. "Then I'd take you up to my hotel room, press you against the window overlooking the street, and give it to you."

He braced for her reaction, and deep satisfaction roared through him when her eyes went wide, her mouth dropped open, and her breathing quickened. Thank *fuck* he'd read the signs right. The way she'd held her pose against that wall until he'd given her permission to move. The way she'd repeated his words back to him, just like he'd commanded. The way she'd melted into his kiss in the middle of the bar.

The way she'd answered his silent question, *Could you possibly want more than this, Olivia?* with a *Yes, please.*

This woman was submissive and she got off on being watched. Which meant she was perfect. Perfect for him.

Liv licked her lips, and her expressive eyes made it clear she was waging some kind of internal debate. But he was in no rush, because if he got her upstairs, he was going to take all damn night.

Finally, she nodded. "Yes, please," she whispered again.

"Say the words, Olivia. Tell me what you want." It'd been a long time since he'd played with someone not in the BDSM lifestyle, or at least exploring entering it, and so he wanted it all spelled out.

"T-take me to your hotel room. And...press me against the window."

He put his mouth to her ear. "And then what, sweetness?" Her floral scent was strong this close. He wanted to drink it down.

"And then...anything, Wolf. Everything."

Wolf had them in the elevator in an instant. He had her pressed against the doors the second they closed. And he had his tongue back in her mouth.

And, Jesus, where she'd been pliant before, now she was aggressive, kissing him back, pulling his hair, grinding against him. Giving him as good as she got.

They spilled into the hallway of the fourth floor. Breathing hard and nearly marching, he guided her down to his corner room, the one he'd reserved in case his interview with the submissive had led to a desire for something that required more privacy.

But never had he imagined *this*. The intensity. The connection. The raging lust.

Between choosing this bar of all the bars in Baltimore, the prospective canceling, and Liv wanting to be rescued—*and* being into what he was into, it was almost as if meeting Liv had been destined.

Wolf believed in signs. And when Liv stood up from that table, she'd given him one.

Maybe what he needed *wasn't* at Blasphemy after all. Maybe it was right here in front of him. In a fucking sexy five-foot-five-inch package, not including the three-inch heels with those seductive little ribbons.

The heavy door to the suite clicked shut behind them. Wolf held his ground as Liv ventured into the sitting room. She moved to the windows, exposed by the open curtains, and he knew exactly what she was seeing. The busy intersection below. Cars driving by on the street or idling at the stoplight. Throngs of people out for the game or heading to the rock concert at the venue a few blocks over.

He turned on one light, then another. It would soon be dark, and that light would draw attention from outside. Would make their window and any other illuminated window stand out in the darkness. Except their window would be filled with their silhouettes pressed to the glass, hot and sweaty and moving.

Should anyone look up and notice.

He came up behind her. His fingers brushed her hair aside and found the top of the zipper to her killer dress. He played with it, not yet pulling it down, not yet exposing her to his eyes—or all of theirs. "I want to fuck you against this window, Olivia. Do you want that?"

She went to turn, but he held her shoulders so that she remained looking outside. He could see her face well enough in the reflection of the glass, and he wanted her focused on being seen. "Yes, I want it," she said. "Though I've never done this before. Picking up a stranger. Um, the window..."

"We won't do anything you don't want to do, and I won't get upset if you change your mind. Now, five minutes from now, or five minutes after that. Do you understand?" he said, needing to be sure. Normally he'd talk to a submissive about safewords and boundaries and hard and soft limits, but that's not what this was. At least not yet. But that didn't mean he wasn't going to make sure she understood that she was in control. No matter what.

She released a breath. "Yes, thank you."

He shook his head and brushed his fingers back and forth along the neckline of her dress. "Don't thank me for that. You should never let someone have more of you than you want to give. And you should never expect less from someone than you'd consider basic courtesy."

"I think I need to get that on a T-shirt, Wolf," she said, chuffing out a small, nervous laugh. "It's good advice."

Wanting to reassure her, he kissed the skin below her ear. "Something else for that Monday to-do list."

Her laughter was real now. "I might need an assistant at this point."

Smiling, he kissed her shoulder, finding it hard to resist her. "Before anything happens, I want you to text a friend. Tell them where you are."

"Okay," she said. "You're...wow." She retrieved the phone from her purse and sent the text. "All done."

"Good," he said, setting her things aside. "I just want you to enjoy this, Liv." Smiling, he tugged at the zipper to her dress. It slid down. Slowly, so damn slowly. She gasped a little breath as the hotel's cool air hit the smooth skin of her back. "All you have to do is tell me to stop or slow down or do something differently, and I will," he said.

Liv nodded. "Don't stop." The dress fell to her feet in a flutter of material, exposing the long, curved slope of her back and the swell of her ass all wrapped in red lace lingerie.

God, she was brave and adventurous and so damn beautiful that Wolf could barely believe he'd found her. That he was going to have her. That she'd said *yes, please.*

He pressed his front against her back and let her feel the bulge of his hard cock against all her softness. "Hands on the glass, Liv," he murmured, lips to her ear.

With a little shiver, she complied. "I'm on the pill, but I want you to use a condom," she said.

"I was planning to, but I'm glad you said something," he said, smoothing his hands from her shoulders to her wrists and back again, then down her ribs, his fingers just skimming the sides of her breasts.

"God, Wolf," she said, another tremor wracking through her. Adrenaline, if he had to guess, which meant she was getting off on just the idea of this. Getting off on it, *hard.*

And her getting off hard was exactly what he intended to ensure. Because something inside him told him that, just like he'd said in the bar, he wasn't going to want to let her go.

Chapter 3

Liv couldn't believe this was happening, couldn't believe that she was about to let a total stranger fuck her against a hotel window. But she didn't want to be cautious or reasonable or respectable. She'd had a lifetime of that, and now she needed something more.

And if *not* doing this was normal, she didn't want to be that, either.

She wanted this. She wanted to know what it was like to *live* her fantasy. She wanted Wolf.

So as his big hands roamed her body, she gave over to having what she wanted. For once.

Running kisses over her neck, her shoulder, her back, he pushed the lace of her cheeky underwear over her hips and down her thighs. They dropped to her ankles.

"Step out of your clothes," Wolf said. "And spread your legs."

The command was so damn sexy, she felt close to orgasming from the words alone. She did what he told her to do, and then stood there in a red bra and a pair of heels. The reflection of herself looking like that would've been arousing on its own, but paired with Wolf's gaze meeting hers in the glass, they were a visual aphrodisiac.

"I want you to come before you take my cock, Olivia. I want you to come on my fingers with the whole world watching." His left hand pressed hers to the glass, while his right smoothed down over her belly and cupped her pussy.

A long moan poured out of her from the shock of the contact. She'd had sex with two other men in the three years since she'd left her ex, but none of them had set her on fire the way Wolf was already doing.

And then his fingers spread her lips, glided through her wetness, slid inside her.

Her forehead sagged against the glass, her hair creating a little curtain around her face that at once left her feeling protected and exposed.

One finger, then two stroked her inside and out, penetrating deep, hitting her G-spot, circling her clit. He ground himself against her ass, and the feeling and the promise of his cock set her immediately on edge. On a groan, she turned her face toward him, and he rewarded her with a deep, wet, claiming kiss, his tongue mimicking in her mouth what his fingers did elsewhere. He tasted so good and he worked her even better, until she was panting and pressing and straining.

"Come on my fingers, Olivia. Come loud enough that the next room can hear you," he said.

And, Jesus, it was like his words had been lifted from her every fantasy. How did he know what she wanted to hear? What she needed to hear? What she'd always dreamed of hearing?

"Yes," she said. "Gonna come, Wolf." The sensation was climbing, tightening, spiraling.

His other hand moved to her chest and yanked her bra down, freeing her breasts so that they just touched the glass.

It was the extra exposure that did it.

She came on a scream. "Oh God, oh God, Wolf!" She slapped a hand against the glass. "Oh, my fucking God."

"Yes, Olivia. Yes," he growled, his fingers still moving, still filling her, still commanding her pleasure.

He kissed her one more time, and then he pulled away, leaving her panting and trembling. Even though his reflection revealed that he was undressing, she peered over her shoulder, wanting to see the real thing.

His chest was lean and broad, muscled but not ridged. His shoulders and biceps were works of masculine art, and she'd always had a thing for those parts of a man's body. His stomach was flat and...

She licked her lips as he pulled down his jeans. And oh man, his cock was freaking glorious. It jutted out from trimmed dark blond hair, long and curved upward, a bead of come at the tip. Because of her.

He retrieved a condom packet from his wallet, tore it open, and rolled it on. There was something about watching a man do that, particularly one she didn't know well, that felt so damn intimate. It was possibly a ridiculous thought, given that she was standing there mostly naked, but she still felt it. Because it meant that Wolf was about to be inside her.

And she couldn't wait another second.

"Please tell me we'll do this more than once," she said, her mouth running away from her. Her cheek suddenly felt hot against the cold glass.

He grinned. "Why's that?"

In for a penny, in for a pound, she guessed. "Because I can't decide if I want you more from the front or back, and I'm hoping maybe I won't have to choose."

Stroking his cock in that big fist, he nailed her with a scorching stare. "You want me, you got me." He stepped in close.

"Are you even real, Wolf?" she whispered, her head spinning.

"What do you think?" he asked, finding her entrance and sliding slowly, agonizingly, and finally deep.

"Yes. God, yes," she cried at the sensation of fullness.

"Keep your eyes on the streets, sweetness."

She exhaled on a long, tortured moan that made it hard to keep her eyes open at all. "That's so freaking good."

Tugging her hips back, he started to move. Long, smooth strokes that set her whole body on fire. That curve in his cock was pure magic, making his head drag against her G-spot on every single thrust. She dropped her face and breasts to the glass, her hair the only thing between her cheek and the cold surface.

"Damn, you're a fucking dream, Olivia." He gripped her hips harder, and the rhythmic smack of their skin sounded out in the room.

A horn honked on the street below.

Through the curtain of her hair, Olivia watched as people strolled on the sidewalk, crossed the crosswalk, and weaved motorcycles through the traffic. Three cabs waited to turn left, and a bus lumbered through the intersection. *How many of those people see us?*

How many of them just did a double take when they spotted us? How many of them might be taking a picture on their cell phone?

All of that excited her. It was risky, of course. Especially now that she owned her own business. But that was why she'd turned her face to the side and let the length of her hair create a little barrier. They would see her breasts and her stomach and her legs. They might see a man moving behind her. They would *know* what they were seeing. But they wouldn't know it was her. Olivia Foster.

The riskiness got her off. Being seen got her off. Getting away with this got her off.

God, the reality was better than any imagining she'd ever done.

"I'm close again," she rasped, more than a little shocked. Because she'd never been able to come more than once with any other man.

"Good, because I want to feel that cunt clamp down on my dick, Olivia. I want to feel your come on my balls," he said, dirty words and hot breath equally thrilling in her ear. He flattened his palms against the front of her thighs and trapped her more fully against the glass. The change in position had him going deeper, the sensation more demanding, more intense. His thrusts shortened and quickened, forcing panting breaths out of her until she was deliciously dizzy.

The head of his cock created the most perfectly agonizing friction against that spot inside her. And that was what did it. "I'm coming, Wolf. Coming on you!"

"Christ," he bit out as her core squeezed him through five mind-blowing strokes. "You're so damn tight."

In the wake of her orgasm, he didn't let up one bit. He pushed both of her palms upward on the glass, his hands covering hers, and pressed her fully flat to the window.

"You still okay?" he rasped before dragging an open-mouthed kiss against the spot in front of her ear.

"Never better in my whole life," she managed with a breathy chuckle. She wasn't sure if she'd ever felt this alive before, and Wolf had been the one to make her feel this way.

"That's what I like to hear. You're going to make me come so fucking hard." His thrusts were short and hard and fast, his hips tilting as he ground deep. His breaths sounded like they scraped through clenched teeth. His hands and his body and his cock trapped her so that she couldn't move an inch. And she didn't want to. She wanted to be held there for everyone to see, against the window, getting the fuck of a lifetime. "Goddamn, Olivia," he growled. "God*damn*."

"Want to feel it," she said. "Want to feel it inside me."

He came on a shout, his hips moving roughly through the orgasm, his cock jerking into her with each spasm. Afterward, he exhaled against her shoulder. "You're amazing," he whispered.

And Liv was once again wondering if this man was truly real.

* * * *

Wolf got her the ribeye.

Room service had arrived a half hour before, and they'd devoured their picnic dinner sitting on the floor of the little living room, backs against the couch, the coffee table their dining table.

And, of course, Wolf made it even more interesting by demanding that she wear his green dress shirt—and only his dress shirt—when the waiter delivered the food. It *just* covered her ass. Even still, with their clothes in heaps all over the floor, it was perfectly clear what they'd been doing before the food arrived.

Her cheeks had heated at the man's purposeful efforts *not* to look, but she hadn't minded. Something inside her had liked that the man knew. And that Wolf had known that she'd like it.

As they ate, they'd had a million little getting-to-know-you conversations. His last name was Henrikson. He'd been born in Sweden but immigrated to the U.S. with his family when he was ten. He worked in IT and was a specialist in designing, installing, and monitoring high-end security systems. He co-owned that company with a friend. So he was a business owner, like herself. Somehow it seemed appropriate that he kept an eye on people for a living...

"Tell me more about your flower shop," Wolf said.

Liv smiled. "It's called Flowers in Bloom and it's been open for almost three years." She took a deep breath and let the next words fly. "It was the promise I kept to myself when I discovered my fiancé screwing another woman a month before our wedding." The revelation used to shame her, as if she'd done something wrong that had made him betray her, but she was over that now.

"Jesus, Liv, I'm sorry," Wolf said, his brow cranking down over suddenly stormy green eyes. There was always an intensity to his expression, but he could shift to fierce in a second.

"I'm not," she said, shaking her head. "Not anymore. Don't get me wrong, it hurt. But finding out that what I thought we had wasn't real was the best thing that ever happened to me. If I'd married him when he didn't really love me, my life would've been miserable. And I think I might never have left the law, which I was good at but kinda hated, to open my store, which is something I'm actually passionate about. Not only am I my own boss, but I get to help make people's lives beautiful with my flowers. Their weddings, their celebrations, their parties, their dinners. Even their funerals. I think, given the way this world is, we could all do more to create our own kind of beauty in it." She shrugged. "Probably sounds a little corny."

Shaking his head, Wolf tucked a strand of hair behind her ear. "Not at all. It sounds like someone's found her calling." He pressed his lips together and his gaze went distant. "It also sounds kinda familiar…"

Liv shifted her position against the couch and chuckled. "It does?"

His gaze ran over her face. Once, twice. "Did you used to have short hair?"

"Uh, yeah, I did," she said, surprised. "That was my boring-lawyer-hair phase. Wait, does that mean we've met?"

"Holy shit, we did," Wolf said. "At my friend and business partner's wedding. Do you remember Isaac and Willow Marten? Got married about two years ago."

The names rushed a slew of memories to the surface. What a sweet, fun couple Isaac and Willow had been. How amazing they'd looked on their wedding day, his white tux and her white gown, both with silver accents, so stunning against their warm, brown skin. Willow's wedding broom was only the second one Liv had ever decorated. She'd wrapped the handle with silver lace and beaded the handle jack and broom head with Swarovski crystals and tiny pearls, before finishing with a cascade of white roses and gardenias, each tipped with silver glitter. Willow had been so pleased that she'd invited Liv to stay so she could take pictures of her arrangements at the ceremony and the reception.

"Of course I remember that wedding," Liv said, staring at Wolf anew. And then recognition dawned. The groom had worn white, but the groomsmen had worn black, and Wolf had been among them. "We *did* meet! I don't know how I didn't recognize you sooner." Or, certainly, how she hadn't remembered his unusual name. Actually, she had an idea. Back then, Liv had still been so stung by Caleb's betrayal that she'd feared her interest in men had died with her engagement. Back then, weddings had still been difficult for her to do.

"Me, either," he said, smiling. "But damn. This is crazy that we ran into each other like this after meeting before."

"It is," she said with a grin. "And it makes me even happier that I caught Caleb. Because I wouldn't have met you then, and I also wouldn't be here with you now." Her pulse spiked at admitting how much being with Wolf pleased her, but she was thirty-one and had just let this man fuck her against a hotel window, so she saw no reason not to be honest. Putting herself out there was something she was trying to learn to do more of, every damn day.

Wolf leaned in and kissed her lingeringly. He tasted of red wine and buttery steak, a heady combination that had her moving in for more kisses when he tried to pull away. "I'm glad you're here with me, Liv."

His hand slid into her hair and he came over her, forcing her backward until they lay on the floor between the couch and the coffee table, Wolf's long, lean body covering hers. They kissed and writhed, hands wandering, clothes falling away again.

"I love how you submit to me," he whispered around the edge of a kiss.

Do you have any idea what your wedding night is going to be like?

The memory came from out of nowhere. A snippet of conversation between Willow and her bridesmaids from the room where the women had dressed for the ceremony. Liv had been unboxing their bouquets from the protective cartons in which she'd brought them. Laughing and teasing, the women had all stopped dressing to hear Willow's response.

Ladies, I'm a submissive, wife or not. If that man doesn't put me on my knees tonight, there's going to be trouble in paradise.

Liv still remembered how much her cheeks had flamed at the

conversation that had followed. Because Willow and Isaac, and some of the other wedding attendees, it seemed, weren't just a little adventurous in the bedroom. They were all apparently into the BDSM lifestyle and belonged to a club where they could actually be open about that lifestyle with others who shared their interests. That such a place existed had been a revelation, but Caleb's words had still sounded out too loudly in Liv's head to allow her to do more than wonder about it then.

Even more than being a little embarrassed, though, Liv remembered how envious she'd been that Willow had found a man who knew what she wanted sexually—and gave it to her. Enthusiastically, unconditionally, and from the sounds of it, frequently.

Questions suddenly circled in Liv's mind. Questions about Wolf. At various points tonight, he'd commanded her. He'd made her *want* to please him. He'd read and anticipated her most private desires—and made them come to life...

"I want to be inside you again," Wolf said, blazing green eyes peering into hers.

"Yes," she said, unable to think when he looked at her that way. Like she was blowing his mind the way he was blowing hers.

He rose and helped her off the floor, and then he let his gaze do a long, lingering down and up over her naked breasts and bare pussy. "I'm a voyeur, Olivia. I get off on watching other people, and I get off on putting a lover in a situation where other people will watch her shatter because of what I do to her." He paused, letting those words hang there.

She swallowed hard, not shocked to learn this about him because that much seemed clear to her already. Instead, she was shocked because he put it out there so bluntly, so freely, so directly as if...as if it were perfectly normal.

And it was, wasn't it? *Damn you, Caleb.*

"I, uh, like that about you," she managed.

He chuckled. "I suspected you might. Because I think you're an exhibitionist."

"I...I am," she said, summoning the courage to admit this to someone again. *Say it. Tell him all of it. He won't judge you. You can trust him, Liv.* He'd proven that—with the text to her friend, with his encouraging words, with his promise to stop any time she wanted. "I *am* an exhibitionist. And I get off on being watched, on doing things where I might get caught, on the idea that other people might get aroused by watching me." The words spilled out of her in a nervous rush, but still, she'd said them, she'd admitted them.

"Good," he said, accepting her declaration unquestioningly. And damn if that easy, open acceptance didn't make something in her chest go tight and warm. "Then I have an idea that should please both of us."

She shivered at the promise of his words. "You lead, Wolf. And I'll be only too happy to follow."

Chapter 4

The rooftop pool deck was empty. At least for now. And that was perfect.

"It's beautiful up here," Liv said, walking past the closed-down bar and around the pool's edge, to the glass-and-metal railing that encircled the whole area. "City lights below and stars above."

All Wolf could see was Olivia, clad in a white towel tucked under her arms. Beneath, she wore only the red bra and panties he'd stripped from her before. A little coverage in case they ran into anyone on the way up. "Definitely beautiful," he said.

She turned, grinning almost shyly when she realized he was talking about her. "Can I tell you something?"

"Anything, sweetness." He came right up to her and braced his hands against the railing on either side of her. Two towels and her lingerie were all that separated them.

Lovely blue eyes peered up at him with emotions that played with things inside his chest in a way that was new. Powerful. Completely unexpected. He couldn't resist kissing her, tasting her, exploring her with his tongue.

At thirty-five, Wolf had been with his share of women. Working at Blasphemy gave him plenty of opportunities to find partners who shared his interests. But he'd never managed to go beyond playing to find a connection. Sometimes he wondered if that was because, at the club, it was all *so* easy, *so* available, *so*...almost predictable. He enjoyed the riskiness of exhibitionism and voyeurism, too. The thrill of it. The fear, and the overcoming of it. And those were harder to experience in a place where everything was so accepted.

Which was why he'd been wondering about remaining as one of the twelve Master Dominants there. Shouldn't he be more into the whole scene than he'd been lately? Once, it had meant everything to him, back when being one of the founding members had given him a community and a brotherhood and a safe place to be his truest self.

Things that Wolf could possibly introduce Olivia to...

Maybe that's why she intrigued him so much, called to him, made him *want*. In her eagerness and her uncertainty, she reminded him of the excitement he'd once felt. Made him want to feel that way again.

And he *did*, right here and now, with her.

Wolf pulled back from the kiss and loved the lust-drunk softness of her eyes. "What did you want to tell me?"

She licked her lips. "You're the first person who ever made me feel like it was okay. I mean, you know, the exhibitionism."

Satisfaction roared through him, curbed only when he studied her and found that uncertainty in her expression again. "It *is* okay, Olivia. Has someone made you feel otherwise?"

She gave a little shrug with one shoulder. "I told my ex. Asked him if we could try some things. He made me feel like I was being ridiculous and irresponsible. That it wasn't normal."

Anger clawed down Wolf's spine. That. That right there was the reason why he'd gotten involved with Blasphemy. He firmly believed that anything two consenting adults were into was not only okay and normal, but also absolutely no one else's business. Not everyone had that kind of tolerance and acceptance in their lives, though. He certainly hadn't. Blasphemy gave people a place to find it. And the fact that her asshole of an ex-fiancé had made her feel ashamed of her sexuality unleashed a fierce protectiveness inside Wolf toward her.

He wanted to tell her all that and more—and he would. But first he wanted to *show* her.

"I'm sorry he fed you that judgmental bullshit, Liv. You put yourself out there and he threw it in your face. What we did in my room... Did that feel abnormal to you?"

"God, no," she whispered. "I'd never felt more alive in my life. More...I don't know...myself."

Wolf nodded, the conviction in her words making him hard. He wanted her to feel all of that again. Because of him.

"Good," he said, tugging at her towel until it puddled at her feet. "Elbows on the railing."

Liv swallowed hard and her gaze cut to the right, toward the direction of the door from the elevator lobby. And then she complied.

"You sure?"

"Yes," she said. "Whatever you're going to do, I want it."

God, she was brave. And willing to be bold. It called to those same parts of himself. Nodding, he went to his knees. "Good, because what I want is your come in my mouth." As she gasped, he pressed kisses to her stomach, her hip bones, her thighs.

And then he pushed the red lace of her panties to the side and licked his tongue firm and flat over her clit.

"Oh, shit," she said, going up on her toes. "Oh, shit, that's so good."

Her praise drove him on, made him ravenous. He licked and licked, sucked and nipped. Gripping her ass in his hands, he canted her hips forward, allowing his tongue to venture deeper between her legs, to probe and plumb at her opening. She moaned and gasped and ground herself forward, sagging against the railing until he was half holding her up. He didn't mind one bit.

He sucked at her clit and flicked it fast with his tongue. Her thighs trembled. Her muscles strained. Her hand fell to the back of his head and held him down. All of which had his cock tenting the towel wrapped around his waist and him struggling to hold back from taking himself in hand.

"Wolf, Wolf, Wolf," she chanted.

He sucked her harder, willing her, forcing her, silently commanding her.

"Ooh, f-fuck," she rasped as her orgasm hit. He lapped up everything she gave him until her arousal coated his tongue and his chin. It was fucking glorious.

When she was steady again, Wolf rose to his feet. Making sure she was watching, he wiped at the wetness he wore with his hand, and then licked his fingers clean. "I could eat you all fucking night."

"Oh, my God," she whispered, a little tremor rocking through her. "Fuck me," she said, her gaze flickering toward the door again.

"Please fuck me. I need you in me now."

He scooped her towel off the ground and led her to the furthest chair at the bar. He covered the metal lattice seat with the terrycloth and guided her panties off. "Sit. Now. Legs apart."

Damn, it was gratifying to watch her follow a command. Did she even realize how submissive she was? How much pleasure she received from being commanded and obeying? Wolf didn't think so, not when that close-minded asshole of an ex wouldn't consider ways of giving her even a little of the public sex she craved.

He glanced toward the door again, but couldn't see it from this last seat, angled as it was in the corner created by the curve in the bar top. Wolf suspected Liv would've gone along with sex standing right where they'd been, but he'd read enough partners' expressions and body language in his life to know that she was just the wrong side of concerned about being spotted over there.

He wanted her to be able to concentrate on pleasure. And nothing but. That was part of the reason why he'd had her send that text.

Removing the condom packet from where he'd tucked it beneath the towel at his waist, Wolf held out his arms. "Undress me."

Those blue eyes flared, and Liv couldn't hold back a little smile. "Gladly." She bared him, dropping the towel near his feet.

He rolled on the condom, then crowded in against the chair until his thighs hit the front of the seat. "Put my cock inside you."

Liv's mouth dropped into an oval. Grasping his length, she shifted forward and ran his head through the pink lips of her pussy. Finally, she lined them up and tilted her hips to take more of him inside.

Wolf's jaw clenched at the goodness of it. "Brace your hands on the seat and fuck yourself on me. Use me, Olivia."

Lighting him up inside, she did as he asked. Clutching the seat on both sides of her ass, she rocked her hips in a steady rhythm until she'd coated his length with her slickness.

"Fuck," he growled, watching her cunt swallow his cock again and again. "That looks so goddamned good."

"Are you...are you getting off watching me fuck you, Wolf?"

He nailed her with a stare, torn between wanting to reward and punish her for that taunting tone. Either way, he loved it. "How could I not? My cock was made for your cunt."

"Oh, Jesus," she rasped.

"Say it," he said. "Say that my cock was made for your cunt. Tell me."

She licked her lips. "Your cock was made for my c-cunt."

"Again," he said, the strain of letting her lead this pushing him to his breaking point. "Say it a-fucking-gain."

"Your cock was made for my cunt!" she nearly yelled.

"Better fucking believe it," he said, suddenly shifting to hunch himself around her. He hauled her ass just over the edge of the seat and leaned forward, using the leverage of the chair's back and a hand in her hair to hammer himself into her once, twice, balls fucking deep.

On the fifth hard stroke, she came on a scream, her pussy squeezing so hard she threatened to take him over the edge way before he was ready to fall.

"Come as often and as loud as you can," he rasped, using the position to grind against her clit on every thrust.

An airplane flew overhead. Car horns blared in the distance. The chair screeched against the concrete. But sweetest of all was the steady stream of moans and murmured declarations and ecstatic cries of *I'm coming, Wolf!* that spilled from Olivia's beautiful mouth. He wanted in there, too.

One hand still around the chair, he moved his other fingers to her mouth. "Suck me while I fuck you, Olivia."

Opening her mouth, she accepted two of his fingers. Sucking, licking, stroking with her lips and tongue. He nodded, loving the way it looked. The visuals were *everything* for him. And Olivia Foster was like a feast for his eyes. The pleasure and passion in her gaze. The way her full breasts bounced, splayed over the disheveled red lace, his cock penetrating her core.

He pushed his fingers a little deeper, testing her. One of her hands flew to his wrist, not to resist, but to anchor. And something about that little gesture shoved him hard toward release. "Take me as deep as you can, Liv. It looks so beautiful."

The backs of his fisted fingers bumped her lips, and her eyes watered as his fingertips touched the back of her throat. She gagged but held him there, her watering gaze on his.

Wolf flew apart. He came on a shout that made him more goddamned light-headed than he'd ever been before. Withdrawing his hand from her sweet mouth, he clutched her tight and drilled his cock deep, deep, deeper until she'd wrung him dry. And then he kept going because Olivia was suddenly clawing at his back and crying his name, another orgasm wracking through her at the hard frenzy of his own.

God, he didn't want this to end. The sex, this night, or his time with this woman.

Chapter 5

Wolf was still buried deep inside her, still nearly hard, and Liv was still panting when he lifted his gaze and nailed her with that brilliant green stare. "Spend the night with me here. I really don't want to let you go."

Butterflies spinning in her belly, Liv nodded. She didn't need to think about it. It was crazy how comfortable she felt with Wolf. How...connected, even. But maybe that's what it felt like when you finally found someone who accepted you for exactly who you were, kinky fantasies and all.

Of course, it didn't hurt that Wolf was seriously one of the hottest men she'd ever seen. That their conversation over dinner had come so easily, so naturally. That he understood her so fundamentally that he seemed to know she'd been uncertain about having sex against the railing. And that he was a freaking *fantastic* lover. With a magically curved cock. Couldn't forget that.

My cock was made for your cunt.

No way was she ever going to hear those particular c-words again and not remember this night, this sex, this man.

"That was amazing, Liv," he said, withdrawing from her. "*You're* amazing." He kissed her sweetly, slowly, appreciatively.

"If I am," she whispered, "you bring it out in me, Wolf."

"Sweet, sweet woman." He held out a hand and helped her down from the tall stool, and then he wrapped her in the towel again. "Care for a swim before we go down?"

Smiling, she ventured to the pool's edge and dipped her toes in. "Oh, my God, it's really cold."

"That's why you're supposed to just jump in," Wolf said, laughing. "Now you're thinking about it being cold."

"No, Wolf, seriously. Feel it." She gave him a challenging look.

Smirking, he moved toward the pool, then picked up speed and dove in over the six-foot marker, his lean body a work of masculine art. Liv's jaw dropped. He was going to regret that. Like, *seriously* regret it.

He came up on a shout. "Fucking hell."

Liv burst out laughing. "I told you."

He turned in the water, his expression like he was half in shock. "It's...it's not b-bad," he said, not selling it at all when his teeth clattered like that. "I grew up in the coastal town of K-Karlshamn and spent my summers swimming in the Baltic Sea. This is n-nothing."

She wasn't buying that for a second. "Uh huh. I think that's the first lie you've told me, Wolf Henrikson. And I'm not falling for it for a second." She backed up from the edge as he swam closer, because no way she was getting pulled in there.

He licked droplets from his lips. That man was sexy even when he was freezing to death. "Water's fine. I'm a s-stout Swedish man. I have ice in my blood."

She shook her head, still chuckling. "Yeah, well, I'm a skeptical American woman and I call bullshit." Man, she enjoyed him when they weren't having sex, too. He was playful and funny and so easy to be around.

Grasping the ladder, he reared up out of the pool, water cascading off of his naked body. Now there was a mental image she wasn't going to forget anytime soon. Except before she could replay it in her mind's eye, he shook out his short hair and stalked toward her. "Can I have a hug, Olivia?"

She backed up. "I don't think so. I'll take a rain check, though," she said, giggling again.

He moved faster. She weaved to put a table between them, though his cock being out in the open was super distracting to her agility.

"Just one hug, Liv. Is that so much to ask?" he said, smiling too.

Shaking her head, she pointed to ward him off. "You keep your icy Swedish hands off me until they warm up. I warned you."

He feinted right, so she went left, but then he bolted the other direction and caught her around the hips. She screamed and tugged, but he held fast, and then he molded himself to her. Ice. He was like ice.

"Fuuck, you're warm," he moaned. The grit in his voice would've been sexy as hell if his touch hadn't almost been painful.

"Aaaah! Get off me," she said, laughing and twisting and fighting. "You're a human Popsicle!"

"Keep grinding against me and I'll give you a Popsicle," he said, laughing.

"I don't like Popsicles!" she shout-laughed as she gave him a shove.

But he held tight. "You like *my* Popsicle," he said, guffawing.

Giggles devolving into super sexy snorting, she kept struggling. "How can you have a Popsicle after that water?"

"Because you're the hottest woman I've had the pleasure of meeting in longer than I can remember," he said.

Liv nearly gasped at the compliment, at the sentiment, at the sudden seriousness in the midst of their horseplay. When had any man made her feel so sexy, so brave, so wanted? She twisted to face him and cupped his face in her hands. "Jesus, Wolf. What's happening here?" she whispered. Because it felt like a lot more than what should be possible after just one evening.

He shook his head. "Something good, Liv. That's all I know for sure."

"Yeah," she managed, emotion thick in her throat. Definitely something good. And it was such a surprise to her. She'd thought she'd gotten over Caleb, and she had. Mostly. But she hadn't realized until tonight—maybe even until this moment—that he'd still held some sway over her. Because Wolf's interest in her, his acceptance of her, his desire for her all chased something away she hadn't even realized she'd still held onto—a little niggle of doubt about whether she'd ever find any of that after everything that'd happened with her ex.

Wolf shivered.

Liv chuckled, and the sound was all lightness amid the strong rush of affection she was feeling for him. "So, stout Swedish man. How about a hot shower before you die of hypothermia?"

He gave her a wink. "God, yes."

They showered together, an intimacy Liv hadn't shared with anyone in so long.

"You can have the water first," he said, backing her under the rain-style shower head as he kissed her.

"No, you first," she said. "You need warming up. Seriously, Wolf. Your skin is still freezing."

"It's more important to me to take care of you," he said, tilting her head back and running his fingers through the length of her hair. Aw, man, this guy knew just what to say to make her melt. He reached for the shampoo. "Turn around." She did, and then he washed her hair for her. No man had ever done that before, and it felt so good she had to brace her hands against the shower wall in front of her to keep from swaying. "You're so damn sexy, Liv."

His voice roughened, but his hands kept strictly to washing her. Her hair, her body.

"Your turn now," she said. And damn, Wolf showering was something to see. He closed his eyes and tilted back his head. The water had turned his blond hair dark, and his position—hands at his reclined head—made all kinds of interesting muscles pop out and flex. "I wouldn't mind a camera right now," she mused, watching him.

His eyes popped open, and his cock stirred. "See something you like?"

She allowed herself a slow, lingering look. "Yes, sir, I do."

He was suddenly totally hard. "Jesus, Liv."

After that, he washed in a rush, toweled them both dry, and secured a towel around his hips again as she wrapped one under her arms, knotting it above her breasts. Then he guided her into the living room, where her dress still lay on the floor.

"Wolf, did I say something wrong—"

He whirled on her, his expression intense. "Olivia, get on your knees."

For a moment she gawped, her brain struggling to make sense of his behavior and his words. But everything inside her told her to just do it. *Kneel first, ask questions later.*

She knelt.

The tenting of his towel became more pronounced.

"Christ, you are..." He held out a hand to her. "Rise, please."

"Wolf, what is going on?"

"Would you come sit with me, Liv? There's something else I need to tell you."

* * * *

"No, you didn't do anything wrong," Wolf said, guiding them to sit on the couch. "In fact, you did something *so* right it's making me a little insane. So right for me." God, when the word *sir* had come out of her mouth, it'd been all he could do not to put her on her knees right that very second. And then he had, and she'd taken to the command without question or hesitation. "Olivia, I'm not just a voyeur, I'm also a Dominant."

"A sexual Dominant? Like, in BDSM?" she asked, her expression not as confused or as surprised as he expected.

"Yes, exactly."

"I wondered about that," she said. "I remember Willow and some of her bridesmaids talking about...stuff. And then when you reminded me that we'd met when you were one of Isaac's groomsmen, I wondered..."

He was going to need to send Isaac and Willow a fruit basket. Or offer to babysit their new little three-month-old. Because Liv's presence at their wedding was going to make this conversation go much better than it might've. A handful of times, Wolf had shared this about himself with women he'd met outside the lifestyle, and the reactions had run the full gamut. Repulsion. Disinterest or a feeling that it wasn't a fit. Or interest even though the woman wasn't truly submissive.

And true submissiveness couldn't be faked.

"How much do you know about dominance and submission, Liv?"

She gave a little shrug. "Not a lot, really. I mean, I've, er, watched some porn..." Her cheeks went pink at the admission.

"Come here," he said, putting his back into the corner of the couch and opening his legs to create a place for her to lay against him. "I need you closer."

Liv shifted so that her side was to his back, in his arms but still able to look him face to face. They smelled of the soap and the shampoo they'd shared, their bodies still warm from the shower. "Are you a member of their club, too?"

He chuckled. "The ladies were talkative that day, weren't they?"

Her expression dropped. "I'm not getting them in trouble, am I?"

"No, no. Not at all," he said, appreciating her protective instincts toward his friends. "I'm not just a member of the club, though. I'm one of Blasphemy's founders and owners. There are twelve Master Dominants who run it. Isaac, too. He and I joke that we're partners in both our day and night jobs. Each of us has areas of expertise on the operational side that we take turns managing. I work with Isaac on maintaining and overseeing the security systems and procedures."

"Okay," she said, suddenly frowning. "Wait. If you live in Baltimore, why did you have a hotel room?"

God, Wolf hoped this didn't make a difference to her, but she had a right to know. "Often, a Dom will meet prospective submissives in public places just to talk about their interests. Then, if things go well, they might come to some agreements about what they want and decide to do a scene. It doesn't always work that way. Sometimes, you just don't hit it off or you find your kinks or expectations aren't as well aligned as it seemed. Just in case the meeting does go well, I usually reserve a room, and I'd been stood up just before we met. In fact, I was getting ready to leave when I ran into you."

"Oh," she said.

Wolf studied her expression, a niggle of concern stirring in his gut. "Talk to me, Liv."

"I…I guess…that all makes sense."

"Damnit, I'm sorry if knowing I had other plans tonight makes you uncomfortable. I can only say that I truly believe this night went exactly as it was meant to be."

Liv shook her head. "Wolf, I was on a *date* when we met. I'm not upset that you'd had other plans, too. It just makes me realize how close we came to almost missing each other."

He kissed her because he felt the same way. "That would've been a tragedy, Liv."

She chuckled and nodded, running a finger down his bare chest, his abs, the semi-erect ridge of his cock beneath the towel. "Can you tell me more about what it means to be a Dominant?"

"First and foremost, it means that it's my responsibility to take care of my submissive in every way that she requires it. Her safety, her health, her pleasure. In a sexual scene, it's my job to read a submissive's body, her needs, her boundaries, and to create a connection through that scene that brings us both pleasure. It's more than just a role I play, though. It's an instinct, a need inside me, sexually and otherwise. It's just…who I am."

"That makes sense," she said. "And why did you tell me to get on my knees?"

Wolf just looked at her to see if she'd make the link herself. He really didn't think he had to spell it out.

"You think I'm a submissive?"

He rewarded her with a soft, deep kiss. "I think you *are* submissive. To know exactly what that means and what the expectations are within the lifestyle, though, would require training. But, yes, you're a natural."

"Even though I'm not shy or reserved?" she asked.

He rubbed his hand over her arm. "It's not about your personality, exactly. Strong men and women can be sexual submissives, Liv. One of my best friend's submissives is a former Marine. Submissives are often people who derive pleasure from obedience or being commanded. Or they derive pleasure from serving and pleasing another, or from being freed from decision making. For some, submissiveness is just what they need to achieve release. For others, it's not even about the sex so much as it is about being in service to another, in every way that might be required. Submission is a gift a submissive gives to a Dominant, and even though the Dom gives the commands, the sub can put a stop to it at any time. The submissive is in control because nothing happens without her or his consent."

"I see." Liv shifted on his lap, creating a gap in the towel between his legs. "You commanded me tonight, several times. And I… I liked it."

Wolf nodded, appreciating the methodical way she was approaching this, like she was taking apart what she knew and examining it from different angles. "You did."

"I-I've never had multiple orgasms during sex before," she said. "Is it awkward that I'm telling you this?"

He nearly groaned. "Not at all, Olivia. None of this works without open communication. That's why couples in the lifestyle often meet to talk about interests, limits, and expectations before anything sexual ever happens."

"Okay," she whispered. "Wow. This is...wow."

"Good wow or bad wow?" he asked, his gut clenching in case he was reading her wrong.

"Good wow," she said, with a little smile. "It's just...a lot to take in."

No doubt, and probably even more so when a lover had once made her feel bad about her sexual interests. "I'm not trying to push you into anything you don't want to do or explore, Liv. As you saw tonight, I don't have to be in full Dom mode to have sex or be dominant. But I also wanted you to know."

"I'm glad you told me, Wolf. And I'm definitely curious. I guess I sorta feel a little like Alice in Wonderland, except Wonderland was where I was always meant to be. I just didn't know how to get there. Or even if it was really real."

He nodded, appreciating the sentiment. "You're welcome down the rabbit hole with me any time, little Olivia."

She shifted again, and her voice came out husky. "You in full Dom mode must be...something."

He chuckled even as her words heated his blood. "If I were to put my fingers between your legs, would I find you wet?"

A shiver ran over her skin. "Yes," she finally answered.

That knowledge made him want to plant his face between her thighs again, but he wasn't getting distracted from this conversation until she'd asked every question she had. "What's turning you on, exactly?"

Pink filtered into her cheeks, and she ducked her chin. "Being close to you, for one."

He lifted her face with his fingers. "Look at me. I want you to see that there's nothing but acceptance here. Acceptance and interest, Liv. Okay?"

"Yes," she said, her eyes searching his. *Yes, Sir*, he heard. "Also, imagining what might go on in your club. All those eyes that might see what we do. And imagining how much more intense sex with you might be when you're in Dom mode."

"Would you like to find out the answers to those questions some time?" He nearly held his breath in anticipation of her answer.

"It's a little scary," she said. "But I think...yes. I would."

"Then you just name it. Any night you want. I'll take you to Blasphemy. And I'll introduce you to anything you want to explore."

Chapter 6

Liv applied the last touches to her makeup, her hands trembling just a little. Because she was going to a sex club tonight.

All week, she hadn't been able to stop thinking about what Friday night would bring.

Actually, that wasn't true. Half her thoughts were occupied by wondering about Friday night, the other half had been consumed with daydreaming about the incredible weekend she'd spent with Wolf.

Weekend. Not just night.

Neither of them had wanted to say good-bye on Saturday, so he'd extended his hotel reservation until Sunday, and they'd spent the time talking and walking around Baltimore's Inner Harbor and eating good food. Not to mention having more amazing sex. Against the window again. In the sauna at the gym. Against the door to the hotel room, so rough and loud there was no way people in the hall or other rooms hadn't heard.

Liv had loved every second of it. On some level, she'd feared that the seductive bubble in which they'd been secluded might burst once they were apart. But Wolf had allayed that concern by texting her throughout the week. Just to check in. Just to make her laugh. Just to tease.

And the result was that she'd been out of her mind with distractions and anticipation. So much so that, just this morning, she'd made an entire arrangement of red roses when the order was for pink.

She stepped into her heels just as the doorbell rang and spared herself one last glance in the mirror. Earlier in the week, she'd taken a picture of herself in a dress to make sure Wolf thought it was appropriate—because what did people wear to sex clubs???—and he'd told her that if she didn't wear it, he'd punish her.

Liv had no idea what that would entail exactly, but she'd worn the dress. A black vintage-inspired number with a formfitting cross halter top with a princess neckline, and a flared A-line skirt that ended just above the knees. She grasped her purse and rushed for the door.

And there Wolf was. Just as sexy as she remembered. Maybe sexier, standing as he was on the front porch of her townhouse wearing a pair of gray dress pants with shiny black shoes and a black button-down shirt. Rolled-up sleeves exposed his forearms.

"That picture did absolutely no justice to you in that dress, Liv," he said, drinking her in. He stepped right up to the threshold, took her face in his hand, and kissed her. A slow, exploring, lingering kiss, like he was tasting her, or sipping at her. It unleashed butterflies in her belly. "Hi," he said.

"Hi. And thank you." She grinned and suddenly felt on the verge of giddiness. For getting to see him again, for getting to go to Blasphemy, for getting to *be* with him again, whatever that might entail tonight. "Would you like to come in?" As he entered, she admired his ass in those pants. "Next time, though, I think you have to send me a picture of your outfit, too."

He arched a brow. "Why's that?"

She smirked. "So I can have a picture of..." She waved her hands at him. "...all *that* on *my* phone."

He chuckled and gave her a challenging look. "You can have any part of me on your phone that you want, Liv."

Her cheeks were hurting from smiling so much. "I'll keep that in mind."

"You do that," he said, surveying her living room. She tried to see it through his eyes. Large, framed Georgia O'Keeffe prints dominated her walls. *Petunias. Red Poppy. Jimson Weed.* The furniture was all neutrals, a cream-colored couch and chair and mission-style dark brown tables, to allow the flowers to stand out. A few framed photographs of family and friends filled one of the bookshelves. Once there had been more, but a lot of her friends had been Caleb's or law firm friends, and somehow, she'd lost or drifted apart from many of them when her relationship fell apart.

"Would you like the nickel tour?" she asked.

Wolf nodded. "I'd love to be able to picture you at home when we can't be together."

Gah! He took what could've been a simple *yes* and multiplied it by like a sexiness factor of at least a gabillion. At the back of the house, the kitchen and dining room were bright and airy, filled as they were with the rays of the setting sun.

She was just about to lead him to the staircase when she noticed him frowning at the vase of red roses on her table. Lest he get the wrong idea, she lightly rested her hands on his waist. "Today, I was so distracted that I made a client a bouquet of red roses when he'd ordered pink. I brought the mistake home to enjoy."

Those green eyes blazed at her. "Distracted, huh?"

"Very." She stepped in closer, until her breasts pressed against his chest. "Thinking about you is very distracting, Wolf."

His lips quirked in a crooked grin. "What if I said I liked you being distracted by me?"

Liv shrugged one shoulder and peered up at him. "Then I'd say keep doing what you're doing."

He licked his lips. "I think you'd better give me the rest of this tour before we never make it out of your house tonight."

Smiling, she led him upstairs. "Just my bedroom, a bathroom, and my office up here." She showed him the latter two before leading him into her bedroom. With her queen-sized bed, comfy reading chair, and two dressers, the room had never felt spacious. But now it seemed even smaller with Wolf there, eyeing her space like he was evaluating how and where he might take her. In point of fact, she was kinda looking around at the possibilities herself...

"You have a nice place, Liv. Comfortable and homey," he said.

"Thanks. I like it here. I can walk to the park and a coffee shop, and it's just a few bus stops to Flowers in Bloom."

He eased his big body to sit on the corner of the bed, then reached for her, bringing her to stand between his spread knees. "Do you have any questions before we go?"

She took a moment to think it through. He'd sent her information to read on Blasphemy, including the rules and membership information, which he informed Liv he'd be covering on her behalf; and on BDSM and submission, including instructions on safewords. He'd also sent her a list of activities for her to consider for her limits, which she'd checked off and stowed in her purse. "I'm sure I'll have a bunch of questions, but I feel like I won't know what most of them are until we're in the moment."

"Fair enough," he said.

"Can I still call you Wolf at Blasphemy?" she asked.

He pulled her to sit on his knee. "No. Please call me either Master Wolf or Sir. You should address all the Doms you meet this way. Sir is always safe if you're not sure."

Liv nodded, hoping she didn't mess up. Because there was a protocol to even speaking to Dominants or attached submissives that people observed. "I don't want to do anything to embarrass you."

"Not even possible, Olivia. I'll introduce you around, and everyone will understand that you're new and learning. And I won't leave you alone. Not even for a minute."

She smiled. "Okay, I'd appreciate it."

"Doing it as much for me as for you. If those roses made me temporarily insane, I can only imagine how I'd feel if another Dominant offered to play with you." He let the evidence of his possessiveness hang there until she was a little dizzy with it, and then he kissed her again. "Damn, sweetness, we gotta get out of here. Because I can't sit on your bed another second and not want to strip you down and bury myself deep."

"I'm not sure which you're trying to motivate me to want. Going or staying," Liv said with a little chuckle. She really adored how free Wolf was with his compliments, his praise, his desire for her.

"Tell me about it," he said. "But let's go. I want to show you off."

The words set her body on fire through the car ride across the city. Then they passed briefly through a public dance club called Club Diablo and spilled out into a private courtyard in front of an old church building. Liv spun around, taking in the nearly private oasis behind what appeared to have once been an old factory building. "No one would ever know this was here."

"The church was abandoned and in bad shape," Wolf said, squeezing her hand. "The city was going to tear it down. But my friends and I bought most of the block for both clubs. We thought this was perfect for the privacy our members want at Blasphemy."

"And it's beautiful," Liv said, looking up at the old steeple and the circular stained-glass window beneath it.

"Wait 'til you see it from the inside. The glass throws rainbows everywhere."

Inside, she gave Wolf—Master Wolf now—her checklist and stowed her purse in a locker, and then he led her out to a reception area where an intimidating-looking man sat behind the desk.

"Master Alex," Wolf said, greeting him. Which was when Liv noticed the black cuff around Wolf's wrist. Soft and worn. With an embroidered Gothic M. "I'd like to introduce you to Olivia Foster. She's my guest here tonight."

"Olivia," Master Alex said, standing. He had dark hair and darker eyes, almost piercing in their intensity. There was no denying the man was handsome, but there was something about him that, despite his politeness, was *too* intense for Liv. His gaze was hard to hold. "Welcome to Blasphemy."

"Thank you, S-Sir," she said, feeling a little self-conscious, like everyone would know she'd never done this before. She finally gave in to the urge to lower her gaze, and that's when she noticed that Master Alex wore a black cuff identical to Wolf's.

She sat and signed some paperwork while Wolf read over her checklist, and then Master Alex pulled out a drawer full of narrowed cuffs, a row of white and a row of red. He turned to Master Wolf, one eyebrow arched.

"Red," her Dom said.

Her Dom. The idea that he was hers, or could be hers, skittered tingles over her skin. "May I ask the difference? Sir?"

Wolf took the red leather into his hand. "White means unattached. Red means attached. I'd like you on your knees when I put it on your wrist."

Attached? He wanted her to wear something proclaiming her as his? She remembered what he'd said in her bedroom and how he'd looked upon seeing her roses, and part of her wasn't surprised. But it still spoke to a seriousness that made her feel like she could float.

"Now, Sir?" she whispered, half rising from the chair at the desk. She felt Master Alex's eyes on her, but she knew that she shouldn't look anywhere but at Master Wolf.

"Now, Olivia."

She sank directly from the chair to the floor, knees apart, like she'd read about, and eyes up on him.

"God, that's beautiful," Master Wolf said, seemingly comfortable saying such things in front of the other man. "Present your wrist, please. Right."

She held up her hand, and he fastened the red leather snugly around her skin. It was one of the most fascinating things she'd ever seen, because it made her feel claimed in a way she hadn't felt in so long. Possibly even ever. "Thank you, Sir," she managed.

He helped her rise and pressed a kiss to the soft spot above the cuff on the inside of her wrist. "You feel ready?"

"As ready as I can be. I'm a little nervous, but as long as we're together, I'll be fine," she said, being completely honest. Because she was excited, but she was also a bundle of nerves. About what she might see, about who she might see, about what might happen on the other side of the doors across the room, from which the bass beat of music was just audible.

"Count on it, sweetness," Master Wolf said.

"Olivia?" Master Alex said.

She peered at the other Dom, a cautionary awareness tingling down her spine. What was it about him that set her so on edge? "Yes, Sir?"

"Have a good night," he said. "It was nice to meet you."

"Thank you. You, too," she said.

Master Wolf shook the other man's hand, then led them through two sets of double doors until they finally entered the back of what was once the church. Olivia gasped. It was *gorgeous*.

At both ends of the vaulted ceiling, large circular stained-glass windows cast colors over the space—and the sun was setting. She could only imagine what the place would look like during the height of the day, when the side windows might be illuminated, too. Soaring frescoes covered the walls, and a large circular bar sat in the center of what had once been the nave. Leather couches and chairs sat here and there, some of them made private by arrangements of large-leafed tropical plants—palms, philodendrons, and bromeliads, to name a few. Against the beauty and elegance of the setting, the decadence of the music, people's costumes, and various sex acts happening where Liv could see or hear them, it was hard to know where to focus first.

She was at once enthralled by everyone's openness and a little shocked by it. Once, Caleb had made her feel ashamed for wanting to play out a fantasy with the man who was going to be her husband, and here was a whole club devoted to playing out fantasies—right out in the open where everyone could see.

"This is just the main floor of the club," Wolf said, pointing a few things out to her. The locker rooms, the public bathrooms, some dungeon furniture, a stage now used for demonstrations where the altar had been, a hallway down which private play rooms were located on multiple floors. In the middle of the space before the stage, a crowd of people danced under flashing lights to the pulsing, chanting, electric music.

"It's a little overwhelming," she admitted as he brought her to the bar. With the marble countertop and iron accents, it had an interesting vibe that was both modern and antique.

"I've got you, Olivia. I promise." He found a seat for her and raised his hand to the bartender.

The man headed their way, and he quite possibly had the best smile Olivia had ever seen. One that seemed a second from splitting into a grin or a laugh. One that might just as easily indicate he was up to no good. "Master Wolf," the man said gregariously. "How the hell are ya?"

"Master Quinton. I couldn't be better tonight. I'd like to introduce you to my Olivia." *My* Olivia! Liv didn't think she was imagining the pride—or the pleasure—in Wolf's voice.

"My, my, little Olivia. Welcome to Blasphemy. Where has my good friend been hiding *you*?" Master Quinton asked, holding out a hand that requested hers.

She looked to Wolf, and he gave her a nod, so she returned the shake. "Hi, Master Quinton. It's nice to meet you." He was a good-looking guy, but it was his humor and personality that created at least half of his charm, which was overflowing.

"Of course it's nice to meet me. I'm the awesomest. So awesome I'm sure Master Wolf hasn't been able to stop talking about me," he said, arching a brow.

She couldn't help but laugh. Where Master Alex set her on edge, Master Quinton put her right at ease and made her feel like an old friend, two things good bartenders often did quite naturally. "I'm very sorry to say, Sir, that Master Wolf has been otherwise indisposed."

Quinton barked out a laugh. "I like you, Olivia. You take care of this guy, okay? He's one of the good ones." He winked at Wolf and took their drink order, a whiskey for Wolf and a glass of champagne for Liv. The club had a two-drink-per-player maximum, but Liv didn't want more than the one. She wanted her senses about her tonight so she didn't miss a thing.

"Otherwise indisposed, indeed," Wolf said, giving her a smile. He led her to a couch partway between the bar and the dance floor, and guided her to sit between his legs as he had in their hotel room. Their position gave her a nearly three-sixty view of the club's main space—and the various activities in it. "Liking what you're seeing so far?" he whispered against her ear.

Liv nodded as she sipped at her champagne and tried to take it all in. A woman in spiked boots danced with a man wearing assless pants, and it was clear from the red handprints on the man's skin who was in control of that relationship. A man gave another man a blow job against the wall just past the dance floor. And a woman was tied spread-eagled to an X-shaped piece of furniture while two of the Master Doms—judging by the black cuffs they wore—tormented her with what looked like pleasure, given the woman's cries. "It's weird that I've had this hang-up when everyone here is so open."

Nodding, Master Wolf's gaze trailed to the threesome on the big X. "That's a St. Andrew's cross, and those are Master Jonathan and Master Cruz. They usually dominate a submissive together. How would you feel to be in that submissive's place?"

"With two Doms?" Liv asked, her gaze cutting back to the three of them. The blond-haired Dominant was on his knees, using his mouth and his hands between the woman's legs, while the dark-haired Dom smacked her breasts with a short instrument full of soft-looking black tails.

"Does that intrigue you?" Master Wolf asked.

"I..." She swallowed hard, her pulse picking up. "I wouldn't mind being her, being tied down and exposed to everyone. But two men seems a little…more than I'm ready for."

He turned her in his lap enough that they could see eye to eye. "It took me so long to find you, Olivia. I have no intention of sharing you." Relief flooded through her, and she nodded. "But I'm intrigued at this idea of tying you down and tormenting you while everyone watches. Maybe someday—" He pointed to the stage at the far end of the room. "—I'll get you up there and make a whole show out of you."

Liv's pulse spiked just imagining it. "Okay, Sir," was all she could manage to say.

Master Wolf laughed. "Don't worry. We'll work up to that."

She smiled. "Yes, please."

"Mmm. I remember the first time you said those words to me." Wolf pulled her to him for a kiss, forcing her to turn until she was straddling him on the couch. A million pairs of eyes landed on her back, watching them kiss, watching Wolf's hands run over her thighs and under her skirt. On a groan, he pulled away long enough to place their drinks on the end table. And then he was right back to her, penetrating her mouth with his tongue, dragging rough hands over her skin.

Knowing people were watching and hearing moans and cries of ecstasy from all around her, Liv was quickly needy and wet and a little dizzy with lust. And then Wolf's hands landed on her ass, rubbing and squeezing, his fingers digging in and making her wetter. "Wolf," she moaned.

Smack! His hand landed hard and unexpectedly against her left butt cheek. "How do you address me here?"

Oh God! "Master Wolf. I'm sorry," she said. The surprise of the spank unleashed twin reactions through her—a little humiliation and a whole lot of arousal. The latter confused her, even as she couldn't deny it. "I'm sorry, Sir."

His fingers curled into the waistband of her panties. "Rise and remove these. And bend at the waist when you drag them down your legs."

Liv's heart was suddenly a runaway train in her chest, racing fast and picking up steam. He helped her off his lap, and then she was standing in front of him. But not before she'd met the curious, interested gazes of a few of the onlookers around them. With a shiver, she met Wolf's gaze, too. His eyes were green fire.

It bolstered her. She bent over, reached under her skirt, and grasped the black silk-and-lace boy shorts. And then she slowly dragged them down her legs until she stepped out of them, one leg at a time.

He held out his hand, and she placed the panties into his palm. "Do you remember your safewords, Olivia?"

"Yes, Sir," she said.

"Use them if you need them." He arched a brow.

She nodded. "I will, but I don't need to, Sir."

"Good." The sternness on his face was so damn hot. "Then lift your skirt and turn around in a circle. I want to see what I'll be having tonight."

A shiver rocked through her, especially since she had a little surprise for him. Eyes on Wolf, she lifted the covering material up around her waist. If she thought she'd been wet before, it was nothing compared to how she felt now that she was standing in the middle of a room full of people showing off her bare ass and newly waxed pussy.

Wolf's eyes went wide. "Very nice, Olivia."

She turned in a circle, realizing that he'd made her do this so she'd see the audience that they were drawing. Her face and her body were equally on fire as she turned back to him.

He rose, made a big show of folding her panties and slipping them into his pocket, and then nodded. "You may drop your skirt."

Shakily, she let the material go, and felt torn between relief and regret.

He stepped in close. "That disappointed you, didn't it? Covering back up."

Relief or regret? Relief or regret? "A little, Sir," she was forced to admit.

"Hmm." He stepped back again, crossed his arms, tilted his head. Looked at her like he was evaluating. "That dress, it's all wrong, I think."

"What?" She looked down at herself, even more confused now. "You don't like it, Sir?"

"Too much, I think. I don't want anything to happen to it." Suddenly, he unbuttoned his own shirt. One button after another, with fast, furious flicks of his fingers. He whipped the black cotton off his shoulders, leaving him bare from the belt up. *God*, he looked freaking good. Cocky and confident, like a powerful businessman about to fuck his secretary on the conference room table in front of the entire board. Shirt in hand, his eyes narrowed. "Where did you go just now?"

"Here. I'm right here, Master Wolf," she said, her body's responses overwhelming. She'd never felt so aroused in her life, and it was almost too much to handle.

He shook his head. "Tell me. What were you just thinking about? I saw it on your face, Olivia. I want to know."

For just a second, she squeezed her eyes shut, and then she let the words spill. "It just...it just flashed into my mind when you took off your shirt. That you looked like...*oh God...*" She opened her eyes again.

"What?" he asked, nailing her with a hot, demanding stare.

"Like a powerful businessman about to have sex with his secretary on the conference room table in front of his board," she rushed out, face flaming.

His grin was slow and sly. "That's a hot fucking fantasy. I do love how your brain works, little Olivia." Without another word or any other preamble, he reached under her skirt and swiped his fingers between her legs.

She nearly screamed at the contact, so startled by it that she had to clutch at his biceps to steady herself.

He brought his hand between their faces. His fingers glistened with her arousal. Watching her watch him, he sucked the wetness into his mouth.

A little moan spilled unbidden from her throat.

"God, you're hot for this, aren't you?" he whispered.

"Yes, Sir."

"Just how far can I push you, Olivia?" he asked, his eyes searching hers. "Just how far are you willing to go?"

The question made her shiver again. As if her nervous system had been plugged into an electrical outlet, she couldn't seem to stop. Still, she knew she didn't want this night to end with her regretting that she hadn't been brave enough to go for something she wanted. And she wanted this. She wanted Wolf. She wanted him in full Dom

Chapter 7

Wolf hadn't planned to push Olivia so hard so fast, but he also hadn't expected her to get so hot so fast. He suspected that if he'd left his hand between her legs for five more seconds, she could've come just from that little contact.

He fucking *loved* how turned on she was. Her breathing came fast. Her pulse jumped at her throat. Her eyes were dilated. And she couldn't stop shivering from the adrenaline he guessed absolutely flooded her system. She'd been so wet that she'd soaked his fingers from just one touch.

So he was going to push her, all right. Because he was suddenly ravenous to learn just how far he could take her, how far they could go *together*. He was flying because of how high *she* was flying, as if they were connected on a physiological level, as if her heart pulsed his blood. Damnit all to hell, but the connection they shared was blowing his mind. Because he hadn't been sure he'd ever find anything like it.

And then he met Liv.

On a shaky exhale, she reached for the zipper under her arm and undid the bodice of her dress. As she slipped out of the straps, he realized she wore no bra beneath it, which meant that disrobing immediately bared her beautiful, full breasts with their tightly erect nipples. Just like he'd requested before, she bent at the waist to push the dress down over her legs, and then she stepped out of the circle of material and rose again, clutching it to her front.

He shook his head and held out his hand. She gave him the dress. And then Wolf debated how he wanted to make her come.

"Too bad I don't have a boardroom table here," he said with a wink. Her cheeks flushed brilliantly, making him chuckle. "God, you're fucking beautiful."

She swallowed hard, and Wolf dropped her dress and his shirt to the couch, then went to her, drew her into his arms against him, and turned her so that his body mostly shielded hers. Now the crowd's eyes were on his back, but that meant that Olivia was forced to face everyone watching them.

"Wrap your arms around my shoulders," he said.

She hugged him, removing the last of the distance between their chests.

"Keep your eyes open while you come," he whispered, grinding his hard cock against her hip. He wanted her drunk with the pleasure that feeding her exhibitionist fantasies could provide. He wanted her to *see* exactly what they could be. Together.

"Sir?" she asked.

He cupped her pussy in his hand, pulling something close to a scream from her throat. "And say my name when you do," he growled, his fingers circling her clit.

The first orgasm hit almost immediately, and Olivia nearly shrieked, "Master Wolf!" as it made her shudder and moan.

"Again," he said, his movements alternating between firm circles against her clit and long strokes between her thighs that skimmed her opening.

"Oh God," she said, more of her weight hanging on his shoulders as her legs grew weak. "I'm going to...oh God." He pressed harder, faster. "M-Master Wolf, I'm c-coming," she nearly cried.

While her body still trembled, he kicked her stance wider. "*Again.*" He penetrated her pussy with his middle finger, using the heel of his hand to provide friction against her clit. She was soaking wet, slick and so damn tight. It was all he could do to avoid taking her to the couch and fucking her right there.

But it wasn't time. Not yet. He wanted to draw this out for her. He wanted to give her the whole fantasy. He wanted to let her experience that for which another man had made her feel ashamed.

So he let his fingers have what his cock badly wanted, masturbating her there in the club, his hand and her thighs wet with her come. "Christ, feel that pussy, Olivia."

Her hold tightened on his shoulders, her fingers digging in. "They're all watching," she rasped.

"Because your orgasms are fucking beautiful. Give them something else to see. Do it now," he said, finger fucking her hard, grinding his palm more firmly.

She thrust her hips to match the strokes of his hand. "Yes," she whined. "Yes, yes, yes."

The third orgasm stole her legs out from under her, and he caught her with an arm around her waist while she was still coming, while her pussy was still squeezing at his finger inside her. "Master Wolf," she chanted. "Master Wolf, Master Wolf."

"Jesus," he rasped, more turned on by her shattered surrender than he'd possibly ever been in his life. Scooping her into his arms, he cradled her against his body, and then he carried her to a more private grouping of seats on the far side of the room, away from the dance floor, tucked behind a wall that separated the old nave from a side hallway. He sat with her in his lap, his hand stroking her hair as the aftershocks of her orgasms continued to roll through her. "Just rest. I've got you."

It only took a few moments before one of the submissive waiters came to check on them. "A blanket, right away," Wolf ordered. "And when you have a chance after that, please retrieve our clothes from the couch behind the bar and bring us two bottles of water."

"Yes, Sir," the shirtless, shoeless young man said. He wore only a pair of Spandex short shorts and the white cuff that identified him as an unattached submissive. In less than a minute, he assisted Wolf in covering Olivia with a black fleece blanket. And within another five, he'd returned with the other requested items.

"I feel a little drunk," Olivia said when the man left them. Her bright turquoise eyes peered up at him, soft and sleepy. "I didn't think I had that much champagne…"

He smiled, adoring the way she was looking at him. "I think you're flirting with subspace, sweetness. Enjoy it."

"What's that?" she asked, the words a little slurred.

Subspace, for sure. "It's an intense, altered headspace some submissives achieve from the intensity of a BDSM scene or the intensity of release. It can feel like a lot of different things, from being sleepy to feeling drunk to almost becoming trancelike."

"Oh," she said with a breathy laugh. "I see. Master Wolf?"

"Yes?" He stroked the hair back off her face, loving being close to her, holding her, basking in the trust and affection plain in her expression. They'd only known each other for a week, but Wolf still felt a surprisingly strong connection to her, an unexpectedly deep desire for her. And not just sexually, though that was there in spades.

"When can we do that again?"

He burst out laughing, setting her off chuckling, too. "Eager, are we?"

"For that? Yes, Sir. Very eager, Sir." She grinned up at him. "Super. Eager."

"Greedy little submissive," he said, trying but failing to give her a stern look. He handed her some water and watched with satisfaction as she drank down half of the bottle. It made him want to feed her, to watch her eat from his hand, to sate her needs in another way. In *every* way. "What did you think of what we just did?" he asked after a moment.

Her gaze went distant. "It was...amazing. Overwhelming. A little scary at first, but then it was like, I don't know. I knew the people were there and that they were watching, but it became nearly impossible to concentrate on that. All I could feel was you and your hand and the way your words impacted my body. I never wanted it to stop but I also felt like I might die if it went on another second." She blinked. "Does that make any sense?"

"Total sense. I think you're articulating all this very well." And Wolf really appreciated that—that she could tell him with such specificity exactly what she was experiencing. It confirmed just how into this she was—and therefore just how right they were together.

More than that, the fundamental pleasure she got from this reminded him of how it all used to make him feel, too. Blasphemy was still new and risky and overwhelming to her, the people all strangers, and therefore, the stakes were high for her here even though it was a safe environment for her to play out these fantasies. And it not only reminded him of the edgy thrill he used to feel more of, it made him actually feel it again, too. And he cherished the hell out of that. He really did.

Being with Olivia Foster was giving him back something he'd been starting to fear he was losing. It was like getting a piece of *himself* back. And that played with things in his chest that hadn't stirred in a very long time. Maybe not ever.

And it was all because of the beautiful woman in his arms.

Right where he wanted her to stay. "Think you'd be up for dancing?" he asked.

"Like this?" she asked, her eyes going a little wide as she peered down at the blanket covering her nudity.

He chuckled. "Not naked, no. Though I don't dislike the idea, Olivia. Not one bit."

Smirking, she nodded. "I'd love to, then."

They rose, and she reached for her dress, but Wolf shook his head and pointed to the black cotton beside it. "Wear that."

"Y-yes, Sir," she said, slipping into his dress shirt. It was long enough that it just covered her ass in the back and the soft bareness of her pussy in the front.

"Just one button, I think," he said, securing the center one for her. "I meant to put this on you earlier, but then you distracted me with your dirty thoughts."

"I think you like my dirty thoughts," she said, a little shyly.

"I *know* I like your dirty thoughts." He winked, then he stood back and drank in the image of her like that. His shirt and a pair of high heels and the submissive cuff that proclaimed her as unavailable to anyone else but him. Damn. He wouldn't be forgetting *that* any time soon. "I love you in dresses, but I have to say, I'm a sucker for you wearing my shirts."

"I like it, too," she said softly.

"Do you now?" he asked, getting closer.

"Yes, Sir," she whispered.

"Those words from your lips make me so hard," he whispered back. Wolf pressed her palm over his pants against his hard cock.

She licked her lips and swallowed. "I like this even more."

"Jesus," he bit out, putting her hand in his. "Dance floor. Now."

They moved to the center of the large Friday-night crowd and swayed to a slower song, her loose breasts and hips brushing up against him so damn good. Then the music changed to a faster techno song with a grinding beat that was all sex set to music. She rubbed her ass against him. He made her ride his thigh as they swung their hips to the beat. Her shirt gaped open and drew up as she moved, earning them stares and appreciative glances that were setting Wolf's blood on fire.

Hers too, judging by the wetness he found when his fingers explored between her thighs.

Given how aroused he was, dancing with Liv was a beautiful torture. And it made his mind whirl with possible plans. He was going to fuck her tonight. The question was how and when and where.

He spun her so her back was to his bare chest again, and then he wrapped his arms tight around her front, molding her to him. Keeping them moving, he pressed his mouth to her ear. "I could fuck you right here in the middle of all these people. Just pull my hard cock out and sink deep."

"God, yes," she moaned, her head falling back to his shoulder. "Please, Master Wolf."

"I can almost feel it. How tightly your cunt would squeeze my dick, both of us standing up, our hips rolling and grinding. And then when I couldn't stand it anymore, I'd make you brace your hands against your knees, grab you by the hips, and hammer my cock into you so hard and fast you'd scream my name as all these people watched."

"I'm so close already," she whimpered. "So close, Sir."

"Yeah?"

She gave him a fast nod and pleading eyes.

He reached out and tapped on the shoulder of the Dom dancing immediately in front of Olivia. Wolf didn't know the man well, but that didn't matter. He just wanted an audience. Up close and personal. "Excuse me, but would you and your submissive be willing to watch my submissive orgasm?"

My submissive. Wolf fucking loved the way that sounded. He hoped she loved it, too. Even more, he hoped she might grow to want that with him.

The man looked at his little one and nodded. "It would be our pleasure."

Olivia moaned and a breath shuddered out of her.

"Thank you, Sir," Wolf said, and then he placed one hand on

Olivia's throat and the other on her cunt, his fingers delving immediately and forcefully deep. "Don't come until I tell you to. And say *thank you* when it's over. Understand?"

"Yes, Sir," she nearly shouted as her fingers fisted in the sides of his pants.

He circled and stroked and tipped his middle finger inside her until she was babbling and begging and writhing against him. He didn't want her to fail, so he knew this couldn't last long, but he was going to draw it out as long as he could. For her.

"Don't come, Olivia. Not yet," he growled, their scene drawing more eyes as his hand worked her.

"Please, please, please, Sir," she whined, her hips rocking and straining.

He ripped her shirt open, popping the single secured button, and grabbed one breast in a tight hold. "Now. Come now."

Her body went taut and she held her breath for long seconds, and then she shuddered from head to toe, a high-pitched moan ripping out of her. "Thank you, thank you, thank you, M-Master..."

Flying high from the sheer intensity of her orgasm—and from how she'd just referred to him as if he were *her* Dominant and not just a Dominant—Wolf held her as her muscles went slack.

"Thank you for sharing something so beautiful with us," the other Dom said, a strain in his voice.

"Thank you, Sir," the man's sub said, her expression aroused, appreciative, envious.

"So good," Wolf rasped into Olivia's ear as he turned her into his chest. Despite the fast music, he swayed them gently, allowing her the time to get her legs back under her.

Her hands clutched at his shoulders as if he were her anchor. He wanted to be.

Goddamnit, but every minute he spent with her made that feeling stronger and stronger. Somehow, seven days ago, he'd been stood up and found his forever in one fell swoop.

* * * *

Liv could barely stand, barely think, barely breathe. And it was the best she'd felt in her whole life.

And it was all because of Wolf.

The man seemed to know her better than she knew herself. Because every time she thought, *I don't know if I can do this*, he proved that she could. And that she'd freaking love it.

He got her the way no one else ever had. Even Caleb, whom she'd been with for three years before they'd split. Which just went to show that time wasn't the only—or maybe even the best—indication of how well you knew someone. Or how well they knew you.

Her night with Wolf at Blasphemy had been amazing. The orgasms—obviously. But it was more than that. Wolf in full Dom mode was something to behold. The look in his eyes. The commanding tone of his voice. Even the way he held himself was slightly different—bolder, fiercer, taller. It spoke to something inside her, a voice she'd never before listened to, but that she now felt as if it'd always been calling out.

They'd danced for a long time after he made her come in front of that couple, until they were tired and sweaty and their voices grew hoarse from talking over the music. He'd introduced her to a few more people. Master Quinton's submissive, Cassia, who Liv hadn't had much chance to speak to because they were leaving to do a scene. Another Master named Griffin, and his submissive, Kenna, the former Marine that Wolf had mentioned. The four of them chatted for a while, long enough to learn that Kenna was assistant director of a veterans' outreach and advocacy association, and that she was interested in talking to Liv about providing the centerpieces for some of their events.

By the time they'd left, Liv couldn't wait to return. God, she really hoped they would. As Wolf drove his sleek Audi A8 away from the valet stand, he took her hand and held it against his thigh, giving her the courage to voice those wishes. "I really enjoyed myself, Master Wolf. I hope we can go again some time."

He brought their hands to his mouth and kissed her knuckles. "It's just Wolf now, Liv. And I'd like to take you there regularly, if you were interested. I'd like you to be mine."

The words unleashed a fluttery warmth in her chest that she hadn't felt in so long. But she knew what it was. Affection. Maybe even something more. *Probably* something more. "To be yours?" she asked.

"Yeah," he said, cutting a heated glance her way. "And not just at Blasphemy, either."

She squeezed his hand, not needing to think about it. Not with the way he was making her feel. There was something important happening here. Something big. Something good. Whatever it was, she wanted it. "Okay."

"Okay?" He arched a brow, green eyes flashing in the passing city lights.

"Yes. I'd like that, too."

"All right, then," he said, shifting his hips and making it clear he was aroused.

Which reminded her of the only thing she might've changed about the night—they hadn't had sex. And despite all the orgasms she'd had, she ached to feel Wolf inside her, for him to experience the same intense satisfaction that she had. Especially after what they'd just said to each other.

She leaned over and pressed her head to his shoulder. "Wolf?"

"Yeah, sweetness?"

She smiled at the term of endearment. "I want to make you come."

"Jesus," he said, shifting his hips again and chuckling. "You're killing me, Liv. I'm so fucking hard I can barely stand it."

She peered up at him, wanting to see the desire she heard reflected on that handsome, angled face. And it was. Oh, it was. She squeezed his cock through the pants, and the groan that spilled out of him was a heady thing. "I could suck you."

"Oh, Olivia, I will definitely be taking you up on that. But not tonight. Tonight, I'm going to be balls deep in your pussy. But we're both just going to have to be patient for a few more minutes." He removed her hand from where he throbbed but didn't let her go.

So, of course, now she burned with curiosity about what he might have up his sleeve. Was he going to take them back to her place and make her bed smell of hot Wolf and hotter sex? Because she wouldn't object to that at all. Or was he planning something else?

It only took another ten minutes before she found out.

Chapter 8

Patterson Park was just three blocks from Liv's house, a big green space in the middle of Baltimore, and one of the main reasons she'd bought a house where she did. Liv loved the park's community garden, its boat lake, the many events held there, and the beautiful Pagoda building that rose high enough that you could see down to the water and over to Fort McHenry from the top of it.

But Wolf didn't guide her to any of those locations. Instead, he took her to one of the pavilions filled with picnic tables and lit only dimly by the occasional path lights. Tension thick between them, neither of them spoke until the moment Wolf sat heavily on one of the benches in the middle of the pavilion, undid his pants and sheathed his cock, then pulled her to him.

"Fucking ride me, Olivia. Ride me so goddamn hard."

She was nearly trembling with need and adrenaline. She cast a glance at their surroundings, lifted her skirt over her still-bare ass, and centered herself over him. "Oh my God," she groaned as she impaled herself on his hard length.

His hands clamped down on her hips, holding her deep, forcing her to take all of him. Anyone who happened upon them would see a woman in a 1950s-style party dress sitting on a man's lap, never knowing she was stuffed full of his cock. But, *God*, Liv was just that. And it was so damn good.

"Move," he growled. "Fuck me."

"Yes," she moaned, bracing her hands on his knees as she lifted and lowered herself on his thick erection.

"Been dying for you all night," he rasped as they moved. "Been dying to make you mine."

Moaning, she kept up the deep ups and downs, her gaze scanning for witnesses, her mind half hoping to find them. Cars passed just a half block over and a couple's dark silhouette moved across a distant path. On such a nice night, all kinds of people were likely to be out, though the lateness of the hour would play in their favor.

Still, Liv could barely believe she was fucking someone in the middle of the park.

Or that she was so aroused that she was going to have to bite her lip to keep from screaming when she came. It didn't seem to matter that she'd come so many times earlier, because her body was winding up hard. From the risk of what they were doing. From the way Wolf's hands dug into her sides and hips and thighs through her dress. From the curses and dirty words spilling from his mouth.

"Christ, that pussy is so tight this way. I can't fucking get deep enough," he said, slamming her down and forcing a loud moan out of her.

Suddenly, he stood them up, bent her over the picnic table opposite them, and slapped a hand over her mouth. With his other hand, he flipped up her skirts, baring her ass to the night. And then he drilled her mercilessly hard and fast. All she could do was brace against the table and take what he gave her until she was screaming against his palm and he was groaning against her back, his hips jerking through each delicious spasm of his release.

"Fuck," he panted, dropping his forehead against her spine. "Jesus fuck."

His voice sounded wrecked, and it was the best thing she'd ever heard. She was so happy that tears suddenly sprung to her eyes and truths spilled out of her she hadn't even fully thought through. "This was the best night of my life, Wolf. Thank you."

"Aw, sweetness," he said, withdrawing from her and putting their clothes back together again. And then he drew her into his arms and held her close, his hand in her hair, his face pressed to hers. "Me, too, Liv. Something in you calls to something in me so strongly that you make me realize that my life hasn't been as complete as I thought. Not until now. I'm sorry if that's a lot to admit already, but—"

She shook her head. "It's not. Because I feel it, too." And so much more besides. All that emotion seemed like it should've been impossible already, but that didn't make the warm pressure in her chest any less present.

"I'm so damn glad," he said, tilting her head back for a sweet, tender kiss. "Let's get you home now."

"You could stay the night…if you want. I make a mean pancake," she said, her belly giving a little flip. Because he was right; despite the admissions they'd both made, this thing between them *was* moving fast. And she didn't want to overstep.

"I'd love nothing more than to fall asleep with you in my arms," he said, melting her heart. Then he grinned. "And to make your bed smell like me."

"Hmm. I was hoping you'd make the bed smell like *us*."

"Damn, Liv. You are perfect for me. You know that?"

She beamed at that, just a little bit. Perfect. It was the right word for how they seemed to fit together. That was amazing. But it was also kinda dizzying—how could she have found something this right, this true, this real…so fast? Could it truly be real? And could it truly last when three years with Caleb had ended in betrayal and humiliation?

"And pancakes would be amazing. Or I could take you to a restaurant and make you come underneath the tablecloth while the waiter watches," he deadpanned.

His voice chased the insecurities away, and Liv guffawed. "Well, that's an idea, too." They both laughed. And they were still laughing a half hour later when they crawled into her bed, her back spooned to his front, while he told story after story about funny things from his childhood, and that'd happened at Blasphemy, or that his friends had done. Just getting-to-know-you kinds of stories you told about your life and all the things that'd come before you met another person. Liv adored how much she enjoyed talking to Wolf, hearing about his life and his friends and his family, and how much they laughed, too.

She fell asleep mid-sentence, or maybe he did. Liv wasn't sure. Either way, she drifted off smiling with the knowledge that, despite their exhaustion, neither of them had wanted to give up on the magic of the day or the amazing connection they already shared.

* * * *

"Knock, knock," came a man's deep voice from behind him.

For maybe the tenth time, Wolf turned from the bank of computer monitors in Blasphemy's security control room to see who needed him for what. Tonight was one of their quarterly Blasphemous Friends nights, an open house of sorts where current members could invite pre-vetted prospectives for a special night exploring everything the club had to offer. Those who demanded strict privacy avoided these nights like the plague, but the events were a main way they expanded their membership base—and Blasphemy's operating income. And they required a shit-ton of advance work the day of the event to ensure they'd provided for every pleasure—and planned for every contingency.

But instead of some new problem walking through his door, Wolf found Isaac and Willow and a not-so-little baby boy in Willow's arms. "Three of my favorite people, right there," he said, rising from the chair.

He shook Isaac's hand and gave Willow a hug around the baby. Wolf had always thought her name was perfect, because she was tall and thin and so damn graceful she almost seemed to float. The two of them had met during a masquerade ball at the club three years ago, gotten married two years ago, and had this little bruiser here four months ago.

"Vaughn, my man, are you going to be Blasphemy's thirteenth Master?" Wolf asked, taking the chunky babe into his arms. "Because I bet you're already in charge at home." In response, the boy blew bubbles and Isaac laughed proudly.

"Pardon my saying so, Master Wolf," Willow said. "But bite your tongue. What is it with you Doms, trying to corrupt my sweet boy?"

Grinning, Wolf shrugged. "Sex on the brain?"

Isaac nodded. "Sounds about right."

"Well, Vaughn does *not* have sex on the brain," she said, crossing her light brown arms and giving both of the men in the room some serious stink eye.

"*Baby*," Isaac said to Willow. "You see how much he likes his penis. I'm just saying…"

Wolf busted out laughing. "It starts that early, huh?"

Willow rolled her eyes. "Apparently. Boys and their penises. If you don't cover the dang thing up quickly when you're changing him, you either get peed on or he manages to grab it in his little fist."

This time, Isaac and Wolf said it together, "Sounds about right."

"Oh, respectfully, Sirs, you two are hopeless. I'm going to go show him off to Master Quinton. He won't try to corrupt him."

Which set the men off laughing again. It was possible that Quinton was worse than any of them. In all the best possible ways.

Isaac dropped into a chair and scrubbed at his face. "What's new? You've been doing so much covering here and at our shop for me that I feel out of the loop."

"You've pulled plenty of weight, Isaac. Your priorities are right where they should be with your new family. Don't even give it a second thought," Wolf said, truly happy for everything his friend had found with Willow and Vaughn. Wolf himself should be so lucky, which of course had him thinking of Liv…

Nearly a month had passed since their first night at Blasphemy. And they'd been back at least once a week since. But they saw each other much more often than that, because for the past two weeks, they'd taken to spending many nights together at one of their houses. They'd have dinner and end up together. Or they'd stay up late watching a movie and fall asleep on the couch. Or they'd be so goddamned horny for each other that they just couldn't stand to part.

And, damn, the sex. The sex was a freaking revelation. And not just scenes at Blasphemy, either. The more Wolf exposed Olivia to, the more she wanted to try. They'd had sex in one of the bathrooms at Club Diablo, in the back of an otherwise empty matinee movie, on his sixth-floor apartment balcony overlooking a busy city street, and in her stock room during the workday. He'd fulfilled the threat of making her come at a restaurant more than once—with his fingers and with a remote-controlled bullet vibrator. And she'd blown him in a clothing store dressing room and in his car too many times to count.

Liv's excitement and enthusiasm made him feel alive again, making him realize just how much he'd been coasting these past few years. And he loved her for it.

He loved her.

Jesus, he really did.

"Wolf? Earth to Wolf." Isaac waved a big black hand in front of Wolf's face, then laughed when he blinked out of his thoughts. "What is *with* you?"

Unusual heat filtered into Wolf's cheeks, which of course Isaac noticed and ribbed him about. The fucker.

Chuckling, Wolf scratched his jaw. "I met someone."

Isaac's eyes went wide. "That's all I get? Spill, brother. Come on, now. Don't hold back on me."

So Wolf did. He laid it all out there. From the way they met, to the fast way they fell, to the fact that Wolf had been questioning whether Blasphemy was still right for him before Olivia helped him find himself again. "You've actually met her before," Wolf said, chuckling when Isaac frowned. "Liv Foster, owner of Flowers in Bloom. The florist at your wedding."

"No shit? Wait. I don't remember you hooking up with her there."

"We didn't. I didn't even recognize her at first. But it clicked that we'd met before when we finally got around to talking." He shrugged, his nonchalance masking just how damn special that night had been to him. The sex. The conversations. Hell, the whole weekend they'd spent together, and the connection it created. "But she's amazing, Isaac. Brave and sexy and smart and successful. This thing I've found with her, I think it's the real deal."

"Have you told her all that?" his friend asked.

"Some of it," Wolf said, his thoughts venturing where they'd been starting to venture more and more these past days. To questions of what came next... "But I haven't laid it all out there that directly. Yet. I'm starting to get a handle on exactly what I want with her, which I think could be everything. But we haven't been together that long. I don't want to make her feel rushed into anything, especially because she's been in a serious relationship before that went bad. Douchebag cheated on her a month before their wedding."

Isaac nodded. "Damn, that sucks. But it sounds like you know exactly what you want, Wolf. Given that, why wait? Who cares how long it's been if you feel like it's right?"

Wolf chuckled, appreciating the hell out of the sentiment and the straight talk. "Where the hell have you been again?"

"Neck deep in diapers, I kid you not," he said. "Wait 'til you have a baby. Because otherwise you'll never believe how much pee and poop something that little can generate. Hand to God."

The rest of the night alternated between speeding and dragging by. Wolf was busy as hell, working out processing glitches in prospective members' registrations, manning the cameras, and tracking the scrolling roster of players on the floor. Those with enough clout had scheduled interviews with some of the Masters, wanting a more personal introduction to the club before handing over their platinum credit cards for the most elite memberships, and Wolf had a couple of those on his schedule, too.

And all that was in addition to the fact that Olivia would be coming to the club herself sometime after ten o'clock, the final entry window for the event. Hopefully he'd get to spend time with her because he really didn't like the idea of her being alone out on the floor, but it all depended on how many fires arose that needed his particular brand of extinguisher. And she insisted that she could hang with Master Quinton at the bar or with some of the submissives with whom she'd begun to make friends.

All Wolf knew was that he was dying to see her. Because when the craziness of this night was over, he was taking Isaac's advice and laying it all on the line.

His feelings. His hopes. His wants.

Because Olivia Foster had finally taught him exactly what those were.

Chapter 9

Liv arrived at Blasphemy excited as ever, and maybe even more so than usual. Because the vibe tonight was electric, almost frenetic, from the collective excitement of all the new people experiencing the club for the very first time. Not that she was an old pro, by any means, but Liv still clearly remembered how she'd felt during her first visit here—that potent mix of anticipation and fear, arousal and adrenaline, surrender and flight.

And the club was packed.

A shiver ran over her skin. So many eyes…

Making her way through the press of the crowd, Liv finally managed to get close to the bar. But trying to find a seat there was a hopeless endeavor.

A hand fell on her arm. "Hey, Liv. Wanna join us?" It was Kenna, looking absolutely stunning in a silver-and-black sequined cocktail dress that matched the sleeve on her prosthetic arm. She'd lost everything below her right elbow while serving in Afghanistan, and Liv was so damn impressed by her that she already cherished her as a friend. "Some of the other subs and I claimed some couches in the hallway."

"That sounds great," Liv said, smiling at being included. After losing so many friends when she and Caleb fell apart, it felt really good to be making new ones again. New ones who knew the real her. "It's crazy in here."

"I know," Kenna said, leaning closer. "Cass and I were just saying we want our club back." They laughed.

"I don't know if I've belonged long enough to share in that

sentiment, but I totally do."

Finally, they reached the grouping of couches located further down the same hallway where Master Wolf had cradled Liv in his lap that first night. *Some of the other subs* turned out to be about fifteen women and a few men, too. Liv didn't know them all. But she saw Kenna and Cass and Master Kyler's submissive, Mia, who ran an art gallery in town, all of whom she'd hung out with here a number of times.

And Liv also saw Willow, with whom she hadn't yet had a chance to reunite. "Willow!" Liv said, making her way through the tight-knit group. "It's so great to see you."

"You know, Isaac told me that you'd been brought over to the dark side in here. If I'd have known, I'd have happily made that happen two years ago," Willow said with a chuckle and a hug.

"Tell me about it. I wish *I'd* known what I wanted back then," Liv said, realizing how far she'd come in so little time. All thanks to Wolf offering to help a stranger caught up in the world's worst date.

Willow nodded, her soft curls a dark halo around her glowing, new-mother's face. "It's a process, trust me. Now that we have Vaughn, we're figuring out our relationship all over again."

"That sounds exciting and scary," Liv said.

"Little bit," Willow said. "But anything's possible when you're both in it together, you know?"

Liv appreciated that sentiment, especially because she felt like she had that kind of a relationship with Wolf. Or, at least, they were well on their way to building it. "And where is Vaughn tonight?"

"Believe it or not, he's asleep upstairs in the Masters' lounge." With a chuckle, Willow pointed at the coffee table where a baby monitor Liv hadn't noticed sat mixed in among the drink glasses and appetizer plates.

"Haha, training him early, are you?" Liv teased with a wink.

"Oh, my God, lady. You and Master Wolf must be a perfect match, because he said nearly the same damn thing."

Heat filled Liv's cheeks, but only because Willow was so right.

A warm body pressed to Olivia's back. "My, my, who have I found here?"

She smiled and turned in Master Wolf's arms. "There you are."

"I saw your name on the roster and then spotted you on the

feed," he said, pointing up at the corner of the ceiling where a security camera perched.

"Mmm, were you watching me, Master Wolf?" she asked, heat stirring in her body from being in his arms again and from imagining him watching her when she didn't even know it. It made her want to perform for that camera. Undress for it. Orgasm in front of it. All knowing he was on the other side. His eyes on her every move.

"Always, Olivia. And this is giving me some interesting ideas," he said, eyebrows waggling.

She laughed. "All you have are interesting ideas, Sir. That doesn't tell me much."

He smirked and leaned in for a kiss. "I'll take that as a compliment," he murmured as his lips claimed hers.

"So do you have time to hang out or are you completely slammed?" she asked when they parted again.

"I have about fifteen minutes before I have to do an interview," he said.

"Fifteen minutes, huh?" She hoped her expression adequately feigned innocence as she peered up at him, even though her mind was all *Please have some dirty, dirty plans for those fifteen minutes!* "And what are you going to do with those fifteen minutes, Sir?" she teased.

He pressed his mouth to her ear. "Different crowd in here tonight. How adventurous are you feeling?"

Her belly did a flip-flop. He wasn't wrong, and that was both a little overwhelming and a lot intriguing. "I know you wouldn't push me to do something you didn't think I could handle, Sir."

"Mmm, you *are* feeling adventurous." His gaze ran over her dress—a white modern, mid-thigh number with sheer cutouts here and there that offered glimpses of her skin beneath. "And that dress is a fucking wet dream."

She grinned and did a spin, eager for him to see the cutout located almost dangerously low on her back.

His expression went all stern and intense, evidence that *full Dom mode* was now in effect. And she freaking loved when that happened.

Honestly, she loved every version of Wolf.

She just...loved *him*. Every time she admitted that to herself, it felt like her chest might burst open with the feeling.

"Come with me," he nearly growled as he took her hand and

pulled her into the middle of the mayhem, to a padded wooden bench set up near the dance floor and the couch where they'd sat that first night. "Hands and knees on this bench right now. Head up, eyes forward. And don't move a muscle until I return."

Confusion and curiosity swamped Liv as she got into the position, but that was quickly washed away by the sea of eyes suddenly lighting up her skin with awareness. It was clear to everyone that something was happening, or about to happen, and so she drew a crowd even as Master Wolf melted away into it.

Thank God he told me not to move and how to hold myself, she thought, because otherwise she'd be hard pressed to resist the nervous energy flowing through her, not to mention the urge to duck her gaze.

Long—very long—minutes seemed to pass before Master Wolf finally returned. He got right in front of her face, something in his hand she couldn't quite make out when she knew she wasn't supposed to shift the position of her head or eyes. "You think you can tease me into taking you before I'm good and ready, little Olivia?"

Her mouth dropped open. "No, Sir. Of course not."

"Because that seemed exactly like what you were trying to do. Tease me into giving you the satisfaction you wanted right when you wanted it." He held up his hand. "And so I thought, if teasing is what interests you, I'd be happy to oblige."

Her heart tripped into a sprint, especially when murmurs and chuckles ran through the assembling crowd. It was a small dildo vibrator on two straps with a second vibrating piece those straps would hold tight to her clit.

Oh, God. He was going to torture her. For fun. In front of all these people. For...for *hours*.

"I'm sorry, Master Wolf," she rushed out, because she *was* sorry, and she was also hoping he might give her a reprieve. The last time he'd made her wear a bullet vibrator at a restaurant he'd been especially evil, turning it on every time the waiter stood at their table, forbidding her from orgasming until she was sweating and shaking and damn near to crying. And when he finally had allowed her to come, he'd made her do it so many times that he had to help her walk out of the place—*and* he'd had to walk behind her, because she'd soaked her dress.

And, yeah, Master Wolf had made sure the waiter had seen his fair share of it *all*.

Between that and the hundred-dollar tip her Dom had left, she imagined that waiter had a pretty damn good night. And that kinda got her off, too.

Damn Wolf. Maybe he knew her *too* well. Or at least it seemed so as he grinned and arched a brow. "I'm going to make sure all these eyes are on you tonight, Olivia. I sure know mine will be."

He moved behind her.

Rucked up her skirt. He'd instituted a no-panties rule for her club attire weeks ago, so his actions immediately bared her ass to the crowd.

Then he slid the straps over her heels and up her legs, forcing her to lift her knees one at a time as he went. Finally, he inserted the dildo, centered the butterfly-shaped flat vibrator over her clit, and secured the straps.

He smacked her ass for good measure, two good swats on each cheek, before putting her skirt back in place again.

He hadn't made a big show of it, and that almost made it worse—*more* humiliating—because he wasn't doing this for pleasure. This was his evil brand of voyeuristic punishment.

Liv was developing a love/hate relationship with it.

Oh, who was she kidding?

"Rise, assume the waiting position, and thank me," he said, voice stern and so damn sexy.

With as much grace as she could, Liv followed his command, coming to stand with her feet shoulder-width apart, her hands behind her back, her head up but her eyes down. "Thank you, Master Wolf."

He pressed a kiss to her cheek. "I'll see you in a little while, Olivia." He took one step back.

The vibrators turned on.

Both of them.

Strong.

The high-pitched gasping moan ripped out of her unbidden, and she nearly pitched forward from the sudden surprise of it.

A murmur of humor and appreciative approval rolled through the crowd, but she kept her gaze on her Dom. It was easy when he was so freaking hot in a pair of black dress pants and white dress shirt with the arms rolled up, and a silver vest. Her sexy businessman fantasy brought to life again.

But it was those green eyes that always sucked her in most. Watching her, appreciating her, loving her. Did he feel it as strongly as she did?

"You're dismissed," he said, with a wink. "Go have fun."

* * * *

Thirty minutes later, Liv sought some privacy in one of the little nooks off the opposite hallway from where she and the other submissives had been hanging out. Because Master Wolf was making her insane.

She'd come twice in front of her friends—not to mention the strangers who'd been keeping an eye on her after her Dom's little show. Her friends understood. Hell, they even envied her, and she'd taken her fair share of teasing because of it. Liv was weathering it with as much good humor and chagrin as she could muster, because they'd *all* been there. And because she also knew that if she stood in front of one of the cameras and clearly mouthed the word *Red*, it would be over in a heartbeat.

Liv was in control.

But even with all that, she needed a moment to compose herself because he'd had the vibrator set at one of its higher settings for the past five minutes, and she couldn't decide if she wanted to cry or scream from the torment. What she did know was that her thighs were now wet from her orgasms, and the sensations twisting up tight in her body threatened that the next one might take her to her knees.

Finally, she found an unoccupied couch toward the front corner of the church and collapsed onto it. Closing her eyes, she could almost imagine that Wolf was there with her, whispering dirty little commands in her ears, using those big hands between her legs, that hard, curved cock pressed against her thigh, promising to make her feel so good.

She rolled her hips. His torture was going to make her come again. God. So close. She held her breath.

The vibrations stopped.

"No!" she cried to the empty room.

"So *this* was what you wanted? To be humiliated while everyone watched?"

Liv's eyes flew open, and her whole body went cold.

Caleb.

"What the hell are you doing here?" she asked, flying to her feet. It'd been about a year since she'd last run into him, at a restaurant in the city. And he looked exactly the same. A few inches taller than her, brown hair and eyes, boy-next-door good-looking. But she never in a million years expected to see him *here*.

"I'm friends with one of the Masters. He thought I might be curious," he said, standing in the doorway to the little nook where she'd sought refuge.

Only to actually *be* humiliated by her ex-fiancé all over again. His words made her want to vomit and cry and run, but she wasn't letting him see any of that.

"You? Really?" She steeled her spine and crossed her arms, making sure her red cuff was visible.

He shrugged with one lazy shoulder as his gaze ran over her dress. And now she really did want to vomit. "I think about you sometimes."

She scoffed and headed for the doorway. "Gee, thanks. I *don't* think about you, Caleb. And I haven't in a long time. Now if you'll excuse me."

He stepped in front of her, blocking her way. "I watched what he did to you. I just can't believe that's how you want a man to treat you."

Shaking now, from anger and embarrassment and a whirl of emotions she couldn't even begin to name, Liv chuffed out a humorless laugh. "What I do is none of your business. Hasn't been for years. And why you'd think I'd care what *you* think about how a man should treat me after you'd been fucking another woman for months while we were planning our damn wedding, I can't begin to imagine!"

"Olivia," he said, grasping her arm.

She yanked away from him. "You don't get to touch me, Caleb. Now move out of my way."

"You used to want me to touch you. Maybe I just needed to do it how he does it. Maybe it would've been better between us then. I could turn you over my lap and spank you so hard. That what you like now?" He stalked toward her, and ice tingled down her spine.

"Don't touch me again," she yelled, glaring. "You twisted, pompous, close-minded *asshole!*"

Finally, someone heard them.

And not just any someone.

Master Alex. The most intimidating Master she'd yet met. She'd learned he was a sadist and that she was far from the only one who trembled in his presence. "Submissive, on your knees right this minute," he ordered.

Oh God. This was an order she did *not* want to obey. Not in front of Caleb. Not in a million years. But failing to disobey an order from any of the Blasphemy Masters was crossing-red-line territory for the club's submissives, and it would earn her discipline at Master Alex's hands and reflect poorly on Master Wolf, too. She was equally scared of both.

Liv knelt. Knees spread, back straight, hands on her thighs, head down.

"Jesus," Caleb muttered.

"What's the problem here?" Master Alex asked.

"I'm sorry, Alex," Caleb said. "We were just talking about playing together."

Her head whipped up. "We were *not.*"

Master Alex's dark eyes narrowed. "Talk out of turn again and I will take you over my knee."

Shaking with rage and bone-deep humiliation, Liv bowed her head. And got even madder when tears pooled in her eyes.

"I really did appreciate you inviting me, so I am sorry," Caleb continued. "I thought she was interested."

What the hell? Her mouth dropped open and words were out before she'd even thought to say them. "I can't believe you said that. That's a lie. I'm with someone else now!"

"Olivia!" Master Alex barked.

"But, Sir—"

"Caleb, please wait at the bar."

"Oh. Sure," he said. With one last glance at her, he was gone.

The first tear finally streaked down Olivia's face. And then another. She watched as Master Alex punched a text message into his cell phone, a deep scowl on his face.

God, he was so mad at her. This was bad. Really bad. And, Jesus, if Caleb was Master Alex's guest, of course he was going to take his side. And all she wanted was Master Wolf. Where was he?

After what felt like forever, Master Alex pocketed his phone and stood right in front of her. The hems on his worn blue jeans were frayed over a pair of black work boots.

"Look at me." She did. "Tell me what happened."

"He...he found me here. Made some unkind comments about my choices and...interests. Then came on to me despite my telling him not to touch me and to let me leave. What he told you, none of that was true."

A storm rolled in over Master Alex's expression. "I'll handle him. But what am I to do with you?" Liv knew enough not to answer. "You spoke out of turn repeatedly. Didn't trust me to protect you. Did it never occur to you that I'd be able to tell that he was lying? How many times have I seen you and Master Wolf together? Besides which, you're wearing a red cuff. No other players should even be approaching you to do a scene."

Oh. He was right. More slow tears fell. What a mess this whole thing was. "I'm sorry, Master Alex."

He shook his head. "I know you are, but that might not be enough. I'll let Master Wolf decide."

"Decide what?" her Dom said, rushing into the room. "What the hell happened?"

Chapter 10

All Wolf knew was that his Olivia was crying, and he couldn't not touch her. He went right to her, a hand on her shoulder. "Liv, are you okay?"

"No," she said, more tears falling as her face crumpled. "Not okay."

Whatever Alex thought she had to be sorry for could wait. Wolf scooped her into his arms and carried her to the couch. He gave the other man a look he hoped communicated every bit of the anger coursing through him. Because some shit had clearly gone down and he was livid.

And at least some of that anger he directed at himself. Because he should've been with her. He should *know* what'd happened. Fucking open house night.

"I've got you now," he said, wiping her tears. God, she was so damn beautiful, and those tears were breaking his fucking heart. "And I'm sorry I wasn't here."

"I know," she whispered, visibly trying to pull herself together. "I'm sorry. I know this is probably embarrassing to you."

He cupped her face and kissed her, a firm press of lips to prove he was there, to make her *feel* it. "You could never embarrass me, Olivia. Don't ever say that again."

"A prospective member propositioned her," Master Alex said.

Oh, hell no. Beyond the possessiveness flooding his veins at the fact that this woman was *his*, Olivia wore a red cuff. And every person in the place—new or old-timer—had been made aware of the rules. Red cuffs equaled attached and therefore unapproachable for play by anyone but the submissive's Dominant. Period. "Has his ass been escorted out? Because if not, I want to be the one to throw him the hell out the door."

Alex nodded. "I just notified Quinton to pull him off the floor, and then he'll have to be out-processed." He gave a troubled sigh. "I'm sorry to say this is partly my fault."

Wolf glared. "Explain, please."

"Caleb was my guest," Master Alex said. "I know him professionally. I never would've expected this behavior from him, and I'm sorry. I knew he was in the wrong the minute he started talking, but then Olivia disobeyed my orders to remain quiet so I could get to the bottom of the situation. That's what you heard us talking about."

"Caleb?" he bit out, then peered down at Olivia. In that instant, the name was too fucking unique for his liking. What were the chances?

She nodded, her eyes glassy again. "Yes, it was my ex. He…he saw us earlier. And then he found me here and…" She gave a helpless little shrug that shredded Wolf's insides. "…he said a bunch of stuff. Wanted to spank me and wouldn't let me by him to leave."

Christ. *Christ.*

He wanted to get up in Master Alex's face because the man had made a fucking colossal error in judgment that had put his submissive in jeopardy, but he wasn't letting her go to do it. Not while she was still trembling and teary, and definitely not when she thought her efforts to defend herself—whatever they were—might reflect badly on him. As far as Wolf was concerned, whatever she'd done had been all the way in bounds. "Master Alex, that man was Olivia's ex-fiancé, whose behavior was not honorable while they were together."

The other man blanched, which was impressive given how stoic he typically was. Master Alex was a total hardass, a closed-off wall of a man who rarely showed emotion and was damn hard to get to know. The submissives—men and women—who craved masochism worshipped him, but he wasn't one of the Masters with whom Wolf had gotten close over the years.

"Damn, Master Wolf. I'm sorry, to both of you."

Wolf nodded, all the acknowledgement he could muster just

then. "I hope you'll understand I won't be punishing Olivia. Not for anything that happened here."

The other Dom held up his hands, his expression unreadable. "I'll leave it to you." He left.

Hugging her tight to his chest, Wolf pressed a kiss against her hair. "I'm so fucking sorry, Olivia."

"Not your fault," she whispered. He held her for a long moment, just needing her in his arms, proof that she was okay. "Can you please remove this toy from me?"

"Oh, hell," he said. "Of course." He made quick work of it, setting the vibrator on the floor beside his feet. And then they sat knee to knee on the couch's edge, their foreheads leaning together, their hands entangled. "Are you okay?"

"Better," she said. "I was scared."

"Of what, sweetness?"

"Just...that I'd really messed up," she said, peeking up at him. "That I'd reflect badly on you. I know how important this club is to you—"

"Liv, please look at me," Wolf said, waiting to go on until she finally did. The tears had made her eyes startlingly blue, and he felt like he could fall into that gaze forever. "I need you to see that I don't think you messed up here. More than that, I need you to know. If it came down to you or this club, you'd be my priority, Olivia. I'd choose you. Every damn time."

She sucked in a breath, and her expression went so damn soft and sweet. "Master Wolf," she whispered. "I like playing with you here. The other Doms. Kenna and Cass and Mia. I feel like I have friends for the first time in a long time. A community. I adore that we share that. And that's saying nothing of the fact that this is a business for you, too. I don't want to make you choose."

He shook his head. "You're not, because you did nothing wrong. Your asshole ex did, and Alex did, and I did, but you did not. But I just wanted you to know."

She frowned. "You did nothing wrong, either."

"I should've been with you."

Liv squeezed his hand. "You can't be with me all the time. That's not how relationships work. Besides, I defended myself against Caleb just fine. If he'd have taken things one more step, I would've screamed my head off and brought half the club running."

Her words eased him and made him admire her so damn much. "My girl is always so brave."

"Your girl feels like kind of a mess," she said, and he loved hearing her call herself that.

She was his. And after all of this, he needed her to know.

"I'd wanted to do this differently," he said. "Make a moment of it. Make it romantic."

"Do what?" she asked, peering at him.

He took her face in his hand again, unable to stop touching her, holding her, being close. "Tell you that I've fallen in love with you. I love you, Liv."

Those turquoise eyes went wide and shimmery. "You...oh, my God, Wolf. I love you, too. I do. For weeks now. God, maybe even since the night at the park."

"Jesus," he rasped, pulling her into a tight hug. "I didn't want to make you feel rushed, but I've been feeling it, too. For so long. Damn, Liv, for me it might've been that very first night."

They laughed and kissed, soft, sweet, claiming presses of skin on skin.

"I want so much with you, Olivia. I just want to be in your life, and for you to be in mine, in every way."

Smiling so damn pretty, she nodded. "I want that, too, Wolf. I have never been happier in my whole life, and I'm so grateful you rescued me that night."

He chuckled. "Fate was looking out for us."

She grinned. "It totally was."

"Liv," he said, moving closer to her. "Would you consider moving in together? I want to go to bed with you and wake up with you and have meals with you and come home to you. You can move into my house, or I'll move into yours. Or, hell, we could look for a new—"

"Yes," she said, pushing him back against the couch and straddling him. "Yes to all of it. To any of it. I want to be the person you come home to, and I want you to be that person for me."

"Sweet, sweet woman," he whispered around the edge of a searing kiss that quickly flashed hot.

But he was done sharing Olivia with a million other eyes. At least for tonight. "Let's get out of here," he said.

"I'd like that."

He guided her through the club, taking a few of the security corridors back to registration to avoid the crowds.

"I have to grab my purse from the lockers," Liv said.

Wolf nodded. "Meet you right back here."

She'd barely left the room when the office door swung open and Master Quinton and Master Alex stepped out, deep-set scowls on their faces. A third man followed. Wolf didn't need to be told who it was.

The anger he'd restrained suddenly flashed through his blood, and he stalked toward them. "You Caleb?"

The guy's eyes went wide as he hung back at the door. Not so brave now, was he? "Yes, listen—"

"No, you listen—" Wolf ran into the wall of Quinton's chest as the other Dom blocked him from getting any closer. It didn't keep Wolf from trying as he jabbed a finger at the other man over Quinton's shoulder. "You don't come near Olivia. You don't talk to her. You don't get in touch with her. You see her on the street, and you turn around and go the other way. Understood? And if you say a word about anything that happened inside these walls tonight, this club will sue you for everything you have and then some."

"I'm a lawyer. I understand what an NDA is," he said, his tone laced with poutiness and fear.

"Time to go," Master Alex said, looming over Caleb as Alex escorted him to the door, then pushed it open. Crisp fall air spilled in. "I'll be seeking a new firm on Monday morning. That doesn't begin to reflect everything I'd like to do to your ass, but it's all, unfortunately, I can do. Security, see this man off the property."

Then the asshole was gone.

"Taking the trash out is my least favorite chore," Quinton said, a valiant but ultimately failed attempt at lightening the mood.

Wolf laced his hands on top of his head and unleashed a frustrated breath.

"Sirs?" came Olivia's quiet voice from the side of the room. "Is everything okay?"

"Aw, hell," Wolf said. "Come here, sweetness." The second she was at his side and in his arms, he felt better. "Everything's just fine."

"Is Caleb going to cause trouble for the club?" she asked, peering up at him.

But before Wolf could reassure her, Master Alex said, "He wouldn't *dare*. Between the three of us, we made sure of it. And I'm sorry for the whole damn mess, Olivia. I hope you can forgive me."

"I just heard you fire him for what he did here tonight," Liv said, wrapping an arm around Wolf's back. "That was pretty gratifying to watch. So please believe me when I say you are more than forgiven, Master Alex."

With a glint of appreciation in his dark eyes, the Dom gave a single nod and left.

"Champagne's on me next time, little Olivia," Master Quinton said with a wink as he made for the club again.

"Sorry, Sir, but as good as I'm sure that would be, I don't think Master Wolf or Cassia would approve," she deadpanned.

He blinked, then broke out into a guffaw. "Well played, subbie. I knew I liked you." He gave a wave and disappeared through the doors.

Here she was cracking jokes after the disaster of the past hour. There was only one thing Wolf could say about that. "I love you, Liv. So damn much."

"I love you, Master Wolf. Can we go home now?"

It was exactly what he wanted, too. So he took her home, spread her out in her bed, and gave her a glimpse of what their forever was going to be. All night long.

Epilogue

That night, Liv had told Wolf she'd never been happier, and that had been true. The amazing thing though? Each day of the month that passed after it, it was even more true than the day before.

She arrived at Wolf's office building and went up to the seventh-floor suite of M&H IT Security Services. She and Wolf had settled on a new place last week—deciding that both of their places were too small—and now they were painting and updating it before they moved in. And that meant they had a thousand decisions to make.

"Surprise, it's me," she said, knocking on Wolf's office door with a bag of take-out in one hand and a folder of paint samples and catalog inspirations in the other.

"Hey, Liv," he said, his face breaking out in a big smile. "Best surprise ever." He rose and emptied her hands, then took her into his arms for a lingering, playful kiss.

"Hopefully you'll still think that when I make your mind go numb trying to choose between atmospheric blue, vast sky blue, and bluebird feather."

He chuckled as they set out their Chinese food and sat side by side behind his desk. "Who knew there were this many shades of blue?" he said, using his chopsticks on a mouthful of lo mein.

"Wait 'til I show you the whites." She laughed as his eyes went wide and panicked.

As they ate, they settled on paint colors, furniture to order, and made a few calls to set up appointments for some of their other house-related chores. "I wish I could take care of some of this today," she said, "but I need to get back to the store soon. I want to try to finish the arrangements for Mia's gallery opening today so I can deliver them first thing in the morning." Between Kenna's association events, Mia's art shows, and Blasphemy's big masquerade costume ball coming up in just a few weeks, she'd gotten even busier at Flowers in Bloom. Busy enough that she'd hired some part-time help and might be able to bring on another person in the new year, too.

"We'll work through the list, don't you worry."

"I know," she said, cleaning up their lunch and finishing the rest of her water.

"Exactly how much longer do you have before you have to go?" Wolf asked, a look in his eyes that set off tingles in her belly.

She grinned and pressed the button on her phone to display the time. "Ten minutes. Maybe fifteen, tops."

A slow, evil smile grew on his face. "Plenty of time for what I have in mind."

She arched a brow. "And that is?"

Without another word, he took her hand, guided her down the hallway past his and Isaac's team working in open-concept cubicles, and through another door, which he closed behind him. Then he drew the vertical blinds to the interior windows, blocking out the hall beyond. Mostly.

"I can't have a meeting in here without thinking of your fantasy. And wanting to bring it to life." He nodded to the big conference table behind her.

Liv's body immediately heated. "Now? But your employees—"

"Which is why you'll need to be quiet and I'll need to be quick. Hands on the table, Olivia."

"Holy shit," she whispered, but she totally did what he said. Because who was she kidding? Just thinking about doing this, and that someone could walk in at any second, had her wet.

He roughly pulled down her jeans, but left them hanging at her thighs. And then he was behind her, parting the fly to his jeans and bumping her ass with his fist as he rolled on a condom.

"Hold on tight, sweetness, because this is going to be hard and fast." He filled her in one punctuated thrust.

She slapped her own hand over her mouth and went face down to the table.

"That's it," he whispered. "That's fucking it."

While she hung on to the edge of the cool wood, Wolf hammered at her with fast, hard, rough strokes that had her wanting to scream at how good it was. Instead, she pressed her hand tighter to hold the threatening sounds in and imagined a half dozen men in sharp suits filling the chairs around them. Watching. Nodding. Maybe even wanting a turn.

"Oh, already, Liv?" he asked on a dark, hushed chuckle. "You're squeezing my cock so damn tight."

A whine spilled from her throat.

"Quiet," he bit out. "They'll hear you. They'll come and see your cunt filled with my dick, Liv. Jesus, it looks so good, too."

He grabbed her hips, yanked them out from the table, and absolutely drilled her.

She came on a smothered scream, her body shaking and thrashing against the wood.

Wolf was right behind her, jerking and shuddering until he collapsed down on her back.

And then the only sound in the room was their panting and the rush of her own pounding blood past her ears.

"God, Wolf," she whispered, absolutely shattered in the best possible way. "I have to lay here forever now. I can't move."

"Oh, sweetness, I think that can be arranged," he said, kissing her cheek.

They chuckled and dressed quickly, and then Wolf was guiding her back down the hall again, past the friendly faces of his colleagues, most of whom she'd at least said hello to before on previous visits.

Did they know? Had they heard? And would Wolf ever stop making her feel so damn alive?

She didn't think so, and it was the best feeling ever.

He handed her the folder of materials and her purse, then walked with her to the elevator. "Have a good day, Liv. See ya tonight." He kissed her softly.

She loved knowing he'd be coming home to her. "You, too, Wolf. I love you." She stepped into the elevator.

"Love you more," he said, with a wink.

And she couldn't stop smiling the whole rest of the day.

* * * *

Also from 1001 Dark Nights and Laura Kaye, discover Hard As Steel, Hard To Serve, and Ride Dirty.

About Laura Kaye

Laura is the New York Times and USA Today bestselling author of over thirty books in contemporary and erotic romance and romantic suspense, including the Blasphemy, Hard Ink, and Raven Riders series. Growing up, Laura's large extended family believed in the supernatural, and family lore involving angels, ghosts, and evil-eye curses cemented in Laura a life-long fascination with storytelling and all things paranormal. Laura also writes historical fiction as the NYT bestselling author, Laura Kamoie. She lives in Maryland with her husband and two daughters, and appreciates her view of the Chesapeake Bay every day.

Learn more at www.LauraKayeAuthor.com

Join Laura's Newsletter for Exclusives & Giveaways!

Also By Laura Kaye

The Blasphemy Series
HARD TO SERVE
BOUND TO SUBMIT
MASTERING HER SENSES
EYES ON YOU
THEIRS TO TAKE

The Raven Riders Series
RIDE HARD
RIDE ROUGH
RIDE WILD

The Hard Ink Series:
HARD AS IT GETS
HARD AS YOU CAN
HARD TO HOLD ON TO
HARD TO COME BY
HARD TO BE GOOD
HARD TO LET GO
HARD EVER AFTER
HARD AS STEEL
HARD EVER AFTER
HARD TO SERVE

The Hearts in Darkness Duet
HEARTS IN DARKNESS
LOVE IN THE LIGHT

The Heroes Series
HER FORBIDDEN HERO
ONE NIGHT WITH A HERO

Discover More Laura Kaye

Ride Dirty
A Raven Riders Novella
By Laura Kaye

Caine McKannon is all about rules. As the Raven Riders' Sergeant-at-Arms, he prizes loyalty to his brothers and protection of his club. As a man, he takes pleasure wherever he can get it but allows no one close—because distance is the only way to ensure people can't hurt you. And he's had enough pain for a lifetime.

But then he rescues a beautiful woman from an attack.

Kids and school are kindergarten teacher Emma Kerry's whole life, so she's stunned to realize she has an enemy—and even more surprised to find a protector in the intimidating man who saved her. Tall, dark, and tattooed, Caine is unlike any man Emma's ever known, and she's as uncertain of him as she is attracted. As the danger escalates, Caine is in her house more and more – until one night of passion lands him in her bed.

But breaking the rules comes at a price, forcing Caine to fight dirty to earn a chance at love.

* * * *

Hard As Steel
A Hard Ink/Raven Riders Crossover

After identifying her employer's dangerous enemies, Jessica Jakes takes refuge at the compound of the Raven Riders Motorcycle Club. Fellow Hard Ink tattooist and Raven leader Ike Young promises to keep Jess safe for as long as it takes, which would be perfect if his close, personal, round-the-clock protection didn't make it so hard to hide just how much she wants him--and always has.

Ike Young loved and lost a woman in trouble once before. The last thing he needs is alone time with the sexiest and feistiest woman he's ever known, one he's purposely kept at a distance for years. Now, Ike's not sure he can keep his hands or his heart to himself--or that he even wants to anymore. And that means he has to do whatever it takes to hold on to Jess forever.

* * * *

Hard To Serve
A Hard Ink Novella

To protect and serve is all Detective Kyler Vance ever wanted to do, so when Internal Affairs investigates him as part of the new police commissioner's bid to oust corruption, everything is on the line. Which makes meeting a smart, gorgeous submissive at an exclusive play club the perfect distraction…

The director of the city's hottest art gallery, Mia Breslin's career is golden. Now if only she could find a man to dominate her nights and set her body—and her heart—on fire. When a scorching scene with a hard-bodied, brooding Dom at Blasphemy promises just that, Mia is lured to serve Kyler again and again.

Then, as their relationship burns hotter, Kyler learns that he's been dominating the daughter of the hard-ass boss who has it in for him. Now Kyler must choose between life-long duty and forbidden desire before Mia finds another who's not so hard to serve.

About the Blasphemy Series

**12 Masters. Infinite fantasies…
Welcome to Blasphemy**

Books in Series
HARD TO SERVE
BOUND TO SUBMIT
MASTERING HER SENSES
EYES ON YOU
THEIRS TO TAKE
ON HIS KNEES

Theirs to Take

A Special Crossover Release with Jennifer Probst's Reveal Me, *A New Book in Her Steel Brothers Series*
Two Hot Fantasies. One Night at Blasphemy. Coming September 19, 2017.

She's the fantasy they've always wanted to share…
After serving in the navy, best friends Jonathan Allen and Cruz Ramos become partners in their sailboat building and restoration business and at Blasphemy, their BDSM club. They share almost everything—including the desire to dominate a woman together.

All Hartley Farren has in the world is the charter sailing business she inherited from her beloved father. So when a storm damages her boat, she throws herself on the mercy of business acquaintances to do the repairs—stat. She never expected to find herself desiring the sexy, hard-bodied builders, but being around Jonathan and Cruz reminds Hartley of how much she longs for connection. If only she could decide which man she wants to pursue more…

As their friendship with Hartley grows, Jonathan and Cruz agree that they've finally found the woman they've been looking for. Her reactions make it clear that she's submissive and attracted to them both. But as they introduce her to their erotic world, will she submit to being theirs to take…forever?

Mastering Her Senses
Blasphemy Book 2
By Laura Kaye

He wants to dominate her senses—and her heart...

Quinton Ross has always been a thrill-seeker—so it's no surprise that he's drawn to extremes in the bedroom and at his BDSM club, Blasphemy, where he creates sense-depriving scenarios that blow submissives' minds. Now if he could just find one who needs the rush as much as him...

Cassia Locke hasn't played at Blasphemy since a caving accident left her with a paralyzing fear of the dark. Ready to fight, she knows just who to ask for help—the hard-bodied, funny-as-hell Dom she'd always crushed on—and once stood up.

Quinton is shocked and a little leery to see Cassia, but he can't pass up the chance to dominate the alluring little sub this time. Introducing her to sensory deprivation becomes his new favorite obsession, and watching her fight fear is its own thrill. But when doubt threatens to send her running again, Quinton must find a way to master her senses—and her heart.

* * * *

The quip on Quinton's tongue died when a flashing red light under the bar's edge caught his eye. An emergency in one of the rooms. He glanced at the tag over the light to determine which one, then slammed the drinks down in front of his friends harder than he'd intended. "Shit, G, sorry. Emergency in the dark room. Get someone to cover?" he said, moving without waiting for an answer. He knew Griffin would have his back.

Quinton moved as fast as he could without calling undue attention. Their members knew that the Masters and a team of other Doms who worked as monitors responded to all sorts of problems around the club, some as mundane as an equipment malfunction and others more delicate situations involving disputes between players in a scene. Hell, a few months ago, Quinton had responded when Kenna broke down during a bondage scene, and Griffin had called for help extricating her from his intricate ropework. Sex at the extremes was bound to run into a few issues, which was why consent and safety were hallmarks of BDSM and Blasphemy itself. But none of that meant any of them wished to distract players from their pleasures with worry or curiosity, either.

Off the main floor, Quinton picked up his pace as he moved down the long hallway off of which most of the themed play rooms were located. The dark room was at the far end. Master Wolf came up beside him. "Hey, man," he said.

Quinton gave him a nod. "Didn't know you were on tonight, Wolf. Good to see you."

A little taller than Quinton, the guy had dark blond hair, the brightest green eyes you'd ever seen, and a chiseled Scandinavian face that turned heads all over the club. "Running the security control room. Relieving Isaac because the baby's sick," he said, referring to Isaac Marten, their head of security operations, who had a two-month-old son.

"Damn. Sorry to hear that," Quinton said as they closed in on their destination. The dark room was actually a series of three interconnected rooms. In the center was a pitch-black bedroom, accessed only through two changing/waiting rooms on either side of it—one of which let out into this hallway, and the other of which let out into a different hallway so that the players couldn't run into each other before or after the anonymous scene. The dark room was very popular, and given Quinton's interest in sensory deprivation, it was one he'd used many times.

He heard someone in distress before they even got inside.

Quinton and Wolf burst through the door to find one of the monitors trying to calm a woman curled on the floor, gasping like she couldn't breathe. She wore a slinky bronze dress that bared most of her legs.

"What happened?" Quinton asked, grabbing a blanket from a shelf and going to his knees beside her. He tucked the soft fleece around her.

"I don't know," the monitor said. I sounded the alarm but she told me not to call an ambulance when I asked."

"She just freaked out. I swear. Nothing hardly happened between us," a shirtless man said from the doorway to the dark bedroom.

Quinton hadn't even noticed him there, but Wolf was already questioning him. He nodded to the monitor, a Dom in his forties, and then peered up at Master Wolf. "You all clear out. Debrief him and get his information."

"You got it, Q," Wolf said, motioning the other men out into the hall. "Call if you need help."

As they left, Quinton brushed the woman's shoulder-length hair back off her splotchy face. "We need to get your breathing under control or I have to call an ambulance."

"No...no...I...it's..." Clenching her eyes, she shook her head and growled as if in frustration.

Damnit, he needed to do something for her. The part of him that needed to care and soothe decided, and he scooped her off the floor and carried her to the couch. Everywhere they touched, her pulse hammered against her skin. If this was a panic attack, it was one of the worst he'd ever seen.

He sat with her in his lap, the blanket still wrapped around her, and cradled her so that they were facing each other. "Breathe with me, little one. Do you hear me? Look at me and breathe with me." Striking hazel eyes with flecks of gold cut to his. Almost familiar...

Focusing, he exaggerated one breath, than another, and another, until she struggled to match her rhythm to his.

Griffin appeared in the doorway, questions clear on his face. Quinton spared him the smallest of glances and gave a single shake of his head. Griffin nodded and closed the door. Quinton had this. The others would be there in a heartbeat if he was wrong, but he didn't think he was.

Because the woman's body was calming. Her breathing was evening out. Her pulse was slowing. Her muscles were losing their tension.

"That's it. That's good. Just watch me and breathe with me. Don't stop. We'll kick this thing, don't you worry." He stroked his hand over her hair, wanting to soothe her. The color was so rich it almost matched the bronze of her dress. Her hair was beautiful and soft. As was the rest of her, all golden skin and pretty curves. Her weight felt good in his arms. She turned her face into his hand, just the littlest bit, and he stroked her hair again. A jagged scar ran along her forehead and into her hairline over one eye.

The scar triggered the oddest thought: *That wasn't there before.*

His gaze cut back to those eyes. Hazel with the gold. And he suddenly knew he'd seen them before. Years ago. Right here at Blasphemy. A name clicked into place.

"Cassia?" he asked. Cassia. As in Cassia Locke, a submissive he'd flirted with quite a few times and was once supposed to play with…but she'd stood him up the night of their scene.

"Y-yes, Sir," she whispered. "H-hi, Mas-ter Q-quinton."

So she recognized him, too. Did she remember that night? He shook off the thought. Their history wasn't something to deal with just then.

"Hi yourself, kid." He gently scratched his fingertips against her scalp and concentrated on taking slow, deep breaths that she mimicked. Studying her, Quinton noticed another scar on her right shoulder. Her hair was also much longer than the almost boyish style she used to wear. Finally, Cassia went limp in his lap, and her ease unleashed a satisfaction in his blood. "Feeling better?"

She gave a long sigh, the sound exhausted and defeated. "As better as I can feel after utterly humiliating myself. Sir."

He shook his head. "No such thing happened. Not as far as I'm concerned."

Her gaze skittered away.

"Did I tell you to stop looking at me?"

Cassia's eyes snapped back to meet his. "No, Sir."

Her obedience unleashed even more of that satisfaction. The attraction of BDSM, to him, was as much about the psychology of it as the physicality of the acts. Her reaction—that obedience—represented an ingrained instinct, a need to serve, a desire to surrender. And that fucking heated his blood. He arched a brow and nodded. "Good girl."

She shifted in his lap, but kept her eyes on his. The movement reminded his body that he'd been planning to find a partner, but he locked that shit down tight. First, because she'd been through something tonight he didn't entirely understand. And second, because given that she'd stood him up and never bothered to follow up to explain, he wasn't sure what to make of her anyway. And trust was kind of a thing, for him. Well, for most Doms, really. Which meant he needed to know.

"Now, tell me what happened," he said, nailing her with a stare. "And tell me the truth."

Sign up for the 1001 Dark Nights Newsletter
and be entered to win a Tiffany Key necklace.

There's a contest every month!

Go to www.1001DarkNights.com to subscribe.

As a bonus, all subscribers will receive a free copy of
Discovery Bundle Three
Featuring stories by
Sidney Bristol, Darcy Burke, T. Gephart
Stacey Kennedy, Adriana Locke
JB Salsbury, and Erika Wilde

Discover 1001 Dark Nights Collection Five

BLAZE ERUPTING by Rebecca Zanetti
Scorpius Syndrome/A Brigade Novella

ROUGH RIDE by Kristen Ashley
A Chaos Novella

HAWKYN by Larissa Ione
A Demonica Underworld Novella

RIDE DIRTY by Laura Kaye
A Raven Riders Novella

ROME'S CHANCE by Joanna Wylde
A Reapers MC Novella

THE MARRIAGE ARRANGEMENT by Jennifer Probst
A Marriage to a Billionaire Novella

SURRENDER by Elisabeth Naughton
A House of Sin Novella

INKED NIGHT by Carrie Ann Ryan
A Montgomery Ink Novella

ENVY by Rachel Van Dyken
An Eagle Elite Novella

PROTECTED by Lexi Blake
A Masters and Mercenaries Novella

THE PRINCE by Jennifer L. Armentrout
A Wicked Novella

PLEASE ME by J. Kenner
A Stark Ever After Novella

WOUND TIGHT by Lorelei James
A Rough Riders/Blacktop Cowboys Novella®

STRONG by Kylie Scott
A Stage Dive Novella

DRAGON NIGHT by Donna Grant
A Dark Kings Novella

TEMPTING BROOKE by Kristen Proby
A Big Sky Novella

HAUNTED BE THE HOLIDAYS by Heather Graham
A Krewe of Hunters Novella

CONTROL by K. Bromberg
An Everyday Heroes Novella

HUNKY HEARTBREAKER by Kendall Ryan
A Whiskey Kisses Novella

THE DARKEST CAPTIVE by Gena Showalter
A Lords of the Underworld Novella

Discover 1001 Dark Nights Collection One

FOREVER WICKED by Shayla Black
CRIMSON TWILIGHT by Heather Graham
CAPTURED IN SURRENDER by Liliana Hart
SILENT BITE: A SCANGUARDS WEDDING by Tina Folsom
DUNGEON GAMES by Lexi Blake
AZAGOTH by Larissa Ione
NEED YOU NOW by Lisa Renee Jones
SHOW ME, BABY by Cherise Sinclair
ROPED IN by Lorelei James
TEMPTED BY MIDNIGHT by Lara Adrian
THE FLAME by Christopher Rice
CARESS OF DARKNESS by Julie Kenner

Also from 1001 Dark Nights

TAME ME by J. Kenner

Discover 1001 Dark Nights Collection Two

WICKED WOLF by Carrie Ann Ryan
WHEN IRISH EYES ARE HAUNTING by Heather Graham
EASY WITH YOU by Kristen Proby
MASTER OF FREEDOM by Cherise Sinclair
CARESS OF PLEASURE by Julie Kenner
ADORED by Lexi Blake
HADES by Larissa Ione
RAVAGED by Elisabeth Naughton
DREAM OF YOU by Jennifer L. Armentrout
STRIPPED DOWN by Lorelei James
RAGE/KILLIAN by Alexandra Ivy/Laura Wright
DRAGON KING by Donna Grant
PURE WICKED by Shayla Black
HARD AS STEEL by Laura Kaye
STROKE OF MIDNIGHT by Lara Adrian
ALL HALLOWS EVE by Heather Graham
KISS THE FLAME by Christopher Rice
DARING HER LOVE by Melissa Foster
TEASED by Rebecca Zanetti
THE PROMISE OF SURRENDER by Liliana Hart

Also from 1001 Dark Nights

THE SURRENDER GATE By Christopher Rice
SERVICING THE TARGET By Cherise Sinclair

Discover 1001 Dark Nights Collection Three

Discover 1001 Dark Nights Collection Four

On behalf of 1001 Dark Nights,

Liz Berry and M.J. Rose would like to thank ~

Steve Berry
Doug Scofield
Kim Guidroz
Jillian Stein
InkSlinger PR
Dan Slater
Asha Hossain
Chris Graham
Fedora Chen
Kasi Alexander
Jessica Johns
Dylan Stockton
Richard Blake
BookTrib After Dark
and Simon Lipskar

Made in the USA
Middletown, DE
10 June 2018

From *New York T[...]* auth[...]
Tessa Bailey, Elisa[...]e. Fo[...]
Four Sensual Stor[...]

SOMEHOW, SOME WAY: *A Billionaire Builders Novella by Jennifer Probst*

When an opportunity to transform a dilapidated house in a dangerous neighborhood pops up, Charlotte Grayson goes in full throttle. Unfortunately, she's forced to work with the firm's sexy architect Bolivar Randy Heart (aka Brady), who's driving her crazy with his archaic views on women. Somehow, some way, they need to work together to renovate a house without killing each other…or surrendering to the white-hot chemistry knocking at the front door.

TOO CLOSE TO CALL: *A Romancing the Clarksons Novella by Tessa Bailey*

A fairytale college career skyrocketed Kyler Tate to the NFL draft. Adoration and opportunity are thrown in his direction wherever he goes, thanks to being chosen in the first round by the Los Angeles Rage. None of the accolades mean anything, though, without his high school sweetheart, Bree Justice, by his side. Four years ago, she walked away from Kyler, choosing a quiet life over the flash and notoriety his career would someday bring. Now he's back in their Indiana hometown, refusing to leave for Los Angeles without her.

HUNTED: *An Eternal Guardians Novella by Elisabeth Naughton*

Erebus was Hades' secret weapon in the war between the immortal realms until Hades lost him in a bet to Zeus. For the last hundred years, Erebus has trained Zeus's Siren warriors in warfare and the sexual arts. But he's never stopped longing for freedom. Lately, he also longs for one Siren who entranced him during their steamy seduction sessions. A nymph he quickly became obsessed with and who was ripped from his grasp when her seduction training was complete. One he's just learned Zeus has marked for death.

EYES ON YOU: *A Blasphemy Novella by Laura Kaye*

When a sexy stranger asks Wolf Henrikson to rescue her from a bad date, he never expected to want the woman for himself. But their playful conversation turns into a scorching one-night stand that reveals the shy beauty gets off on the idea of being seen even if she's a little scared of it, too. As Wolf introduces her to his world at Blasphemy, Liv finds herself tempted to explore submission and exhibitionism with the hard-bodied Dom.

Every *Dark Nights* tale is breathtakingly sexy and magically romantic.

EVIL EYE
CONCEPTS

www.1001darknights.com

ISBN 9781948050685

9 781948 050685

90000